I0649585

# Marrying Elizabeth, Books 1-3 Compilation

# Marrying Elizabeth, Books 1-3 Compilation

A Pride and Prejudice Variation Series

## LEENIE BROWN

LEENIE B BOOKS

HALIFAX

No part of this book may be reproduced in any form, except in the case of brief quotations embodied in critical articles or reviews, without written permission from its publisher and author.

This book is a work of fiction. All names, events, and places are a product of this author's imagination. If any name, event and/ or place did exist, it is purely by coincidence that it appears in this book.

Cover design by Leenie B Books. Images sourced from Deposit Photos and Period Images.

*Marrying Elizabeth, Books 1-3 Compilation* © 2019 Leenie Brown. All Rights Reserved, except where otherwise noted. Books in this series were previously published as individual titles.

ISBN (print) 978-1-989410-39-4 ; (ebook) 978-1-989410-38-7

# Contents

# Delighting Mrs. Bennet

## Loving Lydia

## Dear Reader,

It all started with a picture of a sunset and a writing exercise on my blog (leeniebrown.com). However, what was supposed to be a few minutes of practice, grew and stretched and became something much larger.

Those writing exercises have now produced several published works, including the collection you hold in your hands.

While some things about how I create these stories have evolved since that first writing exercise, the tradition of posting a portion of a work in progress continues. In fact, there might be a new story posting there now.

Happy Reading!

Leenie B.

# Confounding Caroline

*He thought his future was bleak, but a well-orchestrated misstep might just bring Darcy the happiness he seeks.*

# Chapter 1

Fitzwilliam Darcy handed his coat and beaver to his friend's butler, while that friend, Charles Bingley, leaned nonchalantly against the sitting room's door frame. The soft glow of a lamp, which remained lit, shone behind him, indicating that Bingley had been engaged in some activity in the room before which he now stood.

"I had hoped you would be home, but I did not expect it," Darcy said in greeting. It was not Bingley's normal wont to remain at home. "Reading?" he queried with some surprise as he took note of the book in Bingley's hand.

Bingley shrugged. "I do read on occasion."

"I would not wish to keep you from your amusements." Darcy smirked slightly. If he knew his friend, Bingley would likely not mind the disruption since Bingley preferred people to books.

Bingley shook his head and chuckled. "Come, my study would be more comfortable than the sitting room and less likely to be invaded by females should Caroline return early."

"I am surprised you did not accompany her to the Grahams' soiree," Darcy said as he followed Bingley into the study.

"I have had my fill of ferrying Caroline around only to have her turn up her pert little nose at every gentleman she meets, so I sent her with Louisa and Hurst."

He tucked his book away on a shelf behind his desk, and then opening the door on the right side of his desk, he pulled out a bottle of amber coloured liquid and two glasses.

"I find I tire of society. It is always the same. The same ladies in different dresses with different coloured hair and hats, but the same gossip, the same weather, the same pleasantries. It's just so much of the same, over and over and over and over." He handed a glass to Darcy and smiled. "Besides, if I am not mistaken, I will not be the only one who will enjoy this Caroline-free evening."

Darcy chuckled "The quiet is agreeable to me, but you have never enjoyed silence so much as I." There was something different about Bingley the past few weeks. He did not smile as much as was his usual wont, and he seemed to tuck himself away in his study more and more. Darcy swirled the liquid in his glass and threw one leg over the other. The leather squeaked as he shifted in the chair across from Bingley.

Bingley sighed. "I find I am longing for the country, but Caroline will hear nothing of leaving town when there are so many functions to attend." He took a draught from his glass. "If I thought she meant to find a husband, trotting her around to the various venues might not be so bothersome, but she is not intent on snaring anyone but you."

Darcy knew that fact very well. Caroline had never been reserved in demonstrating her preference for him over every gentleman she met. "A title and a larger fortune might dissuade her."

The hint of bitterness in Bingley's laugh surprised Darcy almost as much as Bingley's wishing to leave town and avoid society. These were not Bingley actions. They were behaviours that were more likely to be attributed to Darcy rather than his gregarious friend.

"She is as stubborn as a mule," Bingley muttered, "and almost as bright."

Darcy's brows rose. He was not surprised by the fact that Bingley was complaining about his sister. He had heard Bingley complain about Caroline before — many times. However, he had never heard Bingley complain about anything more than her incessant need to purchase fripperies and dresses or the way she nattered on about this person or that. There was something decidedly wrong with his friend, and Darcy had a sinking feeling that he knew just what it was.

"You surprise me," Darcy said, not wishing to broach the topic of the cause of the change in Bingley but knowing it was necessary. "Was it not you who claimed to be happy wherever you were, be it town or country?"

"That was before," Bingley said over the rim of his glass.

"Before what?" Darcy prodded.

"Before I took an estate." Bingley shifted in his chair uneasily, studying the painting above the fireplace for a few moments before allowing his attention to return to his friend. He sighed deeply as his gaze fell to where Darcy's foot slowly bounced up and down.

Surreptitiously, Darcy glanced at his friend. He recognized Bingley's sigh, for it was the same groan of uncertainty that had taken up residence in his own chest. It was a new and unwelcome feeling, and it was not something that, though he had tried, he could command away. He had not been able to erase it with busyness, nor had he been able to wash it away with drink. There remained only one option for dealing with such uncertainty and its pretty reason. It must be acknowledged for what it was. The root of it must be exposed, then left to wither away with time — at least, for him. For his friend, he hoped for a different outcome.

"Is it the estate or the society in Hertfordshire that you miss, my friend?" Darcy's voice was quiet, and he fixed his eyes on the wall beyond Bingley's head. A small smile played at his mouth as he contemplated the image of smiling eyes and an impertinent grin that always came to his mind when he thought of Hertfordshire. "Netherfield seems like a fine estate, and the neighbourhood was not without its enchantments." He sipped his drink and then swirled it again, watching the liquid swirl up the sides of the glass.

"I thought you loathed the inhabitants of Hertford-shire." Bingley's voice was filled with incredulity. "Is that not why you and my sisters were so hasty in joining me in town — the people are beneath us, there is no society worth keeping, that sort of thing?

Again, Darcy's brows rose at the rancor in Bingley's voice. He sighed heavily, and colour crept up his cheeks. This would not be a pleasant discussion.

"I did not loathe all of the inhabitants. I found some of them to be quite delightful — so delightful, in fact, that leaving seemed safer than staying." He rose and walked to the window. Admitting his folly and weakness would be easier if he were able to move about and not have to face the friend whom he had, he suspected, unknowingly injured.

Bingley drummed his fingers on the arm of his chair and raised a brow in anticipation of an expected explanation.

"She is here in town." Darcy placed his empty glass on a side table and allowed his eyes to remain on it rather than look at his friend.

"Who is here in town?"

Darcy drew a deep breath and spared Bingley only a

glance before returning his gaze to his glass. "Miss Bennet."

"Miss Bennet?"

Darcy nodded.

"How do you know?" Bingley was on his feet and pacing. "Have you seen her?"

Darcy shook his head and sighed. "No, I have not seen her, but your sisters have." He turned once again toward the window. Bingley's reaction to the news was as expected and proved to Darcy how deeply attached his friend was to Miss Bennet.

"My sisters?" Bingley stood beside his friend, his brows drawn together in question.

Darcy turned toward him. "This afternoon, while you were out, I came by to drop off those papers." He pointed to the packet sitting unopened on the somewhat cluttered desk. "Caroline informed me that Miss Bennet had called."

"She was here? Miss Bennet was here?" Bingley's eyes were wide with astonishment. "Why did Caroline not tell me?"

Darcy wished to walk away from his friend, so that he could not see the pain in Bingley's eyes, but he would not. "It seems your sister is actively trying to separate you and Miss Bennet. She seemed to think I would be impressed by her belittling of the inferior society of the country." He paused and drew a deliberate breath. "At one time I would have agreed with her, but I no longer do."

Bingley crossed his arms and studied his friend.

Darcy winced under the examination, but it was not more than he deserved. Unable to bear both his shame and the scrutiny of his friend any longer, he turned back to the window. "I have to make a confession, Bingley. You may wish to throw me out of your home when I am finished, and I will fully understand if you do." Darcy continued to stare out the window, but he could feel the eyes of his friend boring into him.

"I wished to separate you from Miss Bennet when we left Hertfordshire." He closed his eyes as he heard his friend's muttered oath. "I told you she seemed indifferent to you. While it is true that I did not notice any particular regard for you on her part, it is not the reason I wished to separate you from her. It is not even the connection to her family or the supposed inferior society of Meryton that led me to take the actions I did." He swallowed and drew a deep fortifying breath before continuing. "I did not wish for you to become attached to Miss Bennet, for it would place me in an awkward situation. I was being completely and utterly selfish." He turned to look at his friend. "I am sorry," he whispered.

"An awkward situation?" Bingley wore a look of displeasure Darcy had rarely seen. "You would separate me from the woman I loved because it would somehow make your life awkward?"

Darcy nodded slowly. "Yes."

"Explain yourself," Bingley demanded, "for I do not have the pleasure of understanding your meaning."

Darcy shrugged one shoulder. "I thought if we left, if you and Miss Bennet were not allowed to become attached, I could avoid the danger, but I have discovered that the danger is not confined to Hertfordshire. It has followed me here to town. It haunts me day and night." He turned back towards the window as he continued.

"I am expected to marry well, to make a match that will increase the wealth and position of my family. It is what my father and uncle have always taught me."

"You are still making no sense."

Darcy could hear the exasperation in his friend's voice. It was rather how he had felt since leaving Hertfordshire — annoyed, disturbed, and vexed by the memory of Miss Elizabeth Bennet.

"How would my being fortunate enough to marry a lady such as Miss Bennet," Bingley continued, "impose upon some imagined need of yours to marry a lady of wealth and standing?"

"Miss Bennet has sisters," Darcy said to the darkness of the night before him.

"Yes, four," Bingley retorted. "I still do not see —"

"But only one," Darcy interrupted, "with the musical

laughter of a brook, eyes as expressive as any the masters have painted, and a mind that is..." he shook his head "so quick, so very quick and keen."

Darcy blew out a breath. "I imagined one day I would find a woman who would meet all the qualifications my uncle and father had taught me are necessary for the wife of a man of my standing and that we would eventually learn to esteem one another. But, I cannot fathom such a match after..." His voice trailed off.

A hand grasped his shoulder. "After meeting the one person you find you do not wish to live without." It was not a question that Bingley asked but rather a statement of deep understanding.

Darcy gave his friend a sad smile and nodded mutely.

"Now, you know why I am longing for the country," Bingley said softly.

Darcy nodded again. "I suspected as much. It is why I came here tonight — to discover if I was correct. I will not stand in your way. You deserve happiness. You have been a good friend to me, and I would not want to part for any other reason." Darcy turned to leave.

"What do you mean part?" Bingley asked. "I do not hate you for what you have done if that is what has you worried. I am not happy, but I am not angry. There is no reason for us to part."

Darcy stood with his hand on the doorknob. "I do not think I can bear hearing of her, especially when she belongs to another. It is just too much." His shoulders slumped. "You shall always remain my friend, Bingley. I will always be ready to serve you in any way, but please...please, do not ask me to be a witness to that."

# Chapter 2

Bingley crossed the room quickly and, taking Darcy by the shoulders, led him back to his chair. "Sit."

Darcy sighed and did as instructed.

"There is no reason for us to part," Bingley reiterated as he handed Darcy a refreshed glass of brandy.

"But —"

"No," Bingley cut Darcy off. "Duty be hanged." He dropped into his chair. There was absolutely no way while the sun still shone that he was going to lay aside his own chance at happiness with Miss Bennet, but it was equally unlikely that he was going to let a man, who was more brother than friend, walk out of his life. How would he be able to be completely happy if he knew he was the cause of such pain to Darcy?

"Your family —"

"No," Bingley cut in again. "My family, just like yours, expects me to marry well, and I shall." He smirked. "It shall, perhaps, not be as well as a certain member of my family would wish, but it is I who has to live with my choice of bride, not her. At least, I hope Caroline does not always live with me." He shuddered. She would be the next problem he would have to sort out.

"My family expects..." Darcy attempted to speak once again, only to find Bingley talking over him once more.

"I know what your family expects."

He had heard his friend wax eloquent on it many times — usually when explaining why he could not consider this or that lady whom Bingley had suggested. They were all excellent ladies. Very pleasant. Not at all stuffy and overbearing. But, none had interested Darcy in the least. Indeed, even some of the stuffier well-positioned ladies Bingley had mentioned in passing had never gotten more than a sigh and a reluctant agreement to consider them if it became necessary.

Bingley's brows drew together, and a small smile played at his lips. None of them had ever flustered Darcy as much as Miss Elizabeth had. She had drawn him out, caused him to debate, and had even enticed him to dance. And now she was the one woman whom Darcy would regret all his life if he did not pursue and win her.

With a most serious look on his face, Bingley sat forward in his chair, leaning toward his friend. "What would happen if you did not fulfill your family's expectations? Would you be cut off? Disinherited? Shunned by society? What would the consequences be?"

Darcy shrugged and sipped his drink. "I suppose it would cause a family rift."

"Meaning you would have fewer functions to attend because they would not invite you?"

Darcy nodded. "Yes, there is that."

"Who would refuse to see you?"

Darcy drew a deep breath. "I cannot say with any certainty who would do so besides Aunt Catherine."

"But," Bingley persisted. "She will be displeased no matter whom you marry unless it is her daughter. You have said so yourself. Do you intend to marry your cousin?"

"No, I have no desire to marry Anne."

"Then marrying Miss Elizabeth would be no different from your marrying some duke's daughter." Bingley cocked his head to the side and settled back into his chair.

"It might make it more challenging for Georgiana when she comes out if my connections are not of the first circles," Darcy argued.

Bingley shrugged. "Will she not still have her thirty thousand?"

"Of course, she will."

"Will your family's ties to the land and aristocracy not still be of long standing?"

Darcy shook his head. "That is a foolish question. How would my heritage change?"

Bingley smiled. "I do not know, but you seem to think that marrying a gentleman's daughter will somehow change how a prospective husband will view Georgiana." He shrugged, rose from his chair, and paced to the window before presenting his next argument. "Actually, I am rather surprised that you would even consider a gentleman who offered for your sister only because she would be a feather in his societal cap."

Darcy's head pulled back, and he blinked.

Bingley smiled. The comment had done its work. It had startled his friend and would hopefully get him to begin to see duty for what it was — a weight that could drag a person down into wretchedness. Perhaps Darcy would consider such a fate for himself, but he would never do so for his sister.

"You must consider her happiness," Bingley continued, leaning against the bookshelf that was near the window. "I know people often think of me as obtuse — do not deny it," he challenged as Darcy opened his mouth to speak. "To be fair, I often am. I am not so quick to catch on to things as some, but I am not oblivious to the world around me. I do spend time in observation and contemplation." He smirked. "Not so much as you, my friend, but I do practice the skills occasionally."

Darcy chuckled.

"You know I care for Georgiana, though not as my sister would wish for me to care for her," Bingley said.

Again, Darcy chuckled, and Bingley joined him. They knew that Caroline wished for not just one connection to the Darcy family through marrying Darcy herself. She also wanted her brother to marry Darcy's sister. To her, there was no better way to ensure they had risen above their roots in trade than to secure ties to the aristocracy and ancient lands and money.

"I care for her as a brother might care for her. I would not wish to see her harmed in any fashion." Bingley came back to where Darcy still sat swirling and occasionally sipping his drink. "She still feels the weight of disappointing you, Darcy. I can see it in her eyes when she looks at you when you are unaware." Darcy had shared with him about Georgiana's ordeal with Wickham at Ramsgate.

"But she has not disappointed me. I have failed her." Darcy's brows furrowed as he shook his head.

"Yet, she perceives she has disappointed you, and it still plays upon her spirit. Imagine how her spirit would suffer if she were to learn you had given up happiness for her. You know as well as I that she would never be happy no matter the match you might make for her." He shrugged. "And what match will you make for her? Will it be one of duty and obligation, or do you wish for her to find felicity and love? And with time, might you not grow to resent the fact that you gave up the possibility of your own felicity for your sister?"

Darcy gaped at his friend. "I had not thought of it in those terms. But, I fear, it does not matter. Miss Elizabeth would not have me anyway.

*17*

"Why would she not have you? I see no reason for her to reject you." Bingley knew he was close to securing a solution. He had learned from his father that there were always a few nagging details which threatened to sink any negotiation. Hopefully, this obstacle would be easily overcome, although, with Darcy, even a small barrier could become nearly insurmountable when he was in a dour state of mind, such as he was this evening.

"She believes George Wickham." Darcy drained the remaining liquid from his glass and placed it firmly on the table next to him. "Which means he has once again stolen from me that which is dear."

"He has not," Bingley refuted. "He did not succeed with Georgiana, and he will not succeed with Miss Elizabeth either."

Darcy's jaw clenched as he shook his head. "He has already influenced her against me."

"How do you know?" With any luck, there would be a great leap that had been made by his friend, who could be overly pessimistic about things at times and see one small error as the ruin of a project.

"She questioned me about Wickham at your ball."

Bingley leaned back in his chair and bit his cheeks to keep from smiling with satisfaction. He had heard about Miss Elizabeth's questioning as Darcy had vented his frustration on an innocent set of billiard balls. It might be challenging to overcome the obstacles of George Wickham and Miss Elizabeth's poor opinion of Darcy, but from Bingley's position, when considering the whole scheme of Miss Elizabeth and George Wickham, there was at least one way in which he knew he could very likely prod Darcy into action.

"Ah," Bingley began, "so that is the real reason why you were in such a rush to return to London. You were unwilling to fight for Miss Elizabeth. Do you really think of yourself so meanly when compared to him? I must say it is rather startling that you do."

Darcy bristled as Bingley knew he would. Not even the staid Mr. Darcy could keep from reacting with displeasure when his masculine sensibilities were challenged. In fact, Bingley knew that Darcy's sense of honour was likely more honed and, therefore, more easily provoked than most gentlemen in the higher echelons of society.

"I do not trust him to behave in a way which will not bring harm to all those I care about." Darcy's voice was satisfyingly close to a growl. "It is safer for her if I do not fight him. He could not only harm her but her family as well."

Bingley shook his head. He knew that his friend would not allow any about whom he cared to be placed in harm's way and would sacrifice himself to see them safe, but his logic, in this case, was sadly lacking. "Have you listened to yourself?"

Darcy's brows furrowed in question.

"Tell me. Exactly how is Miss Elizabeth safer with him than with you?"

Darcy huffed in disbelief, and Bingley waited patiently for him to explain.

"He will leave her alone as long as he does not think I am interested in her," Darcy explained. "Why do you suppose he singled her out to befriend after our meeting on the street in Meryton? She was acquainted with me, and my shock upon seeing him may have left me unable to hide my jealousy. Wickham knows me well. He would not miss such a thing. However, she has no money to tempt him into anything more than a light flirtation, and he would never risk being tied to a woman that would not provide amply for his expenses."

Bingley shrugged. "True, but I still do not see how she is safer. What if she does lose her heart to him? While he may not marry a penniless woman, he is not above taking the little she has to offer." His brows rose as he gave his friend a pointed look.

Darcy groaned and ran his hands through his hair. "Surely, she would not succumb to his charms. She is far too intelligent."

"And Georgiana is not?"

Darcy was on his feet and pacing. "What do I do? Ride back to Longbourn and tell her stories of his past?" He sighed and shook his head at such a foolish idea. "She does not like me. I am sure I cannot convince her of his failings. I will only look like a vengeful fool."

"So, do not convince her," Bingley replied. "She has a sister in town, and there is always the possibility of a well-worded letter placed in the hands of a man she respects such as her father or Sir William. I am sure Wickham has amassed a fair number of debts within the past months. Let her see his character for what it is. She is intelligent. She will see the error in her judgment."

Darcy stopped mid-stride and turned to look at his friend. Relief suffused his features. "Bingley, I do not give you enough credit for your depth of understanding. You are positively wise tonight. Where do you suggest we start? With Miss Bennet?"

Bingley chuckled softly at his friend's exuberance — a word not often associated with the man standing before him. "As much as I would love to start with a visit to Miss Bennet, I rather think a visit to your cousin would be better."

Darcy's cousin, Colonel Richard Fitzwilliam, was well-known and respected by many. He also happened to despise Wickham. Both were items that could help their cause.

"Perhaps Richard could have some influence with Wickham's commanding officer? Colonel Forster may wish to know of Wickham's tendencies to gamble and dally with the ladies — not all turn a blind eye to such behaviors, you know. You do not even have to mention Miss Elizabeth to Richard. You just have to let him know where Wickham is. I doubt your cousin needs any further incentive to make the man's life as miserable as possible."

Darcy's lips curled in a knowing smile. "Richard would need very little incentive to relieve Wickham of his life. If you will allow me, I will send a note to him now, letting him know I need to speak with him."

Bingley motioned to his desk. "Whatever I have is at your disposal."

# Chapter 3

"Darcy," Bingley said as Darcy finished his missive to Colonel Fitzwilliam, "perhaps you could help me with a little problem?"

Darcy glanced up from the paper he was folding and preparing to seal. "Anything."

"My sister..."

"Except that," Darcy interrupted with a chuckle.

Bingley shook his head. "I would not foist her on you. If that were my intention, I would have done it long ago instead of suffering through these years with her airs."

Darcy inclined his head in acceptance. He was thankful his friend had the good sense not to throw his sister in Darcy's path. Caroline Bingley was not the sort of lady that he had ever considered. She was too... His brows furrowed, what was she exactly? Devious, practiced, lacking in warmth? Any of those would do, he supposed. Put simply; she did not possess a nature that appealed to him.

"I do not know what to do about her hiding Miss Bennet's call from me," Bingley continued. "You know I am not the best at knowing how to deal with Caroline." He sighed. "I wish she would just marry and be someone else's problem."

Darcy lifted a brow. "You care for her," he reminded him.

Bingley shrugged. "Not so much at this moment as I did before I knew she was trying to keep Miss Bennet away from me. I would rather fob her off onto the first chap to seem welcoming than have to keep her and act appropriately."

"You would not fob her off on the first chap," Darcy contradicted with a smile. His friend really did care for both of his sisters, no matter how much they annoyed him. "You would see her well-settled, at least."

Bingley blew out a resigned breath. "Then what do I do?"

"Nothing," Darcy replied. "Call on Miss Bennet." He rose and returned to the group of chairs where he and Bingley had been sitting before and where Bingley was now. "Tell your sister nothing about it. Continue as if nothing has changed."

Bingley's eyes grew wide. "Is that not rather a lot of disguise?"

Darcy pondered the question for a moment and then shrugged. "Tell her if you must or if she asks, but it will not aid your cause."

"But you hate –"

"Normally, yes," Darcy interrupted, "however, it seems necessary at the moment."

Bingley's brows furrowed as he nodded his agreement.

"I will even go with you to call on Miss Bennet," Darcy offered.

"You would do that?" Bingley's eyes were wide in surprise. "Her relations are in Cheapside."

Darcy shook his head. "No, they are near Cheapside," he corrected. "On Gracechurch Street, if I am not mistaken."

"That is well-removed from Grosvenor Square," Bingley cautioned.

"I know where it is," Darcy retorted, "and I am not so priggish as you seem to think."

Bingley shrugged and gave his friend a look that said he was not entirely convinced that travelling to that portion of London would not be a trial. "If you are certain, I would be happy for the company."

"Then, it is settled. We will call on Miss Bennet together."

Bingley smiled as understanding dawned on him. "You wish for her to write to her sister about your visit."

"Of course." Having Jane write to Elizabeth about the fact that he had brought Bingley to Jane and had visited her relations in Gracechurch Street would have to earn him some small amount of merit, would it not?

"Very well," said Bingley, leaning forward with eagerness, "do you know exactly where her relations live?"

Darcy shook his head. "I only know it is on Gracechurch Street."

Bingley scowled for a moment, his brows furrowed in thought. He took the letter Darcy was tapping on the arm of his chair and went to the door.

"Jenkins," he called down the hall and then waited for his butler to join him. "Has my sister received any letters from Gracechurch Street?"

Jenkins was a most fastidious butler, and if a piece of correspondence had entered the house, he would know when it arrived, to whom it was addressed, and from whence it had come.

"Yes, sir, she has."

"Do you remember the number in the direction?"

"Of course, sir. It was eighteen."

"Eighteen Gracechurch Street?"

"Yes, sir. Will there be anything else?"

"Would you see that this is delivered?" Bingley handed Darcy's message to him.

"Tonight, sir?"

"Yes, as soon as can be managed."

Bingley closed the door behind Jenkins and rejoined Darcy.

"So, tomorrow, you will accompany me on a social call?" He could not help the smirk that he wore.

"Happily," Darcy answered.

Bingley chortled. "Happily? I repeat, this is a social call, and you will be required to be affable."

Darcy shook his head and smiled. "I know that such a thing is not my strongest suit, but I have a vested interest in your success. For, it seems, I am most anxious to be allowed the chance to disappoint my family's expectations."

As Darcy was speaking, the door of the study was flung open and Darcy's cousin, Colonel Richard Fitzwilliam entered, followed by a flustered Jenkins.

"I am sorry, sir," the butler apologized. "I tried to get him to wait."

Bingley chuckled. "We are all sorry at one time or another for Richard, Jenkins. Think nothing of it." Bingley clapped Richard on the shoulder. "I did not think you would receive Darcy's message so soon."

"Message?" Richard questioned. " I did not receive a message. I stopped by Darcy's, and his butler told me that he was here, so I came. What message was I to receive? Does it have anything to do with my cousin disappointing his family?" Richard smiled wickedly at Darcy.

"This is why one waits to be announced," grumbled Darcy. "There are things that you are not supposed to hear."

At that moment, Jenkins re-entered the room. "A message for you, sir." He bowed, handed an envelope to Richard, and was gone.

Richard broke the seal and scanned the contents of Darcy's message, looking up from it in surprise. "You wish to discuss an old acquaintance?"

"Yes," Bingley took out a third glass and filled it with an ample amount of brandy. "It seems that an old acquaintance of yours has surfaced in Meryton, which is near my estate in Hertfordshire." He handed the glass to Richard. "You may wish to drink this first."

Richard eyed Bingley and Darcy suspiciously. "And who might that be?"

"Wickham," said Darcy.

Richard muttered and took a healthy gulp of his drink.

"Bingley's neighbour has five daughters, and he is concerned for their safety." Darcy felt his ears warm at the half-truth. Hiding Bingley's call on Miss Bennet call from Caroline gave him no qualms but hiding anything from Richard always did, and while it was accurate that Bingley wished to see the Bennets safe, he was not the only one who wished it.

"Five daughters?" Richard whistled softly. "And would one of these be your new angel?" he asked Bingley. "You do still find an angel in every town, do you not?"

"If things go well," Darcy answered before Bingley could, "I think this may be Bingley's last angel."

Richard let out another slow whistle. "She must be quite the lady."

Bingley grinned, utterly undaunted by Richard's teasing

tone. "She is," he said, "and she has four sisters that need protection from Wickham."

Richard tipped his head and looked from Bingley to Darcy and back. "Your angel has been seen in company with you and Darcy?"

Bingley nodded. "As have certain of her sisters." Bingley winked slyly at Richard.

Darcy groaned inwardly as he shook his head. Of course, Bingley would not keep that information to himself.

Richard's brows rose as an impish grin spread across his face. "Has my cousin singled out any sister in particular?"

"Yes, your cousin has," Darcy answered. There seemed no need to try to deny it. Richard would know the truth and to tell him directly was better than to be taunted by both his cousin and Bingley. "Miss Elizabeth Bennet."

"Miss Bennet's next youngest sister," Bingley added.

Richard rubbed his knuckles against his jaw. "And Wickham knows this?"

Darcy nodded. "I believe so. Therefore, we have decided that Bingley will inform Miss Bennet that Wickham is not to be trusted with the hope that she will then impart this information to her sisters; although, I am not sure the information will be immediately accepted by all." He shifted in his seat. "Bingley thought that perhaps you could inform Colonel Forster of Wickham's penchant for cards and women. He has been in the area long enough to have accrued a fair amount of debt, both with the merchants of the area and other members of the regiment. Your word would go a long way in helping me refute the stories that I am sure he has been spreading about me."

Richard blew out a breath. "Miss Elizabeth believes Wickham?"

Darcy nodded slowly. He wished it was not true, but it was.

"Which means she is set against you, and you are besotted with her enough to consider going against familial duty." Richard surmised.

"I would not say besotted," retorted Darcy.

"I would," Bingley muttered.

Richard threw back his head and laughed. "It is about time."

"Why were you looking for me tonight?" Darcy asked before Richard could continue down a road that Darcy was certain he did not wish to have traversed.

Richard lifted his glass. "A drink, a game of billiards, some conversation, and a comfortable bed."

Darcy's lips twitched. "There are beds at Matlock House that are quite comfortable. In fact, there is one there reserved for you."

"There is also one at Darcy House." He consumed what remained in his glass. "However, your home lacks one thing that my parents' house does not."

"Your mother?" Darcy asked with a grin.

"Precisely. I have no desire to hear her concerns regarding my lack of a wife." He placed his glass on the table next to Darcy's and lay a hand on his cousin's shoulder for a moment. "If you will forget family expectations and for once pursue your own happiness, then, I might be inspired to do the same, and my mother will be delighted."

He continued as Darcy rose from his chair, ready to take his leave, "Do you know how many times I have heard Father and Mother speaking about how they wish to see you happy?" He chuckled as Darcy shook his head. "Neither do they, but it is a great number, to be sure. They will be pleased for you. It is only Aunt Catherine who might pose an issue. But then, when is she not an issue?"

Darcy and Bingley both chuckled along with Richard. Lady Catherine was known for voicing her opinion about many things quite loudly, and the more her opinion was ignored, as it often was by her brother, the more vocal she would become until eventually, her arguments would expire in a huff.

"It is not only Lady Catherine about whom you need worry," said Bingley. "I have a sister who is not easily dissuaded and is intent on securing Pemberley."

Richard shook his head. "Is she still at that?"

"Stubborn, is she not?" Bingley said as he nodded his answer to Richard's question.

"Extremely," Darcy muttered.

Richard clapped him on the shoulder. "We should take our leave unless you wish to encounter her tonight."

"You will contact Colonel Forster?" Bingley asked as they moved into the corridor.

"I will send him a letter tomorrow, and I am certain Darcy will see that it travels by express?"

Darcy rolled his eyes. If there was one thing that Richard was good at, aside from his role as colonel, it was weaseling out of extra expenditures. For one who had grown up in a house filled with plenty, he had a strong miserly bent as well as an eye for investment to increase his holdings. A strategic mind, he called it and said it was what made him proficient in his profession.

"I will call for you tomorrow before I head toward Cheapside to call on Miss Bennet," Bingley said to Darcy as they reached the front door.

"Cheapside?" Richard whistled low. "You do mean to disappoint the family." He laughed and slapped his cousin on the back.

"It is where her uncle lives. She is a gentleman's daughter," Darcy argued.

Richard moved down the steps briskly and prepared to mount his horse. "You may tell me all her excellent qualities over a game of billiards." He swung up into his saddle and with a salute was off.

"You know you will have to tell him everything, do you not?" Bingley asked.

Darcy nodded. Along with having a miserly streak, Richard Fitzwilliam was also persistent, and much like a starving dog might latch onto a piece of meat and refuse to let go, if there was something that Darcy's cousin wished to know, he was going to discover it, using whatever means he could. "As long as he lends his help, I will bare my very soul."

"Thank you," Bingley said as Darcy climbed into his carriage, "for telling me about Miss Bennet's call and all."

Darcy leaned forward in his seat so that he could see out the door to where his friend stood. "It is I who should thank you — first, for not tossing me out and, then, for helping me to see reason."

"My happiness could not be complete without yours," Bingley said. "And I promise you, we will find ourselves happy, in spite of my sister."

# Chapter 4

Darcy and Bingley stood just inside the foyer of a neat but modest home on Gracechurch Street, waiting for their cards to be presented to the mistress of the home and her niece.

"The Gardiners do not appear to be destitute or even wanting," Bingley whispered. "This paper is new." He nodded toward the wall. "Caroline has admired it and has begged me to allow her to redecorate the front sitting room with it. However, I prefer paint over flowers." He pursed his lips as he studied the paper on the wall. "Unless of course my wife prefers flowers, and then I shall prefer them as well."

Darcy chuckled. "I have not considered my preference one way or the other. I simply wish my surroundings to look..." His brow furrowed as he thought of how best to describe his taste in decor. It really was not something he considered often. He knew what he liked and what he did not, but he had not put significant effort into deciding how he would decorate a home. His mother had done that sort of thing, and now, if a space needed refreshing, he simply deferred to the opinion of either Georgiana or Lady Matlock. He shrugged. "I prefer my rooms to be welcoming and not garish, homely and not ostentatious."

"Which is why my sister should not be allowed to decorate your home or mine," Bingley said with a smirk. "Are you prepared to see if it is possible to convince a Bennet lady to take on such a task?" he whispered as they followed behind the maid who directed them to the sitting room on their right.

They had discussed how they would approach this interview as they had travelled together today. It was decided that the folly of both Caroline and Darcy should be broached directly as neither gentleman wished to be left wondering as to their position in hoping to attain their happiness.

"Mr. Bingley, Mr. Darcy, it is a pleasure to meet you," a lady, dressed in the current fashion of the day and appearing to be no older than Darcy, if she was even that, greeted them as they entered the room.

"The pleasure is ours, Mrs. Gardiner," Bingley said as he took her hand and bowed over it. "It is a pleasure that should have been ours much earlier had we known your niece was in town."

Mrs. Gardiner barely contained a grin. "That is a welcome sentiment, is it not, Jane?" she asked as she extended her hand to Mr. Darcy.

"Indeed, it is," Jane replied.

"Please, be seated while I arrange for tea." Mrs. Gardiner slipped behind Mr. Darcy and into the hall for a moment but was back before either gentleman had settled into his chair completely.

To Darcy, she rather flitted about like a bird, happily doing all that needed to be done. She tucked away some material that lay on a work table and pulled the table out to be used, he assumed, for the tea service. Then, she perched lightly in her chair, looking at ease but ready to fly away again if she should be needed for something.

"Mr. Bingley, I understand that you have been considering an estate in Hertfordshire," Mrs. Gardiner began, directing the conversation to exactly where Darcy and Bingley had hoped it would eventually fall. "Will you return to it once the season draws to a close? I understand you are in town because you have a sister in need of a husband."

Darcy found the way the lady's lips twitched with amusement to be telling of what she had likely heard about Miss Bingley, and the way that her eyes danced reminded him of Elizabeth. He was certain he would enjoy having this woman's acquaintance.

"Of course, you are also unmarried," she continued, "so I suppose you might also be looking for a wife while squiring your sister to this function and that."

Even Darcy could not mistake the meaning of Mrs. Gardiner's words when accompanied by the pointed look she gave Bingley. It was apparent that Mrs. Gardiner was not the sort of lady to play games but came directly to the point, and that fact made him like her all the more.

"I should not say it, but I will be beyond elated when my sister finally marries," Bingley admitted. "She is no small trial."

"Oh, we all have relations like that," Mrs. Gardiner said with a grin. "Some are born to us while others are attached by marriage. I do hope she finds a husband who does not add to your affliction."

Bingley chuckled. "I most heartily hope the same."

"And what of you, Mr. Bingley? Has the season been kind to you — aside from the trials of a sibling?"

Determined and not to be thwarted in her pursuit — Darcy added these qualities to the list of items that recommended Mrs. Gardiner to him.

Bingley held Mrs. Gardiner's gaze. "Not until this moment," he said before darting his eyes toward Jane and returning them to her aunt and adding, "I hope."

"Very well said," Mrs. Gardiner replied with no small amount of approval in her voice. "We had heard you had intentions of a marriage in the future when a particular lady was finally presented to society." She stood to pour the tea as the maid laid out the service for her.

"You speak of my sister."

Mrs. Gardiner acknowledged the veracity of Darcy's words with a nod of her head.

"Neither Bingley nor I have ever harboured such a wish for any such joining of our families."

Bingley gave his fervent agreement. "I assure you that I view Miss Darcy as nothing more than the sister of a very good friend. If our families are ever joined, it shall not be through either of our sisters." He turned to Jane. "I must apologize for the actions of my sister. I only learned last evening that you were in town and that is only because Darcy told me."

Jane looked between the men in confusion.

"Miss Bingley told me of your call when I stopped to deliver something to Bingley yesterday afternoon." Darcy accepted a cup of tea from Mrs. Gardiner and then began his painful confession. "She thought I would be delighted about how she had snubbed you. I was not, of course, although I admit to not remonstrating her for her actions but only accepting her account and fleeing as quickly as I could."

Bingley chuckled. "You must forgive him for that. Darcy knows my sister's intentions in regard to his marital state and has no desire to encourage those attentions or to find himself unwarily caught in a trap from which his honour will not allow him to escape."

"You do not like Miss Bingley?" Jane asked Darcy in surprise.

Darcy grimaced and looked at Bingley apologetically. "Not particularly. However, there was a reason for her to think I would find her actions towards you acceptable, and for that, I must apologize. You see, I supported Miss Bingley's desire to leave Netherfield and persuade her brother not to return." He closed his eyes and shook his head in self-remonstration. "I abhor disguise, Miss Bennet, and yet, I prevaricated most grievously. I agreed with Miss Bingley that a connection between her family and yours would not be beneficial to her brother."

He stood and placed his untouched tea on the tea tray. He knew admission of his failings would be difficult, but to see the pain in the eyes of a woman as kind and sweet as he knew Miss Bennet to be made the task far harder than he had imagined.

"I will admit to having certain reservations about your family." He grimaced. "They have nothing to do with your ties to trade. They are — were solely based on what I have perceived to be improper behavior." He shook his head again. "Not even I can deny how arrogant that sounds." Indeed, as he said the words here, in the sitting room, standing before both Miss Bennet and her relation, the words sounded like those of a pretentious fool. "Please forgive me."

He drew a breath. He needed to complete his admission of guilt, no matter how painful it might be to do so. "I worked to keep Mr. Bingley from returning to Netherfield as he wished." He smiled sadly at Jane whose eyes had grown wide at his comment. "He wished to return to you. However, I had made a promise to remain with him at his estate until he had decided on either purchasing or moving on and then, if he purchased, until he had enough knowledge to stand on his own as master of his own domain. However, I could not return." He shook his head slowly as he returned to his seat. "I simply could not be there."

"I should not have allowed myself to be persuaded," Bingley said softly as Darcy retreated into his chair to allow Bingley to make his own apology to Miss Bennet.

"No," Jane agreed, "you should not have."

"Was it an unpardonable error?" Bingley's heart thumped wildly, and his palms became moist while drawing a breath became something about which he needed to think. How he would survive a negative response without making a complete cake of himself, he was uncertain.

Jane's cheeks grew rosy, and she took a slow sip from her cup. Then, as she returned her cup to her saucer with only a small clatter, she answered. "It is only unpardonable if your intentions in calling today are less than sincere or if you should be so easily persuaded once again."

"I promise my intentions are both sincere and unwavering," Bingley replied, passing his cup to Darcy. "I fear I will drop this if I must hold it any longer." He rubbed his hands on his breeches. "If you will allow me, Miss Bennet, I will request an interview with your uncle to gain his blessing in your father's stead to court you. I know this is not exactly the most fitting setting for such a discussion. I should have asked to speak to you in private. However, I came today determined to discover if I had any hope of winning you, and I am willing to openly suffer any humiliation my offer may bring." He smiled sheepishly. "Although I would be lying if I said I did not hope to avoid the humiliation of rejection."

"You may speak to my uncle," Jane said with a smile.

Bingley grasped Jane's hand which was not holding her cup and lifting it, kissed it. "Thank you," he whispered, returning her smile.

"My husband will not be home for many hours," Mrs. Gardiner said. "He is to dine with an associate this evening."

"Tomorrow would be soon enough," Bingley replied. "Unless it would not be too offensive for me to visit his place of business today."

Mrs. Gardiner chuckled. "You do not do things by halves, do you, Mr. Bingley?"

"Not when it is of such importance as this," Bingley replied with a smile. "Now, if you were to ask me to muck out the stables, I might not be so eager."

"I shall ask you to do no such thing." Mrs. Gardiner's left brow rose with an impertinence that reminded Darcy once again of Elizabeth. "However, there are four children in the nursery, and I would not be above shuffling one or more of them off on you so that both their nurse and I might have a nice quiet cup of tea and a read."

Bingley shrugged and settled back into his chair. "I am fond of both children and toys, especially if there might be a tin of biscuits involved."

"Oh, boys and their biscuits!" Mrs. Gardiner cried. "My youngest son is forever attempting to sneak an extra treat when his nurse's back is turned." She chuckled. "He is only two, so, though I reprimand, it is forgivable." She held out a plate of almond cakes to Bingley.

"Mr. Darcy," she began as Bingley selected two cakes from the plate, causing her to smile. "You are like John," she said to Bingley before turning back to Darcy. "You said you could not return to Netherfield, and I admit to being curious as to the cause of your reluctance — nay — refusal to return." She offered him an almond cake and refused to move from her spot until he had taken one. Then, she gathered his cup from the tea tray and returned that to him as well. "I will not have you leave without refreshment," she said kindly before returning to her seat. "Would I be correct in assuming it had something to do with another one of my nieces?"

Darcy washed down his bite of cake with some tea. "Yes," he replied simply.

# Chapter 5

"Were you much attached to Lizzy?" Jane asked, causing Darcy's eyes to widen in surprise.

The Miss Bennet he was witnessing today in this drawing room clashed with the one he remembered from his time in Hertfordshire. This Miss Bennet was much bolder. However, from the pink that stained her cheeks and the way her eyes did not hold his for long before dropping away, he knew that the effort was not without cost.

"Surprisingly, yes," he admitted. "Although I did not realize just how much until I returned to town and could not rid myself of her memory."

"She likes you," Jane's voice was no more than a whisper.

"I am sorry to disagree with you, Miss Bennet, but your sister most certainly does not like me," Darcy returned.

"Oh, no," Mrs. Gardiner said, "our Lizzy is quite taken with you. She just does not realize it."

For the first time since his arrival, Darcy saw the woman

relax into her chair and take a leisurely sip of her tea rather than the quick ones she had taken thus far.

"You will have to explain that to me," Darcy said. "I was left with the distinct impression that she did not approve of me any more than I approved of such a connection at that time."

"How will your family receive her?" Mrs. Gardiner asked.

Darcy shook his head and shrugged. "I do not know, but first –"

"Do you love her?" Mrs. Gardiner interrupted.

Darcy drew a deep breath and released it as he nodded his head. "But I do not see how –"

"Good," Mrs. Gardiner interrupted again.

It appeared that the lady was determined to be the only one asking questions and directing the conversation, so Darcy leaned back and waited expectantly.

"No more protests, Mr. Darcy?"

The familiar twinkle had returned to Mrs. Gardiner's eyes, causing the right side of Darcy's mouth tipped up in a half smile. "You are very much like her," he commented.

Mrs. Gardiner finished the tea in her cup and placed it to the side. "I cannot deny that. However, the fact that you have recognized it speaks to how much you must admire her to have noticed such a thing. Tell me, because my curiosity must be satisfied: what makes you say that Elizabeth and I are alike?"

Darcy tipped his head. "You would leave your children in the care of Bingley to have a cup of tea and a read. Therefore, I assume you enjoy reading as much as she does."

With a tip of her head, Mrs. Gardiner accepted his statement as true.

"You are determined and unafraid to speak your mind. You challenged both me and Bingley."

"One of my faults," Mrs. Gardiner said with a smile.

"No, I do not find it to be a fault. I prefer directness to prevarication and pandering." He watched the light dance in the eyes of the woman before him. "Her eyes sparkle and dance just as yours do, and her brow raises in much the same fashion as yours is now." A smile spread across his face. "And, her lips purse and twitch just like that when she is trying to contain her amusement."

Mrs. Gardiner clapped her hands in delight. "Oh, you do love her!"

Darcy nodded. "But –" He stopped as Mrs. Gardiner held up a hand.

"She would not dislike you so much as she does if she did not like you."

Darcy's brows furrowed. How could dislike equate to like? "I beg your pardon?"

Bingley chuckled.

"Do you understand her meaning?" Darcy asked his friend.

"I think I might," Bingley replied. "The lady doth protest too much, me thinks."

Darcy's eyes grew wide. "Shakespeare?"

"I said I read occasionally," Bingley retorted.

"He has the right of it," said Mrs. Gardiner, "does he not, Jane?"

Jane nodded. "Oh, indeed. Lizzy avows her dislike far too much for it not to indicate how much she wishes for your good opinion."

Darcy's brows furrowed as he shook his head trying to rid himself of the perplexity such statements brought. "But she has my good opinion; she does not have to wish for it."

"Oh, she knows she has your *tolerably* good opinion," Mrs. Gardiner said as she rose and gathered empty cups. Both of her brows rose as she took Mr. Darcy's cup from him. "I am afraid she heard your comment at the assembly. In fact, I am quite certain everyone who knows and is close to Lizzy has heard your comment from the assembly. I had it in a letter not two days after it was spoken."

Darcy blew out a breath and closed his eyes for a moment. "Then, if she is so set against me, do I have any hope?"

Mrs. Gardiner placed the cups she held on the tea tray and then, as she crossed the room to summon someone to clear the things away, she stopped and lay a hand on

Darcy's shoulder much like Richard's mother would at times when attempting to reassure him of something.

"Hope is not lost until she is married to someone other than you. Until that time, we must not faint." She gave his shoulder a pat and then rang for the maid.

"Now, we must decide how to proceed," she said as she returned to her seat. "I am not a matchmaker, mind you. However, I do long to see my nieces well-settled."

Her smile and accompanying laugh were infectious, filling the room with a lightness it had not had for several minutes.

"I might be able to persuade her to visit," Mrs. Gardiner said. "And then you can call just as you are now, and she will see that you are not as she thinks." She winked. "I will be certain to sing your praises if she should disparage. An unhappy Lizzy is known to allow her tongue to get the better of her good sense. Aside from getting Elizabeth here and allowing Mr. Darcy to confuse and then charm her, are there any other contentious items that need our forethought?"

"I am positive she has heard some very disparaging stories about me," Darcy said. "Mr. Wickham is not a champion of the Darcy name. I am right, am I not?" he asked as he noted how Jane drew her lower lip between her teeth and dropped her gaze.

Jane nodded.

Darcy shook his head. "I cannot tell you all that has

passed between us, but I can assure you that it is not Mr. Wickham's normal wont to speak truthfully regarding how things now stand between us. He is not to be trusted."

"Indeed, he is not," Bingley affirmed gravely.

"I have not believed him," Jane said with a smile. "He spoke too freely with an acquaintance of a short duration. I told Lizzy to be wary, and I do not think she is completely convinced by his words. Did she not ask you about him at the ball?"

"She did."

"If you would but answer her, her opinion might be swayed. I know you could not on a dance floor, but she is not thinking clearly. You have unsettled her." Jane paused and then continued. "There is, however, one item about which I should like to ask."

"Whatever you wish to know, Miss Bennet," Darcy offered.

"Are you betrothed?"

Darcy shook his head. "No matter how much my aunt insists that it happens, I am not betrothed to her daughter, nor will I ever be betrothed to her daughter. It will come as a great disappointment to her, I suppose," he added sardonically.

Jane's broad smile at the comment was, Darcy recognized, the equivalent of another more vocal lady's chuckle. He was beginning to recognize in the short time they had spent together this afternoon that her emotions were conveyed in small, subtle ways that required greater attention than he had given them in Meryton. She was not a fawning lady of the ton but a gracious and demure lady of quality. His friend would do well to secure her.

"My mother was quite disappointed with Elizabeth in such a fashion recently."

"I beg your pardon?" Darcy asked as his heart began racing and his stomach twisted. Wickham would not offer for a lady of little wealth — not even to spite Darcy. Would he?

"Mr. Collins, our cousin, made an offer. My mother was beside herself demanding that Elizabeth retract her refusal. The whole house was in an uproar until Mr. Collins removed himself to Lucas Lodge, where he found a lady who was more amenable to his offer."

"Mr. Collins? The large man with an excess of words and an inability to dance without injuring his partner?"

At this, Jane actually giggled as she nodded. "Yes, that Mr. Collins. A most ridiculous match, is it not?"

"Indeed," Darcy muttered. How would anyone with half a morsel of sense think that a lady as intelligent and quick-witted as Elizabeth would make a good match for a bumbling fool like Mr. Collins? The idea was far beyond ridiculous. It was ludicrous, and he was happy that it appeared Elizabeth's refusal had stood.

"He married Miss Lucas," Mrs. Gardiner added. "But it is not Mr. Collins we wish to see married, now is it?"

Darcy found himself chuckling at her pointed look.

"No," he replied. He hoped to see both Bingley and himself happily leg-shackled before his annual trip to Rosings at Easter, where he would both have to endure his aunt and Mr. Collins. A smile settled firmly on his lips. Perhaps if he were fortunate to secure a bride before Easter, he would not be required to visit Rosings at all since his aunt's displeasure would undoubtedly take some time to quell.

"Do you think you can persuade Miss Elizabeth to visit soon?" Darcy asked. "It may take some time for me to convince her that I am not so unworthy as I portrayed myself."

"Oh, I should think she would be very willing to visit soon. I imagine that there is a fair bit of unpleasantness to be endured at home since her mother is displeased to know that Longbourn is not to fall to one of her daughters but to Miss Lucas. I will write today, and perhaps Jane will add a note of invitation as well?" She cast a questioning look at her niece.

"Please tell her that I came to call," Bingley said as he rose to leave. "And that it was at Darcy's insistence. In fact, it is through Darcy that I learned of Miss Bennet's being in town. That should do some good in shedding a bit of a rosy glow on my friend, should it not?" He looked from one lady to the other.

"It will," Jane said quietly.

Mrs. Gardiner, followed by Jane, rose to see their guests

out of the room, and after a few words of parting and Bingley managing to get the directions to Mr. Gardiner's warehouse, the two gentlemen stepped out onto the street, feeling very hopeful.

# Chapter 6

"Gentlemen," Mr. Gardiner rose and greeted the two men who entered his office. "How might I be of service to you today?" He made a sweeping motion to the chairs that stood before a desk, covered with a few small boxes on one end and a stack of account books and papers on the other. He tucked his ink and pen away and straightened the few documents that were before him into a neat pile.

Darcy noted the emblem that graced the tops of several of the papers and was stamped on the side of one box that was facing him. Though the lady who looked at him from that box did not always appear in the same dress — what lady did — there was no mistaking her identity. Mr. Gardiner was, apparently, a member of the Mercers' Company.

"We have just come from calling at your home," Bingley began.

Mr. Gardiner, a good-natured-looking gentleman of no more than five and thirty, leaned back in his chair, a small smile playing at the corners of his mouth. "Indeed? I hope you were not too disappointed to find I was not home." His lips twitched with barely contained amusement.

Bingley laughed. "Seeing as my goal was to call on your niece, I was not disappointed in the least."

A grin spread across Mr. Gardiner's face. "I had hoped you were calling for her and not me," he replied. "I also hope you are calling on me now because of her." He tipped his head and smiled. "I am not a man to shake the bushes in hopes that for which I am searching falls out. I prefer to come to the point where it is prudent." He propped his elbows on the arms of his chair and clasped his hands in front of him. "We have heard much about both of you gentlemen." He grimaced. "I wish I could say it has all been good, but I am not the sort to bear false tales."

"Well-deserved criticism," Darcy assured him, causing the gentleman's eyebrows to raise.

"Indeed?"

Darcy nodded. "I have made my full confession of folly to your wife."

"As have I," Bingley added.

"And was your folly forgiven?" Gardiner's eyes shifted from Bingley to Darcy and back.

"Yes," Bingley replied with a grin.

"By your wife and Miss Bennet," Darcy added. "And I hope, eventually, to be forgiven by Miss Elizabeth as well."

"Hmm," Gardiner muttered as he nodded his head in a

pleased fashion. "I am certain my wife will apprise me of the details when I return home this evening."

"I am certain she will," Darcy agreed.

"So, you do not dislike our Lizzy, then?"

The smile he wore told Darcy he knew the answer to that question, but Darcy answered anyway. "I like her very much."

Gardiner chuckled and turned to Bingley. "And I assume you like Jane?"

Bingley's cheeks grew noticeably red. It was one of the hazards of having a fair complexion. "I love her," Bingley answered, "and I would like to have permission to court her."

"Done," Gardiner said with a sharp nod of his head.

"Done?" Bingley repeated. "Do you not wish to ask me my intentions or about why I have not called before now or ... or ... or ... something?"

Gardiner chuckled and shook his head. "My niece is not foolish. I trust her judgment and that of my wife. You would not be here if you had not gotten past Addie and been sent to me; therefore, you have passed the only test I require."

"But what of my wealth and standing?" Bingley questioned.

"You have five thousand a year, your father was in trade — something that does not concern me in the least — and you are planning to purchase an estate eventually —

although might I caution you not to consider Netherfield. Is there anything else I should know?"

Bingley shook his head. "No, I believe that covers the high points. Why should I not consider Netherfield?"

"You have met my sister, have you not?"

"Mrs. Bennet?"

Gardiner nodded. "In my experience, she does not improve with acquaintance, but then, she is my sister. However, I know she will be on your doorstep every second day at least." He grimaced. "I was not blessed with sensible sisters."

"Neither was I, " Bingley commiserated.

Gardiner shifted forward in his chair. "It is best to see them married and well-settled as soon as possible and at a distance that allows them to grow dear to you." He winked. "A half-day's journey is the least I would recommend. Now, was there anything else I could do for you, gentlemen?"

"There was a matter of some delicacy that we had hoped to discuss with you at some point," Darcy said.

Mr. Gardiner pulled his watch from his pocket and after giving it a quick glance, said, "I have an hour before I have to be anywhere, and I would welcome the diversion from my books."

"Have you heard of Mr. Wickham?" Darcy asked.

Mr. Gardiner nodded. "Elizabeth has mentioned him in her letters, and Jane has told us some about him."

"He is not what he appears," Darcy began, "but in revealing his nature, I will have to expose some things that are very personal and which I would not reveal for any other reason than to see Miss Elizabeth and her sisters safe."

Mr. Gardiner's features grew grave. "He is so bad?"

Darcy nodded. "I am afraid he is."

For the next half hour, Darcy related to Elizabeth's uncle all the details of Wickham's dissipated predilections, his refusal of the living at Kympton, the squandering of his fortune, and finally, his scheme to elope with Darcy's sister.

"This is very serious indeed," Gardiner said at the end of Darcy's narration. "You think he has singled Elizabeth out to befriend because of you?"

"At the risk of sounding arrogant, I do," Darcy replied. "I do not deny he might have selected her for her beauty and wit, but I fear that I might be an added reason for his preference."

Gardiner's head bobbed up and down slowly as he thought. "I am not certain how I can help."

"Mr. Bennet seems a sensible sort of man," Darcy began. "Perhaps, a few words of caution regarding Wickham's tendency to acquire debt might set him on guard."

Gardiner shrugged. "It is worth an attempt. I shall find a way to mention it." He paused. "Might I hint that Mr.

Wickham is a seducer? I would not mention your sister, of course."

Darcy nodded. "It is a general fact."

Gardiner blew out a breath. "And this is the man that has captured Elizabeth's attention?" He shook his head. "She is usually discerning."

"He is very practised. It is no fault of hers."

Gardiner shook his head. "Practiced he may be, but there is some fault on her part. She has chosen to listen. I blame my sisters for that. They are the worst gossips — always listening for some tantalizing tale to share and then imparting their stories with great embellishment. A child should not be subjected to such a demonstration from her mother." He rose from his chair. "I have cautioned Bennet about that on more than one occasion. Even the brightest will be influenced to err on occasion." He took his great coat from a hook on the wall and smiled reassuringly at Darcy. "Do not fear; Elizabeth is not like her mother. She has just forgotten her good sense in her dislike of you." He held the door open. "Not that she actually dislikes you, according to Addie."

"So, I have been told," Darcy replied.

Gardiner clapped him on the back. "Do not be discouraged. The female mind it is a delicate and complex thing. It is my belief that we gentlemen could study it all our lives and still only feign an understanding."

Darcy and Bingley added their agreement as they accompanied Mr. Gardiner out to the street.

~*~*~

A light rain was beginning to fall as Bingley reached his home after delivering Darcy to his and spending an hour or so discussing the afternoon and the changes that they hoped would soon be coming. Darcy was, understandably, more concerned for his fate than Bingley would ever be, now that he knew Jane would welcome his addresses. Bingley climbed down from the carriage and, pulling his collar close, hurried into the house.

"The Hursts are here," Jenkins said as he greeted his employer. "And Miss Clark. They are having tea in the drawing room with Miss Bingley, sir."

Bingley thanked him for the information and then stood for a moment in the corridor pondering what he should do. It would be the polite thing to greet his guests and relations, but he had very little desire to do so. His day had been rather pleasant to this point, and Caroline was guaranteed to put a damper on his mood.

"Colonel Fitzwilliam called earlier." Jenkins' voice penetrated Bingley's deliberation.

"Will he be returning?" Perhaps if he were, it could be an excuse to see Caroline for a very brief amount of time without raising her suspicion that he was put out with her — which he was.

"No, sir. He grumbled something about his mother forcing him to attend a soiree and asked if I would allow him to leave you a message. The missive is on your desk as he requested." The butler gave Bingley a significant look and lowered his voice. "He did not wish for the information to be seen by any but you."

Bingley smiled. "Very good. Then, I suppose I shall have to attend to that before I greet my sister?"

His butler shook his head. "I should think it would be better to greet your guests for a few moments before begging off to attend to duty. Your name has been bandied about a good deal."

Bingley cocked his head to the right and studied his butler. "My sisters are scheming?"

Jenkins' brows lifted and lowered, nothing else on his person or in his expression shifted, but it was enough of an answer for Bingley.

"Miss Clark?"

Again, the butler's brows gave his acknowledgment.

Bingley sighed. "Very well, I shall make my appearance and be gone as quickly as I can be. See that some tea finds its way to my study and ensure there is a bit of brandy to add to it."

Jenkins bowed and went to do as instructed.

"Blast," Bingley muttered as he straightened his sleeves and prepared to enter the drawing room. Caroline would never be satisfied until she had directed every last morsel of his life. First, she kept him from returning to Hertfordshire with suggestions that Miss Bennet did not like him — a fact which Miss Bennet had made perfectly clear was false with her admission that he should not have been persuaded away from Netherfield.

Then, Caroline had treated a friend, as she had insisted Miss Bennet was, in such a contemptible fashion. Most likely, it had been in an attempt to embitter Miss Bennet against him in case they should ever chance to meet.

As he pondered his sister's behaviour, he felt his displeasure with her growing to the point it had been last night when her perfidy had been discovered. Drawing a deep breath, he pushed the door to the room open. Caroline might think she was in control of how his future would unfold, but she was not. And, if she were not careful, she would also not be in control of her own destiny, for he would make certain she was well-settled in some gentleman's home as quickly as could be, just as Mr. Gardiner had suggested.

"Charles!" Caroline cried in delight as he entered. "We had begun to despair of seeing you at all."

Bingley placed a kiss on the hand she held out to him and then greeted Louisa and Hurst before waiting to be introduced to Caroline's friend, who had begun fidgeting with her skirt and moistened her lips when he entered.

"Have you met Miss Clark?" Caroline asked. "We spend at least a portion of every soiree in each other's company, but I cannot remember if you have been properly introduced."

Bingley narrowed his eyes and scrutinised his sister's friend with a slight scowl on his lips. It was rude perhaps, but the lady was wearing a very cat-like expression and looking at him as if he were a bowl of cream. "No, I do not believe we have been introduced. Welcome," he finally said. There were several other things that he wished to say, but he clamped his mouth shut and kept his speculations about her standing and wealth to himself. He knew his sister did not befriend anyone who was anything less than a gentleman's daughter with a sizable fortune. He cursed himself silently. Such a fact should have alerted him to his sister's insincerity toward Miss Bennet. For though Jane was a gentleman's daughter, she was not wealthy and held no sway in the ton.

"Miss Clark is attending the Johnson's musicale tonight just as we are," Caroline continued.

"The Johnson's musicale?" Bingley repeated. "Are you attending with Hurst and Louisa?"

"And you." Caroline laughed lightly.

Bingley shook his head. "I do not remember accepting any invitation."

"Oh, but you did. Last week. I asked if I could attend, and you thought it would be an excellent thing." Caroline explained.

Bingley shifted from one foot to another. "And I suppose it is, as long as you go with Hurst and not me."

"But I accepted for both of us. Mrs. Johnson and Marietta will be exceedingly disappointed if you do not attend."

Bingley shrugged. Marietta Johnson was another of Caroline's friends whom his sister kept mentioning on a regular basis. Apparently, her father's estate was old enough, and Miss Johnson's dowry was large enough for him to consider her as a possible wife. "Tell them I have a sore throat or a headache or some such thing."

Caroline gasped.

"I have been out all day and have business that requires my attention and am in no mood to sit about and listen to song after song." He turned to Hurst. "You are escorting Louisa to this musicale, are you not?"

Hurst shrugged and nodded. "It seems I am."

"There you are, Caroline. You may go and see and be seen as you wish, and I can have a quiet night with my ledgers."

Caroline had crossed her arms and was pouting while Miss Clark was looking curiously between the two of them.

Bingley grimaced. He had gone too far in being disagreeable it seemed.

"I say, you have become a right stodgy old bore," Caroline grumbled.

"Yes, well, the delights of town do not enthrall me as much as you, and you know my dislike of sitting for hours."

"Yet you will sit behind your desk all night?"

He shook his head. "No, I shall pace a fair bit between bouts of sitting."

"My brother does not favour being idle either," Miss Clark interjected. "He often stands along the wall when he attends musicales with me. You could stand with him."

"An excellent idea!" Caroline cried.

Yes, Bingley thought to himself, that would set a few tongues to wagging if Miss Clark were to attend a soiree with Caroline while he stood along the wall and conversed with the lady's brother. Every interested wag would have them at the church's door before the fourth piece of music had ended.

"And who will tend to my business whilst I stand about looking foolish?"

"You will not look foolish," Caroline said with a laugh. "You will be amiable and charming as you always are. You will not lack for entertainment."

"I do not wish for entertainment."

"Please?" Caroline begged. "You have not attended a soiree in over a week. People are beginning to talk."

Bingley tipped his head. "About what?"

Caroline bit her lip and ducked her head as she stole a

secret look at her friend. "That you have been jilted and are wallowing in heartbreak."

Bingley crossed his arms. "And my being seen at a function with one of your friends on my arm will put these rumors to rest?" His tone did not disguise his disbelief.

"Of course." Caroline blinked wide eyes at him. "You must be seen in the company of someone if you wish for the rumors to stop."

"Precisely why should I care about these rumors?"

"A man who has been jilted for who knows what reason the gossips create will find it hard to secure a good match."

Bingley chuckled. "Not if he has my fortune. Now, if you will excuse me, I have business that needs my attention." He turned and hurried to his study.

The tea he had requested and a small glass of brandy were on his desk. He eased himself into his chair and pulled the missive addressed to him out from under the corner of the tea tray.

B-

*Letter sent. Should have a response within the week.*

*Mother insists I attend the Johnson's musicale tonight. Your sister said you were attending. Johnson's library is good for escaping the ordeal. Curious to hear about your mission. Bring Darcy.*

*R-*

Bingley sighed, took out his pen, and scratched a note to Darcy on the paper below Richard's message. Then, after folding, addressing, and sealing it, he rang for Jenkins to have it delivered.

He shook his head as he stood in front of his desk and poured a healthy dose of the brandy into his tea before finishing what remained in the glass. Caroline would be far too pleased to have him capitulate to her demands so soon after having refused. He rounded his desk and sank into his chair once again. There was no need to tell her until dinner. He would savour this cup of tea, push around a few books, and consider his happy future until then.

# Chapter 7

Bingley stood near the door in the Johnson's music room. He had seen his sister to her seat and then left both her and her friend in Hurst's care. Caroline had, of course, protested in her teasing, cajoling fashion. However, he had reminded her that Miss Clark suggested that he stand, and she had agreed that her friend's idea was an excellent one.

He smiled even now, as he found a piece of wall to lean against, at how her jaw had clenched in displeasure as she attempted to remain pleasing should anyone hear their conversation. He was certain she and Miss Clark were equally as displeased that he had not gone to stand with Mr. Clark. In fact, Bingley had made certain to stand on the side of the room opposite of that gentleman. Wagging tongues would always wag, but it was not his intent to give them something about which to whisper.

He pulled his watch from his pocket and glanced at it. The music should begin soon. From where he was standing, he could just catch a glimpse of the entry. It seemed as if they were in for a crush this evening. Indeed, every gentleman not already lining the walls would soon be in deference to his lady's being allowed a place to sit. Such a sizable crowd would also make it much easier to slip out of the throng and hideaway.

Ah, there was Richard.

Lady Matlock was whispering something to him. He nodded and then followed behind his parents, stopping when they did to greet the few people who had not yet entered the music room.

"Pardon me," a footman said as he slipped in front of Bingley on his way to help another open the doors that joined this room to the drawing room beyond. Unsurprisingly, the drawing room had been rearranged so that its furniture and, Bingley imagined, a few extra pieces from the other room were facing the instruments positioned in the alcove created by the large bow window on the front of the house.

Mrs. Johnson was a seasoned hostess. She had kept the room small until the numbers had begun to look impressive. Only then, had she thrown open the doors to the room she knew she would need to add. It was a bit of staging — a few dramatics that lent themselves to how successful her soiree had been. After all, the room was not large enough to hold the attendees. Almost inevitably, tomorrow, there would be someone in all the most important drawing rooms in town commenting on her success.

Bingley shook his head and chuckled. Some of these

society matrons would make shrewd businesswomen. Presenting things to best effect, scheming to arrange meetings, wrangling willing daughters and less-than-willing gentlemen into life-long contracts — yes, they would likely own all of England and a half or better of the West Indies in a very small space of time should they put their minds to such a task. And heaven help the poor fellow who attempted to stand in their way! Even Prinny would find it difficult to contain such a movement.

A shoulder pumped against Bingley's, drawing his attention away from the way Mrs. Johnson was fluttering about with her daughter close behind her.

"Where is Darcy?" Richard asked.

"I assume he will be here in," Bingley drew his watch out once again, "two minutes as the music is to begin in five."

Richard chuckled.

Both men knew that Darcy did not like to be tardy to any engagement, but he also did not like to arrive early since arriving early meant he would be expected to stand around and converse politely about trivial matters.

As if the mention of his name had conjured him, Bingley caught a glimpse of his friend at the entrance. "He's early," Bingley said, nodding his head toward the door. "What were your mother's instructions?" Bingley snapped his watch closed and tucked it into his pocket. "I saw her speaking to you in the hall."

"I am not to sneak out to the garden, and I am to be

civil to at least three ladies this evening." Richard smirked. "I have already spoken to three ladies so that requirement is met. As for the garden, I have no intention of strolling about the garden with its dimly lit areas where a compromise could be affected when we could retire to the safer confines of the library."

"You think there are ladies here who would try to trap you into marriage?" Bingley asked with a chuckle.

Richard shrugged. "It would not be the first attempt. There are those who wish for a connection to my father, but I have no desire to sacrifice myself just to elevate some lady to daughter-in-law of the Earl of Matlock."

"Unless, of course," Bingley added with a smirk, "she has a fortune that is as handsome as she is."

Richard nodded. "Precisely. I shall throw myself on no matrimonial swords unless the conditions are in my favour. Darcy," he greeted as his cousin joined him. "Quite a crush, is it not?"

"My favourite sort of event," Darcy replied grimly.

"Two songs," Richard whispered. "My mother will stop looking back here after that, and then we can make our escape."

"Am I going to run afoul of your mother?" Darcy asked.

"Most likely," Richard replied with a grin. "Consider it practice for when you make your intentions known regarding a certain young lady."

Darcy shook his head. Teasing words seemed to roll off

his cousin's tongue as easily as butter slid from a heated knife. There was seldom a time when Richard found himself without a witty rejoinder. It was something Darcy had always envied, for, to him, ease in conversation only came when he was with a small group of intimate acquaintances. A room filled to overflowing, as this one was, made him uneasy and often muddled his thoughts.

His father had stressed to him the need to never bring shame to the Darcy name. With that in mind, every word needed to be measured carefully before being spoken.

Darcy shifted, moving his weight from his right foot to his left, as their hostess welcomed the assembled masses and introduced her daughter, who was to begin the evening with a piece performed on the violin.

Perhaps if he had considered his words more carefully in Meryton, he would not now find himself loving a lady who had very little liking for him.

For the duration of two songs, he pondered his various meetings with Miss Elizabeth. Then, when the third song began, he followed his cousin and Bingley out of the room and down the hall to the library.

The library was not wholly unoccupied. Mr. Johnson gave the young gentlemen a smile and a nod as they entered.

"Your mother will be displeased if you spend the whole of your time in here," he said to Richard.

Richard allowed it to be so but assured the gentleman

that they were only attempting to find a quiet spot to have a bit of a tête-à-tête and would not be overly long.

Mr. Johnson chuckled as if he knew very well that the three men would be in his library as long as they thought they could stay. "I have a daughter," he said. "This room could be yours at every function my wife holds."

"It nearly always is now," Richard returned with a grin. "The desk is a very nice addition."

Mr. Johnson shook his head. "Fitzwilliam, why do you attend if you are only going to hie off to the library."

"My mother," Richard replied as he took a seat in a group of chairs as far removed from the door as the room would allow.

"I know my Marietta is not the incomparable of the season, but she is not without her charms," he tried again.

"She is lovely," Richard said.

"And well dowered," Mr. Johnson interjected.

"Indeed," Richard agreed. "However, these two have their hearts set elsewhere, and I, no matter what my mother might say, am bound to my commission and, as such, am not at present looking for a wife."

"Very well," Mr. Johnson replied with a smile. "I should like to know more about the ladies that have turned your friends' heads, but I will refrain. Unless…"

Richard chuckled. "We are not at liberty at this time to divulge any particulars, sir. The campaign has only begun, and we dare not rouse too many suspicions before the plan of attack is set in motion."

"Very well, men, carry on." Mr. Johnson gave a jaunty salute and returned his attention to his book. "I am only allowed to remain here until the intermission," he added, "and I will direct your mother here if she inquires after you, Fitzwilliam."

"Understood, and thank you, sir," Richard replied. He and Mr. Johnson had held many discussions in this room during soirees. Mr. Johnson was a reasonable man, and if his daughter were not so much like her mother and more like her father, Richard might have considered her just to gain a man like Mr. Johnson as a father-in-law. They got on quite well together.

"Your mission was successful?" Richard asked as he turned his attention to Bingley and Darcy.

Bingley smiled broadly. "Extremely. I have both Miss Bennet's and her uncle's permission to continue calling on her."

"Excellent! And Darcy?"

"Mrs. Gardiner is going to attempt to persuade Miss Elizabeth to come for a visit," Darcy replied.

"So, until then, we wait on that front," Richard muttered.

Darcy nodded.

"Tell me about the aunt and uncle," Richard said, settling back in his chair and preparing to listen to a full account of everything Bingley and Darcy had observed, and he was not to be disappointed. Bingley spoke highly of everything, as Richard knew he would. Bingley was easily pleased when there was no reason not to be, and from everything that his cousin added, there appeared to be nothing that would be displeasing.

"And you told him the whole story regarding Wickham?" Richard asked in surprise.

Darcy nodded. "He can be trusted."

"You are certain?" Richard questioned.

"Yes."

There was no moment of pause, no falter in tone that spoke of any unease on Darcy's part. "Very well," Richard replied, "Then, I will trust your judgment."

"Come meet him," Darcy offered. "I know you will agree." He smirked. "It would be good to have you on my side when I have to defend a tradesman to your father."

Richard chuckled. "You'll have little trouble with Father. Aunt Catherine, on the other hand..." He paused and raised his hand in acknowledgment of Mr. Johnson's leaving. "We will have to prepare ourselves for her, eventually, when you are finally successful, that is."

Darcy knew it was true. "As soon as I am successful, I will write to her and inform her of how things stand."

"And you expect her to just accept your words?"

No, Darcy did not expect anything of the kind. He expected a vocal protest either by post or in person. Lady

Catherine was never one to be put off easily about the smallest thing, and the refusal to marry her daughter and to marry, instead, a lady with an uncle in trade would be tantamount to a call to arms for Lady Catherine.

"Perhaps," Bingley suggested, "you could be married before you wrote to her."

This caused both Darcy and Richard to chuckle and admit that such a plan might indeed be best. A few suggestions — both practical ones and fanciful ones — as to how it might be accomplished were then passed around the group for a time until the library door opened slightly and the three fell silent.

"Your mother?" Darcy whispered to Richard as he could clearly hear that the voice filtering in from the hall was that of a lady.

"Perhaps," Richard returned but then shook his head as he heard giggling. "Mother rarely giggles," he whispered.

"They are either in here, or the garden," a distinctly familiar voice said from outside the half-opened door.

Bingley groaned. "It is worse than your mother. That is Caroline." He rose. "It would be best if we were all in a more populated area if we are to be accosted by her and her friend."

Richard's brows rose. "You do not trust them?"

"If you had seen the way Miss Clark licked her lips and nearly purred in my drawing room when I entered today, you would not trust them either. My sister is scheming."

Darcy and Richard joined Bingley in crossing the room to the door.

"Just stumble on the carpet or catch your toe on the heel of your other slipper. He will not let you fall, and then, when you are in his arms, I will make sure that someone sees it or hears about it."

Bingley stood with the doorknob within arm's length of him and could clearly hear his sister's instructions. He motioned for Richard to open the door. "Open it quickly. Just do not catch her if she falls," he hissed.

And fall Caroline did. Right at her brother's feet and with a rather loud plop when Richard yanked the door open.

"Caroline!" Bingley cried in surprise, extending a hand to help her to her feet. "How many times have you been told not to be listening at doors?"

Caroline allowed him to help her from the floor. Her cheeks burned a brilliant red. "I was not listening at the door. I was looking for you."

"At least, you are somewhat honest. However, you have left out the part that you were scheming. You should know that if Miss Clark or any of your other friends flings herself at me, I will allow them to fall just as you did, and I will not marry her, no matter what it does to either her reputation or mine. I will not be trapped, Caroline." He gave a small bow and began to move around his fuming sister and her stunned friend.

"You must forget her," Caroline whispered as her brother brushed past her.

Bingley stopped mid-stride. "I shall only forget her when my heart stops beating."

"Charles, do be reasonable. She was a pretty plaything. Someone to pass the time. She is not who you need. You will soon come to know I am right." Caroline shrugged under her brother's glare as if not affected by it in the least. "And I am certain I can find the perfect lady for you."

"No," Bingley snapped. "You will not find any lady for me. You will not even suggest any lady to me. If I have not found that for what I wish within a month's time, I am returning to Netherfield and attempting to persuade the lady who holds my heart to have me."

"You cannot," Caroline cried, her eyes darting to Darcy.

Darcy shrugged. "He seems determined," he said nonchalantly. He knew it was not the reply Caroline expected. She likely expected him to support her in her claims that Miss Bennet was not a wise choice. However, having come to understand what it was to have one's heart completely engaged by a lady and to not wish for any other, Darcy would not support any scheme of hers to interfere between Bingley and Miss Bennet. In fact, he would do all he could to ensure that nothing came between them.

Caroline gasped. "I will not allow it!"

"You cannot stop me," Bingley growled.

"I believe I can," Caroline replied with a flick of her head.

"Hurst will see you home. We are through. Darcy, if you do not mind, I should very much appreciate a ride home."

"Certainly. Richard, if you wish to join us, you may."

Richard nodded. "As soon as I find my mother and tell her I am leaving."

"I will wait ten minutes," Darcy said before turning to hurry after Bingley.

Richard waved his acceptance, then turned to Caroline and Miss Clark. "Ladies, I do hope your evening improves," he said with a bow as he took his leave.

# Chapter 8

Bingley made certain not to be available when his sister arrived home later that night, and in the morning, he took his breakfast in his study with strict orders to Jenkins that he was not to be disturbed by his sister. Then, after a few moments of clearing up some accounts and writing instructions to a particular milliner that credit was not to be extended to his sister beyond a certain point, he went in search of her.

He found her at the piano forte, attempting to master a new piece of music.

Standing at the door, he listened for a moment or two before entering. She was not a proficient, but she was every bit as good as the two ladies he had heard last night at the Johnsons' home. Caroline was not without accomplishments, nor was she lacking in beauty. What his sister lacked was sense enough to realize that her ambitions were not to be fulfilled. Even if Miss Elizabeth refused the position, Caroline would never be the mistress of Pemberley. Darcy was not inclined to tie himself to a lady like Caroline for the simple fact that Caroline was grasping, and she lacked the sort of wit that would challenge Darcy. In fact, Bingley was quite certain that Caroline would never dispute with Darcy on much, and no matter how much Darcy liked to be right and in charge of every detail, Bingley knew that his friend craved stimulating conversation and having his opinions questioned — at least, at times. He chuckled to himself. There were moments when challenging an opinion would rile Darcy into a fit of temper. Richard was proficient at marching directly up to that point of breaking and then, with a laugh and a tease, retreating to a safer position. Bingley had witnessed it on several occasions.

At the instrument, Caroline moved the new piece of music to the side and pulled out another.

"I am off. Do not hold dinner for me, for I do not know when I will return," he said as he crossed to where his sister sat. "I have had the knocker removed from the door and have given instructions that it not be returned until I return or Louisa arrives to be a chaperone for any callers."

"Where are you going?" Caroline asked in surprise.

"Anywhere that is not here," Bingley replied with a small shrug. "I find I do not wish for your company at present."

"Charles," Caroline's voice was soothing, "surely you cannot be angry with me for wishing to see you well-matched."

Bingley's smile was tight as he willed himself to remain calm. He knew that the disagreement they had broached last night in the Johnsons' library needed to be revisited and that he needed to make his position regarding whom he married clear, but he had hoped to delay it a bit longer. However, knowing what the note in his hand said, a delay was not actually feasible but merely a wish that was not destined to be granted.

"I am certain I should not be put out in the least if you showed even one ounce of concern about whether I was happy with such a match," he said, taking up the argument of his happiness and wielding it in front of his sister.

"But I do wish for you to be happy," she parried. "Happy and well-matched. If we are to rise above our beginnings and pass that new standing on to our children, we must align ourselves to best advantage." She smoothed the pages of her next musical selection on the top of the instrument. "Do you not wish for your son to be more readily accepted in society than either of us were?"

There had been and still were, at times, sticking points when mixing with some in society. It was why Bingley was actively pursuing the purchase of land. For with the purchase of an estate with its fields and tenants came entrance to that group on the edge of which he could now only circulate because of his wealth and connection to Darcy but to which he could not become a member.

Land. Land was needed to become what his father had

wished him to be — a gentleman in every sense of the word — educated, noble in character, and an owner of land. He knew, however, that even with his purchase of an estate, there would still be those who would think him inferior simply because his father had been a tradesman. That would not change. Though he were to marry the daughter of a king, there would still be those who would remind him of his heritage, for such is the way of some people, people who were only able to feel superior when making others appear and feel less important.

"We cannot erase who our father was," he said to his sister. "And I do not wish to remove his memory from our family. My children will know of their grandfather. He was a great man and an excellent father, Caroline." His words must have struck a chord with her, for she turned her head away, but not before he saw the glint of tears in her eyes.

"He was a tradesman," she whispered.

"Yes, he was, and he always will be. However, he has provided well enough for me to purchase my standing as a gentleman and for you to have a generous dowry that will make it easier for you to marry a gentleman, thereby, raising your standing." He placed the note he held in his hand on the piano. "I would not be lowering myself by marrying a gentleman's daughter such as Miss Bennet. You know this."

"But her uncles are not gentlemen." Caroline lifted her chin, unwilling to admit that he was correct.

Bingley shook his head. Caroline was stubborn, foolishly stubborn. She had been all her life, and he knew that reasoning with her when her mind was set on something was nigh onto impossible. He tapped the note he had placed on the instrument. "Last night you attempted to arrange a compromise and force me into a marriage not of my choosing. This is a copy of a message that has been sent. It is the first of many which I will write limiting your spending at all your favourite shops. Should I even catch a whisper of you scheming in such a fashion again, another merchant will be made aware of your lack of funds."

Caroline's eyes grew wide as she read the missive her brother had written. "But there will be talk of us being poor."

"Perhaps," Bingley replied, "but that is your choice. Act wisely, and you shall retain your privilege to shop as you wish. Behave as you did last night and prepare to be the object of gossip and disdain."

Her eyes narrowed, her cheeks grew red, and she set her jaw firmly.

"I will marry as I choose."

"You will ruin us both," she hissed.

"Have you so little faith in me?"

"You would marry ..." She waved her hand toward the window in a circular motion as she sought for the right word. "A country miss of no standing. No! Less than no standing," she rose from the stool on which she sat. "Jane

Bennet is a nobody, Charles, a nobody with an uncle in trade!" She paced to the window and back, her anger evident in the measured and heavy steps she took. "I suppose you would have Darcy marry her sister as well. I saw how she flirted with him. Pretending not to like him and drawing him along. Why! That is just what Jane did with you. Batting her eyes and smiling demurely! They are fortune hunters, Charles. Nothing more than fortune hunters, trained by their mother to snare the wealthiest man that enters the neighbourhood!"

"Darcy will also marry whom he chooses, and it will not be you." Bingley kept his voice calm, not because he knew it would do little good to raise it, but because he knew that keeping his voice placid would provoke his sister much more effectively. And after hearing such statements about Jane and Elizabeth as his sister had just spewed, he found he wished to provoke her.

"He would marry me if you would promote me to him," Caroline snapped.

"Darcy would not marry you if I offered him twice your dowry." He captured her wrist just before her hand made contact with his face. "You are a tradesman's daughter, but that is not what keeps him from offering for you. You have not caught his interest. You are not what he seeks, and it is time you look for a match elsewhere."

"Pemberley will be mine," she sputtered.

Bingley held her wrist a moment longer. "I will not force

him to do his duty to you no matter what position you might arrange for him to be discovered in with you. I would send you to our aunt and refuse to sign any papers or allow for a marriage. Do I make myself clear?" He released her hand only after she had given a small nod of her head.

"It might be best," he continued as he moved toward the door, "if you were to remove to Louisa's home. I will call on Hurst and see if he is amenable. I do not trust you and your friends not to arrange some folly that will end in some poor lady's ruin and retreat from society along with yours."

He closed the door firmly behind him. He had no desire to stay and listen to her protests, and he knew there would be many. Caroline liked Louisa, but Hurst was not her favourite person with whom to spend time. But then, again, she did not like spending time with anyone who did not always agree with her, and Hurst did not always agree with anyone. His opinion often shifted with his mood, and his ability to recall what he had said before was inversely proportional to the amount of port that had accompanied a discussion. Caroline found it all very annoying. She had complained of it often enough to her brother, but only once to their sister.

Louisa, though having only married for the sake of a good match, had found she did not despise her husband or his odd ways. In fact, on the one occasion when Caroline had complained about Hurst to her, Louisa had made it clear that she not only respected her husband due to his position, but she also found his eccentricities to be endearing. Bingley smiled at the thought of his sister stumbling upon love in a relationship that she had entered as a marriage of convenience.

His horse was waiting for him when he exited the house, and with only one glance at the window to the music room and a small ache in his heart for the rift that had grown between him and his sister, he rode off to call first on Hurst and then to meet Darcy before calling at the Gardiners.

His plans, however, were to be upset in a most pleasant fashion, for when he arrived at Darcy House, he found Mrs. Gardiner and Miss Bennet in the sitting room, conversing with Darcy's sister, Georgiana, as well as Georgiana's companion, Mrs. Annesley, and Richard while Darcy attempted now and again to add to the discourse.

Darcy pulled out his watch and looked at it and then Bingley as Bingley was announced. The others in the room might not have seen the slight rise of Darcy's brow, but Bingley did not miss it. It was the same expression with which Bingley was always greeted when he was late for a meeting with Darcy. Arriving just on time for a social gathering was acceptable as was being several minutes early for a meeting; however, tardiness was always met with disapprobation.

"I have a very good reason for being late," Bingley said

to Darcy after he had made all the proper greetings. "However, I had expected to be on our way to Gracechurch Street rather than here." He smiled broadly. "Not that I am disappointed."

"We were just about to leave for a shopping excursion when Mr. Darcy's note arrived inviting us to call on him here today," Mrs. Gardiner explained, her lips puckering into a small smirk before continuing. "I believe he wished for his sister and cousin to meet me. I did attempt to lure my husband away from his work, but he was unable to be tempted, even for such a treat as this." She waved her hand indicating the room and its occupants.

Darcy chuckled. "I admit it was so my sister and cousin could meet both Miss Bennet and Mrs. Gardiner."

Mrs. Gardiner raised a teasing brow. "Do we pass? Are we acceptable despite our address?"

Richard guffawed. "You are refreshing, Mrs. Gardiner. I do not think I have met another who is so direct in broaching a subject. I quite like it."

Mrs. Gardiner's eyes grew wide. "Oh, I assure you that I am not always so direct. I do know how to be demure. However, with friends — and I do hope we are friends — I find it much better to avoid any sort of equivocation."

"We are friends," Darcy assured her. "And I believe from my cousin's response, you have gained his approval."

Mrs. Gardiner gave a small nod of her head in acceptance and then looked at Miss Darcy and Mrs. Annesley. "I do hope I have not been a poor example."

Mrs. Annesley shook her head. "I have found your manners to be noteworthy, and my charge knows there is a difference between how we act in our homes with our closest friends and family and how we comport ourselves when in a public setting. However, it is good to hear you reiterate what I have taught."

"I find no fault in you," Georgiana said with a smile.

"But it remains a fact that some will, no matter my manners or words or dress. I am a tradesman's wife. He is an honorable man of substantial wealth, but," she held up a finger, "he is not a gentleman. He owns no land, nor does he desire to own any. He is very happy with his life and position. If he were to remove from town for longer than a month or two, he would grow restless and become bored. He was made for making deals and seeing things done. Oh, I know a landowner must possess such skills as well, but he would miss the excitement of seeing a new shipment arrive full of possibilities and promise of gain."

"My father was the same," Bingley said. "He enjoyed so much of what he did. It was not a trial for him to throw himself into his work." He shook his head. "What would tire me just at the thought would invigorate him. That is why he did not seek to purchase land but left it to me to do. I do not have his motivation for such things. I find I would prefer the responsibilities of a landowner."

"Just like our John," Mrs. Gardiner said with a smile. "He will be the one to move his father's fortune from a warehouse and stores to an estate."

"I should like to meet your son sometime," said Bingley.

"As long as there are biscuits?" Mrs. Gardiner asked.

Bingley shrugged. "Perhaps even if there are not."

Mrs. Gardiner laughed. "My husband would scold me for controlling the conversation." She looked directly at Georgiana. "It is a fault with which I struggle."

"I have enjoyed listening to you," Georgiana admitted. "I have felt quite at ease." She darted a look at her brother. "I do not always feel so."

"You are like your brother," Mrs. Gardiner whispered.

Georgiana returned the woman's smile and nodded.

"I should like to hear Bingley's reason for being late," said Richard.

"Caroline," Bingley replied and, with a small huff of frustration, shook his head. "I stopped at Hurst's to inquire about her removing to his house for a time."

Darcy's were not the only brows that rose at the statement. In fact, there was not a brow that remained unaffected by such a declaration.

"I do not trust her after last night." He blew out a breath. "She attempted to find a way to compromise me with one of her friends — a lady she claims would be a good match," he explained to those who had not been in the Johnsons' library. "We had a discussion about it before I left today that did not sit well with her." He held Darcy's gaze. "She claims that Pemberley will be hers, and I have told her that I would never allow it."

When Bingley had finished speaking, silence reigned for several minutes.

"I had hoped to discuss something that I have been pondering since your call yesterday." Jane's cheeks flushed, and her eyes lowered for a moment before rising once again, filled with determination.

"Please continue," Darcy encouraged before Bingley could.

Jane gave him a grateful smile. "When we last spoke, we considered the fact that your aunt will not be pleased if you are successful in winning my sister's heart."

Bingley watched Georgiana's face as Jane spoke to Darcy. From the lack of surprise, he surmised that Georgiana had been told of Darcy's intentions to marry.

"And we must still consider that," Jane continued. "However, I have been considering how best to..." Her brows furrowed, and her lips pursed as she considered her words. She took a breath and smoothed her expression. "How best to prevent Miss Bingley from interfering with either your plan to marry," her lips curled into a smile and her eyes sparkled, "or mine," she concluded.

"You are determined to marry?" Delight filled Bingley as he asked it.

Jane lifted her chin and met his gaze. "I am," she replied

simply. "However, I should not like to have to share a home with a woman who has caused me pain and treated me poorly."

Darcy watched Jane with pleased surprise. The Jane he had met yesterday, who was more forward and less reserved than the one he had met in Hertfordshire, seemed not to have been a figment of a moment but of an enduring nature.

"I can send her to live with our aunt. I do not see Hurst abiding her presence for more than a few months," Bingley replied.

"That would be effective as long as your aunt remains well, but what if the worst should befall her? Then where would your sister reside?"

Bingley blew out a breath and shrugged. "I would hope she might be married," he said uncertainly. Knowing how abominably she had treated Jane, he had no desire to have his sister in his house after he married, for he could see her causing trouble just to prove that she had been correct about Jane not being the best choice of wife.

Jane smoothed her skirt, her eyes watching her hands' motions. "Why hope?" she asked, lifting her eyes to his again.

Bingley could see the unease that mingled with determination in her features, and he admired her courage as he waited for her to continue.

She swallowed and drew a fortifying breath. "It could be arranged."

# Chapter 9

"Arranged?" Bingley repeated the word with no small amount of surprise. Was Jane suggesting that they arrange to compromise Caroline? He had not thought his Jane could be so scheming. While it was shocking, it was not off-putting. In fact, if he were candid about the feelings it stirred within him, it was rather appealing that she would go to such lengths to have a happy future with him and to provide the same for her sister and Darcy.

"I know it is not proper," Jane said quickly, her courage faltering at the startled look on Bingley's face. "But your sister has not treated either you or me well, and I dare say she has not spoken favourably about my sister to Mr. Darcy. If she were to know that we were arranging things so that a match might occur between my sister and your friend, I am certain she would find some way to interfere just as she has between us." As she spoke her anger at how she had been duped into believing Caroline was a friend when in actuality she was nothing more than someone at whom Caroline might laugh rose. She clasped her hands in her lap and squared her shoulders. She would not faint now. She would continue on.

"In fact, I believe the reason she interfered at all between you and me can be set solely on the fact that Mr. Darcy showed interest in Elizabeth. If you were to remain at Netherfield, so would Mr. Darcy. That simply could not be allowed if your sister was to win the prize of Pemberley, which you have just now claimed is her continued goal. Therefore, one and all must be removed from Netherfield and such a danger. And one must not encourage any connection with someone like myself here in town. Why what would happen if you and I should decide to marry, and you would return to Netherfield before she could effectively ensnare her prize? Would Mr. Darcy return to Netherfield with you for a time? Would he be a guest at our home? Would he continue to be enamored with my sister? It really would be far too dangerous to allow any of that."

"She has a point," said Richard. "A very good point." He smiled. "You are just as delightful as your aunt. Are all the members of your family so astute?"

Jane felt her cheeks begin to burn at such a compliment as she laughed lightly. "No, I fear they are not. Elizabeth is to be sure, Mama has her moments, and my father can outshine us all when he is roused to it. However, my younger sisters seem to lack depth. Mary shows potential if she would but see things in degrees rather than absolutes. However, Kitty and Lydia show no desire to think beyond what appears before them unless they are scheming to get their way."

Richard chuckled. "Then I would have to disagree with you, for it sounds like all your sisters could be counted among the great minds of England in some fashion if they were directed properly."

"That is it precisely," said Mrs. Gardiner. "There is much potential in them all. However, there is a sad lack of guidance, and that is all I will say on that subject." She gave a sharp nod of her head to punctuate her determination to speak no further.

"Do you have a plan for how we might deal with Miss Bingley?" Richard could not hide his interest in such as scheme — not that his interest in a scheme came as a surprise to any who knew him.

Jane raised a shoulder and let it fall. "Are there any gentlemen who might catch her eye, and who might be encouraged to pay particular attention to her with the goal of engaging her affections?"

"None that own Pemberley," Darcy muttered.

"She is so fixed?" Jane asked.

Bingley nodded. "Napoleon would more readily give up France to England than my sister will give up pursuing what she wants. She is a very determined sort of person. She always has been." Bingley could not hide the frustration and anger he felt toward his sister.

"It is a good trait if it can be properly directed." Mrs. Gardiner's voice was soothing.

"Indeed, it is," Mrs. Annesley agreed.

Bingley could not help but smile at how both women were attempting to ease his mind. "I am certain it will someday serve her well."

"There is Sir Matthew Broadhurst," Georgiana said quietly. "He has just arrived in town, and from what I have heard, he is rather attractive — broad shoulders, fine legs, wavy brown hair, deep brown eyes, and a pleasant expression. He is also said to be wealthy and heir to a lovely estate in Surrey. And," Georgiana's brows raised to add emphasis as she continued, "he has a title. There is little to dislike about such credentials."

"It does not hurt our cause," Mrs. Annesley added, "that his uncle's will requires him to marry before he can take possession of his inheritance beyond the title. Therefore, he is actively seeking a bride this season."

Jane's brows furrowed. "If he is all those things, why is he still unattached?"

Georgiana grimaced. "Mrs. Allard says he seems rather quiet and reserved."

"Would he be ill-used by a lady who is neither of those things?" Jane asked in all seriousness. She wished to see Caroline married, and married well, but she did not wish to injure an unsuspecting gentleman in the process.

"Oh, no," Georgiana replied. "Mrs. Allard said he is

very fixed and unyielding in his opinions and standards. She suspects that is why he has not found success with the few ladies he has attempted to court in the past."

Jane sighed. "I do not wish to see Miss Bingley tied to an ogre even if he is titled and handsome."

"Not even if she deserves it?" Bingley asked.

"No, not even then." Jane could not be the cause of someone else's misery, even if that someone had caused a great deal of sorrow for her. She would forever feel the weight of such actions.

"There is only one way to decide," said Darcy. "We must meet him. I am certain that, between Bingley and me, we can determine if it will be an amicable match."

"You are not going to discourage us?" Bingley's mouth tipped up in a crooked half smirk.

Darcy shook his head. "I am a bit surprised that my sister is the source of knowledge on such a thing, but I find I cannot fault a plan that will see you happy and clear a portion of the path for me to claim my own happiness." He shrugged and then shook his head. "I startle myself, to be honest, but whatever part I need to play to see this through to the end, I am willing to play it."

So it was settled that, as soon as it was convenient, Bingley and Darcy would find a way to meet Sir Matthew Broadhurst and evaluate his suitability as a husband for Caroline.

It took only two days from the time the decision

was made in Darcy's drawing room for an opportunity for such a meeting to occur.

As the sun was beginning its journey to its height, warming the earth and the people who had ventured out into the crisp air of a clear winter's morning, Darcy and Bingley came upon a solitary rider loping his way through the park with a groom trailing at a good distance behind him. Bingley, as he always did, tipped his hat and wished the gentleman a good morning.

The gentleman returned the gesture and then slowed his horse as he drew nearer Bingley and Darcy.

"I do not believe I have had the pleasure of making your acquaintance," he began. "I am Sir Matthew Broadhurst of Stoningham in Surrey."

"Charles Bingley," Bingley returned, "and my friend, Fitzwilliam Darcy of Pemberley in Derbyshire. It is a pleasure to meet you."

"Indeed, it is," Darcy agreed.

"I have not been to many soirees yet, and it seems I like to rise earlier than most. I believe, you gentlemen make six whom I have met since arriving in town. May I join you?" Sir Matthew drew his horse alongside them after Bingley had assured him that they would be delighted to have his company.

The gentleman appeared to be everything that Georgiana had said he was. His dress was impeccable. He appeared to be of an acceptable stature, neither too tall nor too short. He was handsome with a very pleasant and amiable, if quiet, air about him.

"I have heard that you have just recently come into your title," said Darcy. "My condolences on the loss of your uncle."

Sir Matthew's gave his thanks softly and somberly. "He was not the friendliest of men at times, and he could be demanding. However, my uncle was a good man who took my mother, my siblings, and myself into his home after my father died." He glanced over at the men beside him. "My father was the rector of the parish near Stoningham."

"Do you have many siblings?" Bingley asked.

"A younger brother and two older sisters," Sir Matthew replied. "My sisters are both married and happily settled, and my brother is studying to take orders. He is much like my father. And you, do you gentlemen have siblings?"

"I have a younger sister who has been left in my care," Darcy answered. "She is just sixteen."

"Both of your parents are gone?" Sir Matthew's voice was once again soft and soothing as he inquired.

"For several years now," Darcy answered. "It is something Bingley and I have in common."

"You do not have a parent remaining either?" Sir Matthew asked, turning to Bingley.

"No," Bingley replied. "My father died three years ago, leaving me a fortune and the care of my sisters. Louisa has married, but Caroline has not." He noted how Sir

Matthew's expression spoke of the gentleman's interest in that last fact. "My father was a tradesman."

Sir Matthew's brows rose. "You do not own an estate?"

There was no censure in his tone. He seemed genuinely interested.

"Not yet," Bingley replied. "I have let an estate in Hertfordshire and am looking to purchase one in the near future."

"I wish you well in your endeavour."

There was again a genuineness to the man's words that impressed both Bingley and Darcy.

"I cannot claim my estate until I marry." Sir Matthew shook his head. "My uncle knew that if he did not force me out of the house and to seriously consider taking a wife, I would bury myself within the walls of the estate, seeing to the needs of it and my mother and brother and naught else." He shrugged. "I can be too focused on duty at times."

Bingley laughed. "Darcy can be the same."

"He speaks the truth," Darcy agreed. "Until recently I had only considered marriage in the light of duty just as I considered everything else."

Sir Matthew smiled knowingly. "You have found a lady who makes you question your view of duty, have you?"

"Indeed, I have," Darcy replied.

"I wish you joy," Sir Matthew said.

"I have not won her yet. In fact, I am not entirely certain I will win her."

"He will," said Bingley emphatically. "I know he will."

Sir Matthew's head cocked to the side, and curiosity suffused his expression. "I should enjoy hearing the tale, but I will not ask as it is not my place to be informed of your private matters," he said. "I will only wish you success."

"And I shall wish you the same," Darcy returned. "Do you have anyone in mind for the position of Lady Broadhurst?"

Sir Matthew shook his head. "I do not. It is perhaps unkind of me to say, but the few ladies I have met have been nothing more than a pretty face with feathers for brains." He shook his head. "Such giggling!"

"What do you wish for in a wife?" Darcy asked, casting a sidelong glance at Bingley.

Sir Matthew shrugged. "I likely know better what I do not want than what I want. I suppose I should like someone who would be a good hostess and manager."

"Does she have to be a gentleman's daughter?" Bingley asked pointedly. Caroline was proficient both at hosting soirees and managing everyone's affairs.

"You wish to be rid of a sister?" Sir Matthew asked with a laugh.

The man did not lack perception. That was a point in his favour according to Bingley. He would need to be a man who could see through Caroline's scheming and airs.

"I do."

Sir Matthew eyed Bingley cautiously. "What is wrong with her?" he asked.

Bingley chuckled. "I am not certain I should answer that, for we have had a falling out recently over her disapproval of my choice of bride, and even though she is my sister, I do not know that I would be the most charitable of persons to describe her."

"You are to be married?"

"Eventually," Bingley replied. "As soon as I can rid myself of a sister and help Darcy secure his heart's desire."

Poor Sir Matthew could not hide his confusion, though he did an admirable job in trying to disguise it.

"We are attending the Taylor's ball this evening," Bingley said. "Caroline will be there. You can meet her and judge for yourself if you might be persuaded to consider her."

"She is not hideous," Bingley added in response to Sir Matthew's continued look of skepticism.

"No," Darcy agreed. "She is quite handsome." He smirked. "She has the same colouring as her brother, but is much, much prettier."

Sir Matthew's features relaxed into a smile at the comment. "Very well, if it is just a meeting," he agreed.

"It is just a meeting," Bingley assured him. "And if you are interested, then I will explain over a bottle of Darcy's finest port how both my happiness and that of Darcy hinges on my sister."

"My port?" Darcy said in surprise.

Bingley shrugged. "Very well, we will discuss it at my house over the best I have." He turned to Sir Matthew. "Do we have an agreement?" He held up his hand. "I neglected to mention she has twenty thousand pounds. She does not come empty-handed."

Sir Matthew drew his horse to a stop. "Yes," he said, nodding his head. "Yes, we have an agreement. I will meet your sister and then, if I find her to my liking, you may attempt to persuade me to aid your cause." He held out his hand, which Bingley gave a hearty shake, sealing the deal.

# Chapter 10

Mr. Bennet popped his head out of his study door. "Hill."

"Yes, sir."

"Please inform Lizzy that I would like to see her." He held a very interesting missive in his hand and knew that his daughter had also received some correspondence from town. He was interested to know what Jane and Mrs. Gardiner had to say.

He closed the door and returned to his chair. He propped his feet on a footstool and peered through his glasses once again at Edward Gardiner's surprising letter, giving it a quick perusal and then putting it aside to open the next unexpected piece of mail. Colonel Fitzwilliam? The name did not sound familiar to him at all.

He smoothed the creases out of the letter and began reading.

*Mr. Bennet,*

*Allow me to introduce myself to you. I am the Right Honorable Richard Fitzwilliam, colonel in his majesty's armed* forces and second son of the Earl of Matlock. I am also the cousin of Fitzwilliam Darcy of Pemberley in Derbyshire, whose acquaintance you hold, and am the co-guardian of his sister.

What follows is information that is of a very sensitive nature, and I would request that as a gentleman you guard it with the utmost care.

Darcy has made me aware of the presence in your neighbourhood of a particular scoundrel with a well-practiced charm and ease of manner which will ingratiate him with nearly one and all. However, he is not to be trusted with credit, cards, or the hearts and virtue of young ladies.

Mr. Wickham is, as he will doubtless present himself, an acquaintance of the Darcy family and has been for many years. His father was my uncle's steward and a fine, upstanding man. His son has not been blessed with the same stalwart character. While Mr. Wickham's father served the late Mr. Darcy well, treating him with the respect due to one of his station, Mr. Wickham has treated my cousins poorly and has tarnished the memories of both the late Mr. Darcy and his own father.

There is much history into which we could delve but suffice it to say that W. was a favourite of my uncle, and in homage to the service W's father had provided for Pemberley, my uncle bequeathed W a legacy of one thousand pounds and held for him the living that was in my uncle's power to bestow. The living was to be given upon there being a vacancy and W's taking orders. However, W did not wish to take orders but instead petitioned to be allowed to study the law. My cousin Darcy gave him three thousand pounds in lieu of the living. As it turns out, the law did not agree with W, and he spent his time and fortune in licentious living. When his funds had all been squandered, he returned to Darcy to request that he be allowed the living, which had just fallen open. Darcy refused based on the former arrangement of money in exchange for the living as well as the knowledge that W's lifestyle was not fitting for a man of the cloth. As you may well imagine, W was furious and abused my cousin severely.

Darcy thought that this would be his last interaction with the man, but alas, it was not. And this is the portion of the tale that I impart with trepidation. The sharing of the above is of little significance. However, what I share now is of a graveness that as a father I am certain you will appreciate.

It was just this past spring when W made his appearance and attempted to exact his revenge on Darcy. While Miss Darcy was in Ramsgate with her companion, a woman we later discovered was a friend of W's, Wickham played upon her tender heart and aroused her affection with the goal of persuading her to elope with him, thereby acquiring her thirty thousand and ensuring the misery of her brother. Thankfully, Darcy arrived before the scheme could be set into motion, and his sister confessed the whole of the matter to him. Once again, Wickham did not leave my cousin's presence on friendly terms as you can well imagine.

He is a profligate and a gambler who will likely leave Hertfordshire with many unpaid debts and quite likely a few ruined maids.

I am given to understand, by my cousin's account and that of Mr. Bingley, that you have several pretty daughters. I know that they do not have a fortune equal to what Miss Darcy has, but one of them has something that money cannot buy and would make her of great interest to W. – my cousin's admiration. The possibility of separating Darcy from a lady he admires would please W immensely.

I have written a letter to Colonel Forster regarding W's propensity to dally with the ladies and be less than genuine with the merchants. I have done all this at my cousin's request as he does not wish to see the residents of Hertfordshire harmed by Wickham. He would have made his case known while in the area if it were not for fear of Miss Darcy's folly being exposed and his fear that he could not calmly and rationally relate his knowledge of the man since *the wound caused to his sister is still not one which has healed.*

*Again, I would petition you, as both a gentleman and a father, to protect this information. Please notify either myself or Darcy should any merchant find that he has fallen prey to Wickham's liberty in purchasing and lack of the same in paying his debts. Darcy has given his word that he will settle such accounts should the need arise.*

*God Bless,*

*R.F.*

Mr. Bennet sank back in his chair. First, he had received a missive from Gardiner mentioning both that there were wealthy and upstanding gentleman who admired and wished to court his eldest daughters and that there was a man in the militia of whom he should be cautious, and now this letter repeated much of what he had heard though it delved more deeply into the harm that Wickham had caused the Darcy family. He shook his head. He could not pass such damaging information off as being the dis-like of one man to another, for what gentleman would place his sister's reputation in such a potentially damaging position without cause?

"Come," he called in response to the knock at his door.

"Hill said you wished to see me." Elizabeth entered and took a seat near her father.

He nodded and gave her a fleeting glance. His mind was still turning over the information he had just read. He placed the letter in his hand next to the one from Mr. Gardiner on the desk. "I understand you received a letter from Jane. How is she?"

Elizabeth drew a folded piece of paper from her pocket. "You may read it."

He shook his head. "I trust you to tell me all that I must know. Has Mr. Bingley called on her?"

"He has!"

Mr. Bennet loved the way Elizabeth's face would shine when she smiled as she was now. He watched as her brows furrowed, and the smile faded into puzzlement.

"It is the strangest thing," she said as she unfolded her letter.

"How so?" He was certain he knew what or, more precisely, who made Mr. Bingley's call strange.

"Mr. Darcy called with him."

Mr. Bennet feigned surprise. "He did? Is he interested in courting Jane?" He bit back a smile as his second eldest daughter shook her head and looked at him with more confused astonishment than he had ever seen on her face. Perhaps Mr. Darcy would be good for her if he could challenge her way of thinking as he seemed to be doing. Elizabeth needed a husband with a keen mind and a will that was not easily bent. From what he had gathered of the man while out hunting, Mr. Darcy seemed to possess both fortitude and intelligence.

"According to Aunt Gardiner, he hopes to court me."

"He is not Mr. Collins, and you must eventually marry." Mr. Bennet chuckled as Elizabeth's eyes grew wide. "He is a worthy gentleman, my dear."

Elizabeth shook her head. "You do not find him disagreeable?"

Her father shrugged. "He has a tendency to be dour, or so it seems. However, our acquaintance was of a short duration, and we do not know what he would be like at his own home." Her head cocked to the side, and he knew that he had likely gone too far in his acceptance of the man.

"What are you not telling me?"

He chuckled. She was perceptive even in her current befuddled state. "I have received two missives of my own with some startling information in them. However, before I share them with you, I must tell you that I am sending you to your aunt and uncle."

"Why?" Caution — or was it trepidation that coloured her tone? Whichever it was, it caused Mr. Bennet's lips to twitch in suppressed amusement. She was such a delight!

"Ten thousand a year is not a sum of money a lady refuses without due diligence in deciphering a gentleman's character."

Elizabeth's mouth snapped closed. "You would have me marry him?"

He shook his head. "No, I would have you make an informed choice." He passed her the two letters that lay on his desk. "One is from your uncle, and the other is from Colonel Fitzwilliam."

She blinked and looked at her father in confusion.

"He introduces himself far better than I ever could," he replied with a wink.

She began reading the colonel's letter just as he knew she would. If any of the information in any of the four letters they held between them were to sway her opinion of Mr. Darcy and provide the man with a second chance, it was the colonel's letter. "It seems our Mr. Darcy might have had just reason to be so unpleasant."

He settled back and watched her face as she read the letter twice before proceeding to read her uncle's letter.

"It seems Jane will be married soon," he said as she began reading the second letter. "And you could be as well."

Upon completion of her perusal of both letters, Elizabeth flopped back in her chair and expelled a whoosh of air.

"What say you?" her father asked.

Her head shook slowly from side to side. "I do not know what to say." She handed him the letters she had received from Jane and her aunt. "The Mr. Darcy described in these letters is not the Mr. Darcy I met." Her brows drew together. "Can Mr. Wickham be so bad?"

Her father shrugged. "It appears he can be."

Another whoosh of air escaped her.

"Your aunt and Jane have both included an apology from Mr. Darcy for his words at the assembly?"

Elizabeth nodded while one shoulder lifted and lowered in a small half shrug.

Mr. Bennet returned her letters to her and gathered his two from her. "You will not say anything about what you read in these." He knew she would not, but he felt he must say it.

"No, of course not." She folded her letters and put them back into her pocket. Then, she just sat there, her eyes fixed on the shelf of books behind her father.

Her head occasionally shook, and she grimaced, letting her father know that she was attempting to reason everything out while quite likely remonstrating herself for her lack of discernment about the character of not only Darcy but also Mr. Wickham. There was one thing in regard to that last gentleman that he needed to know. Elizabeth had spent a great deal of time in Wickham's company and seemed to enjoy it.

"I must ask," he began, "for I must know the full extent of things. Has Mr. Wickham touched your heart?"

Her eyes grew wide. "No, I counted him a friend but

naught else." She shook her head once again. "However, it appears he might not have even been that."

"Sadly, yes." Mr. Bennet drew a deep breath and expelled it. "I found him very pleasant and had thought he might even make a good son." He shrugged. "But, I would not consign any of my daughters to a marriage with one who can squander money as readily as it seems he does."

Elizabeth nodded.

"You may go. I can see you need time to ponder."

Elizabeth rose slowly from her chair and moved toward the door, but she turned back instead of opening the door and exiting as her father expected. "Mr. Darcy admires me?"

There was so much disbelief in her tone that it caused his heart to pinch at the thought of not having her here to visit him in his study. However, Derbyshire was not so very far away. What was a couple days journey when it took you to where your child resided?

"It appears he does."

Her lips curled upwards, likely of their own accord since the expression in her eyes was still distant.

"I will take you to town myself," he said, causing her eyes to become focused and her lashes to flutter in surprise. "Tell your aunt that we will arrive in a se'nnight. And not a word to your mother about Mr. Bingley. I shall tell her that news when it is closer to our time to depart. Jane does not need her mother descending upon her or her Mr. Bingley before the papers are signed." He chuckled at the way Elizabeth rolled her eyes and shook her head. "Nor do we wish her to know that there is a gentleman with ten thousand a year who would like to persuade another one of her daughters into the matrimonial state."

"Papa!" Elizabeth chided.

"I am merely stating things as I see them. Now, off with you to consider what you have learned and to decide if your old papa is correct in his suppositions." He waved her away. "I look forward to hearing your conclusions," he called as she pulled the door shut behind her, and he was left to consider for himself the truth of two daughters married.

# Chapter 11

While Elizabeth considered what to make of the letters that she had read, Darcy and Bingley were introducing Sir Matthew Broadhurst to Caroline. They did not do so directly, of course. Bingley was still not on speaking terms with his sister, and she was equally as put out with him.

"Hurst," Bingley greeted his brother-in-law as he sat down at the table which had just been vacated by the men who had been playing cards with Mr. Hurst.

Hurst grunted something of a greeting. "I cannot tolerate her." He waved his glass at a footman for a refill. "Louisa, I can abide on most days, but Caroline?" He shook his head. "And she does not have a pleasing effect on her sister. It is not right that I should be saddled with both of your sisters." He took a large gulp from his fresh glass of port.

"She is here?" Bingley asked calmly. He could understand the man's displeasure. Caroline was demanding and often in a foul mood if things were not done as she wished them done. He could only imagine just how cantankerous

Caroline was at present with her spending curtailed, her residence moved, and her schemes to see him married to one of her friends at an end.

"She will be at any venue where there is a chance of foisting her off on some poor swain," he replied with no little amount of determination.

"Do you think you could pretend she is not the extreme burden she is for a few moments?" Hurst in his current state would be of no help in convincing Sir Matthew to meet Caroline.

Hurst lifted a skeptical brow. "Is there a good reason for such a performance?"

Bingley smiled and nodded as he settled back into his chair. "Indeed, there is. His name is Sir Matthew Broad-hurst."

Hurst's head tipped to the side, and his glass returned to the table without a drop of its contents being consumed. "Continue."

"Sir Matthew is in need of wife before he can claim the entirety of his inheritance. We are in need of someone – anyone – to marry Caroline. He is willing to meet her, but I am sure you can see how my introducing him to her would not make his acceptance a possibility of even minuscule size."

Leaning back in his chair and wearing a half-pleased expression, Hurst cradled his port in his hand, taking a small sip before stating what both men knew to be true.

"She'll not have him no matter who introduces him to her. He's not Darcy."

"She will never have Darcy."

"Aye, we both know that, but she's as daft as a duck trying to swim in a frozen pond."

Bingley chuckled. Caroline was not a fool about everything. However, when it came to her ambitions to gain Pemberley, she made the residents of Bedlam seem perfectly rational.

"Does he know she will not come willingly?" There was a calculating look in Hurst's eyes that Bingley had expected to see. Hurst was not without the ability and desire to scheme himself into better circumstances, and Bingley knew that being relieved of Caroline as a house guest was the best circumstance that could occur at the moment.

"He is only meeting her. He has not agreed to take her off our hands just yet," Bingley cautioned. "Hence the need to tread carefully."

"Aye, let me meet the fellow. I shall not hide her flaws, but I will not parade them before the man either."

Bingley looked toward the door and nodded to Darcy. "The sooner we get on with this business the better, do you not think?" Bingley replied to Hurst's startled look as Darcy and Sir Matthew approached. "She is never returning to my house."

Hurst scowled and then smiled. "Tie 'er up and toss her in a carriage bound for Gretna Green on the hour."

"Perhaps we should not move quite so quickly as that," Bingley replied with a laugh.

"You only say that because she is not at your house," muttered Hurst.

"Sir Matthew, my brother, Mr. Reginald Hurst. Hurst, Sir Matthew Broadhurst of Stoningham in Surrey. I have explained to Hurst that you would like an introduction to Caroline, and he is willing to provide you the service."

"Anxious to be rid of her?" Sir Matthew asked pointedly.

"Like the pox," Hurst grumbled.

Bingley gave his brother's shin a solid kick.

"I prefer to have my wife to myself," Hurst added, moving his legs outside the range of Bingley's boot.

Sir Matthew's expression grew grave. "I am no fool. I know if both brothers and a good friend of the family wishes to be rid of a lady, there is a reason, and that reason must have to do with a deficiency of some sort."

Hurst sighed and lifted his glass to his lips, taking a swallow before continuing. "She is determined to have Darcy," he said. "And like a filly who wishes for the grass in the meadow rather than the feed in the stall, she is stubborn and kicking against the constraints of reality."

"That is no doubt part of what you wished to tell me if

this meeting between myself and Miss Bingley is to my liking?" he asked Bingley.

Bingley nodded. "I did not wish to drag Darcy's situation out to just anyone, but yes."

"A harridan?"

Bingley's heart sank at the word. How would he ever persuade a chap to take on Caroline? She was every inch a harridan.

"She's not always been," said Hurst. "She just has the notion in her head that she is going to marry Darcy and rise above her roots. She can be very agreeable about most other things. She does like to have her way and can cause a scene if she does not get it, but she is among the most accomplished ladies as you will find." He placed his glass on the table and, leaning forward, put up a finger to punctuate his point. "And you must remember that she has been training herself to be the mistress of Pemberley, which is no small estate. I do not know your estate, but I dare say she could have it ticking along like a newly wound clock."

"But a bit of a harridan?"

"Yes," said Darcy.

"Needs redirecting?"

Darcy nodded. "Please, I beg you."

Sir Matthew chuckled. "Dead set against her as a wife, are you?"

"Yes."

"He has his eye on a pretty little thing from Hertford-shire." Hurst took another drink of his port. "She is much better suited to Darcy than Caroline." He shrugged. "I am not always sleeping," he said with a wink. "Now, shall we play a game first or get straight to it?"

"I am not much of a card player," Sir Matthew admitted.

"Do you dance?" Hurst asked as he rose.

"I actually enjoy the activity. I have an affinity for music, you see."

Hurst's brows rose. "Caroline does like music." He gave the man next to him an appraising look. "You're hand-some and you have a title, so those will stand you in good stead." He paused. "She is a schemer at times. How stal-wart are you?"

"My mother has often said there are few less yielding than I, but I cannot see it." The corner of his lips tipped upward in amusement.

"Then, you will do fine," said Hurst, clapping Sir Matthew on the shoulder. "I should hate to present her with anyone weaker than immovable."

"Since you have not run away at such a comment, then I am to assume you are not easily frightened," said Bingley with a laugh.

"It is just a meeting," Sir Matthew reminded them.

"We are a hopeful lot," said Hurst.

"Or desperate," said Sir Matthew with a grin.

"Aye, there is that," Hurst agreed. "I wish my wife to run

my house and not my sister, but that is neither here nor there at the moment. Come along, Sir Matthew. Let's see how you like her."

"No matter how this meeting goes, I will call on you gentlemen in three hours time. That should give me enough of an opportunity to have danced with her and watched her with others."

"We will await your arrival with eager anticipation," said Bingley. Then, he and Darcy slipped out of the Taylor's ball, for neither wished for their presence to place any hindrance on this meeting.

Bingley blew out a breath as his carriage pulled away from the curb. "Our happiness could be closer to our grasp in three hours."

"Or just as remote," Darcy added, causing Bingley to shake his head and chuckle.

~*~*~

Three hours later, just as promised, Sir Matthew arrived at Bingley's home and was shown to the study. Glasses of port were poured, and the four gentlemen settled in front of the hearth where a fire burned brightly, driving away shadows and filling the room with welcome warmth.

It was four gentlemen, not just three, for Richard had called at Bingley's and discovered that Sir Matthew was arriving later and could not be persuaded to leave under any circumstances, save for a man from his unit delivering orders that needed immediate attention. And since no such man appeared with said orders, he had waited with an open book on his knee and his head resting against the back of his chair while he dozed. Darcy, knowing how ill his cousin tended to sleep at night, kept his voice low while he and Bingley pondered the future and recalled the past.

"So?" Bingley's question cut through the air of anxious anticipation which hung in the air.

"I wish to know more about your situation and that of Darcy's before I come to a conclusion," said Sir Matthew. "She is pretty just as you said," he said to Darcy. "There is that in her favour."

"What do you wish to know about Darcy?" Richard asked with a grin.

"I can speak for myself," Darcy retorted.

"Both you and Darcy said that you have your eyes on possible wives, did you not?" Sir Matthew directed the question to Bingley.

"That is correct," said Bingley. "As you know, my wealth comes from trade and was left to me by my father with the hope that I would use it to secure an estate and elevate my family. To that purpose, I leased Netherfield, an estate in Hertfordshire, at Michaelmas. Darcy joined me there to help me evaluate its condition and teach me some of what I will need to know."

"And this is where you met your lady?" Sir Matthew stretched his feet toward the fire.

"Yes, Miss Jane Bennet. Her father owns the estate next to Netherfield."

"A gentleman's daughter," Sir Matthew nodded in approval. "It seems just the sort of young lady one who is aspiring to be a gentleman should marry as she will know what is expected of her role as his wife."

"That is not why I chose her," Bingley said. "It frankly mattered not to me what her origins were. Miss Bennet is one of the most beautiful and kind ladies I have ever met."

Richard chuckled. "And Bingley is well-versed in beautiful ladies. His charm has gained him access where his ties to trade would keep him out."

"If only we all could be so fortunate," Sir Matthew said with a laugh. "I confess I do not possess a great deal of charm. Never have and, most likely, never will."

"But you have a title," said Richard. "One does not need copious amounts of charm if one has either a title or a fortune the size of Darcy's." He chuckled. "If you have both, as my brother the viscount does, then you could be the ugliest, grumpiest curmudgeon in all of the empire and have women flocking to you." He shook his head.

"Your brother is neither ugly nor a curmudgeon," Darcy argued.

"Aye, but the ladies do gather."

"He should marry and be done with it," said Sir Matthew. "He is not married, is he?"

"No, but my mother insists it happens this season, so by summer he may be."

"And then she will begin harassing you twice as much as she does now," said Bingley.

"I am hoping my brother refuses to comply." Richard drained the last of his port and rose to refill his glass. "But, we are not here to discuss my marital state," he said as he removed the stopper from the bottle. "Bingley, continue to tell Sir Matthew why your sister is set against Miss Bennet."

"Right. Miss Bennet. She is the eldest of five daughters."

"Five?" Sir Matthew said in surprise.

"No brothers," Darcy added.

"Indeed?"

Bingley nodded. "Five pretty daughters." He grinned. "Miss Mary might make an excellent Colonel's wife," he teased.

Richard shook his head. "Not unless she has a fortune. Remember, I am the second son, not the heir." He settled back into his chair.

"We are not here to see Miss Bennet's sisters married," said Darcy.

"One we are," Richard said into his glass as he lifted it to take a drink.

"Miss Elizabeth Bennet is the second eldest daughter and the lady who has captured Darcy's heart," Bingley explained. "And that is one reason why my sister is opposed to my marrying Miss Bennet. For if I am married to Miss Bennet, then, Darcy will necessarily be thrown into the path of Miss Elizabeth, and Caroline suspects that Darcy is besotted."

"Which he is," Darcy added.

"I do like hearing you admit it," Richard muttered.

"As do I," Darcy replied. "Miss Elizabeth is not the only objection Bingley's sister has raised. Miss Bennet's family is..." He paused. "Well, there is no particularly polite way to say it. There are those of her family who are both ridiculous and improper at times. They also have an uncle who is a country solicitor and another who is a tradesman here in town. However, I do think these objections would be overlooked if I were to offer for Caroline. Then, she would willingly allow her brother to marry as he chooses." He sighed.

"She is so set, is she?" Sir Matthew asked.

Darcy nodded. "She has never attracted my attention in such a fashion. She is not what I wish for in a wife. We are not companionable."

"And companionship is important to you?" asked Sir Matthew.

"It is."

"I see." The port in Sir Matthew's glass swirled up and around and down, up and around and down, as he thought. "If you were to marry – both of you – and Miss Bingley remained single, why would that be an issue?"

"I would not wish to subject Miss Bennet to having to host her. I could see Caroline causing problems for my wife, resulting in misery for her. Miss Bennet has a sweet, tender constitution. She has already felt the sting of my sister's maneuverings. You see, when Caroline left Hertfordshire, she left a letter for Miss Bennet hinting at my marrying Darcy's sister. Not a word of it was true, of course. Then, when Miss Bennet came to town to visit her aunt and uncle in Gracechurch Street, she paid a call on my sisters. They did not deign to accept her into the house, and I am certain they have no intention of returning her call. A call, I might add, that she concealed from me. I only learned of it through Darcy."

Sir Matthew's head bobbed up and down slowly. "I see," he said once again before slipping back into thought as he watched his port chase itself along the sides of his glass. Then, the glass stilled. He drained its contents and placed it on the table. "Your sister has twenty thousand?"

"More if it is needed," said Bingley.

Sir Matthew smiled. "I am not agreeing to this for your money, but I do wish to have something to settle on children and such, you understand."

"You will take her?" Bingley asked hopefully.

Sir Matthew nodded. "I must marry to take possession of my full inheritance. The lady I met tonight was all that was proper, if a bit cool, in her reception. She mingled with ease amongst the other people in attendance. She did not want for dance partners. Her taste in fashion," he shook his head, "it is good but expensive. That could be an issue. I do not like to be separated from my money, for as you know, it is not my money to dispose of as I wish without thought. There is a duty to those who follow me. To my son who will take up the title. I know that such thinking is perhaps not popular, but it is how I believe."

He rose and picked up his glass. "May I?" he asked.

"Certainly," Bingley said.

"I like you," Sir Matthew said as he crossed to where the decanter of port rested on a cabinet. "You and Hurst have been very open with me about the trial your sister has presented to you, and you have not tried to dupe me into thinking I am tying myself to an angel when she is not." He turned and leaned against the cabinet. "I actually think we could do well together. I could be wrong, of course, and that does concern me for I have always longed for felicity in marriage." He shrugged. "I will call on her at Hurst's tomorrow and invite her to go for a drive. Her acceptance or reluctance of those items will tell us how we should proceed."

Bingley raised a brow.

"I am not opposed to a compromise," Sir Matthew said with a grin. "I see no point in delaying. I need a wife, and you gentlemen need to be free to claim yours without fear of reprisal."

"You will truly take her?"

Sir Matthew nodded. "I will not marry quickly. I will fall into a betrothal with haste, but I do wish for a bit of time to court her after she has been forced to accept such a courtship before we wed."

"Are you hoping that once she can no longer consider Darcy as an option due to whatever compromise we arrange, she will find her more rational self?" Richard asked.

"Indeed, I am," Sir Matthew said. "I would also rather not take an angry hornet home with me. Time should help me with that as well."

"You are a sly one." There was no mistaking the admiration in Richard's voice.

"So I have been told a time or two." Sir Matthew lifted his glass to his lips and hid a smile behind it. "If you are a quiet, focused sort of person, slyness is rarely suspected."

Richard guffawed. "Do you play cards?" he asked.

"Not often."

"But when you do, I suspect you win," Richard said.

"Indeed," Sir Matthew agreed. "Nearly always." He returned to his seat. "Do you wish to speak of marriage settlements now or after our betrothal becomes necessary."

Bingley shook his head and chuckled. "I am certain I am going to enjoy being your brother." He rose and went in search of paper and pen. "I see no reason to delay."

# Chapter 12

"My home has never been so full of handsome eligible gentlemen." Mrs. Gardiner smiled broadly as she settled back into the chair from which she had been presiding over the discussion in her sitting room. "Sir Matthew, it is, of course, a delight to meet you."

Sir Matthew inclined his head in acceptance of her words. "I thank you for accepting me into your home with no prior introduction."

Mrs. Gardiner waved his words away. "Any friend of Mr. Bingley or Mr. Darcy is always welcome in my home."

Darcy thoroughly enjoyed how her eyes danced with pleasure as it once again reminded him of Elizabeth.

"I understand you are from Surrey?" Mrs. Gardiner continued.

"Yes, ma'am, I am."

Mrs. Gardiner did not reply but merely looked at him expectantly.

Sir Matthew straightened a sleeve. "My estate, or what will be my estate, is Stoningham. It was left to me by my uncle, along with the title. He was my father's older brother, but he never married. Therefore, the inheritance has fallen to me." He went on, at her prompting, to tell her about his mother, his sisters, and his brother. She even managed to wrangle out of him details about his sisters' families and situations.

"And you wish to share all this with Miss Bingley?" Mrs. Gardiner had risen to pour the tea which had just arrived.

"I need a wife," Sir Matthew replied.

Mrs. Gardiner replaced the teapot on its tray but did not lift the filled cup to pass to Jane, who stood ready to distribute the tea things. "You have met Miss Bingley?"

"I have."

"And you are satisfied?"

He nodded.

"And your family? Will they also be satisfied?"

He shrugged. "I believe my mother will be happy to have me married."

Mrs. Gardiner lifted the teacup and handed it to Jane. "*I* will be happy to have you married," she said with a laugh, "for I wish for nothing more than to see my nieces well-settled with these two fine gentlemen." She began filling another cup. "However, I would not be able to rest easy knowing that such a thing came about at the expense of your happiness." Her eyes met Jane's. "And I know Jane would also feel such a calamity most grievously, for her heart is amongst the tenderest in the land."

Jane smiled and blushed as she returned from giving Sir Matthew his tea to get another cup.

"You may rest assured, ladies, that I have considered my own happiness very carefully in all of this. I believe, in time, Miss Bingley and I will get on quite well." He hid a smile behind the rim of his cup. "After her sharp edges are smoothed a bit, that is."

"You do not go into this blindly, then?" Mrs. Gardiner asked.

"No, my eyes are fully open. I know there is a risk in what I am doing. A great risk. However, I am not the sort to gamble without thought."

"Very well," Mrs. Gardiner said as she handed Jane a cup of tea and then poured one for herself. "We will proceed with clear consciences."

"As you should," Sir Matthew agreed.

"You called on my sister today, did you not?" Bingley asked.

It was the topic Darcy had hoped to broach as soon as the man entered the room, but as it was not his home nor was it his sister's future being arranged, he had refrained, and instead, he had thoroughly enjoyed watching Mrs. Gardiner interrogate Sir Matthew while feeling quite glad that this time he was not the person of interest to Mrs. Gardiner.

"Mmm hmm." Sir Matthew nodded as he swallowed his tea. "She was agreeable. Very cordial. We had a good discussion, and I did ask her to go for a drive tomorrow." He paused, and his brows furrowed. "She has agreed but not with alacrity. I think she would have refused if Hurst had not entered the room just prior and made a point of gaining her attention with a cough when she did not immediately reply." He took another sip of his tea. "Drawing her along will take far too long. I think it best if we move toward limiting her choices to all but me. She can be convinced of my worth after she has accepted my offer."

There was a constant calmness about this man that Darcy was beginning to admire. There was a matter-of-factness to everything. Possible outcomes were presented – both good and bad – discussed and then put away like papers in folders, each with its own place. Even when Mrs. Gardiner had questioned him, he had replied with ease and directness. This unflappable, intelligent, calculating gentleman might actually be the making of Caroline Bingley. The thought brought a smile to his lips. Who would have ever thought there was such a gentleman? Darcy certainly had not until this moment.

"Then we need a plan," Bingley declared.

"I do not want to be implicated as the source of the compromise," Sir Matthew placed his empty cup on its saucer and set it aside on a table near him. "I do not wish to go into this marriage with any more difficulty laid at my door than necessary."

Darcy watched Mrs. Gardiner hide a smile. "That seems wise," he said.

Mrs. Gardiner nodded her head in ready agreement.

The room fell into silence for a moment, each occupied with his or her own thoughts.

"I should not mind being the source," said Jane.

All eyes turned toward her.

Though she bit her lip and her hands were clasped tightly, there was a sparkle in her eyes that Darcy found surprising, but then, the Jane he had met here in town had surprised him several times already.

"Are you certain?" Mrs. Gardiner asked.

Jane drew in a deliberate breath and pulled herself the tiniest degree more upright. "This whole thing was my idea. Any blame and displeasure which arise should be mine to bear." Her lips curled up slightly. "Besides, though I know it is not proper to seek a reprisal, I do find I would not mind causing Miss Bingley some discomfort, for she has caused plenty for me." Her smile grew. "And I would have her know that though I smile often and am obliging, I am not without resolve."

"That should stand you in good stead for after you are married," Sir Matthew said.

"Aye," said Bingley. "I am not opposed to sharing in Caroline's displeasure."

"Oh, no!" Mrs. Gardiner cried, clapping her hands. "She might suspect you, and a scheme is much more effective if it is accomplished with an element or two of surprise. Jane's being involved will be surprising to Miss Bingley, no doubt, but not nearly so much so if the accident, whatever it may be, is affected with her brother's assistance, since that brother is currently put out with her." Her eyes shifted from Bingley to Darcy. "However..." Her voice trailed off and her eye brows raised. "That is," she added, "if assistance is needed?"

Darcy pointed at himself. "Me?"

Mrs. Gardiner nodded.

Darcy's brows furrowed as he pondered the thought for only a moment. "I am at your service, Miss Bennet. Do you have a plan?"

The sparkle in her eyes grew brighter as she nodded in reply.

"Then, tell me what to do."

Jane looked around the room at each person, then, leaning forward, said in a soft but conspiratorial voice. "First, I will need an invitation to a ball."

~*~*~

Less than a week later, Darcy stood before the Johnsons' grand townhouse, dressed in his finest. It had not been so very difficult to secure the invitations needed to the Johnsons' ball. Mr. Johnson had been eager to assist Darcy with his plan. There was nothing the man seemed to like more than a cunning stratagem. And, Mrs. Johnson had been easily persuaded to part with a few invitations when her husband had suggested that Mr. Darcy's being in atten-dance would without a doubt guarantee that Colonel Fitzwilliam would attend as well as Mr. Bingley. However, he did not share with his wife the plan that was being laid to make her ball the most talked about ball of the season.

Richard huffed as he climbed out of Darcy's carriage. "You do realize that you are indebted to me for this, do you not?" He skewered both Darcy and Bingley, whose carriage stood behind Darcy's, with a displeased look.

Both men nodded.

"She better be worth it," he muttered.

"She is," Darcy said. "I just hope I can persuade her that I am worthy of her regard." He knew that his cousin was not entirely put out with having to dance two sets with Miss Johnson, for Richard had smirked and teased all week about Darcy finally causing a stir in the family by fol-lowing his heart and not his sense of duty. "I think you will agree with me about her worth once you meet her. That is actually why you are here, is it not?"

Richard straightened his sleeves and did not look at Darcy. "I am not sure I understand your meaning."

Darcy chuckled. "Come, shall we get on with the intro-ductions, so that your curiosity might be satisfied? You could have travelled here on your own and arrived fash-ionably late. There was no other need for you to arrive early with us, other than to meet Miss Elizabeth."

His cousin shrugged. It was as close to an admission as

Darcy was likely to get. Richard was a curious sort and had, ever since meeting Miss Bennet, been keenly interested in meeting Miss Elizabeth.

"I am here to watch the theatrics," he replied as they approached the door to the townhouse.

"You do not wish to meet the future Mrs. Darcy?"

Bingley's question was met by a small growling noise.

"Admit it. You are curious," Bingley said with a laugh. "She has three other sisters," he whispered.

"Very well. I will admit to curiosity if you refrain from attempting to marry me off to one and all. It is bad enough that I must dance twice with the same lady." He gave Darcy a pointed look. "There will be talk, and it will reach my mother."

"Your sacrifice is duly noted."

"Good. Now, lead me to the rare creature who has enchanted the dour and disapproving Fitzwilliam Darcy. I wish to know that my sacrifice is not in vain."

"Darcy, Bingley, Fitzwilliam." Mr. Johnson looked as eager as a schoolboy on Christmas day waiting for his Christmas pudding.

"Mr. Bennet and his daughters are in the library." His eyes twinkled. "My wife was called away to attend to something just as they arrived." His brows flicked upward. He nodded his head toward the interior of the house and began walking in the direction of the library. "Quickly, while she attends to another emergency."

Reaching their destination, Mr. Johnson opened the door. "Mr. Bennet, Miss Bennet, Miss Elizabeth, your gentlemen have arrived." Turning to the gentlemen behind him, he added, "I can see why you are so determined to be rid of your sister, Mr. Bingley. Miss Bennet is quite the beauty and her sister?" His eyebrows flicked up as he looked at Darcy. "Well worth a bit of scheming. She's delightful." Then, before allowing them entrance to the room, he said, "My Marietta is still unattached, Colonel."

Richard shook his head. "I will dance my two, but I am attached to my commission at present."

"Ah, well," the man said as he stepped aside, "you cannot fault a father for trying."

"No," Richard agreed. "I would fault him if he did not."

Darcy and Bingley were both inside the library before Richard had finished his exchange with Mr. Johnson.

"Colonel, it is good to see you," Jane greeted as he entered the room. "Thank you for helping us with this plan."

"It is my pleasure to be of service."

Jane lifted a brow, and her lips curled upwards in amusement.

"A small prevarication," he whispered, causing her to laugh.

"Colonel, I would like you to meet my father, Mr. Thomas Bennet. Father, this is the Right Honourable Colonel Richard Fitzwilliam."

"Ah, so I do get to meet the writer of the letter. I thank you, sir, for alerting me to the true nature of Mr. Wickham."

"I cannot say it was my pleasure that it was necessary to impart such information, but I am glad it has been welcomed."

Mr. Bennet nodded. "It is never easy to relate unpleasant news, which makes it all the more appreciated. I have shared it only with my Lizzy." He drew the pretty lady next to him forward. "Colonel Fitzwilliam, this is my second daughter, Elizabeth."

Richard bowed. "I am delighted to finally meet you." He glanced at his cousin. "I have heard much about you."

"Aside from what I could glean from your letter, I know very little about you," Elizabeth replied with a smile.

"There is very little to know," he assured her. "I am but a poor soldier."

Elizabeth laughed. "Yes, a Right Honourable poor soldier."

Richard shrugged. "Far poorer than I wish to be."

"We could all say that," said Mr. Bennet with a chuckle.

"I should very much like to sit for a while," Jane interrupted before Richard could reply. She took her father's arm and gave it a soft tug while she caught Darcy's eye and tipped her head toward her sister.

Darcy nodded. "Would you care to take a turn around

the room?" he asked Elizabeth. "I am no Miss Bingley, but I do think I can circle a library just as well."

Elizabeth smiled, though her brow furrowed. Jane had claimed that the Mr. Darcy she had met in town was different from the one she had met in Hertfordshire, and it appeared she was right. This Mr. Darcy seemed nearly at ease. "I should like that, Mr. Darcy."

"Allow me to begin our conversation with a long overdue apology," he said as she placed her hand on the arm he offered her. "I behaved abominably while at Netherfield. I had my reasons and considered myself justified. However, there is no justification for such poor behaviour." He drew a breath. "I slighted you, looked down on the neighbourhood, and connived to separate myself and Bingley from the area."

She was watching the floor before them.

"I should like to make reparations for my words and actions if you will allow it." He covered her hand with his, drawing her attention up from the red and orange of the carpet. "Can you forgive me?"

Elizabeth lifted her eyes from his hand to his face. "I can. Can you forgive me for listening to Mr. Wickham and speaking poorly of you?"

His smile as he nodded caused Elizabeth's breath to catch and her heart to flutter.

"Yes, yes, I can, and I am certain I deserved most of what you said about me."

"That does not make it right," she protested.

"I will allow that," he replied, "but it does make it understandable. My behavior is harder to comprehend."

They had made a full circuit of the room. Music was filtering in through the door, and they could hear people walking in the corridor.

"If we are to begin again," Darcy said softly, "then, allow me to ask you for a dance as I should have at our first meeting, for I cannot resist the temptation of your loveliness."

# Chapter 13

"Have you concluded your thinking about Mr. Darcy yet?" Mr. Bennet asked as Elizabeth took a seat next to him in the library. She and he would make their appearance after the first set, so there was ample time for them to continue the discussion Mr. Bennet had begun when they had entered the carriage. There, he had questioned his daughter regarding her interactions with Mr. Darcy while he was in Hertfordshire, as well as how she might now consider the gentleman's behaviour in light of the secrets contained in Colonel Fitzwilliam's letter.

"He is so different."

"As Jane said."

Elizabeth nodded, perplexity was written across her face in the way her brows furrowed and how she pulled the right corner of her bottom lip between her teeth, and it was echoed in the way her shoulders rose and then drooped as she sighed.

Mr. Bennet knew that look and sigh well. His daughter was not good at admitting small faults. She had a propensity to strive to be absolutely correct at every turn, and it frustrated and angered her when she was not. He suspected that at present, his Lizzy was more than a trifle upset with herself and did not wish to admit it. It had been a trial to persuade her to admit that she had misjudged Mr. Darcy as they had travelled – not because Elizabeth had not realized that fact as soon as she had read the colonel's letter. No, she knew her error, she just did not wish to face the shame that came with the admission. Pride was never a pleasant partner. Eventually, it would demand its dues, and payment usually was extracted in the form of mortification.

"You like him," he offered to her the words he suspected she wished to say.

Her head bobbed up and down slowly. "I do, or I think I might."

Mr. Bennet sat quietly as his daughter pondered that thought for a moment.

"He was not at all proud just now." She stared across the room toward the door. "He apologized." She turned her eyes to her father.

"For what?"

"For his comment at the assembly, how he behaved while in Hertfordshire, and for attempting to separate himself and Bingley from the area." Her head tipped to the side, and her eyebrows drew together.

Mr. Bennet chuckled. "Indeed, why would he attempt to separate himself from the area?"

Elizabeth blinked.

"Ah, my Lizzy, your eyes have always spoken to me. There was a flicker in them just now as you spoke of his leaving Hertfordshire." He patted her hand. "When your head tips after such a flicker, I know you are questioning something about whatever it was you were saying. I am not so unobservant as I appear." He sighed. "I should appear observant more often. For that, I must apologize. I have not done my duty as a husband and father." He straightened his waistcoat. "It is something I intend to correct, though I do fear I will not be successful. I am too given to taking my ease."

"Oh, Papa!"

"No, it is true. I do enjoy peace and solitude, and though I love your mother and your sisters, they try my patience greatly." He shook his head. "What gentleman who is as fastidious as Mr. Darcy would wish to be tied to such a brood as mine?"

Elizabeth gasped.

"No, not you, my dear, nor Jane. I speak of your mother and younger sisters. They are precisely the opposite of Mr. Darcy, and I would venture to say he finds them as trying as I do. However, he lacks the love I have for them, for they are not his kin." His lips turned up in a small smile. "Yet."

He chuckled at her gasp. "I did tell you to consider it. I

will not force you to marry against your wishes, but he is a sensible fellow, and he is not poor."

"Papa!"

"Be reasonable, my dear. You do not wish to be married to someone who will leave you in the hedgerows upon his demise. Such a worry can addle the mind."

"Oh, Papa." Elizabeth grasped his hand. "You will not leave us in the hedgerows. Mama exaggerates, does she not?"

His head bobbed up and down slowly as he gave her hand a reassuring squeeze. "She does, but knowing I cannot provide for her as I wish has been a heavy weight to bear. I tell you this because I would have you consider your future with your head as well as your heart." He squeezed her hand once again. "The man loves you. It is plain to see. And you are not indifferent to him. See how your cheeks grow rosy at the mere mention?" He chuckled. "Allow him to court you, Elizabeth. Study his character. Grow to like him more. I think you will be happy, but if I am wrong, do not accept his offer. However, I cannot allow you to shy away from this for fear of bearing reproof for not having judged fairly or some other foolish and proud reason without doing my best to persuade you to give Mr. Darcy a second chance. I love you far too much to do that, even if it means eventually having to give you away. Promise me you will consider what I have said."

Elizabeth's lips quivered, and her eyes filled with tears. "I will," she promised him.

He squeezed her hand once more. "Good, now before we become even more missish and you become a watering pot, we should take our places to observe the proceeding. Hopefully, there will be a few gentlemen left to partner you for dances. Your mother would be rightfully put out with me for not having you dance every set with someone. To think you are here in town with so many wealthy young men and instead of dancing, your father has you sitting in a library."

Elizabeth laughed. "It is not you who has us sitting here; it is Jane."

"Of all my daughters, I never thought it would be my Jane scheming her way into a betrothal," he said with a laugh as he stood. "But then, it seems many people are not the same in town as they are in Hertfordshire."

"Except Miss Bingley," Elizabeth added with a smirk, causing her father to laugh again as she took his arm. "I am curious to meet this Sir Matthew," she whispered as they crossed the room. "Who would willingly wish to marry her?"

Her father winked. "We shall soon see, shall we not?"

"Indeed, we shall."

~*~*~

Jane took her place at Mr. Darcy's side, her hand on his arm, while Mr. Bingley followed Mr. Johnson down the corridor and into the ballroom from a door that would not draw notice. It was the same door through which her father would later enter with Elizabeth. Later – after Caroline's fate had been sealed.

Jane blew out a breath. Her heart was racing. She had never caused even a small stir at a ball before this, but she knew that entering the ballroom with Mr. Darcy was just the beginning of the attention she would draw this evening. She scanned the room as she entered. The light from numerous candles sparkled from the chandeliers and danced from mirror to mirror. Everything from the arrangement of the plants and chairs to the size of the floor and the number of musicians in the alcove was breathtaking. Everything was so much finer than anything she had experienced in Hertfordshire. The opulence and number of people in attendance at this ball even outshone Netherfield.

"Are you ready?" Darcy whispered.

She gave a small nod of her head and allowed him to lead her into the room. They circled to the left, passing a window with a set of chairs tucked into its alcove.

"She is just ahead of us," Darcy whispered.

"And Sir Matthew?" Jane attempted to peer through the crowd to where Mr. Darcy was looking, but he, having the greater height, had the advantage, and she would have to rely on his information for the time being.

"He appears to be just approaching to collect her for a dance."

"Precisely on schedule," Jane muttered.

"I do admire that about the man," Darcy replied.

Jane smiled and turned impertinent eyes up toward him. "As do I. Although I find his most endearing quality is his willingness to marry Miss Bingley."

"Indeed," Darcy agreed with a chuckle. "Here we go. Three steps and she will see us."

There was a hint of glee in Mr. Darcy's voice that surprised Jane, though only slightly. She had come to know the gentleman better since her arrival in town. He was not so dour as he had at first appeared. He was proper and given to meticulousness, but he was not without a playful bent. It might not be displayed so often as some such as Mr. Bingley might display such an inclination, but it was there, and it was delightfully surprising every time he displayed it. Elizabeth would be glad for it, and Jane suspected, her sister would likely draw that part of Mr. Darcy's character out. They would do well together, and from the way Elizabeth had fidgeted while waiting in the library and from how she welcomed Mr. Darcy tonight, Jane was certain that her sister was not unaffected by the gentleman – despite her pleas as they had talked last night that she was uncertain how she thought or felt about Mr. Darcy.

Jane heard her quarry before she saw her. The gasp Miss Bingley uttered was exceptionally pleasing.

"Miss Bingley, Mrs. Hurst," Darcy said in greeting. He looked blankly at Sir Matthew. "Have we met?"

For a man who despised all forms of disguise, Mr. Darcy seemed rather adept at prevarication.

"Sir Matthew Broadhurst of Stoningham in Surrey," Sir Matthew replied with a bow after which Darcy introduced himself and then Jane.

"A delight to meet you both."

Sir Matthew's expression was pleasant, and, if Jane were not mistaken, there was a glint of amusement in his eyes. He seemed to be enjoying himself, which was good since Jane still worried that she was asking him to take on a life of misery by marrying Caroline Bingley. Oh, she knew what he had said about knowing what he was taking on, but still, her heart was not wholly at ease.

"You did not tell me you had such a lovely friend," he said to Caroline. "Miss Bennet, I am promised to Miss Bingley for this set, but I would be honoured if you would allow me to claim the next dance. Unless, of course, it is already spoken for?"

"I am afraid the next set has been claimed, but perhaps the one after that?" Jane replied.

Sir Matthew knew right well that Mr. Bingley had claimed the set after the one with Mr. Darcy. These gentlemen, who seemed so honourable, were surprisingly good actors, and for that, Jane was exceedingly glad.

Caroline narrowed her eyes at Jane and stepped closer to Sir Matthew while casting an expectant glance at Darcy.

"I see someone to whom I wish to introduce you, and then we must find your father so that he does not think I have absconded with you," Darcy said to Jane. "I hope you ladies have a pleasant evening." He gave a small bow and led Jane away toward where Mr. Johnson was standing with Richard and a pretty young lady, whom, Jane guessed, was Miss Johnson. The colonel and Miss Johnson did seem to look well together.

"Miss Bingley did not look pleased when I did not request a dance, did she?" Darcy asked.

Again, there was that note of glee in his voice. "No, she did not, and did you notice how she attempted to lay claim to Sir Matthew when he requested a dance from me?"

Darcy chuckled. "Just as you said she would. You are very clever, Miss Bennet."

'Thank you," Jane replied with a smile. She was often complimented for her beauty but rarely for her wit. Cleverness was Lizzy's forte, so it was gratifying, for once, to be commended for intelligence and not beauty. "You played your part admirably."

Darcy inclined his head in acceptance of her praise.

They had reached Mr. Johnson and, therefore, their discussion ended. Jane was introduced to Miss Johnson and, for effect, the colonel. Then, as the musicians began to play, she, Darcy, Miss Johnson, and Richard took their places in the group of dancers with Caroline and Sir Matthew.

"Are you well?" Darcy asked as he took his place next to her.

Jane smiled. "I am. Are you?"

He gave a sharp nod of his head.

Jane looked across the circle to where Sir Matthew stood. She smiled but allowed her eyes to carry her question. He returned her smile as he gave her a slight nod. Gathering her fortitude as the first notes of the song began, she turned and curtseyed to the gentleman on her right before turning to Darcy on her left. Then she skipped and hopped her way through the steps, pausing to watch as others took their turns.

Finally, the ladies joined hands and went around in a circle in one direction and then the other. Jane's heart was beating far faster than the dance steps dictated as Darcy took the hand which was not holding Caroline's.

As she skipped towards him the second time, he gave her a tug causing her hand to slip from Caroline's. She stumbled slightly but being prepared for it, she did not fall. Caroline, however, was not so fortunate and found herself clasped tightly to Sir Matthew's chest as they tumbled to the floor.

"Are you injured?" Sir Matthew asked.

"Let me up," Caroline demanded, wiggling to break free of his hold.

"Not until I know you are uninjured," Sir Matthew said.

"I am well," Caroline sputtered.

"Are you certain?" Sir Matthew smoothed an imaginary hair from Caroline's cheek as his other arm clasped her firmly in place on top of him. "You look flushed."

"Let me up," Caroline insisted once more.

"You are very light," Sir Matthew said.

Caroline's eyes grew wide.

"Allow me to help you." Jane extended a hand to Caroline. "I feel just dreadful that I lost my grip."

"Do not touch me," Caroline hissed.

Jane drew her hand back. "Very well. I do apologize, Sir Matthew."

Sir Matthew smiled up at her. "No harm done."

"No harm done?" Caroline sputtered as he finally released her and allowed her to scramble off of him.

"That is what I said." Sir Matthew rose from the floor and brushed his breeches and then his sleeves before tugging on his waistcoat. "I am in need of a wife, and you will do nicely."

"A wife?" Caroline squeaked.

"Yes, as well as a mistress for my estate – it is quite large — and mother for my children – we will need to have at least two. Boys preferably."

"I see no reason to not let you have her."

Caroline spun around. "Charles, be reasonable. It was a stumble, a misstep."

Bingley nodded. "Indeed, it was. A very fortuitous one." He took Jane's hand and pulled her to his side. "I'll expect you in my study tomorrow," he said to Sir Matthew. "Hurst," he said to his brother-in-law, who had just ambled up with Louisa, "Caroline is getting married."

"I am not." Caroline crossed her arms and glared at him.

"You do not wish for a large estate and fortune?" Hurst asked in surprise. "I had thought that was precisely what you were looking for. I am certain I have heard you declare such to your sister on many occasions. True, it is not Pemberley, but I hear Stoningham is impressive."

"Reginald," Louisa whispered loudly. "She is not a fortune hunter."

Hurst harrumphed. "Is she not?"

"Stop speaking. I shall be ruined," Caroline whispered.

"No," said Bingley, "you shall be married." He nodded toward the door. "Shall we continue this discussion in the library?"

"Certainly," Sir Matthew agreed, taking Caroline's elbow and gripping it firmly as she attempted to pull it away from him. "Smile and look as if you are pleased," he whispered, "that is what you want them to comment on when you are gone rather than calling you all manner of unpleasant things."

Caroline stared at him for a moment, then, smiled. "Of

course, my dear, you are correct. I was merely rattled by the fall." She lifted her right foot. "In fact, I believe, I have injured myself after all. If you would be so good as to allow me to lean on you until I can find a place to rest."

"Ah, see. That was not so difficult, was it?" he replied as she wrapped her arm around his.

Jane gave Bingley's hand a final squeeze and then released it.

Bingley shook his head and extended his hand to her again. "Come with me."

Jane looked at Mr. Darcy. "Do you mind?"

Darcy shook his head as a grin split his face. "I have never much cared for dancing, and besides, there is someone standing by that door over there whom, if I am to dance, I would dearly like to have as my partner."

Jane followed Darcy's gaze to where Elizabeth stood with her father. "I wish you well," she said as she took Bingley's arm. "Remember to tell her – "

"I know," Darcy interrupted. "I shall do my best not to blunder."

# Chapter 14

"Miss Elizabeth, I believe the next set is ours," Darcy said as he came to stand with her and her father. "However, we must wait for this set to conclude." It was perhaps the first time he had ever wished for a dance to begin quickly rather than dreading the moment when he would have to place himself across from a lady and present himself as charmingly as he was able, which, in all honestly, was a meager offering on most occasions.

"That was as fine a performance as any I have seen," said Mr. Bennet. "I had not thought you the actor sort, but it appears I am wrong." Amusement danced in the gentleman's eyes.

"I cannot say that I have ever aspired to the role of actor," Darcy admitted, although, it had not been deplorable to take part in the charade which had just transpired. That was rather surprising.

"We are all actors at times, are we not?" Elizabeth interjected.

Her eyes were sparkling in that transfixing way they

always did when she began a debate. Darcy waited with eager anticipation for her to present her argument.

"I, for instance," she continued, "must perform my roles as daughter and sister as well as niece, cousin, and friend."

"But there is a truth to such roles," Darcy retorted, his lips twitching with the pleasure that accompanied refuting her claim with one of his own. "The actor who dons a smock and frolics about the stage becomes what he is not while you are you no matter if you are with friends or family. There is an element in each role you portray that is real. Your lines are not scripted nor are your emotions contrived."

"Well said," Mr. Bennet agreed.

"Perhaps." Elizabeth motioned to the dancers. The sparkling in her eyes had ignited into a spark, steady and sure. "Do you suppose that all of the ladies and gentlemen in attendance are presenting themselves as they truly are? How much of the genuine person is on display, and how much is hidden? Will the lady who fears to have it known that she enjoys studying the stars rather than Mr. Ackermann's drawings reveal herself as she is or as she is expected to be? Will she enter into a conversation with quickness or will she defer? Will she appear to be happily amused by a gentleman's conversation about trivial matters or will she interject a subject of substance?"

She shifted a step away from her father and closer to him as she immersed herself completely in her thoughts.

"And what of the gentleman with an estate that is ailing and in need of propping up? Will he not hide the true state of his affairs? Will he pursue where his bank accounts lead, or will he chase after his heart?" She shook her head. "It is as the bard said. We are all players on this great stage of life."

"That is also well stated," Mr. Bennet agreed. "And I would add one additional thought. Is it not possible that the fellow who prances about a stage in tunic and tights finds a bit of himself in the role he portrays? Might he not find himself comparing his own character to the part he plays?"

Darcy looked from daughter to father and back. Their brows were furrowed in thought in an almost identical fashion while their eyes held no censure but only genuine curiosity – the sign of a quick and hungry mind.

"I will grant you may both be correct," he said. "There are, no doubt, many in attendance who are very unlike who they truly are. Some will have noble reasons for their performance while others seek nothing more than amusement and sport." He paused. "I must admit that I am not at ease enough in a crowd such as this to always act as I am. As much as I say I despise disguise, I find I am often hiding myself behind an austere mien."

"I had not meant to rebuke," Elizabeth said quickly.

"No, I do not believe you were," he assured her. "I am merely extending your suppositions and examining them closely, and as I do so, I find I must consider myself just as you considered your roles as sister, daughter, cousin, niece, and friend. However, in doing so, I find that my original rebuttal remains true. I am not given to frivolity. I tend to be more serious in nature. These things become part of the disguise but remain true to who I am. For another who gads about glibly, one might find that such a one is naturally more free-spirited, and therefore, when he presents himself, his exuberance is merely an extension of his true identity." He shrugged. "The same can be said for character flaws, I suppose. A person given to cheerfulness, who is at ease in many situations and is never at a loss for words, might, when he allows such traits to grow beyond their bounds, become a fellow who seeks to gain favour and even wealth through charmingly teasing words that entice and deceive." He spoke, of course, of Wickham, and from the way, Elizabeth's gaze fell, he suspected she knew it. So, he continued. "And a gentleman such as myself, who is adept at seeing flaws in need of addressing, might become cantankerous and rude, and in doing so, cause hurt through disparagement, for he can only see the unpleasant corner of the stage in which he finds himself rather than the entirety of the theatre."

"And a gentleman who is rarely rattled by anything might become indifferent to those things which should stir him to action," Mr. Bennet added.

"Papa," Elizabeth chided in a whispered.

"No, my dear, it is true. And I will add that a lady, whose mind is quick and ready to debate in a moment, might use such talent to create swords that can cut and pierce even her own heart and mind, blinding her to the truth."

Elizabeth's head dipped, and her cheeks grew rosy.

"Ah, my Lizzy," her father said, taking her hand. "Realizing folly is the first step in preventing any further foolishness and in finding wisdom, and..." He winked at her when she finally looked at him, an action that caused Darcy to smile unwittingly. "I declare, I have never had such a pleasant time at a ball. Not once have either of you spoken of lace or feathers. And for that, I am immeasurably grateful."

"Indeed," Darcy muttered.

"Not a favourite topic of discourse for you either, is it?" Mr. Bennet said with a chuckle.

"It most decidedly is not," Darcy replied.

Mr. Bennet chuckled once again. "Then allow me to conclude our discussion as it appears the next set is forming, and I shall not return to my wife with the news that her daughter did not dance at least once at this ball." Again, he winked at Elizabeth, who shook her head and smiled. "There is truth in both positions. One is not right and the other, wrong. In fact, they work best together. Now." He gave her hand one more squeeze before lifting it in Darcy's direction. "I shall leave you youngsters to the dancing and find myself a glass of something refreshing."

He lifted a brow while amusement shone in his eyes.

"However, I will not be far away. There shall be no absconding or other such mischiefs. I think we have had our fill for one night."

"I believe you are correct," Darcy assured him before escorting Elizabeth onto the dance floor.

"I must thank you," Elizabeth said as they made their way to where a circle of dancers was forming for a cotillion. "What you have done for my sister is quite lovely."

Darcy drew her to a stop just before they reached their places. "I did not do it only for her."

"You did not?"

Her eyes were wide in astonishment.

"No," he replied with a smile, "my motives were more self-serving than that."

She blinked and looked at him with what he thought might be the most charming expression of confusion he had ever seen. Silently, she allowed him to bring her to their place in the circle. He looked around the group and then back at Elizabeth. He bowed as she curtseyed. They spoke not a word throughout the first half of the dance. Then, in the second half, when they joined hands and circled together, he pitched his tone low and spoke so that hopefully only she would hear. "I wished for my friend and your sister to be happy, this is true. I would do most anything to ensure Bingley is happy, even if it meant my own misery, which I was certain it did."

"I do not understand," she said as they parted once again.

"I will explain, but not here," he replied as they joined hands again. He wanted to pull her from the dance floor, through the side door, and to some secluded alcove so that they might talk in private, but he had promised Mr. Bennet he would not. Therefore, they would have to pass the dance with broken conversation about something trivial such as the weather or, he smiled, books.

"Talking of books while dancing, Mr. Darcy?" She playfully chided him as they left the dance floor.

"Too mundane?" He queried in reply. "Would you rather canvas the weather or the flower arrangements?"

She giggled. "I did not know you could tease, sir. In fact, I was led to believe that teasing was beneath you."

"Miss Bingley does not know me so well as she thinks she does," he replied. "I enjoy a small amount of teasing. I cannot say that it is a staple in my conversation, but I have had a most excellent teacher. My cousin, Colonel Fitzwilliam, is proficient in the art. I think you and he will enjoy each other's company."

"He seems very pleasant," Elizabeth replied.

"Mr. Bennet, might I have permission to take your daughter for a stroll in the hall?" Darcy asked as they joined her father. "I believe I know of a comfortable chair where you might enjoy a few moments of relaxation and solitude and yet be able to see the length of the hall in both directions."

"I would like nothing better than a few quiet moments in which I could rest my feet." He waved his hand, indicating Darcy should lead on, which Darcy did with gladness.

"You did not ask if I had a partner for this dance," Elizabeth said as they reached the door.

"I beg your pardon," Darcy replied. "Have I caused another gentleman to be left standing?"

"No," Elizabeth admitted, "but that does not mean you should not have asked." Her lips curled upward, and one brow was arched with an impertinent air.

"Forgive me. I was in error."

"I doubt very much that Mr. Darcy cares two figs if another gentleman was left standing instead of dancing with you." Mr. Bennet winked at her gasp before looking this way and that and spying a chair. "That should do quite nicely," he said with a tip of his head in the direction of the chair. "We are spending a week in town," he informed Darcy before he turned to go take a seat. "If I stay longer, my wife will likely fabricate some reason to join us, and then, I shall never see the inside of my book room until a month has passed and my bank account has felt the adventure most severely." He winked once again and left them alone.

"Then, I shall be returning to Netherfield within a week," Darcy said to the back of the man.

"Very good," Mr. Bennet replied without a look backward. "My wife shall be delighted."

"Will you be pleased if I return to Netherfield?" Darcy asked as he and Elizabeth began their stroll.

"Mr. Bingley will accompany you, will he not?"

His brows furrowed slightly at her response. "Yes, but I was inquiring about if you would be pleased if *I* returned to Netherfield. Bingley could return without me. It would not be ideal, but it is not outside of the realm of possibilities."

"Will his sisters be joining him?" Elizabeth asked.

Darcy shook his head. "I am not certain, but it seems Miss Bingley will likely need to remain in town." He stopped walking. "Unless Sir Matthew wishes to join our party. I shall have to discuss that with Bingley."

"Yes."

"I beg your pardon?" He blinked as he was pulled from his contemplation and looked down at her smiling face.

"Yes," she repeated before adding, "I would be pleased if you returned to Netherfield, provided you are not alone and even if Miss Bingley and Mrs. Hurst must join you." She looked down at where her hand lay on his arm. "You said you would explain your meaning about fearing that helping your friend find his happiness would cause your misery."

He nodded. "I did." He drew and expelled a great breath. "I left Hertfordshire because I believed that my heart was leading me away from where duty said I should go, for I found myself enamoured with a lovely, temptingly handsome young lady, who, though she was all that I could wish for in a wife, was not what I thought my family would expect. She did not have great wealth or connections, but, I realized as I spent many an agonizing hour in town, she had my heart."

His lips curled up into a slight smile. He had thought revealing so much of himself and his desires would be more difficult, but to his surprise, he felt at ease — completely and entirely at ease with Elizabeth at his side.

"I thought that remaining in town would cure me of my infatuation, and so I worked to keep my friend in town with me. How could I return to where her spell would be greatest? How could I encourage my friend to pursue her sister when in doing so, I would be binding myself to either a life of misery in seeing her but never having her or the pain of being separated from one who is as close as a brother?"

They had come to the end of the corridor and so stopped and just stood together looking back down toward the other end.

"As time passed, I came to realize that I could not be so selfish as to risk being the cause of my friend's enduring the same longing I was. My sense of honour would not allow it. It was just at this time when I learned of your sister's call at Bingley's home, and I realized then that my belief of her being indifferent toward him, for I truly had not noticed any partiality on her part toward my friend, was grievously in error."

"You did not suspect her regard for Mr. Bingley?" Elizabeth asked in surprise.

Darcy shook his head. "No, I did not, but once I knew the truth, I also knew I could not conceal my error from Bingley. So, I confessed all to him and prepared to be separated from him forever because I could not witness your loving another who was not me."

Her eyes grew wide.

"Bingley is a good friend and would hear nothing of a separation. He refused to let me leave until I had seen reason. Who is master of me to approve or disapprove of my choice of a wife if I am so fortunate as to ever secure the affections of the one I love? None, save me. My estate is my own, as is my fortune, and I would rather be separated from my relations than from my heart."

"You love me?"

He smiled at her tone of incredulity. "Shocking as it may be, yes. I love you, most ardently."

"But what of..." she clamped her mouth closed as her eyes grew wide.

"My cousin Anne?" he asked. Wickham had likely told her about his supposed betrothal.

Her cheeks grew rosy, and she nodded.

"It is the wish of my aunt that we marry, but we are not

betrothed, nor do I have any plans to ever be betrothed to my cousin."

"I should not have listened to him," Elizabeth whispered.

"I have already forgiven you for that," Darcy replied. "I am most happy to set straight what he has twisted in his attempts to disparage me." He turned to look at her fully. "I wish for you to question me so that I might defend myself with the truth. Please, do not feel ashamed and hide any of it from me."

"Are you certain?"

Darcy nodded. "As surely as the sun shines in the day and the moon, at night."

Her lips curved into a relieved smile. "You are so different from what I thought."

"I am different from the man I presented to all of Hertfordshire, and yet, I am also the same. I am not a man without faults. However, I am a man with faults who would beg you to give him a second chance to prove himself worthy of your regard. Please?" He sucked in a breath and held it as she searched his face.

"You love me?"

He nodded as his heart picked up its rhythm and his cravat suddenly became an uncomfortably warm and restrictive piece of clothing.

"I do not know how," she muttered.

"Nor do I, in truth, but I do," he replied.

She shook her head and chuckled. "My mother will never believe it."

"Does that mean you will give me a chance?" His heart felt like it was going to climb its way up his throat and out his mouth if she did not relieve his anxiety soon.

Again, she shook her head and chuckled before turning a beaming face toward him. "Yes, Mr. Darcy, I should like to see if we are indeed companionable." She bit her lip and tilted her head. "Do we call this a courtship or a friendship?"

He knew a ridiculously large grin was spreading across his face. "Both." He lifted her hand from his arm and kissed it. "Thank you," he whispered.

Down the hall, the library door opened, and Sir Matthew, Caroline, and the Hursts exited before Jane and Bingley, who walked arm in arm with their heads close together.

Elizabeth sighed as she saw it and shook her head. "No, Mr. Darcy, thank you, for being willing to suffer loss so my sister could find happiness." She paused and then looked up at him with merriment shining in her eyes. "And for confounding Miss Bingley, so that Jane and your friend could be rid of her."

He chuckled and pulled her a bit closer to him as they made their way to where Bingley and Jane stood with Mr. Bennet.

"Am I to assume from your happy expressions that I

have not one but two daughters who will be delighting their mother by having secured such handsome and wealthy gentlemen?" Mr. Bennet asked.

"I have not yet secured your daughter," Darcy replied. "However, she has given me permission to make an attempt at delighting Mrs. Bennet."

Mr. Bennet chortled. "I wish you success, young man. Now, shall we depart? Or do any of you wish to dance more?"

It was agreed that no one wished to return to the ballroom, and after sending a footman to locate Richard, Darcy exited the Johnson's house, leaving behind family expectations and moving forward with the lady who held both his arm and his heart into what he hoped would be a very happy future.

# Delighting Mrs. Bennet

*He wished to please her by tolerating her mother. He hadn't expected to find his heart so entangled in her family.*

# Chapter 1

"How is he?" Darcy stopped pacing the sitting room as his physician, Mr. Westcott, entered.

"I have seen worse." He cast a glance at the others in the room but spoke to Darcy. "Mr. Royston had some difficulty setting the bone. I would not move him for at least two weeks."

"He may stay where he is, of course," Darcy assured Mr. Westcott.

"I suspected you would say that." Mr. Westcott turned his hat in his hand and smiled at Darcy. "I have left instructions for Mr. Bennet's care with Mr. Abrams, and he informed me that he would find someone to assign to my patient."

He reached down and scratched the head of the black and tan dog standing at his side. "A fine mess you made, lad," he chided.

The dog cocked his head to the side and seemed to smile, utterly unaware of the damage his racing about in a frenzy of fun had caused.

"Stick to chasing rats," Mr. Westcott added with a pat for the happy beast's head.

"I have never had a pup that was so difficult to train," Darcy apologized. He snapped his fingers at the dog and was completely ignored. Every other dog which had come into Darcy's possession had learned to stop and look when they heard his snap, but not Dash.

Dash was his own dog. It was not that he was incapable of learning commands. No, he was an intelligent beast, wily even, and adept at finding all kinds of mischief into which to toss himself with abandon. He was just unwilling to follow a command unless he determined first that it should be followed.

"Strength of character is not so bad a thing." Mr. Westcott patted Dash's head again. "It is a great asset once it has been properly directed."

Darcy sighed. "That is the struggle." He looked at Dash and made a clucking sound while tapping his leg.

Dash tipped his head so that one ear flopped up as he looked at Darcy and paused for a moment before deciding that standing at Darcy's side would be the thing to do. And he almost made it to Darcy's side before being distracted by a pair of pretty slippers.

"He'll come around," Mr. Westcott assured Darcy. "He's young."

Elizabeth pulled her feet under her chair and, bending

forward, scratched Dash's ear while he looked from her hidden slippers to her face and back.

"Our patient is well-settled?" Mr. Westcott asked Mr. Royston as he entered the room.

"He is, sir. He will likely sleep for some time."

"At present, the more sleeping he does, the better," Mr. Westcott said. "I shall return tomorrow, but if anything changes, you know where you can find me."

"Two weeks," Elizabeth said to Dash as Darcy walked to the door of the sitting room with Mr. Westcott and his assistant. "My father must stay in bed for two weeks, and who knows how long after that it will be before he is walking properly." She leveled a severe look at the animal which was happily accepting her attention. "You were a very naughty pup," she chided.

Dash ducked his head and looked up at her with sad eyes.

"Do not think I will fall for that," Elizabeth said with a chuckle. "You are still a naughty pup."

"Perhaps if you did not scratch his ear while reprimanding him, it might have a greater effect," said Mrs. Gardiner.

Elizabeth sighed. "I cannot help it. His ears just beg to be scratched, and if I do not scratch them, he will attempt to chew my slipper with my foot still in it."

"I should send him to John at Pemberley," Darcy said from the doorway to the drawing room. "John always knows how to get an animal to mind." He shook his head.

"Of course, Georgiana would be sorely displeased if I did. However, I do believe he will be confined to Georgiana's sitting room when we have guests take a tour of the house."

He blew out a breath and crossed the room to sit with the ladies. "I must apologize for the damage Dash has caused. There are no words for how dreadful I feel." How did one make amends for his dog tripping a gentleman and causing him to tumble down the stairs, resulting in a broken leg?

"It is not as if you expected it to happen," Mrs. Gardiner said.

"But if he were better trained..." He stopped his protest at the lift of the lady's brow and the incredulous look she gave him.

"Babies, which Dash is, do not always mind their parent. Trust me. I know. I have four children, Mr. Darcy, and there are days I wonder whose offspring they are, for surely my children would not behave in such an inappropriate fashion." She sighed. "But alas, they are mine. However, each possesses his or her own temperament and will. And Dash, I would imagine, is not so very different." She smiled. "I find biscuits work quite well to encourage proper behaviour."

Darcy chuckled. "Dash does enjoy biscuits."

A footman, carrying a leash, came into the room, and

immediately, Dash scooted between Elizabeth's chair and the wall.

Darcy took a small piece of cake from the tea tray, which had yet to be removed from the room after the commotion of a falling father and the doctor being summoned. Crouching down, he extended it to Dash. The cake proved to be far too tempting for Dash to ignore, and soon, the footman was leaving the room with Dash trotting happily behind him while Darcy returned to his chair and the room fell silent.

"I should like to look in on my father before we go, even if he is sleeping," Elizabeth said.

"Of course," Darcy agreed. "Is there any way you might be able to stay with him?" Darcy knew it was unlikely, but he also knew that Elizabeth would wish to see to her father's care. From the hopeful look Elizabeth shared with her aunt, he knew he was correct.

"I fear there is not," Mrs. Gardiner answered.

Darcy nodded and again the room fell into silence, save for the ticking of the clock on the table in the corner. In Darcy's mind, it was not right that a man should be without at least someone from his family near him when he was convalescing. The someone should be Elizabeth. She would, no doubt, know best how to cheer her father and keep him entertained. However, without some sort of able-bodied chaperone to ensure that things were kept proper, it was not possible for her to attend to her father without risking damage to her reputation. His brows furrowed as he considered asking his aunt to come for a visit, but the countess was a stranger to Elizabeth, and that would not do. Perhaps...

"What if your mother were to come to town?" Darcy asked.

"My mother?" Elizabeth's eyes were wide.

Darcy nodded. "Yes, your mother. Then you and your sister could stay here, and your father would not be alone."

Elizabeth shook her head, her look clearly telling him that she thought he was not thinking clearly. "My mother will bring all of my sisters."

"I know," Darcy admitted, "but I thought you might wish to care for your father, and I cannot think of any other way to make it possible."

"I would be delighted to care for him," Elizabeth replied, "but my mother?" She turned to her sister. "Jane, tell him he does not want our mother here. In town. At his house."

"It is only two weeks," Darcy argued. "I am certain I could perform the part of host admirably for two weeks." He was almost certain that was true. Surely, two weeks would be endurable.

Elizabeth sent a pleading look to her sister.

"Our mother is trying," Jane said. "Darcy House is so peaceful," she grimaced, "but it would not be after the arrival of our mother." She paused. "And sisters."

Darcy knew Jane was correct, but he was determined to do what he thought was his duty.

"No," he said, shaking his head, "I am inviting your mother and sisters to Darcy House." His stomach twisted at the thought. The more he thought about it, the more he did not know how he would tolerate so much noise in his home, but it had to be done. His dog had caused Mr. Bennet's injury, and Darcy would bear the discomfort of Mrs. Bennet's presence in return.

# Chapter 2

Darcy rubbed the back of his neck and reclined in his chair as he studied the letter before him. As much as he had insisted – multiple times – to Elizabeth, Jane, and Mrs. Gardiner that he was capable of tolerating Mrs. Bennet, and as much as he attempted to assure himself that it was true, he was not entirely certain that he had not overestimated his ability to abide so many people in his private domain. He scowled at the dog lying in front of the hearth.

"You look rather displeased," Colonel Richard Fitzwilliam said as he entered Darcy's study.

"Do you ever wait to be announced?"

Richard shrugged out of his coat and unbuttoned his waistcoat. "I do not need an introduction. You know me. We are family, and as Aunt Catherine always says, there is no need to tell my family who I am." He smirked as he tossed both his jacket and his waistcoat onto a chair and crossed to where Darcy kept a decanter of port and glasses.

"You may be known to me, but there are times I would like a few fleeting seconds to gather my thoughts before they are intruded upon." He nodded as Richard lifted a glass in offer.

"So tell me," Richard said as he poured, ignoring Darcy's reprimand, as he often did. "What has you scowling at poor little Dash."

"Naughty little Dash," Darcy corrected. "I have a houseguest for the next two weeks, at least, and I was just writing to invite four more guests to join us, all thanks to that naughty little pup."

The fashion in which his cousin slowly sat the decanter down and methodically turned toward Darcy as if he expected to see something hideous or to be faced with the barrel of a pistol caused Darcy to smile, despite his displeasure with Dash and his misgivings about the invitation which lay on his desk.

"I assure you I have not lost my mind."

Richard lifted a brow. "You just admitted to inviting five people to stay with you. That is not something you do."

Darcy blew out a breath and began folding his letter. "I have no choice, and it might actually be more than five people."

"First, you decide to marry, and now, you are filling your house with guests. Should the home office hear of this, they might rightly send a couple men to ensure you have not been kidnapped and replaced by an imposter." He chuckled as he placed a glass on the desk in front of Darcy.

"Now, just a moment, young pup," he scolded as he saw

Dash leap into the chair on which Richard had tossed his clothing and begin to circle before lying down. "My clothes are not your bed." Richard shooed the beast onto the floor.

"I told you. He is a wayward pup. Nearly incorrigible."

Richard bent and scratched the dog's ears. "He merely wants more instruction."

"Why must everyone give him attention when he misbehaves?" It was as if those ears had some sort of magical pull on everyone who came near them.

"He is doing as he is supposed to at present. My jacket is safe; therefore, he deserves a scratch."

Darcy shook his head. "Your jacket is only safe until you turn your back."

To prove his point, Darcy said nothing when Dash once again sprang onto the chair and made a bed of his cousin's jacket, but he did chuckle when, this time, Richard added a curse to his command to get off his clothes.

Dash, apparently, knew that he had crossed some line and scooted back to the hearth with his ears flattened and his tail tucked.

"And you had best stay there for a time," Richard said to the animal while settling into the chair he always claimed when he visited Darcy in his study.

Darcy chuckled and finished folding and sealing his letter before he made his way to the study door and requested that it be posted express as soon as possible. He was not in a rush to have Mrs. Bennet and her younger daughters descend upon him, but he was eager to allow Elizabeth the opportunity to care for her father.

"What was that about?" Richard asked as Darcy joined him near the hearth. Dash popped up when Darcy approached, but a gruff word from Richard returned him to his place.

"Dash has decided that I am inviting Mrs. Bennet and her remaining daughters to Darcy House."

Richard cocked his head to the side and drew his eyebrows together until they nearly touched.

"While Mr. Bennet and his family were taking a tour of Darcy House this afternoon, Dash decided to break into one of his racing fits. You know how he gets."

Richard nodded.

"He circled the hall in front of the guest rooms, tore down the stairs, toppled something in the blue drawing room, and on his way back up the stairs, darted under Mr. Bennet's foot."

Darcy nodded in response to Richard's look and gasp of alarm. "Mr. Bennet tumbled. His leg is broken, and he cannot be moved for two weeks."

"Dash can be sold." Richard gave the dog a pointed look.

"Not if we wish to keep Georgiana happy. She is quite attached to him."

"Females and their dashed sensibilities," Richard muttered.

"I'd send him to Pemberley were it not for her, but she is doing so well. I should hate to be the cause of any sorrow for her."

His sister had weathered the devastation of discovering her affections, which had been incited in an attempt to claim her fortune, had not been returned. It had taken her months to begin returning to the happy girl he had always known her to be. Even if she was more serious now than she had been before the ordeal with Wickham in Ramsgate, she was not so grave and despondent as she had been at first.

"So, the pup stays," Richard agreed. "As does Mr. Bennet."

Darcy nodded.

"And you are inviting Mrs. Bennet to care for her husband? I had thought she was a silly woman. Is that not how you described her?"

A great sigh escaped Darcy as he nodded again. "What am I to do? The man needs his family near him, and without a proper chaperone, it cannot be either Miss Bennet or Miss Elizabeth. You know how it would be. Two single young ladies staying with a single gentleman — to whom neither is related but who is courting one of those young ladies while his good friend is betrothed to the other — would cause talk."

A slow smile crept across Richard's face, causing a slow burning to creep up Darcy's neck.

"I will not deny that the idea of having Miss Elizabeth under my roof is not a pleasant one, but I assure you that is not why I wish to have her here. She is her father's favourite. Surely, he will feel most content if she is near."

Richard chuckled and nodded. "As will you." He drained the last bit of port from his glass and then held it out for Dash to lick, ignoring Darcy's protests. "The mother comes with more daughters, does she not?"

"Most likely." Darcy blew out a breath. He dreaded the arrival of the younger Bennets almost more than their mother.

"How will you keep them entertained?"

Darcy shrugged. "I had hoped they would bring their own entertainment." His sister was proficient at keeping herself occupied.

Richard made an uncertain sound of disbelief. "There is also the park and the museum," he suggested. "And do not forget shopping. There is not a female alive that I know of who does not enjoy a trip to the shops."

Darcy groaned. Entertaining the youngest Bennets was definitely going to be trying. But, he thought as he emptied his glass, seeing Elizabeth happy would be worth the discomfort. Or so he hoped.

# Chapter 3

"Lizzy," Mrs. Gardiner said softly as her niece rose and paced to the window for the third time in only three times as many minutes.

Elizabeth drew the right corner of her lower lip between her teeth as she turned toward her aunt. How could she not pace and fidget? "Mama will be here soon," she whispered, casting a look toward the bed where her father was sleeping.

"And I am certain all is in order and ready for her arrival." Mrs. Gardiner joined her niece at the window.

Elizabeth shook her head and wrapped her arms around her middle. Having a room ready to receive a guest was not enough preparation for the arrival of her mother.

"Mr. Darcy is not prepared. I know he has said he is, but he is not. Do not look at me like that. I know I am correct." She blew out a breath and turned back to the window.

Her mother would set Mr. Darcy's well-ordered world on its head, and then? Then, she would once again lose Mr. Darcy's good opinion, and that thought caused her eyes to sting with tears and her heart to beat as rapidly as a horse flying across an open field.

"He will still love you despite your mother or your sisters," Mrs. Gardiner whispered as she placed an arm around Elizabeth's shoulders.

Elizabeth's brow furrowed. Her aunt was very good at figuring out what was truly bothering her, even when Elizabeth did not say a word.

Her aunt pulled her close and added, "Should it appear that Mr. Darcy is struggling to keep his equanimity, you need only send word, and your uncle and I will take your mother to Gracechurch Street." Her head tipped to the side. "Of course, that would mean you must also return to us. You cannot stay here unchaperoned."

Elizabeth expelled a resigned sigh and nodded slowly. The thought of leaving her father did not sit well with her. However, the thought of leaving Darcy House did not seem to disturb her only because it meant leaving her father. She had not even been here for more than a few hours each day, and yet, she had found herself growing oddly attached to her surroundings.

There was a soft rap at the door before it opened, and Mr. Darcy, the likely reason why Elizabeth was growing so attached to Darcy House, stepped into the room. Her lips curled into a smile at the sight of him.

"Is your father sleeping comfortably?" he asked softly

once he had crossed to where Elizabeth stood with her aunt.

"He says the pain is not so bad today as it has been," she answered.

"I am glad."

"As are we all," Mrs. Gardiner said.

"Were you watching the street?" Darcy asked with a nod toward the window.

Elizabeth nodded. "She will be here soon."

He extended his arm to her. "That is why I have come. You should be among the first to greet your mother." He turned his head toward Mrs. Gardiner once Elizabeth had placed her hand on his arm. "I have a footman in the hall who will take your place."

"You are very thoughtful," Mrs. Gardiner said with a smile.

Darcy shook his head. "No, I am self-indulgent, for I find myself quite unequal to greeting my guests on my own."

Elizabeth turned worried eyes toward her aunt.

"I am certain you would acquit yourself of the duty perfectly," Mrs. Gardiner said, favouring her anxious niece with a pointed look before she and Jane followed her from the room.

"I am not so confident in my abilities as you are, Mrs. Gardiner," Darcy replied as they reached the hall.

"My mother can join us at Gracechurch Street," Elizabeth offered.

"You are not the only one who is uneasy, Mr. Darcy," Mrs. Gardiner added. "Mrs. Bennet can be a trial at times."

"You are worried?" Darcy asked her.

"Not I so much as Elizabeth," Mrs. Gardiner replied.

"I assure you I am prepared for your mother and sisters to arrive and turn my well-ordered life on its head."

Elizabeth loved the playful smile which accompanied his words — no, they were not his words, they were her words. He was quoting her, after all. How many times had she used that phrase about his well-ordered life when trying to dissuade him from his foolish notion of entertaining not only her injured father but also her mother and sisters?

"Truth be told," he continued with a sheepish grin. "I have made no secret of my desire to one day see you as mistress of this very home."

Elizabeth could feel her cheeks growing warm. The dour and reserved Mr. Darcy from Hertfordshire seemed nearly a thing of the past, for in the days since she had agreed to a courtship when standing in the hall at the Johnson's ball, he had become quite bold in his proclamations regarding their future. The dining room would be the one over which she presided one day. The menu would be hers to approve. The drawing room was no longer his but rather ours. It was nearly too much for her to take in in so short a space of time, but it was not off-putting. She rather liked how he seemed to be claiming her not only as a wife but a partner.

"Therefore," Darcy continued as Elizabeth attempted to keep her thoughts and emotions under regulation, "I thought it only fitting for you to be at my side when your mother arrives." His smile had shifted to something more sly and cunning than sheepish. "And I wish for her to see you at my side. I have been assured that she knows nothing of our courtship, and I find the idea of revealing such a thing in such a way to be oddly tantalizing. I honestly do not know why. It is not my normal wont to taunt and tease. I leave such things to my cousin. However, upon discussing your mother with your father yesterday, I agreed that to alter her view of you could be enjoyable."

Elizabeth's mouth dropped open. Her father, even in his injured state, was still provoking her mother and using Mr. Darcy to do so? Oh, he was incorrigible!

"And Mr. Bingley has arrived to add to the excitement," Darcy added.

"I fear you have lost your mind completely!" Elizabeth declared. "The whole square shall reverberate with her shrieks of delight."

"Or she might just faint away," said Mrs. Gardiner with a chuckle.

"We might want to hope for that," said Jane.

"No," Darcy assured Elizabeth as they reached the bottom of the stairs. "I have not lost my mind, just my heart."

Elizabeth attempted to scowl at him but could not. She was not made of stone. So, instead, she just shook her head while she smiled that foolish smile she seemed to wear whenever he said anything about loving her. It was utterly ridiculous to be so easily swayed from one's indignation by a sweet word. Truly, it was.

While she grinned and said not a word, he led her into the sitting room. Not only was Mr. Bingley present as Darcy had promised, but so were Richard and Georgiana, who was accompanied by her companion, Mrs. Annesley.

"Do you not fear that my sisters will ruin your sister?" she said, attempting, once again, to convince him of his error in inviting her family to stay in his home.

"No." He said simply and led her to a settee. "We could stand at the window if you prefer," he whispered.

She shook her head and took a seat. Pacing in her father's room was one thing. Having her nervous state on display for all to see in the sitting room was something else entirely. She would summon her courage just as she always did when she was faced with a situation in which she suspected her mother or sisters would cause some embarrassment.

"All will be well," Darcy assured her softly, covering her hand, which lay on the settee, with his own.

His touch was reassuring, yet Elizabeth still sent a prayer heavenward that he was correct.

# Chapter 4

For a quarter of an hour, Elizabeth engaged in conversation and allowed her mind to nearly forget the reason why they were all gathered. However, as soon as Mr. Abram, the butler, made an appearance at the door to the sitting room and Darcy rose, straightened his jacket, and extended his hand to her, the reality of the day came flooding back.

Elizabeth paused to draw a quick breath before placing her hand in Darcy's. Good. Her hand was not trembling. Her nerves must only be causing her insides to quiver.

"Mama can stay at Gracechurch Street," she whispered.

Darcy chuckled and shook his head as he wrapped her arm around his and placed her hand on his forearm. "I assure you I am made of sterner stuff than you think."

Her response of "it is not that" fell on purposefully deaf ears, and it was probably just as well. She was in danger of becoming just as annoying as her mother was when anxious, and it would not do to have Mr. Darcy think that she and her mother were alike. They were not. However, her mother had an altering effect on most people after a period of acquaintance, and as Elizabeth stood next to Darcy while the doors were opened, she hoped that whatever change her mother might work on Darcy, it would not be the sort that would drive a wedge between them. She had just begun to learn what a wonderful gentleman Darcy was, and she suspected her heart would shatter into a million pieces if he should decide that he no longer wanted her.

"Oh, Mr. Darcy," Mrs. Bennet said as she entered the house, "I must say I was delighted by your invitation to your home. Not by the circumstances that caused it, of course," she added quickly. "But the honour of being invited to stay in such a grand home as I knew yours must be — which I am now only ashamed I had not imagined to be so truly grand as it is — made the news of my husband's injury nearly bearable. I cannot tell you how often I said just such a thing to one neighbour or another as I was making preparations. It is such a noble gesture, I said. He is the most gracious gentleman, to be sure, I said. And they all agreed."

She had by this time, removed her hat and coat and was smoothing her skirts as she spoke. Then, apparently ready, she extended her hand and froze, mouth hanging slightly agape as she finally noticed her second daughter standing beside her host. She blinked as Darcy took her hand and bowed over it, extending his welcome.

"Did you have a good trip?" he asked.

Her brows furrowed, and her eyes shifted from him to Elizabeth and back. "It was excellent. There was not a thing to put us out of humour." Again, her eyes shifted to Elizabeth.

"We are glad you have joined us," Elizabeth said. "I am certain Papa will be pleased to see you."

Mrs. Bennet's brow rose. "We?"

It was one word. One short word spoken in such a tone of disbelief that Elizabeth knew her mother was beginning to put things together. And Elizabeth had to admit that it was rather tantalizingly enjoyable to be causing her mother's intrigue.

"Yes, Mr. Darcy and I as well as Aunt Addie and Jane." She motioned toward where her sister was standing with her aunt and Bingley.

Again, Mrs. Bennet's mouth dropped open slightly before curling into a delighted smile.

"Mr. Bingley," she said, moving toward him with her hand outstretched, "it is a pleasure to see you. You have been sorely missed in Hertfordshire. But," she looked hopefully at Jane, "then it seems it was far better for you to have remained in town?"

"Oh, most certainly," Bingley replied. "I found town had just the right sort of diversion to keep me from wishing to return to Netherfield."

Mrs. Bennet clasped her hands in front of her chest.

"And is there any happy news?" she asked. "My husband hinted before he left that there might be."

"Indeed, there is," Darcy replied. "However, your husband has made us promise that he be the one to share such news with you."

"He did?" Elizabeth could not catch the words before they flew from her mouth.

"Yes, my dear, he did."

Such a reply could not go unnoticed by Mrs. Bennet.

"My dear?" she cried.

Elizabeth thought from the wideness of her mother's eyes and the gasp that followed her cry of surprise, her mother might expire right there on the spot. However, she did not, and it took only a moment for the questioned words to draw a conclusion from the woman's mind.

"Oh, do not tell me," she exclaimed with obvious delight, "that Elizabeth has captured the affections of a wealthy gentleman." Her right hand tapped her chest above her heart.

"That is precisely what I have promised I would not tell you," Darcy replied. "Now, shall we move to the sitting room."

"I must see my husband," Mrs. Bennet replied. "It seems there is much he needs to tell me." Though she wore a broad smile, she was looking at Elizabeth very carefully, almost suspiciously.

"There are others for you to meet, Mama," Elizabeth said. "And Papa is sleeping."

"But my heart," she protested, tapping her chest once again.

"Your heart will survive a wait of a few moments," Mary muttered.

Mrs. Bennet glared at her third eldest daughter but did not say a word beyond encouraging Mary, Kitty, and Lydia to follow her.

"It is good to see you, Fanny," Mrs. Gardiner said, taking her sister-in-law by the arm as they followed Darcy and Elizabeth into the sitting room. "All is very well. You shall be doubly delighted." Elizabeth heard her say.

It was just like her aunt to add a calming word when needed.

"Indeed?" her mother inquired. "Both Jane and Elizabeth?"

"Oh, that I am not supposed to say. However..."

Elizabeth looked over her shoulder just in time to see her aunt give one small sharp nod of her head which caused her mother to nearly faint away.

"Mrs. Bennet," Darcy began as soon as she and her three youngest daughters were in the sitting room, "This my cousin, the Right Honorable Colonel Richard Fitzwilliam. Richard, Mrs. Bennet, and her daughters, Miss Mary, Miss Kitty, and Miss Lydia."

Elizabeth sighed inwardly as her youngest sisters giggled

softly at being presented to not just a handsome gentle-man but a colonel.

"And this," Darcy continued, "is my sister, Miss Geor-giana Darcy, and her companion, Mrs. Annesley."

Mrs. Bennet did all that was proper in greeting each per-son, though she did keep peering curiously at Darcy and Elizabeth almost as if she needed to reassure herself that she had indeed seen what she had seen.

"Now that we have made all the proper introductions," Darcy said as Mrs. Bennet once again looked his direction, "it might be best if we see you settled into your room and allow you to check on your husband before we have tea."

"Oh, yes, indeed, Mr. Darcy, that might be the best course of action," Mrs. Bennet agreed quickly. "Not that I do not wish to make myself acquainted with your sister and the colonel," she added. "But it has been a long trip."

Elizabeth watched Darcy's lips twitch with amusement. The cunning gentleman was leading her mother down a merry path and enjoying himself thoroughly. Perhaps all would be well.

"I find I always wish for a basin of water and a fresh set of clothes after just about every journey," he said as he led her from the room and to the stairs. "While you are getting settled, I shall look in on your husband and let him know of your safe arrival."

"Yes, yes," Mrs. Bennet muttered as she looked high and

low at the opulence which surrounded her. "That is a very good idea."

"And a maid can show you to his room as soon as you are ready," Darcy continued as they climbed the stairs. It was a suggestion that was met with great enthusiasm.

"Your home is so beautiful," she said as she reached the top of the stairs.

"Thank you. I hope you will also find it welcoming and comfortable."

"I cannot see how we could find it any other thing," Mrs. Bennet assured him.

"These are your rooms," Elizabeth said when they came to a stop. "This one," she said as she opened the door, "and the one next to it adjoin, and Jane and I are just across the hall."

"How lovely!" Lydia cried, pulling Kitty into the room with her.

"Your maid will conduct you to your husband as soon as you are ready, and we shall be below, awaiting your return," Darcy said. Then, with a small nod of his head in acceptance of Mrs. Bennet's words of thanks, he and Elizabeth took their leave.

"Mr. Darcy," Elizabeth said as they approached her father's room, "I must congratulate you on your cleverness. My mother's initial raptures shall be confined to this room while you avoid them in the sitting room."

He shook his head. "I fear I am not that clever, my love."

She felt her cheeks grow warm first at the appellation and then the kiss he placed on her knuckles.

"It was your father's idea. Now, shall we warn him of your mother's impending delight?" He opened the door in front of them and motioned for her to enter the room before him.

# Chapter 5

"One betrothed and another nearly so," Mrs. Bennet said for the fourth time since tea had begun. She had taken a few moments to express her delight when she had arrived in the sitting room for tea. However, it had been a contained excitement for a lady so prone to exuberance as Mr. Darcy considered Mrs. Bennet to be, and then she had ventured into other topics of conversation, deftly guided by Mrs. Gardiner.

That woman still impressed Darcy each and every time he met her.

Darcy glanced at Elizabeth just as he had the three other times her mother had said such a thing. Embarrassment stained Elizabeth's cheeks and caused her head to dip, but her lips wore a smile. He was almost certain he could ask for her hand now and be accepted, but he would not. Not just yet. The way she pulled her bottom lip between her teeth spoke of some worry that she still held, which he supposed was likely about how he would be able to handle her mother and sisters in large doses.

To own the truth, though he had declared he was capable of surviving the visit of the Bennets, he still held a small amount of doubt about his abilities to remain unruffled by the experience. However, when he considered that it was Elizabeth for whom he was making this effort, his confidence rose.

He smiled as she looked his direction, and she returned the gesture. Her smile was one of her most beautiful features, which was placing it at the top of a great mountain of qualities and characteristics she possessed. It lit her face and sparkled in her eyes. It even caused one brow to rise just a fraction of an inch.

He would do nearly anything for her, for he had tasted a small amount of the desolation that his life would become without her. He had not forgotten the ache that had settled into every fiber of his being as he had attempted, and failed, to forget her after leaving Netherfield. He could not, would not face such wretchedness again. He would do everything in his power to avoid it.

"Are you married?"

Lydia's question to Richard snapped Darcy from his observation of Elizabeth. What conversation had she started that he had missed while contemplating her sister?

"No," Richard replied, sparing her only a quick glance.

It was an action Darcy recognized as Richard's way to nearly ignore a female. He had seen Richard use that very technique – a half-turn of his head and a look that was not quite focused on the person who had spoken to him – when actively attempting to dissuade a young debutante from pursuing him.

"Are you courting anyone?"

Richard shook his head.

Darcy smiled. He had moved from a short reply to silence.

"Lydia." Jane hissed.

Lydia flicked her head and turned back to her tea. "Do you have a beau?" she asked Georgiana.

"Lydia," said Mrs. Gardiner, who was sitting near her, "that is not the sort of thing one asks on first acquaintance."

"I do not," Georgiana replied with a smile for Mrs. Gardiner. "I have not had my come out just yet."

Darcy watched as Lydia's brows furrowed and her mouth dropped open.

"My sister will be presented next season. She will be well-prepared by then to present herself to the best advantage."

Lydia's head turned toward him, but she still wore her look of shocked confusion.

"There are many skills in which a young lady must be proficient before she enters the society of the ton. The expectations are great, and if not properly prepared, a young lady might have an unsuccessful first season which, in turn, might lead to her being overlooked."

"Or shunned," Georgiana replied as she nodded her head. "Last week, a particular young lady, whom I shan't name, made a grave error in refusing one gentleman at a ball and then accepting another. She has been the talk in many drawing rooms, and I fear, the subject of many jokes."

Darcy raised a brow in question. He was not certain he cared for the idea of his sister knowing such information. It smacked too much of gossip.

"Miss Allard's mother was reminding us of the rules for balls, both private and public, after we had finished our time with Mr. Hughes." She explained to her brother before she turned to Lydia. "Mr. Hughes is our dancing master." She turned back to her brother. "I would not share such a thing except it illustrated your point of being properly prepared for the season. I should not wish to make such a mistake and be the source of drawing-room tales. There are rules for a reason." Her cheeks flushed, and her head dipped but only just.

He knew she was thinking of how she had narrowly escaped being the source of many drawing-room tales. When she had been taken from school just before the events of last summer had unfolded, she had been adamant that she felt prepared for life in society. She was old enough to make her own choices. She had excelled at every lesson set before her, and she was not a foolish school girl. These things had been said with a sense of confidence. Not a word had been antagonistic. She had merely reported the facts to her brother and cousin with the hope that she would be permitted to make her debut this season. She had not been pleased to be denied the honor, but she had not pouted overly much about it — no more than Darcy expected a displeased young lady might. In fact, he had told himself that his sister had done less pouting over the disappointment than many others, such as Caroline Bingley, would have.

"I would caution you about sharing such a tale even in support of my cause," he said to her with a small smile. "However, you are correct. There are rules for a reason." He tipped his head. "When do you see Mr. Hughes next?"

"He is here tomorrow."

"And will Miss Allard be attending as well?"

Georgiana nodded.

He pursed his lips. "I wonder if it might be too much for the man to have a few more ladies to make up his sets? I know that Miss Lydia and Miss Kitty both enjoy dancing."

Lydia's eyes grew large as a smile of pure delight spread across her face. "Oh, I do. It is perhaps the very best activity in all the world, and I am quite good at it."

"What do you say, Georgiana? Do you think you and Miss Allard would mind sharing your time with the Miss Bennets?"

Georgiana pondered the thought for only a moment

before assuring one and all that a larger group would make for a much merrier lesson.

"Then, I shall send a note to Mr. Hughes today so that he might be prepared." Darcy leaned back and cradled his teacup. One activity was arranged. He would mention the theatre and the opera over dinner, and they could decide on a night for each.

He looked at Elizabeth, who was smiling at him. Yes, yes, he could do this. He just needed to keep her sisters entertained.

# Chapter 6

Later that evening, Richard lowered himself into a chair near the fire in Darcy's study. Bingley sat opposite him, while Darcy pushed around a few papers on his desk, tidying up and sorting in preparation for tomorrow.

"A dance lesson is a good place to begin," Richard said after a few moments of silent relaxing before the fire. "The youngest Bennet wants some direction."

Bingley chuckled but said nothing.

Richard tapped Bingley's foot with his own. "I do not see how you can find that humorous."

Bingley lifted one shoulder and allowed it to drop but did not reply, earning him a glare.

"You are merely stating what we already know," Darcy muttered from his desk.

"You are in a position to improve them," said Richard. "Do they sing or draw?"

"I honestly do not know," Darcy answered, rising from his desk since things were in order. "It was not on my agenda to discover the skills of all the ladies in Hertfordshire when I was at Netherfield. I was there for Bingley."

"Although he did think it his duty to observe at least one lady while he was helping me."

"One is not all," Darcy replied easily as he took his seat. "They will be down in about an hour, I suspect. Mr. Bennet will be sleeping again by then." He pulled his watch from his pocket and marked the time.

"Are you not concerned about what the other Bennet ladies are about?" Richard asked.

Darcy shook his head. "No, I heard them mention some fashion magazine, and Georgiana was going to introduce them to Dash. It is not as if they are infants who need a constant nurse around them."

Richard sighed.

"Why are you so taken with them?" Bingley asked. "It is not like you to be suggesting that we try to improve young ladies. You are usually the one directing us away from the silly debutantes and hiding yourself away so that your mother will not marry you off to one of them."

"The Bennets are different." Richard shifted and stretched before looking at Darcy. "An hour, you say?"

Darcy nodded. "I should suspect they will return no sooner."

"And what will we do when they do return?"

"You are staying?" Darcy asked in surprise.

Richard nodded. "Did you not see my man? I am staying for a few days."

Richard often arrived to take up residence unannounced. So that part of his news did not surprise Darcy. However, the fact that he chose now, when the house had so many visitors, was a bit unusual.

"I thought you could use help," he said in response to Darcy's unasked question.

Darcy smiled. Richard had an uncanny way of reading people, and Darcy in particular.

"I know you do not fear for Georgiana, but I needed to see these young ladies before I could agree," Richard added. "Elizabeth was so concerned that I could not pass it off as completely ungrounded. She seems intelligent and not given to flights of fancy, and that coupled with what Jane told us about her sisters when I first met her, compelled me to decide for myself."

If it were anyone else doubting him, Darcy would have been mildly to severely irritated, but it was Richard. He might be a gentleman with a ready quip and a tease to match his nonchalant façade, but he was not the sort of gentleman to leave things to chance when there might be a better option.

"And what are your thoughts so far?" Darcy asked.

Richard grimaced and shook his head. "She inquired if I was married and if Georgie had a beau."

"Miss Lydia, you mean?" Bingley asked.

"Yes, the other two seemed less forward. Miss Mary is a trifle severe, and Miss Kitty lacks identity."

"I beg your pardon?" Bingley sat forward. "How does a lady lack identity?"

"She makes no decisions on her own," Richard replied. "She follows her younger sister. Therefore, it is the youngest that requires our attention. She is the key to the lot of them doing well or causing some calamity."

"How so?" Eager curiosity suffused Bingley's features.

"Miss Mary would do better to be less severe if she ever wishes to marry." He shuddered slightly. "She is too much of a governess." He chuckled. "Or a bit like my Aunt Catherine, and the world does not need two Lady Catherines."

"Too true," Darcy agreed with a chuckle.

"If Miss Mary did not have silly sisters of whom to disapprove constantly, she might soften her manners and her features – before that scowl becomes a permanent line between her brows." He shifted. "And if Miss Kitty is to follow, it should be someone worth following. Currently, Miss Lydia is not an appropriate leader." He sighed – a great, heavy sounding exhalation. "And I cannot explain it, but I feel as if Mrs. Bennet will calm if her daughters are all well-matched or, at least, prepared in such a fashion as to be capable of making a good match." He shrugged. "I cannot put my finger on it, but that is what my gut is saying."

Darcy propped his elbows on the arms of his chair and, steepling his fingers, rested his chin on them. If there was one thing he had learned in the past year, it was not to question Richard when he said something felt out of place or needed better scrutiny. They had both ignored the gut feeling Richard had felt regarding Mrs. Younge, Georgiana's former companion who had assisted Wickham in his attempt to persuade Georgiana into an elopement.

Richard shook his head. "She is just the sort to fall for one of Wickham's schemes."

"Mrs. Bennet?" Bingley asked in surprise.

Richard's brows furrowed as he shook his head. "No, Miss Lydia. I do not think she has the sense to see through his pretty words. She will see only his charm and handsome features and will do whatever he asks to have him as her beau. She seems rather intent upon having a beau." He might have said more but at that moment the door to the study, which was not quite closed, as Darcy had left it open to hear whatever might be happening in the hall, opened.

"No, no! Come here!"

Dash followed by a flushed Lydia, who was trailed by Kitty and Georgiana entered the room. The young ladies stopped just inside the door when they saw the gentlemen sitting within. However, Dash did not. He circled the room and then hopped onto Richard's lap without so much as a look of invitation.

"Now look here, Dash," Richard scolded as the ladies

at the door giggled, "I did not ask you to accost me. Get down."

Dash immediately laid down on Richard's lap.

"That is not what I mean," Richard scolded as he rubbed the dog's ear.

"Why do you insist on petting him while reprimanding?" Darcy asked.

Richard smiled sheepishly. "How do you not scratch his ear when he looks at you with those eyes."

"I will take him," said Georgiana. "Mrs. Annesley went to her room to retrieve a particular pattern for stitching, and he scooted out with her. I do apologize." She attempted to pick Dash up from her cousin's lap, but the pup growled, causing her to pull back.

"There will be none of that," Richard said firmly and placed the dog on the floor. "No, not even those eyes will save you this time, lad."

A soft clucking and whistling drew both Richard and Dash's attention. Lydia knelt on the floor, removing a ribbon from her hair and calling softly to Dash.

"Do you want it boy?" she asked as she wiggled the ribbon in the air. She held it toward him and then snatched it back when he put his nose forward. She repeated this three times while telling him that he only needed to come to her to have the ribbon. "Please," she added at the end of her third request.

Dash trotted to her, tail wagging, and licked her cheek when he reached her.

Lydia giggled and threw her arms around the puppy. "You cheeky fellow," she scolded while she scruffed the top of his head. "There will be no stealing kisses."

Dash paid no heed and licked her cheek again as she slipped the ribbon she held around his collar and tied it on.

"There!" she declared. "I have won this game."

The entire back half of Dash wagged with pleasure as she gave him a hug and prepared to lead him from the room.

"He seems to be taken with you, Miss Lydia," Darcy said.

"Oh, I am very good with animals," she replied. "It only takes a little persuasion – a tempting treat or toy and then praises and some attention when they respond. It is not hard." She batted her lashes.

"You did make it look easy," Bingley said.

"We will be in the drawing room in about half an hour," Darcy said to Georgiana before the ladies left.

"May we play cards?" Georgiana asked.

"I do not see why not," Darcy replied. He enjoyed a game or two of cards on occasion.

"Oh!" Lydia cried with delight as she followed Georgiana and Kitty from the study, "I am also very good with cards."

"Why do I suspect she uses some of the same techniques she used with Dash to draw gentlemen along and to win at cards?" Richard asked dryly.

Bingley chuckled. "Because, as she said, she's very good at it."

Richard shook his head. "Good she might be, but she wants instruction."

"And you wish me to provide it?" Darcy asked with a laugh.

"I cannot do it all," Richard said, rising from his chair and straightening his jacket before brushing at the dog hair on his breeches.

"Where are you going?" Bingley asked.

Richard turned from the door. "To see that the card tables are placed and to make sure my money is well-hidden." His lips tipped up in a half smile. "I am also curious to see if Dash is still following Miss Lydia around like a green schoolboy."

Darcy looked at Bingley after Richard left the room. "Do we need to worry about him?"

Bingley nodded. "I think we may."

# Chapter 7

"You do not wish to dance, Mr. Darcy?" Mrs. Bennet asked the next morning as she sipped tea and ate toast in the morning room.

Darcy had just been discussing his day with Richard, and while he had mentioned the appointment for Georgiana with her dance master, he had not included himself in the party who would be joining in on the activity.

"No, I do not," he replied simply.

"But Colonel Fitzwilliam is going to dance," Mrs. Bennet encouraged. "It would be so much more fun for the young ladies if there were two gentlemen with whom to dance. They would not have to stand up with each other for every dance that way."

"My cousin is not fond of dancing," Richard replied in Darcy's stead.

"Not fond of dancing! I declare I have never heard of such a thing."

She smiled over her cup of tea, and for a moment, Darcy saw in her eyes a familiar expressive twinkle. He had thought Elizabeth had inherited that particular impertinent expression from her father. It appeared he was wrong.

"Might you be fonder of dancing if I were to send Elizabeth to join you?" she asked.

Mrs. Bennet's lashes batted very much like Miss Lydia did when she was attempting to get her way with either dogs or humans. He had seen Lydia use that expression twice with Dash and at least as many times with Richard while playing cards last evening. The shock of the similarity between Mrs. Bennet and both her second eldest and youngest daughters slowed the smile that curled his lips at such a suggestion.

"I do find it more enjoyable to dance with Miss Elizabeth than anyone else," he admitted, causing Richard to laugh, and Mrs. Bennet to beam.

"Then, I will send her to you."

"Only if she is amenable," Darcy cautioned. "I would not wish to force her to do that which she does not wish to do."

At this Mrs. Bennet giggled, and then, with a slight arch to her right eyebrow — very reminiscent, in Darcy's mind, to another expression of Elizabeth's — she responded in a whisper, "I should not say it, for I would not wish to hinder your regard for her, but there are few who can force Elizabeth to do that which she does not wish to do. She is a very determined young lady and has been so since before she was in leading strings."

To Darcy's surprise, there was a look of pride on the woman's face that seemed to run contrary to her disparaging words.

"Her father has taught her to use that determination to great effect, though I find there is still room for improvement. Elizabeth is not one to be swayed by pretty words and affected airs as some might be. And that is a very good quality for a young lady to possess." She took a sip of her tea. "One does not wish to be tricked into believing things that are not so." She sighed. "I am not so good at that sort of thing as is my husband. That is why he has worked so diligently with Elizabeth. I am certain I would have failed her, for she is far more challenging than any of my other daughters."

"Miss Lydia seems to be in need of some similar instruction," Richard muttered.

Mrs. Bennet's brows rose as did Darcy's. Richard was not usually one to be so open about his disapproval of someone.

"I fear she might fall prey to some of the charmers here in town," he added.

"Do you really think so?"

There was no denying the genuine fear which coloured Mrs. Bennet's tone.

Richard nodded. "I do."

"But she is a sly one," Mrs. Bennet said. "Lydia knows far more than she will ever display. She does not wish to be thought a bluestocking, you see."

Richard's expression did not register belief. "Be that as it may," he said, "you must admit her head is easily turned by a handsome gentleman. She has spoken of little else. Gentlemen, beaus, ribbons, and dresses – and the ribbons and dresses were only mentioned in terms of capturing a beau."

Mrs. Bennet huffed, and Darcy, picking up his cup, leaned back in his chair to watch.

"It is imperative for a young lady to be fashionably attired to show not only her status but also to entice a gentleman to make an offer." Mrs. Bennet wore a stern look as she shook her head. "Any lady's future is dependent upon securing the best offer, and a lady who has little to her name aside from the claim of a gentleman father must make the best use of what is available to her in seeking a secure future."

Richard's head cocked to the side as he studied the woman before him for a full thirty ticks of the clock on the side table. Then, he nodded. "I will agree that what you say is true if you will agree that the young lady in question needs guidance to guarantee that the gentleman who calls on her is not a cad presenting himself as a proper match."

Mrs. Bennet blinked, but then lifted her chin. "I am certain all of my daughters would be able to pick out a cad should one present himself."

Richard shook his head. "They have not. I know it for a fact."

"You cannot know that!" Indignation radiated off Mrs. Bennet in palpable waves.

"What do you think of Mr. Wickham?"

Darcy nearly choked on his tea at the question.

"He is a handsome fellow, very pleasant and promising."

Richard shrugged. "He is handsome and pleasant, but he is only promising if you wish to win his money in a game of card. However, if you are a merchant expecting repayment or a lady expecting an offer of marriage and not just a bit of fun, especially if you have no fortune, he is quite the opposite of promising."

Mrs. Bennet huffed. "He cannot be. Elizabeth found him agreeable."

"We all err at times," Richard said softly. "But, I know for a fact that he is nothing more than a practiced liar and a libertine."

"But Lizzy is always right." Mrs. Bennet's brows were drawn together so tightly that they nearly touched.

"What was her opinion of my cousin?" Richard asked.

Mrs. Bennet's brows sprang apart and upward as she turned wide eyes toward Darcy.

"I was less than civil," Darcy said. "Her opinion was not without justification."

"True," Richard agreed. "But it still stands to reason that she is just as fallible as the rest of us. A person presents himself in a particular manner, and we all determine he is a particular sort of person until evidence refutes our evaluation."

Mrs. Bennet's brows were once again furrowed, and her face was suffused with confusion.

"He means," Darcy began, drawing the woman's attention back to himself, "that until I presented myself as civil and gentlemanly, your daughter saw me as a dour disapproving man, which I was. I did not behave at all as I should have while in Hertfordshire. I have apologized to her, but I should also apologize to you for speaking of your daughter as I did at the assembly. It was wrong. She is lovely and very handsome."

Mrs. Bennet smiled. "I knew you could not be an utter fool. You would have to sooner or later admit that she was pretty, for she is. Perhaps not so handsome as Jane, but Elizabeth is far more than tolerable."

"I would agree." Though his cheeks were warm from the reprimand in her words, he could not help but smile at her assessment of Elizabeth. "She is far more than tolerable. However, getting back to my cousin's point, even if I would find it far more entertaining to contemplate your daughter..."

At that, Mrs. Bennet giggled.

"Mr. Wickham will present himself as an affable gentleman until he has acquired whatever it is that he wishes. Only then will his true character be revealed." Darcy's brows furrowed. He could not tell her about his sister's ordeal, but there must be some bit of information that would help her understand Wickham's lack of character. "What do you know about him?"

She shrugged. "He mentioned he was a friend of your family, but beyond that..." Her eyes grew wide, and she gasped. "Very little," she admitted quietly.

"He was a friend of my family. In fact, he was a favourite of my father. So much so that when my father died, Mr. Wickham was bequeathed one thousand pounds and, should he take orders, the living at Kympton, which was in my father's power to bestow when a vacancy should arise. There are many details that I could add, but I will suffice it to say that the living was refused in favour of three thousand pounds."

"He squandered it," Richard interrupted. "Four thousand pounds gone in a very short period of licentious living."

"Can this be true?"

Darcy could not fault Mrs. Bennet for being so surprised. Wickham was very good at weaving a tale and presenting himself in the best light. "I fear it is. Again, there is more I could tell you, but not without endangering the reputation of a young lady whom we – my cousin and I – know."

Her eyes grew wide. "Did..." she looked around the room and lowered her voice, "did he ruin her?"

Darcy shook his head. "Thankfully, no, but he played with her heart in hopes of securing her dowry."

Mrs. Bennet's hand flew to her mouth as her eyes filled with tears. It was a response which Darcy had not fully expected. Surprise was to be expected, but tears? He saw her jaw clench and relax before she swallowed and spoke softly but with a great deal of anger behind her words.

"From this moment, he is no longer a friend of mine. The heart is a precious thing, and its ruin is..." She shook her head and brushed a tear from her cheek. "What can be done for my Lydia? She is very taken with Mr. Wickham."

"If you allow me, I shall consider it and devise a plan," Richard said. "There must be at least one young man in London who could replace Wickham in Miss Lydia's regard. Between Darcy and I, and with Bingley's assistance, I am certain we can help her forget Wickham."

Relief washed over Mrs. Bennet's whole being. "I would be so delighted if you would."

# Chapter 8

A vision in a blue day dress stood in the corridor. Darcy paused for a moment to appreciate her form as she was unaware of his presence; then he continued toward his destination.

"Miss Elizabeth."

Darcy smiled as he said her name in greeting. Seeing her here in his home was such a pleasure, but she did not have to be present for him to wear this particular smile. Just the thought of her brought a great deal of joy to him. How very different from just a few weeks ago when he thought of her only with sorrow as he contemplated a long and dreary existence without her in his life. Happily, he had been guided by his friend to rethink his position, and now, here he was standing just outside the ballroom — his ballroom — with her.

"Mr. Darcy," she said, returning his smile and dipping a small curtsey. "My mother informs me that I am to participate in a dance lesson?"

"Only if you wish to do so."

Elizabeth laughed lightly. "My mother was most insistent that I wished to dance, and my father agreed! I should not like to return to them and tell them I have not danced."

"But you do not wish to dance?" Darcy's brows rose. He thought she loved dancing.

Her lips twitched as she attempted to affect a serious expression, but it was of no use. She could not keep her amusement from showing on her face. "I would so like to tease that I despise dancing, but I fear I am not so good an actress as that. I do love to dance."

Darcy offered his arm. "Then shall we interrupt and join the fun?"

Her left eyebrow lifted impertinently, and she opened her mouth to speak. However, Darcy spoke first.

"Your mother does that very thing," he said, looking steadfastly at her face as if he had never before seen her. And for a moment, he felt as if he had not. He was not certain how many times he had felt this very same way — as if he was seeing things for the first time — since that moment in Bingley's study when he had confessed first to his part in separating his friend from Jane and then to loving Elizabeth. He needed to pay better attention to people. He had always thought himself a good observer and reader of character, but at present, he found himself wanting.

Elizabeth's brows furrowed. "What does my mother do?"

He had turned to look at her more fully, lifting her hand

from his arm and placing it in his left hand before he ran a finger of his right hand over her left brow. "She lifts this very same brow just as you were doing a moment ago. I assume you were about to tease me." He smiled at her, his hand resting on her cheek. "You often arch that brow when you are about to say something impertinent. It is an enchanting expression. One of many."

She was so beautiful. Her eyes, her lips, and even her nose spoke as plainly as her words did.

"You fascinate me," he muttered.

Her lips were parted as if she wanted to speak but no words would form.

He caressed that one eyebrow once more and then removed his hand from her face. "What were you about to say?"

She shook her head. "I do not know."

"Then shall we join the others and dance?"

Her eyes grew wide.

"You remember," he said with a smile.

"I do." Her lips curled into a smile, and that one eyebrow arched as he waited and watched.

"I was going to say I had thought you did not like to dance, Mr. Darcy."

He could not help himself. He had to touch her cheek again as he responded, "I like to dance with you."

Her cheeks flushed, and her lids lowered as she looked

away from his eyes. "There will be others with whom to dance. You shall not be allowed to dance only with me."

He waited until her eyes lifted to his again before speaking. "The prize is worth the price." It was enjoyable making her lower her eyes and smile that soft smile she was wearing now. "Come, my love. Let us disturb the master."

Inside the ballroom, Lydia, Miss Allard, Richard, Georgiana, Kitty, and Mary were just forming sets.

"Ah! Do we have more dancers?" The slight, blonde-haired master cried in delight, clapping his hands together.

"Miss Elizabeth, this is Mr. Hughes. Mr. Hughes, Miss Elizabeth Bennet."

The man bowed and welcomed Elizabeth.

"Do you dance well?" he asked.

"She dances very well," Darcy said. "I have had few partners who performed better."

Mr. Hughes clapped his hands in delight once more, chortling about his good fortune to have such assistance in instructing his pupils. "An example to follow is far superior to attempting to follow my words. You will stand up together, yes?" he asked, looking from Darcy to Elizabeth and back.

"With pleasure," Darcy assured him. He had always found Mr. Hughes to be a most animated fellow, but today with a room full of dancers, the man was positively beside himself with glee that showed in his every movement and expression.

Mr. Hughes tapped his lip with his finger as he surveyed the room. Then, he flitted over to the group of dancers.

"Here. You will do well to be near Miss Allard and Miss Kitty. Miss Darcy and Miss Mary will stand beside Colonel Fitzwilliam and Miss Lydia."

After Darcy and Elizabeth had taken their places, he clapped his hands three times, pulled himself straighter, and said, "Ladies, I expect great things from you today with so many fine examples to follow." Then, he nodded to his assistant, who began to play the cotillion, *Le Rouët à filer*.

"Circle right," he called as he clapped his hands in time to the music. "No, no, no! Join hands behind. Behind, Miss Mary. Not in front. Ah, better."

And so it continued for a full three repetitions of the same cotillion before the second and final dance of the day, a quadrille was attacked in the same fashion with instructions such as forward, back, and step lightly being given over the music.

Finally, as the second attempt of the quadrille came to an end, Mr. Hughes clapped loudly and shouted, "Well done! Well done! A fabulous day. Simply fabulous."

Darcy chuckled. The gentleman's fair complexion was nearly as flushed as Miss Lydia's who wore a smile as broad as Mr. Hughes did. There was no denying that Miss Lydia found dancing to be the best activity in the world when her enjoyment was so evidently displayed.

"Can we not dance one more?" Lydia asked.

"I am afraid I must be on to another appointment," Mr. Hughes replied. "However, if it is possible, I would welcome you to join me again for a lesson. You are very light and quick on your feet, and so graceful."

Lydia sighed and thanked him, though it was apparent to anyone who looked at her that she was disappointed that Mr. Hughes was leaving.

"Come, Miss Lydia, allow the gentleman to leave," instructed Richard.

Lydia sighed again, a small pout forming on her lips. "If I must."

"You must."

Richard's assurance was met with another sigh.

He pulled his watch from his pocket. "What would you say to taking Dash for a walk?"

Lydia's eyes lit with delight. "I should like that very much."

"Darcy?" Richard asked.

"I see no folly in such a plan as long as Dash's leash is secure." The animal would likely benefit from expending some of his energy in a walk.

"And will you join us?" Richard asked.

Darcy looked at Elizabeth and after getting a nod in

response to his unasked question, told Richard that in half an hour's time, they would all take Dash for a walk.

# Chapter 9

Dash paced the drawing room, stopping to sniff each person, and thoroughly checking each corner before he decided to curl up at Lydia's feet.

Darcy shook his head, both Dash and his cousin had been following Lydia around all day. First, it was the dance lesson – Dash was, thankfully, absent for that. Then, it was their walk where Lydia had one hand on Dash's leash and the other on Richard's arm. After that, they had spent a bit of time in the music room with Georgiana, where it was discovered that Lydia had a most remarkable voice, though she could not play a single song without several stumbles. For dinner, Dash had once again been relegated to his room, but now, as they sat in the drawing room, he was at his favourite Miss Bennet's feet, and Richard was at her side.

"She seems very willing to listen to everything the Colonel says," Jane whispered to Elizabeth with a nod toward Lydia.

"Indeed, she does. It is most remarkable," Elizabeth

replied. "He suggests, and she does. I have never seen her so compliant." She darted her eyes toward Darcy before continuing. "Do you suspect she has set her cap at him? He is unattached."

Jane sighed. "I would say yes if she were to act more..."

A loud giggle cut off Jane's words.

Jane's shoulders drooped, and she changed her answer to a simple yes as she saw her youngest sister playfully swat Richard's arm.

Oh, that was not good. Elizabeth watched Lydia duck her head and bat her eyes. Surely, the colonel would not be swayed by such obvious ploys. He had navigated the ton for many years and yet remained unmarried. He was far too sensible and astute a gentleman to be led along by a pretty young girl, especially one so young as Lydia, was he not?

"I think she fascinates him," Darcy whispered. "He wishes to see her improved," he added when both Jane and Elizabeth turned shocked eyes toward him.

Elizabeth bit her lip. "It is a dangerous game they play."

"How so?" Darcy asked.

"Affections could be aroused without a hope of a future." She spoke softly as she did not wish to have any-one other than Darcy and Jane hear what she had to say.

"You fear Richard will engage your sister's heart with no intention of returning her admiration?"

That was part of it, though she did not expect the colonel to do so knowingly.

"He might also find himself enamoured. It is less likely, but not outside the realm of possibility."

"And if both should become attached, what harm would there be?"

Darcy's brows were furrowed, and to Elizabeth, he looked less than pleased.

"I do not mean to imply that I would object to such a thing, but how could it be resolved happily? I do not know your cousin's situation, but my sister has little..." she grimaced at the next word, "money." It sounded so callous, so avaricious. It felt no better to add her next thoughts. "His father is an earl. Our father is little-known."

"My uncle is an earl," Darcy replied. "Yet, I would happily marry one of your father's daughters."

Elizabeth's brows furrowed. "But it is different," she protested, though she was uncertain how to put it into words. "He is a son. Would his father even approve?"

Darcy shrugged. "Richard is not known for doing things just to please anyone. He is his own man."

"But his inheritance could be threatened."

How could he not see that the colonel pursuing a young lady such as Lydia would be disadvantageous and... well... wrong? That thought brought to mind something about which Elizabeth had been wondering since the day her father had fallen while they toured Darcy's grand home.

"I still do not know why you would choose someone like me when you have so much, and I have so little."

"You are not a pauper begging for food on the street," he replied with a smile. "Your family is not poor."

Her cheeks grew warm. "No, we are not, but compared to this," she indicated the room by looking around, "we are not equals."

"Very well, if you are using things such as money as the measurement for equality of station, then no, we are not equals. However, you are a gentleman's daughter. I am a gentleman's son."

"Yes, but.."

"And I love you," he said, cutting off her words. "As you already know, that is the determining factor as to why I choose you. You may thank Bingley for making me aware of such reasoning, and you may also take up your argument with him if you find the reasoning unfounded."

Were he not smiling while lifting those brows so imperiously, and had he not just declared he loved her – and before her sister — Elizabeth might have been put out with his final words. As it was, all she could do was smile that silly grin, just as she always did when he said something sweet, and think of no logical retort. How did one refute a declaration of love?

"I will admit that my cousin has always said he would marry to better his lot in life," Darcy said when Elizabeth remained silent. "And it would weigh on him to have his inheritance threatened, I will not deny those facts. However, I would not see him do without, and I know he would not desert a lady he loved just for a few more pounds from some other source. He is too honorable for that."

"Which proves my point exactly," Elizabeth declared. "It is a dangerous game they play. How could such a future be happy?"

"You ask the wrong question."

The wrong question? Surely, not. If the colonel and Lydia were to fall in love and wish to marry, there would be strictures placed on them by lack of wealth that would most certainly lead to eventual discontent and therefore, unhappiness.

"I cannot see how I have asked amiss," Elizabeth replied. "Strictures and a reduction in means of living would not sit well with either your cousin or my sister."

Darcy shook his head and smiled.

Was he dismissing her opinion as foolish? She knew her point was valid.

"The question one should ask," he began, still wearing that amused smile, "is not how could their future be happy together in the reduced circumstances you fear, but rather, how could their future be happy without the one whom they love. I pondered that very thing for weeks before Bingley so wisely pointed out the error in my thinking."

Elizabeth knew she was smiling that silly smile again. It

was ridiculous how easily her emotions could be swayed whenever he even hinted at loving her.

"But you are wealthy," she protested. Charming words and whether she felt compelled to smile instead of scowl, did not change the fact that she knew she was correct.

"My cousin is not poor. He is just not as wealthy as he would wish to be."

She lifted her chin. "I still say it is a dangerous game."

"Say what you will, but I will say that it is not so dangerous as you think. And on this, I shall not be moved."

She shook her head and turned away from Darcy's charming smile. She would press her point no further. It was so much easier to debate with him when he was being dour — not that she had any desire for him to become dour once again.

Time and experience would have to determine the winner of this contest, and as Lydia once again giggled at something the colonel said, Elizabeth hoped that she might be proven wrong. For though Lydia was a trial at times, Elizabeth did not wish to see her sister injured, and from the way, Lydia was looking at Colonel Fitzwilliam, injury was indeed a possibility, whether Mr. Darcy chose to acknowledge it or not.

# Chapter 10

The next morning, as Darcy once again started the summation of a column through which he had only made it halfway before finding his mind wandering back to Elizabeth and their conversation about Lydia and Richard, the door opened, and he acknowledged the entrance of his cousin with a nod of his head.

"Miss Lydia seems enamoured with you," he said, glancing up from his books as his cousin settled into a chair. That column of numbers seemed destined to remain as they were – without a total at the bottom. "You are only encouraging proper behaviour and not encouraging an attachment, are you not?"

One corner of his cousin's mouth tipped up, causing Darcy to pause and lay his pen aside. Yes, those numbers would remain without a total for a while longer.

"She is a pretty thing," Richard finally replied.

"And young. And not an heiress."

Richard shrugged and sighed. "True."

"But?" Darcy prodded. Richard rarely capitulated so easily.

Richard shook his head. "I do not know."

Darcy knew just how quickly a gentleman could fall for a pretty Bennet lady. Bingley had been lost before the end of one dance, and he, himself, had not been a whole lot longer in falling for Elizabeth. He had just fought the reality of such a thing happening where his friend had readily accepted it.

The fact that his cousin, who was never without a plan of which he knew the workings forward and back, was currently faltering when answering a question about his plan to improve Lydia Bennet spoke loudly to Darcy that Richard's heart might likely be in danger of being lost.

"She is Georgiana's age," Darcy continued.

Richard nodded. "And in one year's time, Georgiana will be entertaining gentlemen in the sitting room and dancing with them at balls."

"But she will be a year older," Darcy argued. He leaned back in his chair and studied his cousin. It was not that Darcy did not wish for Richard to find a lady who made him happy, nor was his argument actually about Lydia's age. I was more about the fact that he had always thought a more mature and sensible sort of lady would catch Richard's eye. In fact, he had not truly believed that his cousin was in danger last evening when speaking with Elizabeth. A small niggling worry had poked him a time or two, but he had brushed it away each time it did. However, this morning while having his first cup of tea, he had reconsidered his talk with Elizabeth and had decided the best thing to do was to broach the subject with his cousin rather than just guess and suppose.

Richard threw one leg over the other. "Do not fear. I have not lost my heart to Miss Lydia's pretty blue eyes. I am merely helping her achieve her potential, so that she can find a proper husband. I am, after all, married to my profession."

"It concerns me that you know the colour of her eyes," Darcy muttered, causing Richard to laugh.

"I notice things about people."

"Especially if the person is a pretty young lady," Darcy added.

"They are more pleasant to observe than some dour old gent."

Darcy was about to give a final word of caution when Abrams knocked and entered.

"You have callers, sir," said the butler. "Miss Bingley and Sir Matthew are awaiting you in the sitting room. Mrs. Bennet is entertaining them until you arrive."

"And the Miss Bennets?" Darcy rose from his desk and donned his jacket.

"The youngest are with Miss Darcy and Mrs. Annesley. The eldest are with their father."

"If the eldest could be spared from their father's side, Miss Bingley might wish to see them."

He pulled at his sleeves and straightened his waistcoat as Mr. Abrams left the study. Mrs. Bennet was not unfamiliar with entertaining guests in her home. He did not need to rush to see to his callers, yet he felt as if he should. Miss Bingley was not favourably disposed to any of the Bennets – especially after the incident at the Johnson's ball. In fact, he was surprised she had called at his home at all. He had hoped she would be too put out with him and his part in the fiasco leading to her current betrothed state to call on him. His cheeks puffed out as he exhaled.

"This should be entertaining," Richard said from directly next to Darcy, causing him to jump.

"It might well be. I wonder why she has decided to call?"

"Only one way to find out." Richard held the door for his cousin to exit before him.

In the sitting room, Caroline Bingley was perched on the edge of a settee with Sir Matthew at her side. She wore a green gown and a tight smile. There was nothing relaxed in her form at all. She was not, Darcy decided, here of her own accord. He would like to know just how Sir Matthew, who was, as always, relaxed and unruffled, managed to get her to Darcy House.

"Hurst told me that your husband had been injured," Caroline was saying to Mrs. Bennet as Darcy entered. "And Sir Matthew and I, of course, thought it only proper to call to inquire after his health." She paused and raised her chin slightly. "We are to be relations, after all."

"You are too good, Miss Bingley. I had not thought to see you at all while I was in town. I said to Lady Lucas that it would be delightful to see you, but I did not expect it. You would be busy with the season and all that I told her. Yet, here you are. Quite a proper thing, and so kind. Mr. Bennet is resting well, and we hope he will be able to return to Longbourn in just over a week. There have been no complications, no fever, no swoons, or anything else. We have been quite blessed."

Darcy slipped into a chair while Mrs. Bennet spoke.

"Oh, Mr. Darcy," Mrs. Bennet cried upon noticing him, "Is it not just the best treat ever to have Miss Bingley call on us?"

Darcy bit back a smile at how the lady had joined herself to his establishment and referred to him and her as "us." "Indeed, it is."

"And she has the most wonderful news."

"Does she?"

"She does!"

Mrs. Bennet's face was suffused with excitement.

"She is betrothed!"

Again, Darcy bit back a smile as he replied, "I had heard that she was." He darted a look toward Caroline, who, catching his eye, glared at him.

"And to a baronet! Oh, she is a most fortunate lady."

Mrs. Bennet gasped. "Lady Broadhurst! How well that sounds! You must be delighted," she said to Caroline before gasping once again. "Forgive me, I have quite forgotten my manners in light of such wonderful news. Do you know Sir Matthew, Mr. Darcy?"

Darcy nodded. "I do."

Mrs. Bennet looked relieved. "Lady Broadhurst," she muttered once again. "I should be very pleased if any of my daughters were ever to have such a title. Miss Bingley, you have done very well, very well, indeed."

To Darcy's surprise, Caroline's smile shifted from the tight one she had been wearing to one of a lady who was quite pleased with herself.

"I have done well, have I not?" she agreed.

The look she gave Darcy was nearly his undoing, but he bit his cheek and kept his composure. Apparently, Mrs. Bennet's praise of Caroline's status had been a balm capable of changing the glare Caroline had given him before into a look of mild hauteur. While he did not appreciate how she looked down her nose at him, he was relieved to see her more relaxed posture.

"I do believe it is I who has done very well." Sir Matthew sat forward and covered Caroline's hand with one of his.

To Darcy's surprise, Caroline Bingley blushed and dipped her head. If he had not seen it with his own eyes, he would not have believed it possible should someone tell him of it. Sir Matthew had said he thought his odds were good in persuading Caroline to love him, and it appeared he was right.

Richard leaned toward Darcy. "Remind me never to play cards with that man."

Darcy chuckled. "I asked that Miss Bennet and Miss Elizabeth be made aware of your arrival."

Caroline's eyes grew wide. "You did?"

"Yes, I thought you might like to visit with them."

"Of course, we would," answered Sir Matthew. "I should like to get to know them better, especially Miss Bennet as she will be a sister."

"Is that not wonderful?" cried Mrs. Bennet. "I thought for sure when Mr. Bingley left Netherfield, and then his sisters and Mr. Darcy followed, that my Jane would be forgotten." Her brows and chin rose. "Not that any of my daughters are easily forgotten." She shook her head. "But I did think we had lost Mr. Bingley, and he had shown such promise. He is such an amiable gentleman," she directed this last bit to Sir Matthew, "just the sort of gentleman with whom a mother wishes for her daughter to be happily settled."

"And his fortune is not small." Caroline's lashes fluttered as she smiled at Mrs. Bennet.

"Oh, it is not, you are most correct, but then you should be as you are his sister and more intimately acquainted with such things," Mrs. Bennet replied. "A mother does like to see her daughters well-situated. You will understand when you have a daughter or two of your own. It is such a worry. Why a lady's future rest entirely on that very thing – finding, as you have done, a gentleman to lend his rank and keep her in dresses and a home."

Clearly, from the shocked look on Caroline's face, Mrs. Bennet's answer had not been what she had expected. To own the truth, it was not what Darcy had expected either, but it did, strangely, make him happy to be one of the gentlemen who would care for the future of one of Mrs. Bennet's daughters.

# Chapter 11

"I hear Miss Bingley called." Mr. Bennet pushed himself up, pulling his leg along the bed while taking great pains not to move it any more than was necessary to achieve a comfortable sitting position.

"She did," Darcy replied. "Sir Matthew seems quite capable of steering her in the proper direction." Seeing the curiosity on Mr. Bennet's face, he added, "He covers her hand, drawing her attention away from whatever she is about to set upon as a topic of conversation; he replies before she does when there is a danger that her answer might not be pleasing; and he stays as close to her side as is possible. It is remarkable actually. If you were not looking for such actions, one would never suspect he is directing her."

"And does she seem to be warming to him?" Mr. Bennet winced as he shifted once again. "I promise it does not hurt as it did, but there are moments when that injury reminds me it is there."

Darcy smiled apologetically. "Is there anything I can get you for your comfort?"

Mr. Bennet began to shake his head but then stopped as a small smile crept onto his lips. "You could marry my daughter. I should be very comfortable knowing my Lizzy was well-settled."

"I should like to oblige you as soon as possible. However, your daughter is not yet ready for such a discussion. And, to be fair, we are only just becoming well-acquainted." Darcy's comments were met with a resigned sigh.

"I would say that you have all your life to become acquainted after you marry, but..." he paused and looked toward the far corner of the room where a dressing table stood next to a large wardrobe, "sometimes even twenty-three years is not enough for some to learn what they should know about their mate." He drew a deep breath and expelled it. "Though I love her, my wife may never understand me." He shook his head. "Courting for a year rather than just a week and three days would not have changed that fact."

He turned back to Darcy. "It would have, however, helped me prepare for what lay ahead. I knew my Fanny did not possess a keen wit, but I had not accepted that it was part and parcel of who she was. I thought it could be changed." Again, he shook his head. "It seems it cannot be."

He looked down at the blue blanket which lay across his lap and ran his hands over it as if smoothing some imaginary wrinkles from it. "I should have been like Sir Matthew. He knows his future wife's failings, and as you said, he is taking steps to direct them."

Darcy did not know how to respond to such an admission, but he did not have to, as Mr. Bennet continued.

"When we first married, I attempted to engage Fanny's mind. I read her books and asked her questions, but my efforts fell on deaf ears or a dull mind. I tried teasing and prodding. However, she did not know that she needed to move, and so she did not. That is when I retreated to find solace in my solitude and to hide my failure in laughter." He shook his head. "Do not do that. Remember our discussion at the ball – when I said a gentleman who is rarely rattled by anything might become indifferent to those things which should stir him to action?"

Darcy nodded.

"My strength of forbearance became indolence." Mr. Bennet chuckled. "One has a great deal of time to ponder things, when he is confined to his bed, and a tendency to become contemplative, when his daughters are on the verge of beginning their own families. But enough of that. Did you not say you had a chessboard somewhere?"

"I did."

"Then, might not you go retrieve it so we can have

something to do while listening to me meander down my ruminative road?"

Darcy chuckled and rose to call for the chess set.

"How are my daughters?" Mr. Bennet asked when Darcy returned to his chair. "Not my eldest, but my youngest."

"They seem to be settling into their new surroundings well." He paused and grimaced slightly. "I fear I am not the best at entertaining young ladies. We have had a dance lesson and a walk. Tomorrow, I believe, there is talk of a shopping excursion."

This news did not seem to be news at all to Mr. Bennet as he simply nodded and said, "Will you accompany them?"

Darcy shook his head. "Mrs. Annesley will be with my sister, so there is no need for me to attend them. As I heard it, they are only looking for gloves and a pair of slippers for Georgiana."

This was met with a burst of laughter. "I should be surprised if that is the extent of their purchases. My wife is not known for her restraint, and shopping is one of the skills at which she excels."

"My aunt is the same," Darcy replied. "My uncle is forever bemoaning the bills for dresses and hats and the need to redo this or that room. My aunt will hear some bit of news about the latest thing and find it necessary to be the first to adopt it."

"That is not unlike my wife."

The chess set arrived just then, and they paused their conversation while it was set up on a table next to the bed.

"I fear I will not be able to reach every spot," Mr. Bennet said as he surveyed the board.

"Just instruct me on what move you wish to make, and I will see it done. You may begin."

"You never told me if Miss Bingley was warming to Sir Matthew," Mr. Bennet said as he made his first move.

Darcy tipped his head to the left and then the right as he decided which piece to move first. "She blushed and dipped her head more than once at something the man said or did. I do believe he is in a good way of finding himself well liked if not loved."

"Ah, that is good to hear. Felicity in marriage is a wonderful thing."

"I believe you have the right of it," Darcy agreed.

For five minutes the only sound that could be heard in the room was the moving of pieces and the occasional direction of Mr. Bennet as to which piece needed to be placed where when he could not reach to do it himself.

"Returning to my daughters," Mr. Bennet said, breaking the concentration on the game before them, "my Lydia seems enamoured with your cousin, but then she is easily swayed by a uniform."

Mr. Bennet's hand rested on his knight, but he did not move it. "Lizzy says the admiration may not all be on one side." He lifted his horse and placed it ahead and to the left, blocking the advancement of Darcy on his queen.

Again, Darcy's head tipped to the side as he attempted to figure out the best way to get around Mr. Bennet's pieces. "Richard assures me he is only interested in seeing Lydia improve."

"He thinks she wants improvement?"

Darcy swallowed. Perhaps that had not been the best way to respond to the man's question. He nodded. "Yes." What else could he say and remain honest?

"He's not wrong. Did he say why he thought she needed improvement?"

Darcy blew out a breath. "She asked him nearly upon her arrival if he was married and then proceeded to inquire after any beaus my sister might have."

Mr. Bennet made a dissatisfied sound.

"He worries that she would be an easy conquest for a man such as Wickham. There are several of only marginally better morals in town."

"Is that all?"

As Darcy took his turn, he heard the disbelief in the question and felt rather than saw the scrutiny he was receiving from Mr. Bennet. He shook his head. "Richard also feels that Miss Mary would have less to criticize, and Miss Kitty would have a better example to follow if Miss Lydia were to improve. That is why he selected her as the object of his instruction."

He looked up to see Mr. Bennet still pondering him.

"It does not hurt that she has pretty blue eyes," Darcy added.

Mr. Bennet chuckled. "He noticed her eyes, did he?"

Darcy responded with a small shrug and a nod.

"What if he did find her more than just an object of curiosity and a project?" Mr. Bennet asked, leaning back on his pillows, the game forgotten for a moment.

"He is an honorable gentleman if that is what you are asking."

"In part, yes. But what of his future?"

"You mean money?"

Mr. Bennet nodded. "He is a second son, and my daughter has little in the way of wealth. Lydia is not a pauper, but she is not the sort someone in the colonel's position might seek out."

Darcy drew and expelled a deep breath. "He is not without funds and a home. He will also have his retirement once he leaves his position – if he leaves his position – in his majesty's service."

"He is happy in his profession then?"

Darcy nodded. "He seems to be, and there is talk of him joining himself to a position here in town. He has not said more than it would keep him on home soil."

"Nothing is guaranteed in this day and age with so much unrest," Mr. Bennet said solemnly.

"True."

Mr. Bennet leaned forward and moved a piece. "Check."

"Mate," said Darcy after looking at his options to try to escape capture and realizing there were none.

"Oh, well, will you look at that? You are right. I had not thought you so captured. I shall blame that oversight on the laudanum," said Mr. Bennet with a chuckle.

# Chapter 12

Elizabeth wandered around the library, looking first at this book and then that one. There were definitely enough books here to keep her entertained for some months if not years. Some she had read, a few she was certain she never wished to read, and others called to her to pick them up and read them immediately. She sighed. It was as if she had been presented with a full tray of her favourite sweets. How did one select just the right delectable treat?

She moved a few feet from the shelves on the left side of the room to where a large globe stood just at the edge of a group of chairs. Her head tipped to the side, and she leaned forward as she spun the globe slowly, looking at the various forms on it. How she would like to have one of these to look at all the time. She smiled. If she married Mr. Darcy, she would, or at least, she would when they were in residence here.

"I thought I might find you here," Jane said, as she closed the door softly behind her.

"Is this not the most beautiful room?" Elizabeth extended her hands and twirled in a circle.

Jane wrinkled her nose. "You know I do not like reading so much as you do. Therefore, I cannot agree that this is the most beautiful room, for I find many other rooms to be just as inviting." She stood next to her sister, and while Elizabeth huffed her disagreement, she wrapped her arm around Elizabeth's and began leading her around the room.

"If you do not wish to read, then why are you here?"

"To disturb you," Jane replied with a laugh, "and to retrieve a book. Just because I do not enjoy reading as much as you do, does not mean I do not read." She squeezed her sister's arm and lowered her voice. "This could be your library."

"I was just pondering that very thing." Elizabeth felt her cheeks grow warm at the admission.

"So do you love him?" Jane's whispered question was full of hopeful excitement.

It was not the first time, Jane had asked that question of Elizabeth. She had asked it many times since that night at the Johnson's ball. To own the whole truth, Jane had even asked if Elizabeth could love Mr. Darcy before the ball, but it was not until after her reintroduction to Mr. Darcy at that ball when Elizabeth felt it to be a distinct possibility.

"I like him very much," Elizabeth hedged.

"Like? Only like?" Shock and censure coloured Jane's response.

"Very much," Elizabeth repeated before adding two steps later, "and maybe more."

It was the closest she had come to acknowledging what she suspected her heart was telling her. She was uncertain why she could not just admit that she loved Mr. Darcy, but it seemed too grave a thing to declare without proper consideration.

"He loves you."

"I know."

"He has been very good with Mama and our sisters."

"They have only just arrived."

Jane stopped walking and pulled Elizabeth to a settee. "You will not be living with Mama once you are married. Even if Papa were to die, you would not have to house her very often. You will be so far away, and you know how she is about travelling more than a day's journey. She will not wish to make that trip very often, for it will require staying at an inn."

Their mother had a great dislike of staying anywhere that was not the home of a friend or a relation. She worried about being robbed or murdered as well as contracting some horrid disease from some stranger that had used the cups or slept in the bed. It did not matter to her that she could and would carry her own cups and bedding. The idea that someone she did not know had been in that room or eaten at that table caused her to flutter and call for her salts. However, Elizabeth knew that their grandfather Gardiner had died after contracting an illness on a journey, and therefore, her mother's worries were not beyond comprehension.

"She will likely only visit you when you are in town, and then there are so many things to distract her," Jane continued. "You must not let your fear of how vexatious Mr. Darcy finds her to keep you from accepting him."

Jane's arguments made sense. However, it was not just their mother who could be vexing.

"What of our sisters? Mama will expect us to help them find husbands."

Jane nodded. "And we will. Just think how helpful Mr. Darcy was in finding a husband for Miss Bingley."

Elizabeth could not help but laugh at the comment. It still surprised her that Mr. Darcy would participate in a scheme just to see his friend and Jane happy. Her lips curled up in that silly smile he so often caused her to smile. He had not just taken part in Miss Bingley's demise for Jane, he had done it for her – so that he might be free of all fetters to pursue her for his wife.

"I am certain Mama would not be pleased to have any of our sisters fall into marriage as Miss Bingley has," Elizabeth argued.

Jane giggled before countering, "And how many years has Mr. Darcy tolerated Miss Bingley as a friend even when she was so fixed on snaring him for herself?" She shook her head. "You are too fastidious. You cannot know every eventuality before it occurs. He has proven himself loyal and of good character. He loves you, and you love him, though you are too obstinate to admit it. Only good can come from such a match."

Elizabeth leaned back on the settee and looked up at the ceiling. "Am I capable of running so large a home?" she asked Jane without removing her eyes from plaster flowers and leaves that wound themselves around the edge of the room.

"Without a doubt," Jane replied quickly. "Mama has trained us well to run an estate twice the size of Longbourn, and you have the quickest mind of us all. You are perfectly capable of mastering whatever additional skills you might need."

She rolled her head to the side, so that she could see Jane. "Can I help guide a young lady like Miss Darcy?"

Jane smiled. "I think you can. You are forever instructing Lydia on one thing or another, and Miss Darcy seems a far more receptive pupil."

"But I know nothing of town," Elizabeth protested.

Jane turned and took her by the shoulders. "But you know everything about loving a sister. You are very good at it, even when she steals your bonnet and ruins your dress."

Elizabeth's brows furrowed, and her lips puckered. "Or

when she is pushing you to admit what you know to be true."

Jane wrapped her arms around Elizabeth. "Do you admit it then? Do you love Mr. Darcy?"

Elizabeth drew a deep breath and expelled it to drive out the last worries and allow her confidence to fill in those places. "I do. I love Mr. Darcy. I believe I have for some time."

"Since he first insulted you." Jane pulled back and looked at her. "Do not shake your head. I am right as I usually am, though you will not admit it. If Mr. Goulding had said you were not handsome enough to tempt him, you would have laughed and made it a great joke. Do not deny it. I know it is true. But Mr. Darcy was different. You loved him from the moment you saw him."

"I could not love someone I did not know." Elizabeth extracted herself from her sister's embrace and rose. "I found him handsome. And anyone would feel the slight of a stranger far more greatly than that of a friend."

Jane laughed. "If you say so, but I think you are wrong."

Elizabeth rolled her eyes and shook her head.

"You will see," Jane said as she smoothed her skirt and straightened her sleeves. "I am right."

"You are not," Elizabeth muttered.

Jane's response was a smug smile which irritated Elizabeth more than any words might, and Jane knew it. It was how Jane always ended an argument when she thought she was right and Elizabeth was wrong.

"What book are you going to read?" Jane asked.

"I have not decided."

"Good, then, you can help me find a book before you do."

Sisters! Even the most understanding, proper, loving of sisters could be annoying, and yet, Elizabeth would not trade Jane for the world.

# Chapter 13

Darcy nudged his horse to a faster pace. The day was young, and Rotten Row was occupied by several grooms exercising horses for their masters. A few well-dressed gentlemen dotted the trail here and there, but most men of Darcy's class were likely still in their beds. He smiled as he saw Bingley just ahead, and Sir Matthew just beyond him. He knew he would see at least one friend here at this hour. Seeing Sir Matthew would be a bonus. He would make a point of joining up with them soon.

"Darcy."

Darcy's lips curled into a partial snarl as he turned toward the unwelcome rider who had called to him. "Wickham. It seems a rather early hour for you to be out and about. I would expect you to still be abed, not that I expected you to be in town."

"Didn't expect me in Hertfordshire either, did you?" George Wickham teetered just a bit in his saddle. "I'm just on my way home to get some sleep," he added. "Not that I have not been in bed." A wolfish grin spread across Wickham's face.

"And what brings you to town?" Darcy asked, ignoring the implication of Wickham's words. The man was a profligate of the first order. That he had been keeping some woman company for most of the night was not a surprise.

"I am merely visiting some friends for a day or two," Wickham replied.

"I do hope you enjoy your visit." Darcy nudged his horse forward. He had no desire to remain here talking with Wickham. He did not care what the man was doing in town so long as he stayed with his own kind and did not attempt to visit at Darcy House.

Wickham did not, however, seem to be capable of letting Darcy depart with so short a conversation and moved his horse to keep pace with Darcy's.

"I hear you have guests."

Darcy glanced at him. "Do you?"

"I do. A whole house full of pretty ladies."

"And their father and mother," Darcy added. He did not appreciate the suggestive tone Wickham was using.

"I also heard Miss Bennet is to marry your friend."

"She is." Darcy did not like the bent this conversation was taking. The knowledge of the Bennets being at Darcy House was easily explained away. Surely everyone in Hertfordshire knew Mrs. Bennet had been invited. However, the knowledge of Bingley's betrothal had only been shared with Mrs. Bennet after her arrival.

"I suppose you will wish to marry Miss Elizabeth eventually if you can convince her of your worth."

"Why would you say that?" Again, Darcy cast a wary glance at Wickham.

"Come now. We both know you fancy her. I saw how you looked at her when we met in Hertfordshire."

Darcy said nothing in the ensuing silence. He had suspected Wickham knew of his preference for Elizabeth. There was nothing to deny, but Darcy also did not wish to tell Wickham he was correct.

"It is too bad she has heard of your poor qualities. It might make it a great deal more challenging for you to persuade her to accept you."

Darcy wished to kick his horse into a gallop to be rid of the vermin next to him. "She is an intelligent young lady. I am certain she will soon discover your true talent is your deceitful tongue."

"You mean as your sister did?"

Darcy whirled toward him. "You will not mention my sister."

"Georgiana?" Wickham asked with a smile.

Darcy's eyes narrowed. "Yes," he ground out. "Your life depends upon it."

"Does it?"

Darcy wanted to wipe the smirk off Wickham's face with his fist. "My cousin does not make empty promises."

Wickham leaned close to Darcy. "How is the good colonel?" he whispered loudly.

Darcy drew back. The man positively reeked of alcohol. It was a wonder he could stay seated for he must be excessively foxed.

"He is well and staying at Darcy House. Would you care to give me your direction so that he might call on you?"

Wickham laughed and slapped Darcy's back. "No, but I might call on him. It would be good to see Georgiana again. She's such a pretty thing, and Miss Lydia." He whistled. "Very agreeable and lively."

"You are not welcome to visit. Ever."

"Well, that would look right uncivilized of you to turn me away should I come to call on my friends the Bennets. I am certain that would curry you no favours. They already think you disagreeable."

"Go home."

The Bennets may have found him to be disagreeable at one time, but Darcy knew they now no longer did. There was very little fear that Wickham being turned away from Darcy House would do more than cause the youngest Bennet to be perturbed. However, Darcy knew that arguing with Wickham when he was sober was an act in futility, and it was even less productive when he was drunk.

"I may call," Wickham said as he turned his horse toward the park's exit.

"You will be turned away," Darcy replied.

Wickham's only response was to laugh loudly and wave.

"Who was that?" Bingley said as he and Sir Matthew approached Darcy.

Darcy closed his eyes. "Wickham."

"Wickham is in town?" Bingley asked in surprise.

Darcy nodded. "And threatening to call at Darcy House."

Bingley chuckled. "I would like to be there when he does, for I should like to witness the fond welcome he receives from Richard."

"He is not a friend?" Sir Matthew asked.

"He was. At one time," Darcy replied. "However, he has proven himself to be anything but a friend."

"Ah," Sir Matthew replied, "I shall ask no more."

"Thank you," said Darcy.

"Are you going to ride further?" Bingley asked.

Darcy shook his head. "No, I think I should go inform Richard of Wickham's presence."

Sir Matthew's brows rose.

"That man has damaged people close to us," Darcy said in explanation. "He narrowly escaped with his life the last time he and Richard met."

"Indeed?"

Darcy nodded. "If an innocent's reputation were not at stake, I would tell you the tale, but as it is, I cannot."

"As I said, I will ask no more. I shall just remember that this Wickham is not to be trusted."

Wickham was most certainly not to be trusted, and that was the reason Darcy needed to speak to Richard and quite likely Mr. and Mrs. Bennet. He turned toward the exit of the park but then turned back to Bingley. "He mentioned that he knew you were getting married."

"He did?"

Darcy nodded.

"Gossip does circulate quickly," Bingley said with a sigh. "It is not so horrid to have it spread among your acquaintances when they are friends, but..."

Again, Darcy nodded. It was never pleasant when someone who was not friendly knew details about you that you did not wish for him to know. "He mentioned Elizabeth," Darcy added. "He knows I like her."

"Oh," Sir Matthew gasped, understanding dawning in his eyes. "This is that man? The one who has told lies about you and posed a danger to your lady and her sisters due to his debauchery?"

"Yes," Bingley replied.

They had told Sir Matthew some about Wickham after Sir Matthew had agreed to marry Caroline.

"Do you fear he can cause harm now?" Sir Matthew's

mien was somber. It held no curiosity or amusement. He was, as he always seemed to be, sincere.

"I do not trust him to not act rashly," Darcy replied. "However, I do not expect him to be able to do them any harm while they are at Darcy House, for he shall not gain entrance."

Sir Matthew shook his head. "There are so many fools in this world, are there not?"

Neither Darcy nor Bingley could disagree with that.

"If you need anything," Sir Matthew continued, "do not hesitate to ask."

Darcy offered his thanks and set off for home.

# Chapter 14

"Wickham is here? In town?" Richard's fork returned to his plate, still holding its piece of beefsteak.

"I admit I was surprised to see him and not pleasantly so."

Upon returning from his ride, Darcy had found his cousin eating breakfast and had chosen to join him and share his news since no one else was yet in the room.

Darcy took a sip of his coffee. "He knows Bingley is betrothed and that the Bennets are here as well as the fact that I like Elizabeth."

Richard's jaw tensed. "He has always been too good at ferreting out information," he muttered.

"Only when it serves his purpose," Darcy said after another sip of coffee.

Richard allowed it to be true.

Wickham was always attempting to gain information and then twisting it and turning it as needed to achieve his goals — whether that was getting himself out of trouble, placing Darcy in a precarious situation, or charming a young woman into thinking herself in love with him.

"However," Darcy continued. "That is not the worst of it."

"What could be worse?" Richard demanded.

"He said he might call." Darcy watched Richard's face darken. "He said it would be nice to see Georgiana again."

Richard muttered a curse as he shook his head. "Not while I still breath."

"I told him he would be turned away."

"Or worse," Richard muttered.

"Yes, I did tell him you were in residence. I hope it will help him be reasonable, but this is Wickham, and once he's set on an idea, there's little which can shake it from his head. This idea of his of calling here will likely be more firmly rooted in his mind than is normal since he sees this as a way to make certain the Bennets still view me as disagreeable."

"Have you instructed Abram that he is not to be admitted under any circumstances? Because doing harm to you is incentive enough for him to disregard any fear for his life that he should possess," Richard grumbled.

"I did. He will be turned away."

"Good." Richard shoved his beefsteak into his mouth and chewed with vigor as he stabbed another piece.

"Do not break the dishes," Darcy said with a smile. "I know you despise him, but please spare the plates."

Richard shook his head as he replied around his food. "If he were here, I'd not have to abuse your china."

"Then perhaps we will be fortunate, and the blackguard will call this afternoon."

Richard swallowed. "I almost hope we are."

"Good morning," Lydia chirped as she and Kitty entered the room. "Mary and Mama will be along soon, but Lizzy and Jane are likely still with Papa." She slid into a chair next to Richard. "You look a bit like a storm cloud, Colonel. Does he not, Kitty?"

"He does indeed!" Kitty agreed.

Darcy smiled at the exuberance of the two youngest Bennets. Perhaps, he would not need to fear Miss Lydia being put out if Wickham were turned away. He suspected that one word from *the colonel* would make all well in her eyes.

"We were just discussing some unpleasant business," Richard said in his own defense before popping another bite of food into his mouth.

"Well, you should not have been." Lydia poured a cup of tea and placed a roll on her plate. "It is not healthy. One should only think on happy things while eating, or one's stomach will ache dreadfully. And I imagine it becomes even more important to follow such a practice as one gets older. Old people seem to have so many ailments that if one can be prevented, it should be. Do you not think, Colonel?"

She smiled brightly at Richard as he attempted to clear his mouth of food before responding.

"Are you saying I am old?" he asked.

"Oh, goodness, no!" Lydia exclaimed. "Why would you think such a thing? Just because I mentioned your discussion of disagreeable things while eating and then the ailments of the elderly does not make you old." Her brows furrowed. "Does it?"

From her tone of voice, it sounded to Darcy as if she had reasoned her way into doubting her own supposition.

"I'm not old," Richard replied.

"No, but you are older than I am." Lydia was still looking perplexed.

"That does not make me old. You are just young."

"Not so very young!" Lydia now sounded offended. She huffed and then shook her head as she sat straighter and lifted her chin. "We must think on pleasant things," she instructed. "Dash can hold a biscuit on his nose until I tell him he can eat it."

Darcy chuckled at Richard's look of bewilderment caused by the sudden change of topics.

"He will sit just so." Lydia held her finger on her nose as if it was a biscuit. "And then when I say 'good boy,' he flicks it in the air and catches it." She spooned some jam onto her bun. "He is very smart."

"And adorable," Kitty added. "You should have seen

him wearing his cravat last night. I tried to draw it, but he is not very good at sitting still just yet."

"Except for when he has a biscuit that is on his nose," Richard inserted.

"Yes, but he cannot sit forever with it on his nose. Half a minute is all. Longer than that would be torturous. He is just a puppy," Lydia's tone held a great deal of shock.

"But perhaps he could learn to sit with it longer," Kitty said.

Lydia tipped her head to one side and then the other. "Perhaps, he could." She took a bite of her bun.

"Do you think we will get to purchase some ribbons today?" she asked Kitty. "I should like one for my bonnet. Red would be delightful to go with my sprigged muslin dress, do you not think so, Colonel?"

Richard, who had just taken a sip of his tea, coughed. "I really could not say," he managed after a few moments of coughing followed by another sip of tea. "I am not even sure I know what sprigged muslin is."

"It is the one I wore when we had our dance lesson." Lydia's lashes fluttered as she blinked.

It was as if she could not fathom that the colonel did not know to which dress she referred. She might be the Bennet who posed to cause the most disturbance to Darcy's life, but Lydia was also proving to be the most entertaining, and, surprisingly, he was beginning to appreciate her lively mind. Lively, but not logical. He chuckled to himself behind his cup.

"Maria Lucas has always said a red ribbon would set it off nicely," Lydia added.

She said it in such a tone that Darcy could imagine her mother saying that very thing. Lydia was indeed her mother's daughter. He had to admit he was enjoying the chance to learn so many intimate details about Elizabeth's family. He shook his head before taking another sip of his coffee. He never thought he would be enjoying having the Bennets at Darcy House. He had thought he could endure them, but he had not expected to benefit from their stay in such a fashion.

"Well, then it must be true," Richard replied.

Richard did know how to bow out of an argument he was sure to lose.

Lydia huffed as she swallowed the bite of jam covered bun she had taken. "I shall wear it again tomorrow, and you will see."

Darcy chuckled to himself. Richard was not going to get away from the argument without admitting defeat. Miss Lydia was a determined young woman.

"I look forward to being proven wrong," Richard responded with a smile that was returned in kind.

And his cousin, who would have at any other time likely argued his position of not needing to know which dress

Georgiana wore or with what ribbon, was in danger of becoming the pupil rather than the instructor.

# Chapter 15

Elizabeth rolled her shoulders and rubbed her neck. The rest had felt good, but the stiffness that followed was not as pleasant.

"That is not the best place to take a nap," said her father. "Those chairs were not designed for comfort when resting."

Elizabeth smiled. The soreness in her neck could attest to the truth of his word. "How are you feeling?"

"As well as a man who is confined to a room might," he replied with a smirk. "Truly, the pain is not so bad today as it was yesterday. I do believe in another week's time I will be set to return to my study, unless?" His brows rose and then waggled.

"Unless what?" she asked.

"Unless more time is needed at Darcy House?"

Jane laughed from her place near the window where she was keeping a watch on the front door of Darcy House. Elizabeth knew that her sister was hoping for Mr. Bingley to call again today.

"For either of you," her father added.

"I believe Mr. Bingley intends to return to Hertfordshire," Jane replied.

"But will he bring his friend?" Mr. Bennet asked.

"I doubt he could keep his friend from following him."

Jane's answer was met with a chuckle from Mr. Bennet.

"What think you of this, Lizzy?" her father asked. "I have not inquired about your opinion of Mr. Darcy since before taking up residence in this room. I should think I — and that rascal of a dog — have given you enough time to consider all that might need considering. Ah! I am right, am I not? That is why your sister is looking as if she is about to burst, is it not, Lizzy?"

Elizabeth's cheeks grew warm. "Yes."

He clapped his hands. "Does your mother know?"

Elizabeth shook her head. "Only Jane."

"Not Mr. Darcy?" her father asked in surprise.

Again, Elizabeth shook her head.

"But you would be favourable to an offer of marriage from the man?"

Light as a butterfly landing upon a rose in the garden at Longbourn, nerves alighted in Elizabeth's chest. Below the lace trimmed edge of her day gown, her heart raced. There was a slight uneasiness to the feeling but not so unsettling as it had been before she had come to her decision while talking to Jane yesterday. It was becoming a familiar, nearly welcomed, excitement of her senses very like unto how she felt when Mr. Darcy said something about loving her but heightened by the knowledge that she returned his sentiments.

"I would be." She knew that the foolish smile, which accompanied any sweet words from Mr. Darcy, was now scrawled across her face.

"Your mother will be in her glory."

Elizabeth was not sure she had ever seen her father smile so broadly. To her, it looked a lot like her father was in his glory as much as her mother might be on hearing such a thing, though her father displayed his delight in a more subdued fashion.

"To return to Longbourn with two daughters so well-matched," he continued, "she will be the envy of the community. Well, of the ladies of the community that is." He chuckled and then expelled a breath. "Do you think we can find three more such gents before my leg heals? I can insist that the physician recommends I not be moved for longer if necessary."

"Papa!" cried Jane. "You sound more like Mama than yourself."

He only chuckled in response. "Your mother is not your only parent who has worried about your futures."

"Indeed?" The comment surprised Elizabeth. Her father had never appeared to her to be overly concerned with anything beyond the here and now.

"Oh, it is very true. I would do almost anything for any

of girls. I cannot say I look forward to parting with any of you, but it is not so dreadful to contemplate when I know you will be cared for so well."

He chuckled again. "I guess your mother and I have begun to prove the naysayers wrong," he murmured.

Jane and Elizabeth shared a confused look.

"What naysayers, Papa?" Jane asked.

He shrugged and smoothed his blanket. "I did not marry a gentleman's daughter."

Jane and Elizabeth waited patiently as her father found it necessary to smooth the same portion of his bedding before continuing.

"I had relations who condemned me for lowering myself so." He shrugged again. "Fanny Gardiner had more ability to run an estate than the young ladies of my circle. She was not the most intellectual of the lot of ladies, but she knew how to manage things and," he smiled at some imaginary object far in the distance, "she was prettier than any lady I had ever seen before or indeed have ever seen since. Save for my daughters, but then they all resemble their mother."

Elizabeth had never heard her father speak in such an affectionate way about their mother. She had always known he loved Mama, but he had never said so much in praise of her. He often teased about her beauty being enticing to others, but at this moment, there was no teasing tone. His words were spoken in such a sincere and almost longing fashion that Elizabeth could not help but to feel them greatly.

In addition to this new realization of how deeply her father loved her mother, Elizabeth realized that she had never considered how he might have been looked upon for marrying the daughter of a country solicitor. She, herself, had never felt a compelling need to make a great divide between classes, but then that was likely because she had relations in trade.

"Mr. Collins offering for you, Lizzy," her father's words interrupted her contemplations, "was indeed a thing of significance as your mother was never accepted by his father. So, to have his son accept the daughter of my unacceptable wife was a true gesture of goodwill." He shook his head. "Not that he would ever be good enough for any of you in my eyes. He has too much of his father's preposterousness. Not even Lydia, who I must say has the most creative way of reasoning out anything, would be well-suited to such foolishness.

"There were others as well. It is not easy to move from one sphere to another without someone watching and waiting for you to fail."

A whoosh of air from Elizabeth was met with a shake of her father's head.

"You will do well, as will Jane, and, I hope, eventually Mary, Kitty, and Lydia will follow suit." He smiled. "Perhaps we should stay longer so that the colonel has more time to instruct Lydia."

Elizabeth and Jane laughed.

"I appreciate your willingness to see me entertained, but there is a gentleman below who would surely like a few hours of Lizzy's time, and there is also an outing planned. I would not wish to keep you both from such things." He winked and picked up his book.

"I have my bell," he said when they did not immediately rise. "If I have need of anything, I shall summons someone. Now, away with you." He made a sweeping motion with his hand in the direction of the door. "I will be well."

"There is nothing you need?" Jane asked as she rose from her chair.

"Nothing, save a kiss for each of my cheeks," he replied, tapping his left cheek for Jane to kiss and then doing the same to his right for Elizabeth before settling into the silence of the room when the door clicked closed.

# Chapter 16

Elizabeth wandered the hall from the sitting room almost to the door of Mr. Darcy's study and back three times before finding enough courage to rap softly at his door. She blew out a breath and was just about to scurry away, assuming he had not heard her knock when the door before her opened.

"Miss Elizabeth."

Darcy's smile of greeting was enough to cause her heart to flutter. It was intoxicating to be met with such pleasure.

"Please, come in," he offered.

"We are to leave shortly," she said as she entered at his invitation. "My father has insisted that he be left alone and that Jane and I go with Mama and the others."

She looked around the room as she was talking. It was not much larger than Papa's study at Longbourn, but it was much more organized. Books did not lie upon shelves. They stood in fine array. Papers were not scattered across the desk but were contained within tidy piles. The room seemed to exemplify the personality of its master – dignified, reserved, and proper.

She took a seat in the one chair that faced the door but was positioned in such a way that its occupant could share in the conversation at the hearth to their right or with Mr. Darcy while he sat at his desk on the left. It was a plush chair with a wide seat of creamy fabric decorated with flowers and vines.

She smoothed her skirt and looked up to see Darcy staring at her.

"Am I not supposed to sit here?" She made to move.

"No. Stay as you are. You are so charmingly arranged." He shook his head. "I am quite overcome with how charming you look there."

Could cheeks burst into flames? If they could, Elizabeth was certain hers were very close to igniting from the pleasure in the tone of his voice and the intensity of the look in his eyes. It was perhaps best if she did not come to his study in the future. It felt far too dangerous a place to be.

"You are going shopping?"

Mr. Darcy moved around his desk and took his place behind it which made Elizabeth feel only slightly better as now she was separated from him by a substantial piece of furniture, yet he looked so... She could not describe it beyond the thought that the position fit him. He filled the chair with such authority and confidence that it was nearly palpable. It was no wonder Mr. Bingley gave such weight to any of Mr. Darcy's advice. How did one not listen to this man?

"I am," she replied when she had found her voice.

He seemed at a loss for how to continue the conversation, so she added, "I am not a lover of shopping as much as my mother or Lydia, but I must say I am eager to view the world in this part of London."

"Have you not shopped in town before?"

She smiled at his surprise. It was understandable. She had visited London many times to visit her aunt and uncle, and Mr. Darcy was well-aware of that fact. "I have, but we have never ventured to Bond Street."

"Never?" His surprise had not receded.

"Never," she assured him. "My uncle has many connections, but I am not certain if they extend to Bond Street. But whether they do or not, we have always frequented shops nearer to his home. Travel time is always a consideration for my aunt. She does have young ones at home, and though she employs a nursemaid, she does not like to be completely absent from their lives."

He seemed to relax into his chair at her words. She knew he liked both her aunt and uncle Gardiner greatly.

"I can understand such a sentiment. My mother insisted on not being parted from me for an overlong period of time when I was young."

He wore a soft smile as he spoke.

"Georgiana does not remember, but our mother was the

same with her until she became too ill to leave her room." He sighed.

"Did you visit her then?" Elizabeth could not begin to imagine the sorrow that having a gravely ill parent would bring to a child no matter how young or old he was.

He nodded. "We did."

"That must have given her great joy," Elizabeth said softly.

He nodded once again but did not speak. How she would like to ask him more about his mother, but she dared not, for she did not know how best to approach such a thing. Her mother refused to speak of her father or mother and had scolded anytime Elizabeth had made a curious inquiry. So, to press the topic felt wrong even if it was not.

Darcy's eyes focused back on her. "I should like to tell you about her sometime."

"I would like that. Very much."

Lydia and Kitty scurried past the open door.

"It looks as if it is nearly time for you to depart."

Elizabeth sighed. As much as she longed to see the people and the shops on Bond Street, she also wished to remain here with him. Her heart and mind seemed a jumble of opposing feelings lately as it tried to decide where it belonged and how it fit in that place.

He rose from his seat and coming around his desk once again, extended his hand to her. "I shall see you off." His lips tipped up on one side. "I realize you must go fetch your things, but I will wait for you and see you to the carriage. I almost wish I was going, so that I could walk about with you on my arm." He wrapped her arm around his. "Maybe one day we will stroll down Bond Street together, and we can even visit one of the auction houses to select a few things for the house."

He was doing it again – speaking as if they were partners in life, as if this were already her home, and as if he valued her opinion and input. And she was wearing that silly grin that accompanied such things. However, this time instead of saying nothing. She smiled up at him and said, "I do hope so."

He stopped short of exiting the room and turned hopeful, yet uncertain, eyes toward her.

She shrugged. "There might be a thing or two that the house could use." Her heart beat wildly at such a proclamation of her affections.

A smile, large, bright, and filled with pleasure, spread slowly across his face. "Do you mean it?"

"I try not to tell falsehoods, Mr. Darcy." She arched a brow impertinently and attempted to ignore the heat which flooded her cheeks. "I should very much like to go shopping with you."

"Just shopping?" His eyes sparkled with merriment.

She shrugged one shoulder. "That is all you have asked me to do, is it not?"

He opened his mouth to speak, but at that moment, a tan and black blur raced into the room and between them.

"Dash!" Georgiana called as she hurried in behind him.

Elizabeth heard Darcy sigh as he turned toward the pup, who was standing on one of the chairs before the hearth. "Always Richard's chair," he muttered. Then, he looked at her. "Shall we discuss more than shopping later?"

"Yes, Mr. Darcy," she replied as her heart skittered and skipped, "I think we should."

# Chapter 17

Inside the cobbler's shop, Elizabeth stood near where Georgiana sat trying on the lovely burgundy silk slippers which had been made for her.

"What do you think?" Georgiana asked, holding out her foot and tipping it this way and that for everyone to admire.

"I could dance for hours in those!" Lydia declared.

"They are beautiful," Elizabeth said.

"Are they comfortable?" Mrs. Annesley asked. "Is the fit good?"

"Oh, yes," inserted Mrs. Bennet. "Pretty shoes are only wonderful if they do not cause sores."

"Stand and give them a try," the shopkeeper encouraged as he stood back and hooked his thumbs on his apron. "My slippers are of the finest quality, as you know. I am certain they will not cause any discomfort." He stood in front of a counter that was piled with leather, fabric, and forms. Behind the counter was a workbench with several partially finished boots and shoes on it.

As Georgiana stood, Lydia took her hands and led her in a few patterns of the dance they had practiced in the ballroom with Mr. Hughes. "Did they make you feel like you could complete that dance over and over?" Lydia asked when she finally released Georgiana's hands. "You performed the figures very well."

Elizabeth shook her head. Lydia had so much confidence. There never seemed to be a situation in which she found herself that caused her to pause and watch warily. No, Lydia threw herself most happily into any fun scheme that presented itself. It was an admirable quality in some ways, for it meant that she was not held back from experiencing new and delightful things by fear. However, it also meant that sometimes she found herself in less than desirable places because she had not first carefully considered where a plan might end. Thankfully, as of yet, none of those scrapes had caused anything more than a few moments of unease for her and her sisters.

"They are absolutely perfect!" Georgiana declared. "I only wish I could keep them on my feet now."

"Oh, you mustn't," chided Lydia. "The streets would see them destroyed before we got to the carriage."

Georgiana giggled. "You could carry me."

"What is the use of a pair of shoes if one cannot walk when wearing them?" muttered Mary.

"She can walk," Kitty shot a displeased look at her sister, "just not on the streets. Slippers are not for out of doors. Everybody knows that." Kitty drew out the word everybody and rolled her eyes as she said it.

"Girls," Mrs. Bennet said sternly.

Elizabeth shared a questioning look with Jane. Their mother rarely scolded in public. In fact, had they been in a shop in Meryton, she might have taken up Kitty's position in reprimand of Mary.

Thankfully, none of Elizabeth's sisters continued the argument, and Miss Darcy was allowed to remove her new slippers and put on her boots while the shopkeeper wrapped up the precious new footwear, which was then handed to the footman who accompanied them.

Elizabeth linked arms with Jane as they made their way among and around the people on the street to another shop not far away. She was glad that she had Jane to guide her, so that she could pay attention to the people they passed as well as to the shop fronts rather than attending carefully to whether they were still following Miss Darcy.

Walking this street on the arm of Mr. Darcy would indeed be delightful. She made a mental note of where particular stores of interest were, so she could mention them to him when next they spoke. It was not that she wished to purchase anything inside of them, it was just that the glimpse through an open door or window was enough to arouse her curiosity.

Her attention turned back to her party as she stepped into a store that sold cases and cases of accessories. Everything was displayed so well, and Elizabeth delighted in watching the various clerks assisting the customers.

"Fanny Gardiner!" Some woman's high-pitched declaration pierced through the din of the store. "I would never have imagined that I would see you here, in this district of town, and yet, here you are."

"Are you well?" Jane whispered to their mother who had frozen and paled. "Mama?"

"Yes, yes. I am well," Mrs. Bennet assured her, but Elizabeth was not convinced she was speaking the truth.

Mrs. Bennet turned to greet the lady who had crossed from where she had been standing at a case to where the Bennet party was.

"It is Mrs. Bennet now." Mrs. Bennet extended her hand to the lady. "I am sorry. I would greet you properly, but I do not know your name. I am sure it is no longer Miss Foster."

Elizabeth watched the exchange of greeting curiously. Her mother's chin was lifted, and her back was straight and stiff. As far as she could remember, Elizabeth had seen her mother assume such a posture only once before when Mrs. Long had said something disparaging about Jane three years ago.

"Indeed, it is not," the woman said with a laugh. "It is Mrs. Salter now."

"Mrs. Salter, it is a surprise to see you after all these

years." Mrs. Bennet motioned for Jane to step forward. "Allow me to introduce you to my daughters."

She waited until the woman before her nodded and motioned for her to continue.

"This is my eldest, Jane. Next to her is Elizabeth, and then Mary. Kitty and Lydia are examining the gloves with our friend Miss Darcy." She motioned to where Georgiana was pulling on a pair of calfskin gloves while Lydia praised them profusely.

"Five daughters?" Mrs. Salter asked.

"Yes."

"Are these all your children then?" The woman continued to look amused by that fact for some reason.

"Yes."

To Elizabeth, it seemed strange that her mother would not inquire as to Mrs. Salter's children. In fact, it was very unusual for her mother to be so silent.

"I do hope your husband's estate is not entailed – he does have an estate, does he not?"

"As you well know, my husband's estate is Longbourn in Hertfordshire, and it is entailed, which you also know."

The woman fiddled with her gloves. "Oh, I had forgotten. It has been what?" She looked at Jane. "Twenty-three years since we last saw each other."

Mrs. Bennet said nothing in reply, but her cheeks turned from their pale colour to a rosy hue.

"I have two sons – an heir and a spare – as they say," Mrs.

Salter said with a laugh. "And one daughter. She is in her second season, but we do have some high hopes that there will be some very happy news for her soon." She lifted her chin as she smiled down at first Mrs. Bennet and then Jane, Elizabeth, and Mary. "I mustn't keep you from your friend – Miss Darcy, did you say it was?"

"Yes," Elizabeth pressed her lips together. It was not for her to answer such a question, but this woman was so gratingly arrogant in that overly pleasant fashion of some catty women that for a moment she forgot herself.

"Well, I see you are still able to worm your way up from your position into one that is higher, but then you were always overreaching your bounds, were you not, Fanny?"

Elizabeth's eyes grew wide both at the accusation and the cold turn of the woman's tone.

"He preferred me," Mrs. Bennet's response was spoken softly. "He still does."

Mrs. Salter smiled tightly. "Yes, well, be that as it may, although that got him what he wanted in the moment, it did not get him what he needed, now, did it?" Again, she looked at Jane.

"I assure you we are perfectly happy with the children the Lord saw fit to give us."

The woman shrugged and sighed as she affected a look of nonchalance. "Such beautiful daughters," she said. "Daughters," she repeated. "It almost makes you wonder if it is not punishment for an indiscretion."

Elizabeth caught her jaw before her mouth dropped open.

"And your daughters seem to have learned well from you," the venomous viper of a woman continued. "I hear one of them caused quite a scandal at a ball recently, but I digress." She waved her words away as if shooing away a servant. "It has been delightful to see you again after all these years. I shall have to tell our friends. They will be overcome with the surprise just as I was when I saw you enter this store." She turned to leave, but Mrs. Bennet's words stopped her.

"Do try to tell them the truth this time. Unlike you did all those years ago."

"I am afraid I do not understand your meaning."

Elizabeth could tell from the way Mrs. Salter's lashes fluttered that she knew precisely of what Mrs. Bennet was speaking.

"Jane, dear," said their mother. "When is your birthday?"

"May 24," Jane replied.

"Just three days before my anniversary," Mrs. Bennet added.

"That does not mean you did not...well, we will not speak of such thing in public. It is not how the well-bred do things."

"No, they prefer to gossip behind closed doors," Mary

muttered. "One is so much better than the other," she added, her tone dripping with sarcasm.

Mrs. Salter gasped. "Such talk! You will do well to see any of your daughters well-matched with such behavior."

"Are you not happy it is not your problem then?" Mrs. Bennet replied with a smirk. "They all take after their father in some way. Mary has her father's love of the sardonic while Lizzy has his wit and teasing nature. Jane has his kind heart, Kitty has his willingness to please those she loves, and Lydia has his determined spirit. If you cannot admire those things in my daughters, then I do not see how you could have ever truly admired their father. But then, you did not. You just did not wish for him to admire me." She turned to her daughters. "Come along. We should not keep our friend waiting." She cast a glance at Mrs. Salter. "It would be rude." Then with a flick of her head that would rival Lydia's best performance, she led Jane, Mary, and Elizabeth away from Mrs. Salter.

# Chapter 18

"But Mama, I really must get a red ribbon," Lydia protested upon hearing Mrs. Bennet's suggestion of returning to Darcy House without entering any other shops.

Mrs. Bennet pursed her lips, furrowed her brow, blew out a breath, and gave a small shrug. "One ribbon?" Her tone was filled with uncertainty.

It was not like their mother to be so brief when shopping, nor was it like her to question Lydia's wants. On most occasions, Lydia had only to hint that she might like this or that, and it was secured if at all possible.

"We could wait for her in the carriage," Elizabeth suggested softly to her mother. "She will be well with Jane and Mrs. Annesley to attend her."

"But that woman – oh, it is too much," Mrs. Bennet dug in her reticule and pulled out her salts. "I do not wish to see her again."

"Nor do I," Elizabeth agreed. "She is most horrid." She placed an arm around her mother's shoulders. "In fact," she said in a whisper, "she is so horrid that she makes Miss Bingley and Mrs. Long look rather pleasant."

Her words did what they were intended to do by causing Mrs. Bennet to giggle. The sound made Elizabeth's heart ache a bit less. While it had pained her to hear that woman speak so cruelly to her mother, the worst of it was how it discomposed her mother. A giggle meant that her mother's usual vigor and cheerfulness would soon be restored.

"She does, does she not?" Mrs. Bennet took one more whiff of her salts before tucking them back in her reticule.

"One more shop," she said to Lydia with a smile. "I think I can endure one more shop."

"I dare say Mrs. Salter will not approach you again," Jane said as they began moving toward the street.

Mrs. Bennet sighed. "Perhaps not today, but..." She shook her head. "She is not the sort to be easily put off. She tormented me for months."

"How do you know her?" Elizabeth held one of her mother's arms while Jane had the other.

"I went to school. It was not a fancy school. It was a good one, but not the sort that Miss Darcy would have attended, I suppose. Your aunt Phillips and I were sent to polish a few skills which might help us rise above our beginnings. I managed it. My sister did not, but then I have always been more accomplished at the skills necessary to man-age a home, and, well, not to be too very arrogant, I have always been the prettier of us two. You know your aunt well, and I am sure you can see the truth in what I am saying."

Elizabeth had to admit that if she were to compare her aunt Phillips and her mother only on beauty, her mother was most decidedly the prettier sister, and, if she were to pause and consider the soirees held at her aunt's home and compare them to what was had at Longbourn, she would also have to admit that her mother was indeed more skilled than her aunt Phillips at entertaining. However, until this moment, she had never stopped to ponder such things. Her mother had always just been her mother and her aunt, her aunt. She had not thought about them as sisters who might compete with each other or as young women learning skills and hoping to make a good match. Elizabeth wondered if when she had a daughter, she would also be viewed as just Mother and nothing else?

"Mrs. Salter is from Hertfordshire, or she was. Her family has since moved to smaller accommodations." Mrs. Bennet looked around her and lowered her voice. "They had to cut expenses, you see. Her father liked to gamble, and he was a very poor player." She raised her eyebrows and gave her daughters a look that spoke of how absolutely dreadful such a thing was.

"But if Mrs. Salter was from Hertfordshire, how did you not meet her until you were at school?" Jane asked what Elizabeth was also thinking.

"Oh, I did not say I met her there," Mrs. Bennet said with a laugh.

"Did you not?" Elizabeth queried. Had her mother not answered the question of how she knew Mrs. Salter with the information that she had gone to school?

"No, I simply was beginning my tale. I knew Mrs. Salter for years. She was always a jackanapes." Here she paused to shake her head and cluck. "Always thinking so highly of herself. Oh, my, the airs she put on."

"So, you were not friends?" Jane asked.

"Goodness! Never! I was polite to her because my father needed me to be welcoming to all. His business was only profitable if he was sought after, and one will not seek out a solicitor whose daughters are rude."

"I see," Elizabeth muttered, again being struck by how she had never truly considered what her mother's life might have been like as a young girl.

"Well," Mrs. Bennet continued, "when Mrs. Salter – Miss Foster then – turned sixteen, she took a liking for the young gentleman at Longbourn." She sighed. "He was a handsome fellow, and he still is." She winked at Elizabeth. "A little older but no less handsome."

Elizabeth could not help but smile at her mother's comments and be reminded of how her father had spoken so lovingly of her mother earlier that day. There was no doubting what she and her sisters had always known –

despite their differences, eccentricities, teasing, and nagging, their parents loved each other.

"Miss Foster, who is a year older than I, was at the same school I attended, and she attempted to outdo me in most things, which in some areas was not so great a task. I shall never be an accomplished musician, for instance. But there were areas where, try as she might, she could not earn the praise I did, and to make matters worse, the young man she wished to have call on her, showed a preference for me."

That part, Elizabeth had guessed from the conversation between Mama and Mrs. Salter.

"Oh, this shop is delightful!" Mrs. Bennet cried. She followed behind Lydia and exclaimed over this ribbon or that lace. "And the caps!"

"Will you get one, Mama?" Kitty asked. "That one right there with the rosette. Would not that look divine on you?"

"To be sure!"

Elizabeth knew that the cap was purchased even before her mother asked the shop assistant to wrap it up.

"You should buy some lace, Lizzy," said Mrs. Bennet. "You see Jane is already looking at a fine lot of it there. You may need it if you ever decide to accept Mr. Darcy. I do not know what keeps you from bringing him up to scratch. He is the finest gentleman I have ever met. Well, aside from Mr. Bingley, of course. And your father. And

Colonel Fitzwilliam – he is such a nice gentleman, is he not? And a colonel, too." Her brow furrowed. "Sir Matthew is lovely as well from what I could tell. I am not certain why he would wish to marry Miss Bingley, but then I am not well-acquainted with how they get on."

"You did not like Mr. Darcy," Elizabeth reminded her mother.

"With good reason! He was rude. One of my daughters, not handsome enough? I knew it could not be true. Anyone with eyes can see that my daughters are amongst the fairest in the kingdom." She pulled out a bit of lace and held it up for Elizabeth. "This will be perfect." Then she turned to the shop attendant and had it wrapped up without waiting for Elizabeth to agree or disagree.

"Mr. Darcy is very clever, though. He soon realized his error."

"Yes, he finds Lizzy more than handsome now," Jane teased with a smile, causing Elizabeth to blush. However, she did not refute the statement, for she knew it was true.

"Well, now, if Lydia would just select what she needs," Mrs. Bennet flitted off to give her assistance to her youngest.

A short argument about the correct shade of red as well as the width that would be best broke out as was often the case when Lydia and their mother clashed over something. However, it ended as it always did — and in short order — with Mrs. Bennet purchasing both items and telling Lydia how she would see that her mother was right when they returned home.

"They are very alike, are they not?" Elizabeth asked Jane, who nodded her agreement.

"Ah!" Mrs. Bennet's sigh as they stepped out of the shop was one of relief. "We can now go home having had a most successful outing," she declared.

And they did.

# Chapter 19

Darcy stretched and rose from his chair. He had slipped back into his study after tea and before dinner to complete some instructions that he wished to send off to his solicitor just as soon as he had secured Elizabeth's acceptance of his offer... he smiled... which he would make either this evening should he find the correct moment or tomorrow when he would ask her to take a drive with him in the park.

Her father had already given Darcy permission to make his offer. They had discussed many particulars about marriage settlements and the like while playing a game of chess when the ladies had been out shopping. Mr. Bennet was turning out to be a gentleman who Darcy not only liked but could also admire. The man was sharp and an excessively good chess player. Darcy had yet to win a game.

"I do not know how you will ever choose." Bingley's tone was teasing as he entered Darcy's study behind Richard.

"I shall just see which one she seems to favour, and if I wish for the discussion to stop, I will pick that one. However, if I fancy a bit of a row, I shall then pick the other."

"With whom are you considering starting an argument?" Darcy asked.

"Miss Lydia," Bingley replied. "Apparently, she has decided to wear her muslin to dinner instead of waiting until tomorrow, even if it is more of a day dress than a dinner dress. She just will not be able to sleep if she does not know which red ribbon the colonel prefers. He is the expert in all things red, you see."

Darcy chuckled. "Is he? I did not know."

"It's on account of his uniform," Bingley added. Then, he sat primly on the edge of his seat, clasped his hands on his knees, and batted his lashes as he said, "It's red, you know."

Richard cuffed Bingley on the shoulder. "It is red," he defended. "Miss Lydia is just enamoured with all things uniform. It is not so strange a thing." He smiled as he slipped into his normal seat before the hearth. "And I do cut a fine figure, so you really cannot blame a young woman for being duly impressed."

Bingley dissolved into laughter.

"I must have missed an important discussion," Darcy said with a laugh as he leaned against his desk.

"Oh, it was entertaining," Richard agreed. "Miss Lydia and Mrs. Bennet hold differing opinions on which of the red ribbons they purchased today will look best with Miss Lydia's muslin. You know, the one she mentioned this morning?"

"I do remember that conversation."

"Miss Kitty is certain Miss Lydia is correct while Miss Mary thinks that a ribbon is a ribbon, and it is foolish to be arguing over something so trivial." Bingley tipped his head and waggled his eyebrows as he smirked.

"And that did not sit well with either Miss Lydia or Miss Kitty, I suppose," Darcy said.

"Oh, most certainly not!" said Richard. "They were still discussing the issue when they went up to dress for dinner." He sighed. "We are assured of at least thirty minutes of silence on the topic of ribbons."

Darcy tipped his head and studied his cousin. Richard did not look as put out with the topic of ribbons as his voice seemed to convey. "You could avoid all of this if you returned to Matlock House."

Richard shook his head. "I have to return to my men the day after tomorrow. There are drills scheduled." He reclined in his chair and crossed his ankles. "We may be shipped off soon."

"To the continent?" Darcy asked in surprise. Richard had said nothing of his unit being called up.

"Nothing is certain just yet, but the whispers I heard today were that it could happen." He shrugged. "There is also more talk of unrest at the mills, and Father expects it to get worse before it gets better. So, I could be sent in that direction as well – which is what Mother prefers." He smiled wryly. "She has made her preference known to Father, of course."

"You do not know?"

Richard shook his head in response to his cousin's inquiry. "Not at present." He drew in a deep breath and blew it out slowly through his nose. "You'll have to see to the betterment of Miss Lydia without me."

"I shall do my best," Darcy assured him. "And Bingley can help me once we return to Netherfield."

"I will stand at your side and say yay and nay as instructed," said Bingley. "But I fear I am not the best at directing young ladies. You have met my youngest sister, have you not?"

All three of them chuckled at the thought. Caroline Bingley followed her own path without anyone diverting her from her desired purpose. Well, Darcy amended, that is she had always proceeded in such a fashion until recently.

"Perhaps we should have Sir Matthew join our efforts," Darcy suggested.

Bingley shook his head. "He is busy enough directing my sister. I should not like to tax him with anything else after he has so graciously taken her off my hands." He shook his head again but this time with an air of bewilderment. "Have I told you that Hurst claims she seems happy?"

"So soon?" asked Richard. "The man works quickly."

"It seems he does," said Bingley as he nodded his head. "She has been humming as she works on her stitching, and Hurst has seen her smiling for no reason and looking out the window for moments at a time."

"You must be pleased," said Darcy. He knew that his friend had always hoped that both of his sisters would be happily matched.

"I am."

The room fell into silence for a few moments.

"I spoke to Father about the possibility of resigning my commission."

Darcy's brows rose. Richard had always claimed he would be a military man until he died. He even scoffed at men who had retired from their positions earlier than age and mobility required.

"Might I inquire about why you are considering such a thing?" Darcy asked.

Richard shrugged and again expelled a great breath through his nose. "You may as well. Father did."

"And?" Darcy prodded.

"Georgiana will be out next year. You will be married, and who knows if you will be able to see to her as you ought."

"I am certain I shall be able to care for both her and my wife."

"There is no need to be affronted," Richard said with a smile. "What if your wife is pregnant with your heir? It is possible."

Darcy rubbed the back of his neck. He had not thought about that scenario. The left side of his lips tipped up in a half smile. It was not that he had not thought about his wife being pregnant. No, he had considered that aspect of marrying. He had just never considered that it might interfere with Georgiana's season.

"Your mother could see to her," Darcy argued.

"Mother?" Richard shook his head. "She would have her married off within a fortnight."

Darcy laughed. "She would not. But I do understand your meaning. She does like to make matches."

"Which is why I should be on home soil to stand next to Georgiana when needed."

"There is no other reason?" Darcy asked.

"None," Richard said.

However, Darcy noted that his cousin's eyes did not lift from their study of the tips of the boots on his out-stretched feet and there was a slight reddening of Richard's ears. Both were signs that Richard was not being straightforward.

"You'll likely need help with one or another of the Bennet sisters as well," Richard added.

Ah, now to Darcy, that sounded as if they were getting closer to the heart of the matter.

"Their mother will wish for them to be presented at some point, and it will not do for them to cause a stir. Your wife and Mrs. Bingley will be in the process of adjusting to their new environment. I would not wish for either of them to be censured for one of their sisters."

"That would be unfortunate," Darcy agreed. It was not completely unlikely that such an event could happen, but he highly doubted that it was the reason Richard truly wished to help with the younger Bennet's presentation to London society.

"And they will be relations of Georgiana's, so we must consider the impact of such a thing on her as well."

And they were very neatly and safely back to Georgiana. Darcy smiled. "I do hope your father discovers a way for you to keep your uniform and still be able to squire around Georgiana and the Miss Bennets, for I am certain at least one of the Miss Bennets would be more inclined to listen to you when you are in uniform than if you were not."

Bingley laughed. "Indeed. Her red ribbon would be for naught if there were not a uniform at her side to compliment it."

"The ribbon is to match her dress," Richard argued. "She did not buy it to match my uniform."

"If you say so," said Bingley rising from his chair. "Shall

we return to the drawing room to await the ladies and our dinner?"

Darcy motioned toward the door.

"She did not buy it for me," Richard said once again.

"No?" Bingley replied. "Then why does she require your opinion and not mine?"

"Because I have better taste," said Richard.

Darcy shook his head and followed his cousin and friend from the room. He would have to take note of how Miss Lydia and Richard interacted tonight if he could keep his eyes off Elizabeth long enough to do so.

# Chapter 20

In the drawing room, tables were being arranged for a game of cards. Lydia was directing the proceeding, but only with the approval of the colonel. Had Richard not picked Lydia's choice of ribbon, his consent might not be so eagerly sought after now. However, he had chosen Lydia's ribbon, and now found himself deferred to on most things since he obviously had *exquisitely good taste*. Darcy chuckled and ducked into the hallway, having seen Elizabeth leave just a moment earlier.

"Are you on your way to see your father?" Darcy asked, bounding up the stairs two at a time and leaving Bingley and Richard to tend to the ladies in the drawing room without him. He had something more important to do than to play cards, and that something involved the lady who was slipping away from her sisters and was alone on the stairs.

Elizabeth halted her ascent and waited for him to join her. "I am. I only wished to see if he needed anything. We have been gone from him so much today. I cannot imagine how excessively tiring it must be to lie in one's bed and look at the same ceiling and walls for days."

"I would think it is rather boring." Darcy offered her his arm. "Are you planning to return to the drawing room after you have seen him."

Elizabeth sighed. "I am not certain I wish to hear my sisters argue over yet another thing." She smiled sheepishly. "You appear to be weathering their visit far better than I."

"I do not know them so well as you. If I did, perhaps I would find the end of my patience more quickly, but as it is, my store of vexation is rather empty compared with yours." The comment elicited a light, musical laugh of pleasure from Elizabeth. "I was hoping we could find a moment this evening to continue our discussion from earlier today."

"About shopping?"

Her question was said softly, but she did not turn away from his gaze as they stood at the top of the staircase. The welcome he saw in those lovely eyes buoyed his heart even further than her visit to his study had earlier today.

"I believe it was *more* than shopping we were to discuss." Much more. Infinitely more important than shopping. His future happiness was to be determined with this discussion.

She looked to her right and then her left. "There is no one in the hall. We could walk and talk, could we not?"

"We managed it at the Johnson's ball," he replied with a

nod of his head toward his right before he started walking that direction with her on his arm.

"Indeed, we did – for a time."

He glanced at her. An impertinent smile graced her face just as the tone of her voice had indicated it did. He knew to what she was referring. At the Johnson's ball, they had only walked to the end of the hall, but that walk and the several minutes they spent standing at the far end of that hallway had been most pleasurable.

"This hall has an end just as the one at the ball," he replied with a smile of his own.

"Oh, so it does!"

Darcy chuckled. He did enjoy her teasing nature. It was so light and urged him to leave behind the heaviness of his more naturally austere temperament. She balanced him in that way, which was likely why he felt so steady in her presence. It was not that he was a wavering sort of fellow — he most certainly was not — but he did often feel awkward and ill-at-ease. But not here. Not with her. Not any longer.

"Did you see any shops we should visit?" he began.

She nodded. "I did. There are several that simply intrigue me too much never to explore them — not that I wish to purchase anything in them," she added hurriedly.

"You may if you wish," he replied. "That is if there are things within the shops that you would like."

"It is fortunate I am not my mother," she said with a

laugh, "or a great number of things – necessary or not – would be added to your account."

He chuckled. "Your father mentioned that your mother likes to shop. Richard's mother is the same."

"And your mother? Did she like to shop?"

"She did. However, she was more cautious with her expenditures than my aunt is. In our family, it was my father who spent more lavishly than my mother."

"Then, you got your cautious nature from her?"

"A great part of it," he replied with a nod. "My father was so sure of himself. He was a bit like Richard in that regard, although I think Richard is more miserly. Not that my father was not a careful manager. He was wise in his decisions, most times."

There had been a few decisions made regarding Wickham which were perhaps more heart than head, but for the most part, his father had been sensible in his thinking.

"Then you have received your wisdom from him?"

Darcy shrugged. "Perhaps."

"Your sister is lovely," Elizabeth said softly. "Someone is responsible for that, and I do not think it is all your parents' doing."

He blew out a breath and looked toward the ceiling. "How do you know she is the reason I doubt my ability?"

It was so unusual to find anyone who understood him even when he explained himself. Bingley still struggled at times to comprehend how Darcy thought about some things. Yet, Elizabeth seemed to have an innate ability to reason out things about his character that were often misunderstood. At least, she seemed to possess that skill tonight even if a few weeks ago her understanding had been clouded by his poor behaviour.

"Because I would feel the same," Elizabeth replied. "Even if it were not my fault that one of my sisters was placed in harm's way, I would feel as if I should have known, as if I should have seen the danger before it was present." She shrugged. "I imagine that is how many people feel about the ones they love."

He nodded and pulled her just a tiny bit closer to his side as they stood at the end of the hall, looking back in the direction they had come. "I love you – so very much," he said softly, "and I would feel even more doubtful of my abilities if I could not protect you from harm."

Elizabeth squeezed his arm and gave him a wavering smile when he looked down at her. "I would feel the same about you."

"You would?" His heart skipped a beat.

She nodded.

"Why?"

"I imagine," her smile turned slightly teasing, "that is how a lady feels about the gentleman she loves."

"You love me?" Oh, he knew he was smiling in a very stupidly broad fashion, but it could not be helped. The one thing for which he had longed for since November had come true. She loved him. And when something as wonderful as that occurs, one does not refrain from showing his pleasure.

"So very much," she replied.

He turned and took her hands in his. "Will you marry me?"

She nodded, her own smile growing with each bob of her head. "I will. Most happily."

He dropped her hands and wrapped his arms around her. "You have made me the happiest of men," he murmured as he held her to his heart.

Her arms wound their way around his waist. The sigh she expelled was a sound that matched the contentment which settled into his soul as he held her – his Elizabeth.

After a few moments, he released her but just barely, holding her in place with one arm.

"May I kiss you?" he asked as he cupped her cheek with his free hand.

Her cheeks glowed a lovely rosy colour as she formed the word "yes" with lips which he claimed before they had finished speaking.

# Chapter 21

"Do you still wish to go see your father?" Darcy asked Elizabeth sometime later as she stood wrapped in his arms.

"I do." She did not want to leave where she was, but she also knew that the longer she stood here, the greater chance there was of someone discovering them and their wonderful news. And that news was something that she did not wish to share with anyone just yet. She wanted to keep this quiet, special moment to herself for just a while longer.

"May I accompany you?" He looked down at her. "He will be happy to know our news."

The smile that greeted her as she looked up at him was the sort that made her heart skip a beat. His face seemed to mirror her own feelings, for he looked completely, perfectly, thoroughly happy, and it was unspeakably wonderful to know that she was the cause of his joy just as he was of hers.

"Only him," she said softly. "I would like for this to be our secret for tonight if possible."

He chuckled. "I cannot promise that I will not give away something of it. Richard and Bingley will know, and I must tell them."

She understood that feeling as well. "And I must tell Jane and Papa, but if Mama and my other sisters could learn about it in the morning..."

"If your father is amenable," Darcy replied.

Then, sadly, he released her and, winding her arm around his, led her to her father's room.

"How do I look?" she whispered before he opened the door. Would her father be able to tell she had been kissing and embracing Mr. Darcy?

"You are blushing, but you look lovely." He shook his head as if he understood her thoughts. "Your father will suspect we have sealed our promise with a kiss, for that is how these things often happen. However, you do not look as if you were being improper." He lowered his voice just a touch further. "It is not improper to kiss your betrothed," he added.

That last comment did nothing to cool her cheeks, but the thought of being able to kiss him again did cause her smile to grow. Oh, how she loved him. She squeezed his arm tightly, and he bent to kiss her lips quickly.

"Ready?" he asked as he turned the handle to open the door.

She nodded as she blew out a breath. Happy anxiousness fluttered in her belly.

"Ah, my Lizzy and Mr. Darcy," Mr. Bennet greeted. "I was hoping for a bit of distraction this evening, but knowing Mr. Bingley is here, I thought I might not be so fortunate."

"We could not leave you alone all evening," Mr. Darcy said as he pulled a chair close to where Elizabeth had taken a seat next to the bed. "Although I must admit it was Elizabeth's idea, I was happy to join her."

"Elizabeth is it?" Mr. Bennet asked with a chuckle.

"Yes," Darcy replied.

"Then you have happy news for me?"

"Only if you can keep a secret from Mama until tomorrow," Elizabeth said.

"I kept our trip to London a surprise until we were nearly gone," he replied. "Are you betrothed?"

"Yes, if you will allow it," Elizabeth replied.

"I would not like to be the one to explain my refusal to your mother! She has taken as strong a liking to your Mr. Darcy as she held a disliking for him after the assembly."

Darcy shook his head. "A foolish, ill-thought-out comment, and utterly untrue."

"Yes, that would be how my wife would describe it," Mr. Bennet agreed with a chuckle. "However, she would not say it so concisely. I do believe she went on about it for a quarter hour upon her arrival home from the assembly and that was not the only time I heard it. But," he scooted up a bit in his bed and grimaced as he pulled his leg along, "that is the past. I am pleased to give you both my blessing. Though I do not like the thought of losing my Lizzy, I know that there is no better gentleman to whom I would see her tied."

"Thank you," Darcy mumbled.

Elizabeth smiled at his apparent embarrassment in being praised. "In this, my father, I do believe you are perfectly correct, for I can think of no gentleman better suited to me," she bit her lip and ducked her head, "or that I could love half as well as I do Mr. Darcy."

"It does my old heart good to hear it, my dear, for you know that your mother and I would do anything to see you girls happy and loved."

"I know," Elizabeth replied. "Now, how can we entertain you?"

"You have guests," her father cautioned.

"We will return to them in a few minutes," Darcy assured him. "For now, we would like to be of service to you."

"A game of chess then?" he asked.

Darcy willingly obliged and arranged the chessboard. "I have suffered defeat enough today. Perhaps Elizabeth would like a turn."

Mr. Bennet chuckled. "What say you, Elizabeth? Shall we play as we talk about weddings and such?" He held up a finger. "But no lace, I will not speak of lace."

Elizabeth laughed. "Mama did find a lovely piece of lace for me today."

"I know," her father said with a pointed look. "I heard all about the lace, the slippers, the gloves." He shook his head.

"And Mrs. Salter?" Elizabeth asked quietly.

His brows drew together. Apparently, her mother had not mentioned that part of their trip to her father.

"Who is Mrs. Salter?"

Elizabeth tipped her head. "Maybe I am not supposed to tell you."

"My curiosity is not going to be satisfied until you tell me more."

That was something Elizabeth had in common with her father. They were both curious creatures.

"Mama said that her name was Miss Foster before she married."

Her father's eyes grew wide. "Miss Foster, you say?"

Elizabeth nodded.

"Well, that could not have been pleasant. Miss Foster was always disagreeable." He shook his head. "Excessively disagreeable. Especially when she did not get what she wanted." He looked at Darcy. "Far worse than Miss Bingley. Miss Bingley appears to have some redeeming qualities should she be directed properly. Miss Foster was not so fortunate." He motioned for Elizabeth to begin playing.

"She was cunning." Again, he shook his head. "What did Miss Foster have to say? And there is no need to tell me of her greeting and such. I just want to know how she attempted to disparage your mother."

Elizabeth sighed. "Will Mama be angry that I have told you?"

He shook his head. "She will tell me later." He smiled softly at Elizabeth. "After she has had time to put her shame and hurt away."

Unexpectedly, Elizabeth felt tears gather in her eyes which caused her to blink. Her father was so understanding of her mother. It was not something that was always displayed, but it did appear now and again. To hear him speak so softly now when her understanding of love for another was greater than it had ever been, she could hear that same love she felt for Mr. Darcy in her father's words.

"She has two sons and one daughter," Elizabeth began.

Her father sighed. "And your mother has five daughters."

It was stated as fact, but there was a small amount of pain in his voice as he spoke. Again, Elizabeth was struck by the love he held for her mother.

"She mentioned that and hoped that your estate was not entailed."

Mr. Bennet looked at Mr. Darcy. "The lady is from Hertfordshire and knows full well that Longbourn is entailed."

Darcy shook his head. "Some ladies can be vicious."

"Miss Foster – what did you say her name is now, Lizzy?"

"Mrs. Salter," Elizabeth replied.

"Mrs. Salter is among the champions of such ladies," he continued speaking to Darcy. "Did she say much else?" he asked, turning back to his daughter.

Elizabeth bit her lip.

Her father groaned. "She mentioned something about an indiscretion."

Elizabeth nodded. "And Mama had Jane tell Mrs. Salter her birthday."

Mr. Bennet shook his head. "That woman! Was that the extent of it?"

"No, she began to say that Jane's birthday was not proof that an indiscretion had not occurred, but she did not complete the full thought, though anyone listening would know what it was. Speculating in such a way, she said, was not what well-bred people did. Mary agreed with her and pointed out that well-bred ladies prefer to gossip in private."

Mr. Bennet chuckled.

"And then Mama told Mrs. Salter exactly how each of us is like you in some way and ended by saying if the lady could not appreciate those qualities, such as Mary's quick tongue, then she could never have truly admired you."

A smile spread across his face. "Ah, that is my Fanny," he said softly.

The room fell into silence for a few moments as father and daughter took turns playing.

"Your mother had gone to visit a friend in town. Someone she had met from school. All was well and good until the young woman's grandmother arrived unannounced." He darted a look at Darcy. "She was a lady of quality who did not approve of the smallest tie to trade."

Darcy grimaced. "I know some who are like that."

"She turned Fanny out." He blew out a breath. "Fanny cannot tell left from right when travelling. She wandered for hours with her bag in her hand. It was fortunate that I had gone to this friend's home to call on Fanny, for upon hearing what had transpired, I was able to go in search of her." He sighed. "I found her and took her back to my apartment since it was very late, and Gardiner was not expecting her. He was not yet fully his own man in business, you see. It was perhaps a foolish thing for me to have done, but I needed to see her safe."

"And that was the indiscretion?" Elizabeth asked quietly.

He nodded. "There was no indiscretion aside from your mother being alone with me in my apartment, but Miss Foster heard of Fanny's expulsion into the streets and discovered the remaining details to which she added several of her own concoction. Fanny's father demanded that we marry within three weeks, for he could not imagine there had been no true indiscretion. His daughter was beautiful, and he himself was not above flirting with a pretty lady even though he was married." Her father's voice was harsh. "Just because a lady is the most beautiful woman you have ever beheld, does not mean..." His words trailed off as he shook his head.

"It is called self-control," Darcy said firmly, "and respect for the lady you love."

"Precisely!" Mr. Bennet said with some force. "I knew I liked you for a reason," he added with a chuckle.

"Check," Elizabeth said.

"Well, Mr. Darcy, it appears I can be beaten. You shall just have to ask me to share a somewhat troubling tale the next time we play." He laughed and forfeited his king. "Will you send your mother to me when you go below?"

"You will not tell her?" Elizabeth asked.

"Not a word, my dear, but I do need to remind her that she is the one my heart chose."

Again, Elizabeth blinked at sudden tears. Then, rising, she gave her father's cheek a kiss before following Darcy from the room.

# Chapter 22

Later that evening, after Georgiana, Lydia, and Kitty had retired to Georgiana's room to play with Dash and discuss dresses and hats, and who knew what else, while Elizabeth and Jane had gone to visit their father once more before bed, Darcy sat in one of the corners of the drawing room with a snifter of brandy at his side and a book that he had no desire to read on his lap. Bingley had left some time ago, and Richard, who had seen the younger ladies and Dash to their room, was just returning to join Darcy.

"She said yes," Darcy said before Richard could even take his seat.

"You offered?"

Darcy nodded. "I did." A smile spread across his face as he considered his good fortune. "And she accepted. However, she does not wish for her mother to know until tomorrow. She wished to tell Miss Bennet first."

"Betrothed." There was a hint of awe in Richard's voice as he said the word. "I knew it would happen, but..." He shook his head. "Betrothed. Mother and Father will be pleased to know that there will finally be a Mrs. Darcy."

"I hope they are." Darcy knew that Elizabeth was not exactly the sort of lady whom Lady Matlock would have chosen for Darcy to court and marry. Elizabeth was nothing like the ladies to whom his aunt had introduced him. Though she lacked the standing in society which those ladies held, Elizabeth was far superior to any of them.

"They will be," Richard assured him. "Hopefully, Mother will then give up her notion that I need a wife." He tipped his glass and watched the contents sway with the action.

"You do eventually need a wife," Darcy replied. "I had almost begun to think you were considering the need now." He took a sip from his glass as Richard glanced at him. "You were talking about giving up your commission, and I thought perhaps there was more of a reason than just seeing Georgiana through her season."

Richard shook his head.

"No other reason?" Darcy pressed.

Again, Richard shook his head — more firmly this time. "I cannot consider such things until I am no longer married to my commission, and things are so uncertain..." his voice trailed off as if he were actually thinking about some lady and how such uncertainty would affect her.

"She is young."

Richard's head snapped up from his contemplation of the glass in his hand.

"Miss Lydia." Darcy waited for Richard to say something, but he did not, which spoke far more loudly than any protest would have about where Richard's thoughts and heart lay. "Would your mother approve?"

Richard placed his glass on a table and rose. "No. I do not think she would. She has aspirations for her children..." He ran a hand through his hair.

"She will be the sister of my wife."

Richard pulled in a deep breath as he nodded. "She is not at all what Mother would expect. She is not even the sort of lady I would have expected to capture my interest." He shook his head. "It is mere infatuation, nothing more. I will return to my unit. She will return to her home, and all will be as it should be."

Darcy raised a brow but said nothing.

"It will be," Richard repeated, "eventually."

It was Darcy's turn to shake his head. "I hope you are correct, for if you are not, the pain of separation I suffered after leaving Netherfield is not something I would wish on anyone, let alone you. You are my cousin and Georgiana's guardian. I would see you happy even if it were to cause a rift in our family. And, as my wife's sister, I would see that Mis Lydia was settled appropriately into a marriage. I know her father can only provide so much."

Richard shook his head. "I could not accept such charity."

Darcy smiled. "I know, that is why I will give it to her as a gift through her father."

Richard chuckled and rolled his eyes. "I had forgotten you have delved into your scheming nature, but we speak of things that will likely never be."

Darcy shrugged. He had attempted the same sort of arguments with himself before he left Netherfield, and he knew that Richard was no less stubborn than he himself was. Therefore, there was little use in debating the point with the man. He watched as his cousin took two more turns of the room before sitting down. "Not a word of this conversation leaves this room."

"Not a word."

"No matter how Bingley might taunt."

"Not a word," Darcy repeated.

"And no compromises."

Darcy laughed. "None. Unless one becomes necessary."

"She is lively and pretty," Richard muttered before slipping into silent contemplation of his glass once more. "Charming," he said breaking the silence. "She is charming."

"And in want of instruction?" Darcy asked.

Richard nodded. "There is that." He chuckled. "I shudder to think what she might say or do in the presence of my mother's friends. And that is yet another reason why this is not a good idea."

Again, Darcy was reminded of his own arguments against accepting his growing admiration for Elizabeth when he was in Hertfordshire. He had not feared her behaviour causing any raised brows, but he had feared the actions of her family would.

"I like them," he said aloud.

"You like whom?" Richard asked in surprise.

"The Bennets. I had thought I would not. I thought I would merely learn to tolerate them, but the more I know of them, the more I like them."

"Indeed? How so?"

"Mr. Bennet is indulgent, but he loves his family greatly. He knows his faults in that regard and admits them willingly. Only a man of true character would do so. And he is sharp. Such a keen mind!"

"But would not a man of character also take action to amend his ways."

Darcy had considered that very thing. "He may take action once his leg heals."

"And if not?"

That was a good question, and Darcy weighed it carefully. "Perhaps I could lend some aide? Just as you are with Miss Lydia?" He shook his head. "They have been exposed to a limited amount of good society here with you and Georgiana, and they have responded well to the setting.

Granted it has only been a short time, and the setting is new, but if they were to experience society here in town…"

Richard nodded. "It could work. Mrs. Bingley and Mrs. Darcy could see that their sisters were given appropriate instruction and opportunity to be part of a finer society."

"They are not as horrid as I had first thought." Darcy's mouth tipped up on one side. "But then, I was not in any mood to be pleased when I was in Hertfordshire."

Richard chuckled as Darcy knew he would, for Richard had heard Darcy's grumblings about leaving home and spending an extended amount of time with Miss Bingley in the country – country where he knew no one but his host.

"That covers the father and the younger Bennets, but what of their mother?"

Darcy blew out a great breath. "She is not astute, but I believe her heart is good. Do you not remember how she responded to learning about Wickham?"

"That was impressive."

"She wishes to see her daughters avoid the trials she has endured."

Richard's brows drew together in question.

"I cannot say more than that. It would be wrong, but suffice it to say, Miss Bingley is not the only devious woman with whom Mrs. Bennet has been acquainted. In fact, Miss Bingley seems not so bad after hearing the tale Mr. Bennet shared with Elizabeth and me." He shook his head again. "She was a tradesman's daughter who became a gentleman's wife."

The comment was met with an understanding nod from Richard. They both knew how some could, and did, treat those whom they imagined to be their inferiors.

"Aunt Catherine will not be pleased," Richard said.

"Indeed, she will not be."

Their aunt was one who enjoyed feeling superior to all around her. She was the daughter of an earl and the wife of a baronet. Those two facts entitled her, in her mind, to a great deal of deference.

Richard drained the last of the liquid from his glass and rose. "You are getting married."

"I am." The joy that such a thing brought to Darcy's heart and mind was overwhelming. Elizabeth would be his Mrs. Darcy.

"Come along, old man." Richard motioned toward the door. "You and Mrs. Bennet have an exciting day ahead of you tomorrow. You'll need your sleep."

"I am not old," Darcy said as he rose to follow Richard while he hoped, that in his happy state, he would be able to sleep.

"Married, old, are they not one and the same?" Richard teased.

"No," Darcy said as they entered the hall. "They are not the same."

# Chapter 23

Elizabeth lay awake for some time after she and Jane had discussed, at length, their good fortunes in securing the affections of men such as Mr. Darcy and Mr. Bingley. Jane was now breathing softly and evenly next to her, but for Elizabeth, the excitement she felt when she thought of this room being just one of the guest rooms in her home would not allow her to relax enough to join her sister in sleep.

She sighed and closed her eyes.

Mrs. Darcy. It would be a wonderful name to wear, for with it came the love of Mr. Darcy. She pressed her fingers to her lips as she recalled his kisses and wrapped her arms around herself as she imagined being held in his embrace. Why had no one ever told her how lovely such things were? It was likely because once one knew...

Her thoughts trailed off as she heard something in the hall in front of her door.

She sat up in bed and listened.

Yes, there. That was a door, and if she was not mistaken, it was the one directly across the hall. Was her mother or one of her sisters unwell? She put on her slippers and robe before sneaking quietly into the corridor.

"Lydia," she called in a whisper to the disappearing form of her youngest sister. "Lydia," she called again as she hurried toward the staircase. "Where are you going?"

Lydia looked back at her sister and held a finger to her lip, indicating that Elizabeth should be quiet. However, there was no way Elizabeth was going to remain silent when her sister was sneaking around Darcy House in the middle of the night.

Elizabeth scampered down the stairs after Lydia. "Lydia!" she called in a louder whisper as Lydia moved toward the front door. Where was she going and at this hour?

"I will only be a minute," Lydia called back.

She turned into the sitting room, and Elizabeth sighed in relief. Lydia must have left something in there.

"Lydia, you frightened..." Elizabeth did not finish the sentence as she took in the aspect of an empty sitting room with an open window.

"Lydia?" Elizabeth called through the window before exiting the house herself in hopes of finding her sister — which she did. However, Lydia was not just outside the window; she was running down the street. Elizabeth chased after her, turning the corner just after her sister had, but stopped short the sight before her.

"Lydia!" Elizabeth's heart leapt to her throat as a gentleman extended his hand from a carriage, and Lydia climbed in.

"Are you coming, too?" Lydia asked, poking her head out of the still open door.

"I am not getting into a carriage in the middle of the night dressed as I am, and you are getting out."

"Oh, I will get out in just a moment. I only need to give my reply, and then we can return home," Lydia assured her. "But you do not want to stand on the street in the damp night air, do you?" She put her hand out to her sister.

"You must get out," Elizabeth demanded.

"I cannot. Not just yet," Lydia replied.

Elizabeth sighed and accepted Lydia's help into the carriage. As foolish as she knew it was to enter that vehicle, there was no way she was going to let her sister sit in there with some gentleman unchaperoned. Why what if the man drove off with Lydia still in the carriage? She would never forgive herself for not having attempted to see to Lydia's safety.

"It is good to see you," the gentleman occupant of the carriage said as Elizabeth settled into her place next to Lydia.

"Mr. Wickham?" Her shock was so great at seeing him that had a cat batted at her as it did a length of yarn, it surely would have knocked her over.

"At your service," he pulled the door closed and tapped the roof of the vehicle.

"Where are we going?" Elizabeth demanded.

"Scotland," Wickham replied.

Elizabeth clutched the top of her robe at her throat. "Scotland?" she squeaked, her eyes darting from her sister to Wickham in the dim light from the exterior lanterns that filtered through the windows.

"No, we are not going to Scotland," Lydia replied. "That is what I have come to tell Wickham. We had intended to run away and marry. I thought it would be a great lark. However, I have changed my mind."

"What do you mean, you have changed your mind, my dear?"

Wickham's tone did not sound pleased to Elizabeth, and she sent a silent prayer heavenward that Providence would keep them safe.

"I do not love you."

"One does not need to be in love to marry," Wickham argued.

"But I should like to be, and while I do not love you, I think I might love another. And that would make being married very awkward, do you not agree?"

Elizabeth sucked in a breath. Lydia thought she was in love with Colonel Fitzwilliam?

"Has Darcy turned your head?" Wickham asked with a

laugh. "He is rather old and dour for a pretty young thing such as you."

"Oh, no!" Lydia swatted Wickham's knee. "But he is not so terrible as you said. He has been very kind, although that might be because he is in love with my sister."

Wickham threw back his head and laughed heartily. "I suspected as much when I met him in Hertfordshire."

"You did?" Elizabeth pressed her lips together. She should not have said anything.

"You are surprised to know that I knew of his admiration for you, but you have yet to protest that admiration."

"Only because she is as in love with him as he is with her," Lydia explained, much to Elizabeth's dismay.

"Indeed?" An unpleasant smile crept across Wickham's face.

"But Mr. Darcy is not half so gallant as his cousin," Lydia added dreamily.

Wickham's head whipped from his observation of Elizabeth toward Lydia. "Fitzwilliam?"

"Colonel Fitzwilliam," Lydia said with a sigh.

"He is even older and more unpleasant than Darcy," Wickham said.

"He is wonderful, and he is a colonel and the son of an earl."

"After his money, are you?"

Lydia shook her head. "No. He does not have all that much, but it should be adequate."

The carriage drove along silently for a time, making several turns, before Wickham tapped the top of the carriage signalling for it to stop.

"What are you doing?" Lydia asked as he opened the door.

"If you are not going to Scotland with me, then you should not be in this carriage."

"But we are not returned to Darcy House," Lydia protested. "I cannot just get out anywhere you choose."

"You can, and you will. Out!" He pointed toward the door. "I shall have you removed if you do not remove yourself."

Lydia gasped.

"Out!" he shouted inches away from her face.

"You are not nice," Lydia said with a flip of her head before poking Elizabeth in the side. "It seems we must walk home."

"I do hope you can find it," Wickham said with a sneer. "And I hope your colonel and his cousin will still accept you when it becomes known you were walking the streets late at night dressed as you are."

Elizabeth wrapped an arm around Lydia's shoulders.

"They will!" Lydia shouted at the carriage as the door closed. "They are gentlemen unlike you!"

She stamped her foot.

"Oh, of all the rotten things to do!"

"Shhh," Elizabeth said, trying to calm Lydia even as her

own heart and mind raced. "We do not need to attract undue attention." She was not exactly certain how one got to Scotland, but this did not look like it was the correct direction. She looked up and down the unfamiliar street. There was a light in a window not far down the road, and people seemed to be moving about at the door. Perhaps she could inquire as to where they were and from that find her way back to Mayfair.

"Do not tell anyone where we are staying," she hissed in Lydia's ear. "And do not use your name." This did not appear to be an affluent neighbourhood, and she feared what some of the people here might do if they thought she and Lydia had any money of their own.

"Then who shall I say I am if someone asks?"

"You are Grace — it is one of your names — Grace ... Gardiner — after Mama, and I am your sister Ann." Elizabeth's mind whirled as she concocted their story. "We are staying in Gracechurch Street. If we can get there, we can get home." How she longed to be safe inside Darcy House at this moment! "Our carriage broke down three streets back," she whispered. "But I do not know how to explain the way we are dressed. Why did you have to go out at night, Lydia?"

Lydia pursed her lips and glared at Elizabeth. "I am Grace."

Though Lydia's expression was defiant and her chin

lifted, Elizabeth could see the sheen of tears in her sister's eyes.

"I am sorry," Elizabeth replied. "I should not lecture at present."

"I did not think he would toss us out on the street."

Elizabeth could hear the trembling in her sister's voice. Those tears were likely to start falling at any moment.

"That is understandable." She rubbed her sister's arm soothingly while her own heart hammered in her chest. "All will be well," she murmured as comfortingly as she could. "All will be well." She only hoped her words were true.

# Chapter 24

Elizabeth and Lydia trudged a distance down the road before Lydia asked quietly, "Why would he do such a thing?"

Elizabeth could hear the hurt in Lydia's voice and responded gently, "Because, he is not what he appears. The stories he told about Mr. Darcy are lies, and, well..." She paused and pulled her sister closer as she considered how Darcy's sister Georgiana had been duped by Wickham. "I must know something, Lydia."

Her sister nodded.

"Was it your plan to elope or his?"

There was a long moment of silence during which Elizabeth thought perhaps her sister would not answer. However, she did.

"I am not entirely certain."

"What do you mean?"

"I joked with him and his friends once about how I would likely be the first of all five of us sisters to marry. I was only flirting. But then, one day sometime later, Wickham suggested that I could ensure that I was the first to marry if I were to marry him."

"Did he make you an offer of marriage?"

Lydia shook her head. "Not in so many words. It was more of a suggestion and not a request."

"When did this happen?"

"Oh, it was when I was telling him all about the ball at Netherfield. He was very sorry to have missed it and the chance to dance with both you and me and doubly sorry that you had been forced to dance with both Mr. Collins and Mr. Darcy. He laughed for some time about that actually." Her head ducked. "I did, too. It was not nice of me."

"I felt sorry for myself for having had to dance with them both," Elizabeth replied with a smile. "I had no idea just how wonderful Mr. Darcy was at that time."

"Nor did I," Lydia said with a small smile. "He is quite nice, is he not?"

Elizabeth squeezed her sister close and agreed before urging her to continue telling her about Wickham.

"Wickham was surprised at Mr. Darcy dancing with you at first. 'What?' he said, 'Old, high and mighty Fitzwilliam Darcy condescended to dance with someone not in his circle? That is rich,' and then he dissolved into peals of laughter. Then he said, 'Do you know what would be an even better joke than Darcy dancing?' Of course, I did not, and that is when he said we should run away and marry because that would truly be something about which to laugh."

"Marriage is not something about which one should jest." Elizabeth kept her voice soft but firm.

Lydia sighed and rubbed the corner of one eye. "I know that now."

"Do you?" Elizabeth demanded.

Lydia nodded as she wiped her eyes with the sleeve of her robe. "I did not know one could feel anything more than a thrill of being admired until I came to Darcy House."

"Are you saying you love the colonel?"

Lydia's shoulders lifted and lowered. "I think I love him. He... he cares for me." A small silly grin tipped the corners of her mouth. It was an expression Elizabeth recognized, for she often wore it when thinking of Mr. Darcy. Her youngest sister was well and truly besotted.

"And I wish to please him." Lydia shook her head, her smile fading. "And I do not just wish for his admiration of my hair or clothes or anything. I want him to think well of me." She brushed tears from her cheek and once again lifted and lowered her shoulders sadly. "He will not after this."

Elizabeth pulled her sister close. "That is not what you told Mr. Wickham."

"I say lots of things to Wickham that are not true."

They had reached the house with the light in the window, so though Elizabeth wished to know what sorts of lies Lydia told Mr. Wickham and why Lydia seemed to think it acceptable to do so, they could not continue their conversation.

"Pardon me," she said as she stepped around a man who had just exited the house.

"What have we here?" he asked. "You must be new."

His words slurred, and Elizabeth could smell some sort of alcohol on his breath when he leaned close to look at her. He was not old or dirty as she had expected someone from this part of town to be. In fact, the hat and coat he nearly wore – his hat was askew, and his coat was only on one arm while the other arm of the garment dangled behind him – were of an excellent quality as was the cravat which hung undone around his neck.

"Sally!" He called back toward the house. "Your new girls are here."

Elizabeth's eyes grew wide, and she swallowed as she shook her head. "We are not Sally's girls." She was not exactly certain who Sally's girls were, but she had her suspicions and knew that she did not want to be thought of as such.

"Aye, they are a pair of pretty doxies!" the man shouted toward the door.

"Might we just pass?" Elizabeth attempted once again to step around him. "Our carriage wheel broke, and we need to know where we are."

"You are at Sally's," the man said with a sweep of his hand toward the house that nearly toppled him.

"Might we just pass?" Elizabeth asked once again.

"Aye, but not without a kiss."

"I think not!" Elizabeth replied firmly, causing him to laugh and place a hand on her shoulder to keep from falling.

"How 'bout you?" His hand remained on Elizabeth's shoulder as he leaned toward Lydia.

"A shilling for one cheek and a half crown for both."

Both Lydia's reply and her boldness surprised Elizabeth.

"A shilling for a peck on the cheek?" the man exclaimed.

"Or a half crown for two," Lydia repeated.

"And if I do not wish for you to kiss my cheeks?"

"Then you must do without." Lydia batted her lashes and smiled as Elizabeth had seen her do on several occasions when Jacob Lucas was attempting to scheme his way out of doing something for Lydia and his sister, Maria. Elizabeth had to admit that when it came to getting what she wanted, Lydia was a proficient.

Lydia held out her hand. "A shilling for one, a half crown for two, or move aside so we might pass."

The man grumbled, dug around in the pocket of his coat once he had caught the flapping garment, and pushed a shilling in Lydia's hand.

Lydia wrapped her hand around the coin. "Which cheek?"

He turned his head to the right, exposing his left cheek. Lydia pinched his nose which caused him to shout.

"I must guarantee you are not going to attempt to steal more than that for which you have paid," she said before giving his cheek a peck and then releasing his nose.

As he was busy rubbing his nose, Lydia pushed Elizabeth to move around him.

"A shilling for a kiss?" Elizabeth whispered. "Proper young ladies do not charge for kisses, and they do not kiss strangers – or friends." She knocked on the door.

"We are rid of him, are we not?" Lydia demanded. "And we now have one shilling which is far more than what we had a moment ago," she added as she stepped into the house behind Elizabeth.

"Who might you be?" A fashionably dressed woman leaned on an ornately carved cane and gave them both an appraising look.

"I am Ann, and this is my sister Grace."

The woman nodded and waited.

"Gardiner," Elizabeth added. "Ann and Grace Gardiner."

The woman's mouth dropped open and then snapped closed. "Gardiner, you say?" Her eyes narrowed, and she took a step nearer Lydia. "I knew a Gardiner once," she murmured as she scrutinized Lydia. "She looked a lot like you. Her name was Fanny."

"Mama?" The word leaped from Lydia's lip.

"If your mama is Fanny Gardiner who has a brother named Edward who works somewhere in town – near Cheapside, if I recall correctly," the woman replied.

"Oh, it is her!" Lydia cried. "Uncle Gardiner lives in Gracechurch Street, and his name is Edward."

"Hmm," the lady said with a chuckle, "Fanny Gardiner's girls." She shook her head. "Gardiner," she repeated tipping her head. "You say your family name is Gardiner? I had thought she would marry that handsome young man who came in here all a fluster to get her. Bennet was his name."

"Papa?" Lydia's eyes were wide.

The lady chuckled. "Gardiner, is it?" she asked Elizabeth. "Or is it Bennet?" She shook her head. "You do not need to tell me. I understand it might be best if your true names are not known in an establishment such as mine." She waved to a door on the right. "Come. You can sit in my apartment and tell me your tale of woe over a cup of moderately good tea."

She led the way, and Lydia and Elizabeth had no choice but to follow or be left in the entry way where that gentleman from outside might find them again.

"I am very good – excessively good – at keeping secrets," she said with a pointed look for them both before she allowed them to enter her private domain.

# Chapter 25

"Fitzwilliam?"

Darcy rubbed his eyes and squinted through the darkness toward the door to his room. Had he heard his name amid the knocking?

"Fitzwilliam?"

There it was again.

"Please, open the door."

Hurriedly, Darcy donned his robe and padded over to open the door for his sister.

"Are you..." His question about her wellbeing died on his lips as he took in the aspect of tear stained cheeks on the young woman beside her. "Miss Kitty, what is wrong?"

"Lydia is gone. She was supposed to return an hour ago, but she has not?" These words were followed by sobs as Kitty buried her face in her hands.

Darcy nodded toward the chairs near his fire which was burning low and, leaving the door fully open, crossed to his night stand to light another candle. The one which

Georgiana carried was little more than a nub and did not give enough light for his liking.

"Has she told you what this is about?" He asked his sister as he returned to them and placed his candle on the table next to Georgiana's.

Georgiana lifted her chin in a very determined fashion and nodded. Darcy had seen her make that same expression before – usually when she was attempting not to cry. Something was seriously wrong.

"Miss Lydia went to meet someone."

"At night?" Darcy asked in surprise.

Georgiana nodded and swallowed. "Wickham," she whispered, tears glistening in her eyes.

"Wickham?" The question was expelled on a rush of air. Darcy gripped the arm of Georgiana's chair and knelt next to her. He sucked in a breath to replace the one which had been knocked out of him by his sister's revelation.

Georgiana nodded. "Miss Kitty came to me when Miss Lydia did not return, and I suggested we come to you."

"You have not informed Mrs. Bennet or any of Miss Lydia's sisters?"

"No, Mama would be so distressed," Kitty managed to say as she fought to keep from sobbing once again.

"What about Miss Bennet or Elizabeth?" Surely someone in the Bennet family must be told that Lydia was missing.

"I thought of that, but what can they do?" Georgiana

asked. "Mr. Bennet cannot go searching for Miss Lydia, nor can any of her sisters. At least, they cannot go unaccompanied."

"Mr. Darcy," Mr. Abram stood at Darcy's door.

"Yes."

The butler took one step into the room. His brow furrowed slightly as he took in the sight of the Georgiana and Kitty. "I have the unpleasant task of informing you, sir, that a window has been left open in the drawing room. We have conducted a thorough search of the lower levels and not a thing appears to be out of place."

Darcy sighed. "Miss Lydia is out of place. Please have my horse readied and send up my man as soon as is possible."

"Miss Lydia?" Abrams repeated. No amount of training could keep all the surprise and concern out of the Darcys' faithful servant's tone. "Shall I call for a horse for the colonel as well?"

Darcy nodded. "It would be best if I did not search alone." Richard had experience running wayward recruits aground, his assistance would be invaluable.

"Mr. Abrams," he called before his butler had done more than turn to leave.

"Yes, sir."

"Please, rouse the colonel and send him to me."

"Right away, sir."

Darcy turned back to his sister and Kitty and pushed the furry mass that rubbed against him away. "Not now Dash."

Dash poked him with his nose, then sniffed his way over first to Kitty and then to Georgiana before racing from the room.

"Did Miss Lydia tell you what she was going to do?" Darcy asked gently.

"She was supposed to meet Mr. Wickham and tell him that she did not wish to marry him."

"They were going to Scotland," Georgiana added in a whisper.

Darcy clutched her hand firmly. How difficult this must be for her having to remember her own folly and plan to run away with the cad.

"I am well," she whispered. "Truly. But Miss Lydia is in danger."

Kitty dissolved into tears once again at the statement.

"I told her some of what passed at Ramsgate when she came to me. By doing so, I assured her that you would know what to do and would not treat Lydia poorly for her foolishness."

"I will never say a word," Kitty said through her tears. "Just please find my sister."

"What do you need?" Richard rubbed his face as he entered Darcy's room. "Is someone unwell?" he asked when he saw who was with Darcy.

"Lydia is gone," Kitty wailed.

Richard stopped dead halfway between the door and the hearth. "What do you mean 'gone'?"

Dash raced into the room, a piece of paper hanging from his mouth. He sat down in front of Richard and dropped the paper.

"She went to meet someone," Darcy said as his cousin bent to pick up what Dash had delivered to him.

Richard blanched as he unfolded the paper. "Wick-ham?" he nearly shouted.

Kitty burst forth with fresh sobs while Darcy nodded and Georgiana attempted to comfort her friend.

"Scotland? They are going to Scotland?" Richard demanded.

"No," Darcy said, rising from next to his sister. Kitty would be well cared for by Georgiana, and, at the moment, his cousin looked as if he was in greater need of attention. "She went to tell him that she did not wish to marry him."

"She went to tell him that he was not getting what he wanted?" Richard sneered. "That never ends well with someone like Wickham."

"Have a care," Darcy scolded. "Miss Kitty is distressed enough. She does not need you to add to her worry." He grabbed Richard by the arm and pulled him into the hall. "I have sent for our horses, and as soon as we are dressed, we will begin a search."

"Where?" Richard demanded. "We do not know which road he took or if he tricked her into..." His jaw clenched, and he did not continue.

"I was hoping you might know where we could find him

in town. If we find where he was staying, then perhaps we can find out where he has gone or if he returned disappointed."

"He'll pay, and you'll not stop me," Richard's voice was low and dangerous.

"I will not see you hang," Darcy cautioned.

"I shall do my best to leave him living."

"Mr. Darcy," Jane said as she approached him. "Have you seen Elizabeth? Did she pass this way? She is not with our father."

Darcy's heart plummeted to his stomach.

"Do you still wish for him to live?" Richard asked quietly.

Darcy shook his head. "I wish for you to live," he replied.

"Do you know where Elizabeth is?" Jane asked.

Again, Darcy shook his head. "We will search the house, but..." He turned back toward his room. "Is it possible she might have heard Lydia and followed her?"

"What do you mean?"

Darcy had never heard quite so much emotion in Miss Bennet's voice.

"Miss Kitty has informed us that your youngest sister left some time ago to meet Wickham and tell him she did not wish to marry him."

Richard caught Jane by the elbow and, wrapping an arm

around her, held her upright. "We were just going to prepare to find Miss Lydia."

"Georgiana," Darcy called, "please take Miss Bennet and Miss Kitty to your sitting room." He turned to Jane. "I will inform your father of what is afoot before I leave. However, I will need to leave your mother to you. Are you able to care for her?"

Jane nodded.

"Allow me to assist you to Georgie's room," Richard offered.

"What is happening?" Mrs. Bennet stuck her head out of her door.

"Come with me, Mama," Jane said. "There is something I must tell you."

A wave of compassion swept over Darcy as he saw the concern in Mrs. Bennet's eyes.

"Is everyone well?" she asked, clutching her robe at the neck. "Kitty, why are you in Mr. Darcy's room?"

"Come, Mama," Jane repeated. "I will tell you, but not here."

Darcy placed a hand on Jane's arm. "I will return her daughters to her, and I will do my best to see they are unharmed."

Jane pressed trembling lips together and nodded her head. "I know you will," she whispered, "and I will tell her so."

# Chapter 26

Darcy and Richard saw that Jane, Kitty, Georgiana, and Mrs. Bennet were settled in Georgiana's sitting room before they began their preparations. Darcy began his with a brief, though difficult, visit to Mr. Bennet's room while Richard, followed by Dash, returned to his own room.

Richard was, of course, ready to leave before Darcy, and Darcy found him where he knew he would, pacing the front hall, while Dash raced up and down the stairs, along the corridor, and finally into the sitting room where he sat and barked at the window.

"See that he gets to Georgiana's room," Darcy said to Abrams as he joined Richard.

Richard shoved the note Dash had delivered to him at Darcy. "Look at the direction? That is not Wickham's hand. That looks feminine."

Darcy took note of the swooshes and swirls of the writing on the outside of the missive. It did indeed seem to have a feminine quality to it.

"It did not seem out of place," Abrams shuffled from one foot to the other nervously. "If I had known..."

"How could you?" Richard said. "For once, that idiot was clever." He shook his head.

Clever was seldom a word anyone used in conjunction with Wickham's name. However, this time, Darcy had to agree with Richard. This did appear to be a clever ploy. "When did it arrive?"

"This morning, sir."

Dash raced between them and up the stairs, a footman following close behind.

Darcy shook his head. That pup was a ball of energy even in the dead of night.

"Some tea or something slightly stronger might be needed by those above stairs." He put his hat on as he instructed Abrams.

"Of course, sir. We will see that they are well tended."

Darcy rested a hand on his butler's shoulder and nodded. It was a small sign of approval, but one that Abrams understood well. The staff at Darcy House were exceptional at their jobs, and Abrams was one of the reasons for that. The man knew how to lead without being overbearing. The Bennets and his sister would be in good hands while he and Richard were gone, and Darcy wished for his butler to know he knew that. The small smile and nod Darcy received in return let him know his message had been understood.

Richard stood impatiently holding the door open as he waited for Darcy. However, it was Dash who reached the door before Darcy did, planting himself in front of Richard and growling viciously at the footman when he reached for him.

Richard scowled down at the dog, but his reprimand died on his lips when he saw something dangling from Dash's mouth. "What do you have there, boy?" He stooped and took a red ribbon from Dash.

Dash did not remain where he was to reply or to allow Richard to even rise. Instead, as soon as the ribbon was in Richard's hand, Dash ran to the horses, standing at the head of Richard's horse and looking for all the world as if he were demanding the beast's full attention and obedience.

"I think he wishes to help," Richard said with a chuckle as Dash took his eyes off the horse to once again growl at the approaching footman before barking and running forward and then returning to stare down Richard's mount once again.

"Leave him be," Darcy said to the footman. "He will join us on our search."

Richard had swung up into his saddle. "Dash, up," he commanded, patting the front of his coat.

Dash trotted over, looked at the footman expectantly, and allowed the man to lift him up without so much as a whimper, let alone a growl.

"He's very much like Miss Lydia," Richard said as he scratched the dog's ear once he was settled in front of him. "Determined to have his way and compliant once he gets it."

Darcy sighed. "And causing trouble without meaning to do so."

Richard nodded, and the two gentlemen began riding. "We never gave her reason to doubt Wickham was anything more than what he presented."

"We had no reason to tell her anything," Darcy replied. "Where to?" He was confident that Richard had a plan in mind. His cousin would not be so calm as he was now if he did not already know where they were going to begin their search.

"Mrs. Younge's boarding house. If anyone knows where he is, she does. I would bet you a month's wages that she is the one who addressed that letter, but I am not the gambling sort. I do not like to be parted from my money."

Darcy chuckled, and then the two men fell into silence as they road. Darcy knew that if Richard's thoughts were anything like his own, that month's salary, as well as all Richard had, would be given away without a second thought to have both Lydia and Elizabeth back at Darcy House, safe in bed.

Thoughts of Elizabeth being found unharmed as well as thoughts of seeing Wickham laid out on the floor filled Darcy's mind as he rode.

"Ahead on the left," Richard said.

Dash, who had been lying down, sat up, alert to whatever was coming.

"Good boy." Richard scratched the dog's ear. "Bite his leg, and I'll give you a tin full of biscuits."

Dash yipped his understanding as Richard dismounted and reached up to lift him down.

Darcy was already at the door, banging loudly.

"What's the meaning of this noise?" A man shouted from behind the door.

"Open the door," Darcy yelled in response.

"Why should I?"

Richard pushed Darcy to the side and threw his shoulder against the door. "We need to see Mrs. Younge about a scoundrel," he called.

"No need to break the door," the man called back. Locks rattled, and finally, the door opened. "My mistress is abed as are all her guests."

Richard forced his way inside the door, Dash scooting between him and the man who had opened the door. "Is there a guest named Wickham?"

"Yes, sir." The candle the man held trembled slightly as Richard towered over him. "At the top of the stairs."

"He is here?" Darcy asked.

The man nodded. "Only just. Was gone for some time, but he tends to come and go at odd hours."

"Is he alone?" Richard demanded as he moved to the stairs.

"Tonight, he is, and he seemed none too pleased to be so. Took a bottle of port with him to his room." The man placed his candle on the table near the door and fished out a ring of keys from the pocket of his robe, fiddling with them until he had one between his fingers. "My mistress won't want no broken doors." He handed the key to Darcy. "Is it about a sister or a wife? You wouldn't be the first to seek him for such."

"Both," Darcy replied before hurrying up the stairs after Richard. "Wait!" he whispered loudly, holding up the key.

Richard gave a nod of his head and stood aside but only long enough for Darcy to open the door. Then, he entered the room before Darcy but after Dash, who leapt onto the bed with a bark and a growl.

"What the devil?" Wickham cried as he sat up in bed. "Who let this beast into my room?"

"I did," Richard said, leaning close to Wickham.

"What? Who?"

Darcy struck a match and lit a candle.

Wickham's eyes grew wide. "Fitzwilliam?" They shifted to Darcy. "Darcy?"

"You're not in Scotland," Darcy said.

Wickham smirked. "No need. I got what I wanted."

The crack of knuckles against jaw was the reply that greeted his lie.

Wickham scrambled from his bed, placing the piece of furniture between him and Richard as he held his jaw. "She's sweet on you." He wiped blood from his lip with the back of his hand. "And you," he jutted his chin toward Darcy, "it seems, have actually managed to convince a lady to have you."

Darcy nodded. "Despite your lies."

"Where are they?" Richard shouted.

Dash leaned forward from the edge of the bed toward Wickham and growled to punctuate Richard's words.

"I have no idea."

Richard rounded the bed and grabbed Wickham by his nightshirt. "What do you mean you have no idea? Did they not meet with you? Were you not going to Scotland?"

Wickham laughed. "They met with me, but I had no intention of ever going to Scotland." His eyes narrowed as he looked around Richard to Darcy, who was at Richard's shoulder. "Never have had any plans to go to Scotland."

Darcy growled. Richard released Wickham and stood to the side, arms folded as Darcy expelled his displeasure on Wickham's person.

"Where are Elizabeth and her sister?" Darcy asked as he stood over Wickham. His fist throbbed, but it was a satisfying pain.

"I have no idea. I opened the door, and they got out of the carriage." He scooted back toward the wall. "Somewhere between here and the river. Closer to the river."

Richard crouched down. "You best pray we find them within the hour, or we will return." He rose. "We may come back anyway."

Darcy smirked. "Perhaps he should go to Scotland," he said to Richard.

"That might be a good idea," Richard replied, "although I would still hunt him down there if anything – and I do mean anything — untoward has happened to either of them. Dash. Come."

Dash looked at Richard, then lurched at Wickham and growled before following Richard and Darcy from the room.

"Thank you," Darcy said, handing the keys back to the man at the bottom of the stairs. "We may return if we do not find what we are seeking."

The man's head bobbed up and down rapidly. "I'll open on the first knock," he assured them as they left.

Darcy blew out a breath as he stood on the street, looking toward the river. "Between here and the river?"

Richard nodded. "Closer to the river."

"Wandering the streets," Darcy muttered. And frightened, but hopefully unharmed.

Richard wrapped the red ribbon from his pocket around his fingers and knelt next to Dash. "I don't know how good you are at hunting," he said, holding the ribbon out for Dash to sniff, "but I would sure appreciate some help finding Miss Lydia."

# Chapter 27

Elizabeth pulled Lydia toward a rose-coloured sofa in Sally's comfortable sitting room. A book lay open on a table next to a chair near the hearth. Its presence surprised Elizabeth. How did one relax with a book of poetry while drunken men entered and exited one's establishment? She smoothed her robe and made certain that it was done up as well as it could be as she took a seat.

Though the place where she found herself made her feel excessively uncomfortable, Elizabeth would not deny that the warmth radiating from the fire felt wonderful as it wrapped around her, chasing away the coldness of the night and restoring feeling to her nose and toes.

"My name is not actually Sally. Just like you, I have no desire for my guests to know my real name, for various reasons." With a dismissive wave of her hand at her final words, she took her seat. The discussion of identities, as well as Sally's ability to keep a secret, appeared to be at an end. "The tea will be here soon along with some clothes. I think we have a girl or two who are about your size."

"Clothes?" Lydia asked in surprise. "We do not need clothes."

Sally chuckled. "You cannot be delivered to your uncle's home in the middle of the night dressed as you are." She sighed. "I would just allow you to sleep here, but it would not do for you to be seen exiting my establishment in the morning. A young gentleman can afford such whispers but not young ladies. Therefore, the cover of darkness will be to our advantage. We will have tea and then one of my footmen will accompany you to your uncle's home."

The woman tipped her head and looked at Lydia. "You are the very image of your mother."

"You remember her?" Elizabeth asked.

Sally nodded. "I know it would seem nearly impossible for one to remember a lady twenty-some years after meeting her, especially since our meeting was not long in duration, and, well, I do meet a good number of young women." She rose as a tray with three cups of tea arrived, carried by a young maid in a perfectly modest and rather drab dress.

"Your mother," Sally continued as she passed a cup of tea to Lydia and then Elizabeth, "was in quite a state when I found her."

"You found her? Where did you find her?" Lydia asked over the rim of her cup.

Sally chuckled. "Very like your mother. So inquisitive," she muttered before continuing. "She was walking up and down the street. I saw her pass the window there." She pointed to the window that would face the street. "She passed three times before I rose and watched her turn a corner and disappear only to reappear in front of my window not half an hour later." She took a sip of her tea. "She was walking in circles." This comment was followed by another chuckle and a shake of Sally's head before she took a sip of tea.

"I brought her in here, fed her, and dried her tears. Oh, the tears! But it was understandable."

"Why was she crying?" Lydia had moved to the edge of the sofa and was resting her elbows on her knees and her chin on her hands. Her cup of tea had been abandoned to a side table as she had become absorbed in the story.

Lydia had always been easily entertained by a story when just a girl, which was likely why she found gossip so delightful now that she was older.

"She had been turned out of her friend's house because she was not a gentleman's daughter," Elizabeth supplied.

"You know the story then?" Sally asked.

"As much as Papa told me just the other day."

"Papa told you? When?" Lydia asked.

"Do you remember Mama meeting Mrs. Salter when we were shopping?" Elizabeth asked.

Lydia's brow furrowed. "I think I do."

"You were helping Miss – our friend," Elizabeth corrected, "make a selection at the counter."

Lydia nodded.

"Papa told me on that day when I told him how upset Mama was by the things Mrs. Salter said."

"What did she say?" Lydia demanded.

"She hinted that Mama and Papa only married because of Jane." She held Lydia's gaze until she saw the widening of Lydia's eyes as understanding dawned.

"Oh, no!" Lydia shook her head adamantly. "Not Mama. Or Papa!"

"Your mother was no lightskirt," Sally inserted. "She gave a couple of gentlemen a good tongue lashing when they attempted to sit too close or touch her when she was here. No one was allowed such liberties unless he had a marriage certificate in his hand and a fortune in the bank. That's what she said. That and that even with all the gold in England, they would have to be a great deal more handsome, noble, and kind than Mr. Bennet if they wished to succeed with her, and she knew, just knew, that such a thing was not possible." Sally chuckled again. "She was a delight, and I am pleased to meet her daughters. No matter what their names may or may not be." She winked.

"We have three sisters," Elizabeth said. "No brothers."

"Indeed? I take it that your mama and that handsome man who came to collect her married?"

Elizabeth nodded.

"Do not worry. I have never in all my years mentioned your mother's name until I saw you, and you said your name was Gardiner." She shrugged. "I wouldn't have brought you in here if I did not know she was your mother. My girls never enter this room. It is my sanctuary. A step away from the work I do." She shrugged again. "A lady without a gentleman or her own fortune must find her way somehow, and I dislike both cleaning and cooking. Service was not for me." She leaned back with her teacup cradled in her hands. "I know it is not a proper occupation and my reasons for its existence will not meet with the approval of fine young women such as yourselves, but this has been my life. I live well, and I see that my girls are safe – or as safe as can be."

Elizabeth nodded and sipped her tea. She really did not wish to know what Sally did for a living or how well she ran her establishment.

"Ah, gowns," Sally said, sitting forward as the maid once again entered. "Place them on my bed," she instructed.

"Do you ladies have handsome young men who might come bursting through my door ready to cut down anyone who might attempt to stand in their path?" Sally continued.

"Lizzy does." Lydia's eyes grew wide, and she clamped her lips closed.

"I am good at keeping secrets," Sally reassured her before turning expectantly to Elizabeth.

"I am betrothed."

"You are what?" Lydia nearly shouted.

"I was going to tell Mama in the morning," Elizabeth explained. "I wished to keep it a secret until then." She shrugged and smiled sheepishly at Lydia. "I just wished to enjoy the wonderfulness of being his for a night without anyone else, save Papa and Jane, knowing."

"No one else knows?" Lydia bounced in her seat.

"Perhaps his cousin," Elizabeth replied.

"Colonel Fitzwilliam?"

"Fitzwilliam?" Sally repeated. "My, my, Fanny Gardiner's daughters have some high connections."

Lydia's hand covered her mouth.

Sally chuckled. "I swear I will not say a word." She tipped her head. "A cousin?" She waggled her brows at Elizabeth. "I think I know of whom you speak, though I would never expect to see him darken my door. He's not the sort, or so I have heard." She placed her empty cup on the table next to her book.

"Now," she said rising, "we should see you into some more appropriate clothes for travel. We would not want your names bandied about as belonging to this establishment."

"There was a man out front who thought we were," Lydia said as she followed Sally.

It seemed Lydia had already accepted this woman they had just met as a friend. Lydia was like that. Elizabeth welcomed newcomers, but she held them at a distance until she could figure out their character. She shook her head – except when it was a handsome cad in a uniform telling her horrid tales about a gentleman she wished to hate.

"You said my Papa came here to get my Mama?"

Elizabeth chuckled. Of course, Lydia would wish to hear the rest of the tale.

Sally clasped the lovely green day dress she held to her chest. "Your mama saw your papa pass by the window and tripped over a footstool on her way to call to him through the window. I have never seen a lady so delighted to see a gentleman as she was." She passed the dress to Lydia. "And he was so gallant." She shook her head and sighed. "It is the kind of love story about which every young girl dreams – her prince coming to her rescue when she is in distress."

Lydia sighed. "Mama was very beautiful."

"Is," Elizabeth corrected. "Mama is very beautiful."

"Yes, but now she is married, and her beauty is not so important," Lydia replied.

Sally laughed. "You are the image of your mother. You may slip into this behind the screen. You can keep your nightgown on under it since you do not have a proper shift, but we will fold your robe and tie it up like a package. It's better to travel with a package and be a bit chilled than to wear the robe and have your reputation tarnished."

# Chapter 28

"Do we go up this one?" Darcy nodded toward Fish Street Hill. One street was beginning to blend into another as the men searched for Lydia and Elizabeth. A fear that they had already been found by someone unsavoury had settled into Darcy's heart.

Richard blew out a breath and shook his head. "I don't know. Do you see anyone on the street?" He scratched Dash's head.

Apparently, his cousin was also beginning to feel the hopelessness Darcy was attempting to keep at bay. He had to find Elizabeth. He could not lose her. He looked up the street, sitting still and listening while he watched for any sign of movement.

"No," Darcy answered after a moment of watching. "Then we stick to Thames?"

Dash's bark made it impossible to hear Richard's reply, and the creature's popping to attention took a quick hand from the colonel to keep the beast from falling from his perch on Richard's horse.

"What is it, boy?" Richard asked as he attempted to quiet Dash. "That carriage?" He nudged his horse forward. A carriage was moving down the road in front of them.

"It is worth a look," Darcy said as he drew up next to Richard. "I do not think they would have money for the fare, but at this moment, I am willing to look anywhere."

"As am I," Richard replied. "It's stopping at Sally's."

Darcy tipped his head. "Sally's?"

Richard shrugged. "One of the places my brother helps finance with his allowance."

"A brothel?" Darcy knew that the viscount was given to some vices, and Sally's did not appear to be a gambling hall or tavern.

Richard nodded. "The only one he visits."

One was more than any gentleman should visit in Darcy's opinion.

"It is likely just some drunken chap finding his way – No, those are not gentlemen." Richard urged his horse to go faster as Dash once again took to barking.

In the light of the lamp outside the house just two blocks away, Darcy could make out the forms of two ladies in front of Sally's house and being handed into the hackney by a footman while another lady stood at the door giving instructions.

"Lydia?" Richard shouted. "Elizabeth?"

The lady in the doorway waved and the ladies who had just boarded the carriage were removed from it.

It was them. It had to be them. Darcy expelled a breath as relief washed over him at the thought. His Elizabeth was safe. He did not reach the house before Richard, but Dash had only just been handed to Lydia who was exclaiming about being rescued just like her mother when Darcy arrived.

Darcy dismounted and dropping the reins of his horse, rushed to Elizabeth, enveloping her in his embrace. "I found you," he whispered to her hair, "I was afraid I would not."

Elizabeth held on to him tightly.

He pulled back just a little so that he could look at her face. "You are well? You have not been injured?"

"Thanks to Sally, we are well," Elizabeth replied, smiling brightly at him even though her eyes glistened with unshed tears.

Darcy crushed her to him once again. "I am glad. So very glad."

"Fitzwilliam, we are on the street."

"I do not care," Darcy replied.

"You must meet Sally."

Darcy slowly released Elizabeth from his embrace but took one of her hands in his. He would keep her at his side and safe until she was once again within the wall of Darcy House.

"Mr. Darcy," the lady from the doorway had descended the steps.

"Sally?" he inquired.

The older woman smirked. "That is what they call me."

"But that is not her name," he heard Lydia whisper to Richard, who, Darcy noticed, had his arm protectively around Lydia's shoulder as Lydia held Dash. He had to admit in that moment and in the limited light of the lamp and what spilled from the house behind them, Richard and Lydia looked very well-together, perfectly at ease, as if they belonged as they were now.

"Not many know my given name," the woman replied with a laugh. "Come. You may tell your gentlemen your story in my sitting room." She raised a brow at Elizabeth who had just opened her mouth to say something. "It is better to share it there than on the street where anyone who passes or drives a carriage might hear it."

She turned to her footman, who was standing next to the carriage. "Have the driver stay in case he is still needed, remind him that he only gets called because of his discretion, and see to the gentlemen's horses. We will not be long, but I should hate for them to wander off."

The footman nodded, and Sally turned back to lead the group to her sitting room. Once they were in her private quarters and seated, she looked at Miss Lydia. "You might as well begin. I do think you were telling me that this whole adventure was your doing."

Lydia bit her lip and looked from Richard to Darcy and back. "I did not intend for it to be," she began. Then, much to Darcy's surprise, the always bold Lydia Bennet dissolved into tears.

Elizabeth moved to go to her sister, but Darcy held her beside him. Richard could deal with a few tears. Indeed, he seemed to be doing a fine job of soothing Lydia.

"I am sorry," Lydia sobbed into Dash's neck.

Darcy was reminded of another young girl sobbing after being tricked by Wickham, and compassion for Lydia washed over him. He waited a moment until, under Richard's soothing caresses of her back and whispered reassurances, she calmed.

"I will not dismiss any guilt you may hold in this ordeal," Darcy began, "however, both my cousin and I know how artful Wickham can be."

"You do?" Lydia sniffled and peeked up at him, fear and question mingled in her eyes.

Darcy nodded and smiled. He had seen that look before as well. It was a look of a young lady seeking his approval and hoping she had not lost his good opinion. It was something he expected from Georgiana but seeing Lydia Bennet longing for his approval was unexpected.

"You are not the first young woman to need rescuing from him," he replied softly.

"Dash gave us this," Richard said, taking Wickham's letter from his pocket.

"I was not going to go with him. I only went to tell him I could not marry him because I did not love him." She shrugged, and her lips trembled. "I did not know he would not take us home."

Richard placed his arm around her shoulder and drew her to his side. "He has been rewarded for his lack of care for you both. I dare say he'll not trouble you again."

"What did you do?" Lydia's eyes were wide.

"We pummelled him," Richard replied bluntly. "And Dash growled and barked at him."

Lydia's eye turned from Richard to Darcy.

"You hit him, too?"

Darcy nodded. "Several times."

Lydia blinked. "I did not think you knew how."

Richard threw his head back and laughed loudly.

"I may not do it so often as my cousin," Darcy replied with a glare for Richard, "but when you have a cousin such as Richard, you must learn how to fight."

Lydia blinked again. "I had not thought of that. Did you spend a lot of time together when you were young?"

"Lydia, could we focus on the matter at hand," Elizabeth inserted.

Lydia scowled. "I'd rather not."

Darcy chuckled.

"But we must," Elizabeth replied.

Lydia sighed. "Very well. We got into his carriage. I told him I could not go to Scotland with him. He said some rude things and told us to get out." She lifted her chin.

"He did not like it at all that Lizzy likes Mr. Darcy or that I preferred a colonel to a lieutenant."

Darcy saw a look of pure horror wash over Lydia's face as she realized what she had said.

"Do you?" Richard asked with a chuckle.

Lydia's cheeks glowed rosy, but she lifted her chin. "Who would not?" she said without looking at him. "And then we walked here. I made a man give me a shilling for a kiss because he would not let us enter without kissing him, and Lizzy refused. And then we met Sally."

"You did what?" Richard interrupted the stream of words flowing forth from Lydia as quickly as water from an upturned pot.

"I met Sally," Lydia replied.

"Before that." There was a slight growl in Richard's tone.

Lydia huffed. "There was this gentleman who would not let us enter without giving him a kiss. So, I told him I would kiss one cheek for a shilling or both cheeks for a half-crown. He gave me a shilling, so I grabbed his nose," she demonstrated on her own nose turning her head away from Richard as she did, "and pinched it while giving him a kiss on the cheek."

"You grabbed his nose?"

"Of course. I did not want him to turn his head. Our agreement was only for a kiss on the cheek. Nowhere else. And then we met Sally."

"And we had tea, and I found some clothes for them to wear to their uncle Gardiner's." Sally shook her head. "To think I met Fanny Gardiner's girls," she muttered. This, of course, led to a relating once again of the tale of how Mr. Bennet rescued Mrs. Bennet at Sally's house.

A quarter hour later, as Darcy handed Elizabeth into the hackney and waited for Lydia and Dash to be settled inside, he thanked the Lord for directing Mrs. Bennet to this house twenty some years ago, and then guiding Elizabeth and Lydia to the same place tonight.

He turned and looked at Richard as the carriage began to move, and they waited to follow it to Darcy House.

Richard nodded. "I feel exceptionally grateful to have met Mrs. Bennet."

"Who would have thought?" Darcy muttered, a smile spreading across his face.

# Chapter 29

Abrams greeted the returning party at the door to Darcy House.

"How is everyone?" Darcy inquired as he handed his hat and coat to his butler.

"There has been much pacing of the hall from Mr. Bennet's room to Miss Georgiana's and back. I was nearly required to call the physician to inquire after his opinion about whether Mr. Bennet could be moved, but Miss Bennet calmed her mother."

Darcy sighed as he tucked Elizabeth's hand into the crook of his arm. "I can only imagine the worry she must have faced." He shook his head. "Two daughters lost to the night is no small thing."

"It is understandable, sir. We are all happy to see everyone returned safely."

"Oh, Mr. Darcy!" Mrs. Bennet stood at the top of the stairs. "Have you found them?" She waved her handkerchief as she began to descend to them.

"We will come up to you," Darcy replied. "Both Elizabeth and Lydia are well."

"You are too good, sir. Too good."

Jane wrapped an arm around her mother's shoulders
and moved her down the hall.

"Mr. Bennet's room," Darcy called to her. "Your father
will wish to know the full story," he added to Elizabeth.

"He will not rest until he does," she agreed.

"What troubles you?"

Elizabeth's brow was furrowed with grief.

"The distress we have caused." She shrugged one shoulder. "I knew that our being gone would cause worry, but
I am afraid in my focus on seeing us safe, I had forgotten
about the anguish Mama would feel."

"Your focus was just as it ought to have been," he
replied as they mounted the stairs behind Dash. He
stepped to the side to allow Richard and Lydia to chase
after the escaped pup.

"Your mother was in good hands." He blew out a breath.
"We must tell her of our betrothal."

Elizabeth laughed. "If we do not, Lydia will."

"You told Lydia?"

Elizabeth nodded. "It seemed right."

Her head tipped, and he knew she was thinking about
something, so he said nothing, choosing to wait to hear
her thoughts. They climbed three steps before she spoke.

"Lydia's visit to Darcy House has been good for her.

Even our ordeal tonight, though I would not wish it on anyone, was to her benefit." She sighed. "And your cousin and your dog seem to be the reason. She is beginning to think not as a girl but as a young woman. That is why I told her. She seemed to finally understand the solemnity of marriage, but I do not trust her to keep it a secret. She tends to speak before she thinks, much like my mother." She shook her head and laughed lightly. "I do not think that is a lack of maturity but rather just part and parcel of who they are."

"We comes to view others differently when we pause to consider them through a different lens," Darcy said.

They had reached the top of the stairs. There was not a great deal of corridor to traverse before they reached Mr. Bennet's room, and they could only saunter so slowly. Therefore, Darcy spoke quickly to clarify his statement.

"I have come to understand better your sisters and your mother – even your father. Though I would not wish an injury on anyone, your father's fall has been a blessing. I do not know where else I would have been given such opportunities to be intimately acquainted with you or your family." He shook his head at her attempted protest. "In Hertfordshire, I would be at Netherfield, and you would be three miles away. We would not pass hours sitting across a chessboard, hearing tales of the past or sharing banter over breakfast. Nor would we see one another in passing as we retired for the night or rose to face the day." He covered Elizabeth's hand, which lay on his arm with his free hand. "I like her – them. I am pleased to be adding them to my family."

"Truly," he added in response to her shocked expression. "They may still be trying at times, but it is far easier to overlook a few eccentricities in those we care for than it is in strangers."

"Do you mean it?" She blinked her eyes, which were glistening with tears.

"I do." He lifted her hand and kissed her fingers. Then with a nod toward the open door, he whispered, "Are you ready to go delight your mother with the news of our betrothal?" He winked. "After Lydia finishes regaling them with her tale of adventure, that is."

Lydia's voice could be heard telling her mother about how detestable Mr. Wickham was, and Dash was adding his agreement with an occasional bark.

Elizabeth's expression did not say she was ready, but she nodded.

He lifted her fingers and kissed them once more before leading her into the room.

"Sally?" Mrs. Bennet squeaked as they entered the room.

"Yes, Mama. She knew you," Lydia said.

"Sally?" Mrs. Bennet repeated as she fanned her face.

"They were fortunate enough to stumble upon someone who knew you," Darcy inserted. "I must thank you for having met her those years ago, for it was the memory of you and Mr. Bennet which led her to take particularly fine care of your daughters."

"Was it a brothel?" Mary asked.

"Mary!" Jane scolded.

"Yes," Richard replied.

"And someone knew Mama there?" Mary continued to question, ignoring her sister's second scold.

Lydia did not waste a moment in sharing a well-crafted tale of a damsel in distress being rescued first by a kind woman and then a handsome gentleman.

"And that has something to do with that horrid Mrs. Salter?" Mary inquired.

"Yes, there is something there," Mrs. Bennet replied softly, carefully inspecting the hem on her handkerchief.

"And you met her how long ago?"

Miss Mary was not one to just hope to discover details. She seemed to be the sort that actively sought them even if the questions were at times somewhat awkward. Darcy attributed it to a keen mine and an ample supply of her father's inquisitiveness.

"More than twenty years ago!" Lydia's tone was slightly exasperated as if it was not necessary for Mary to have asked such an obvious question.

Mary's brows furrowed, and her lips pressed together as she shrugged. "It is very like Joseph; do you not think? His brothers meant to be rid of him, but God had a different purpose."

"Oh, Mary!" Mrs. Bennet scolded. "Now is not the time for sermons! Indeed, I am not sure when it is the time for a young lady to moralize as you do."

Mary scowled but held her peace.

"She is right, Mama," Kitty said softly. "Your horrible ordeal did provide a blessing just as Mr. Darcy said."

"I would rather not speak of that ordeal," Mrs. Bennet said sternly and then shrugged, "though I am happy it helped my daughters."

"You have always said you would do anything for us, Mama," Elizabeth said with an impertinent grin.

"Elizabeth!" Mrs. Bennet cried.

"Oh!" Lydia's eyes grew wide, and her hand flew to cover her mouth as she looked at Elizabeth.

"What is it?" Mrs. Bennet asked.

Lydia shook her head.

Elizabeth smiled at her. "You may share it."

"Truly? I may tell Mama?"

"Yes," Elizabeth replied.

"Lizzy is getting married," Lydia declared, "to Mr. Darcy."

"Is it true?" Georgiana asked her brother from where she sat next to Kitty.

Darcy nodded.

Mrs. Bennet squealed in delight and jumped from her chair to kiss Elizabeth on the cheek.

"Oh, Mr. Darcy," she said, "you are too good." She turned to Mr. Bennet. "You knew and did not tell me?"

He chuckled. "Your daughter wished to tell you in the morning."

"She does like to vex me," Mrs. Bennet muttered as she took her seat again. The smile she wore spoke loudly of the fact that such a vexation was more a delight than a torment. "We shall have to go shopping. Jane and Lizzy both need wedding clothes."

And with that statement, the ordeal of the night seemed to be over, and the future seemed all important.

"Not today, of course. We shall sleep today and do some quiet activities. And I shall write to your aunt with the news." Her brows furrowed. "We should visit her tomorrow. She will surely know all the best places to procure what we need." Mrs. Bennet rose. "Mary, Kitty, Lydia, it is time for bed."

"I should like to speak with my youngest daughter," Mr. Bennet interjected.

"She has had a trying night, my dear," Mrs. Bennet replied.

"As have we all," her husband said.

Mrs. Bennet pulled herself a little straighter and looked at Lydia. "You heard your father, Lydia. Mary, Kitty, come."

"My good woman," Mr. Bennet called, raising an eyebrow when she turned toward him. "I require a proper parting."

Mrs. Bennet looked around the room uneasily.

"They shall all avert their eyes," Mr. Bennet commanded.

"We shall leave you to your peace," Darcy said with a chuckle. "Do you require Elizabeth?"

Mr. Bennet shook his head. "I should like to hear her thoughts tomorrow, and those of you and the colonel, but I do not require that tonight." He looked at Lydia. "See that Dash is in his proper place and return."

"Yes, Papa," Lydia followed Elizabeth out of the room. "He loves Mama very much."

"He does," Elizabeth agreed.

"And he is very angry with me."

"Is he not right to be?" Richard asked.

Lydia's gaze dropped to the floor as she nodded.

"Come along. Let's see that pup to his bed," Richard held out his arm to her. "He was very worried about you..." His voice faded as he moved away from Darcy.

"I should like a proper parting as well," Darcy whispered to Elizabeth.

Elizabeth looked down the hall. Nearly everyone had disappeared inside a room.

"Very well, Mr. Darcy, but if my mother sees us..."

"I will take full responsibility," he muttered, pulling her

into his embrace and kissing her as he had wanted to do from the moment he saw she was safe.

# Chapter 30

"Ah, Mr. Bennet!" Bingley said as he entered the sitting room at Darcy House two days later. "I see the physician is pleased enough with your improvement to allow you to leave your bed."

"Happily. Yes," Mr. Bennet replied. "Although I cannot rise to greet you."

"I am just pleased to see you in the sitting room," Bingley replied.

"Papa's improvement means we will be returning home soon," Jane said as Bingley took a seat next to her.

"Not until all the lace in London has been purchased," Mr. Bennet said with a laugh.

"Everything will be ordered or purchased by the beginning of the week," Elizabeth inserted. "Mama is very efficient at seeing a plan put into action."

For the past two days, Elizabeth and Jane had been required to follow their mother from their aunt's house to their uncle's warehouse and then to a variety of shops. Gloves, hats, dresses, slippers, whatever Mrs. Bennet thought a new young wife of a wealthy gentleman might require — and Mrs. Gardiner agreed was a necessity — had been listed out and attended to.

Lydia had wished to go with them on their excursions, but Mr. Bennet had required her to sit with him for a portion of each day – the same portion of the day in which her mother would be shopping.

There would be fittings and such in Meryton, but whatever could be acquired in London to quicken the preparations had been purchased.

"I have sent a letter to Mrs. Nichols just this morning," Bingley replied. "Everything at Netherfield should be ready for our arrival. Will you be joining us, Colonel?"

Richard had just stepped into the sitting room.

"I've not seen you in your uniform in days," Darcy commented. Between the uniform and the grave expression Richard wore, Darcy knew that the news his cousin bore was not good.

"I am to be in Manchester by next week," he said simply. "I am to leave immediately." He held up a missive. "There is no time to waste."

"Leaving?" Lydia cried. "Now?"

Richard nodded. "There have been reports of fires and attacks on mills in the north, and the government expects it to only increase. There is a bill..." He sighed and then forced a smile. "This is my profession."

"Will you return?" Lydia was blinking rapidly, yet

despite her best efforts, Darcy saw a tear slide down her cheek.

"Eventually."

"You must come to Netherfield when you do," Bingley offered.

"Yes," Lydia agreed. There was a hint of desperation in the word.

"And call at Longbourn," Mr. Bennet added.

"I would like that very much," Richard replied. "If all goes well, perhaps my journey will not be too long in duration, but with the sanctions that are coming..."

Darcy rose from his chair. "It will not be a pleasant affair."

"It never is a pleasant affair when I am sent to see to it." Richard's attempt at a chuckle was weak. "I will write when I am settled."

"I'd not be opposed to a letter reaching Longbourn." Mr. Bennet shrugged when Richard turned his direction. "My wife and certain of my daughters will worry."

Richard paused.

Darcy could see the indecision on his face. Then, after a quick glance at Lydia, Richard's expression shifted to a look with which Darcy was more familiar — that of a colonel with a mission before him that must be fulfilled.

"Might I send it to Miss Lydia?" Richard asked.

Darcy smiled at the declaration of Richard's intent. It was like him to come directly to the point when a decision had been made. Richard was not one to dance around an issue, and Darcy was glad for it. For Richard to have gone off to Manchester without making his attachment known, or worse — denying it, would have made a miserable job that much more unbearable.

"Do you know what you ask?" Mr. Bennet replied.

"I do."

Darcy's gaze shifted from his cousin to Lydia, who was likely holding her breath from the way in which she was sitting so motionless.

"And what of your family? We are not of your sphere and should things progress favourably, Lydia has little by way of fortune."

Lydia's expression fell, and Darcy turned his observation back to Richard.

"I have considered that, sir, and I cannot say with any certainty what will transpire at such a juncture. All I can promise is that I do not seek such a privileged acquaintance with your daughter without thought, and I am prepared to endure whatever censure may arise."

Darcy had never seen his cousin shift so uncomfortably, but then, his cousin had never, to this point, lost his heart. And from the reluctance with which Richard seemed to be reporting for his duty to the crown – the profession to which he had proclaimed himself happily married – Darcy knew that Richard was more than a little attached to Lydia. He had finally found a reason to leave his life of single devotion to his commission behind.

It still surprised Darcy that it was not some lady of the ton with a fortune as beautiful as her face but rather a simple country miss, who was not always sensible, who had wrought such a change. However, Darcy could not deny the fact that the Bennet ladies held a certain power that no sense of duty or demand of relations could quench.

His eyes shifted to Mr. Bennet. That was likely how a man as seemingly astute as Mr. Bennet had gained a wife so unlike him. His lips tipped up on one side as he considered that perhaps that was why the man knew he did not need a fortune for his daughters. They had inherited something far more valuable than tuppence and crowns from their mother.

Mr. Bennet nodded slowly and then turned to his youngest daughter. "Lydia, would you welcome a letter from the colonel?"

Lydia's head bobbed up and down rapidly, and she smiled through her tears. "Very much, Papa."

"Then I suggest you see the gentleman to his horse and make certain he knows the direction to put on the envelope." He turned back to Richard. "I wish you well on your journey. May you return to us safely."

"Thank you, sir." Richard turned to Darcy. "I will write."

"Take care," Darcy replied. He disliked these times

when he had to part with his cousin and friend, not knowing if the man would return to him or not.

"I saw Georgie upstairs," Richard said.

"Is she well?"

"No, but she assures me she will be." He stooped to
scruff the top of Dash's head. "I shall miss you. Keep my
chair warm." Then with a final word of parting for each of
the others in the room, he departed with Lydia at his side.

"He will be well," Elizabeth whispered as she came to
stand next to Darcy.

Darcy was unsure if she said it to reassure him or herself. Either way, he was thankful for it. It would be a trifle
easier to endure this separation with her presence to cheer
and distract him.

"Walk with me?" he asked.

"Of course." Elizabeth took his arm. "Are you well?" she
asked as they walked down the hall to his study.

Apparently, she had made her comment, at least in part,
to reassure him. He nodded his reply but said nothing
until they were inside the study.

"I will not lie. I worry about him every time he leaves."
He pulled her into his embrace. "But I think I can endure
it far better this time with you by my side." He kissed her
forehead.

They stood silently for a moment, her head against his
chest, arms wrapped around each other as they did nothing but breath and be.

"He's never courted anyone before," Darcy finally voiced a portion of the thoughts swirling in his mind. "He's never even hinted at wishing to court someone before."

"Lydia has attempted to draw several gentlemen along enough to court her," Elizabeth replied with a small laugh.

"They are very different from each other, are they not?" Darcy looked down at Elizabeth and smiled.

"They are," she replied.

"And yet they seem to fit well together."

Elizabeth's cheek rubbed against his jacket as she nodded her agreement.

"Just as we do." He pulled back far enough so that he could look at those captivating eyes of hers which spoke to him even when she didn't say a word. At this moment, they were speaking of happiness and contentment – or was that just his heart reflecting itself in her eyes? Whichever it was, he did not care. "I love you, Elizabeth."

She smiled. "And I love you, Fitzwilliam."

He kissed her once, just lightly, and was about to speak again when he thought better of it and kissed her again. This time he kissed her deeply, and for some minutes. Finally, when his mind was wandering to wishes beyond kisses, and his hands were itching to roam, he leaned his forehead against hers.

"I have spoken to my uncle about our betrothal." This was not news to her, he had told her he was going to visit the earl. "And I stressed that now was not a good time to visit as your father is still recovering."

"Are you afraid to have them meet my family?"

He smiled at her playful tone. "Perhaps," he teased and then shook his head. "His schedule is busy at present. There was no need to push things aside for us. There will be plenty of years for them to get to know you and your family. He gave me his blessing without more than a question or two about who you were. I believe he is just happy that I am finally marrying. Of course, that was my uncle. His sister, my aunt Catherine will be less obliging."

"She is the one with the daughter to whom you are *not* betrothed?"

She was teasing him again, and willingly, he played along.

"Yes, she is that as well as your cousin's *esteemed* patroness."

They both chuckled.

Darcy wrapped her tightly in his embrace one more time before giving her another quick kiss and releasing her.

"We should return to the others, no matter how much I wish to just remain here with you."

She wrapped her arm around his and leaned her head against his shoulder as they walked back toward the sitting room. "It is not many days until we are in Hertfordshire. Do you think you can continue to tolerate my family even in the wilds surrounding Netherfield?"

"I believe I am up to the challenge," he replied with a chuckle.

"My mother will be delighted to have you and Mr. Bingley to reintroduce to the neighbourhood. Are you prepared for that?"

Darcy looked down at her upturned, smiling face. "I believe I can endure anything for you."

"Even Sir William and my aunt Philips?"

"Have I not yet proven myself enough to you?"

She shrugged and pursed her lips as she tried to contain her smile. However, she could do nothing to hide the sparkle of amusement in her eyes.

"Just you wait and see, Elizabeth," he said, pitching his voice low. "I shall perform admirably."

She giggled. "I do not doubt you will."

"Yet you question me most severely." He darted a look up and down the corridor before giving her impertinent, puckered lips a quick kiss.

"Mr. Darcy!"

Had she not been smiling, her scold might have given him a moment of pause. However, she was smiling, so he kissed her again. "That, my dear, is my promise."

"Your promise of what?"

He took both her hands in his and grew serious. "It is my promise that come what may, I shall endure it all, for I love you – and that is a fact which I will not allow you to forget."

"You will not?" Delight shone in her eyes.

He shook his head. "And do you know how I will remind you?"

Her left eyebrow arched. "How?"

He lifted her hands. "By kissing you." He kissed the knuckles of both her right and left hands, and then, leaning forward, he pressed his lips against hers one final time before returning with her to the sitting room where a very delighted Mrs. Bennet was presiding over a discussion of wedding breakfast receipts.

Darcy knew that his life would never be without some amount of liveliness and possible chaos, thanks to his new family. However, the thought of it did not unsettle him as it once might have. Instead, he welcomed it – not with eager anticipation, but with calm assurance. As he had told Elizabeth, he was determined to endure it all, for he could not, would not, face life without her by his side, no matter what might lie ahead.

# Loving Lydia

*He never expected his heart to break over her sister's sorrow.*

# Chapter 1

"Are you certain you will be well?" Fitzwilliam Darcy asked as he leaned against the doorframe while his sister, Georgiana, worked on getting settled into her room at Netherfield, and Dash sniffed his way around the perimeter of the room.

Why he had allowed two young ladies to talk him into bringing that dog, he was not certain. It was likely his inability to say no to two sets of begging eyes. He shook his head. It was perhaps not his sister about whom he needed to worry. It was himself. He was becoming soft – dreadfully soft.

He reached down and scratched Dash's ear when he came to sniff Darcy's boots for the third time.

"I am certain I will survive if I have to see him. I am not without friends or you." Georgiana turned and looked at him while still holding her jewelry box. She always saw to the arranging of her dressing table. "I am not so foolish as I once was. I do not trust him, and I know for a fact that

Miss Lydia and Miss Kitty no longer like him either. You have very little to fear."

"I will worry nonetheless."

She smiled. "Of course, you will. You are most proficient at worrying about me."

It was true. Darcy did excel at worrying about many things – his sister had been at the top of that list, followed very closely by his cousin Colonel Richard Fitzwilliam. However, Georgiana would now find that top position a trifle more crowded. For there was now Elizabeth and her sisters – most especially Miss Lydia – about whom to worry.

"There." Georgiana stepped back and admired her table. "Everything is just as it should be." She glanced around the room. "Where is Dash?"

Darcy sighed and pushed off the doorframe. "He must have escaped."

"Which is not hard to do when the door is standing open," Georgiana teased.

"You have grown a tad impertinent over the past few weeks." Darcy's scold was gentle.

"And your smile says you are not truly displeased," Georgiana said as she crossed the room to where he stood and accepted his proffered arm.

"I cannot say that I am," Darcy agreed. "That is I am not as long as your impertinence keeps its place."

"Which is not in public," Georgiana replied.

"Precisely."

"What is the cause of that sigh?"

Darcy grimaced. He had not meant to sigh, but thoughts of impertinence and worry naturally turned his mind to Lydia Bennet. "I was remembering my promise to Richard."

"What promise is that?"

"I am not certain I should say."

"Is it that dreadful?" Her tone was teasingly horrified.

He chuckled. "That depends on how you receive the information. I know Miss Lydia is your friend."

"Please? I know Richard loves her and that he has asked for permission to write to her while he is away."

Darcy nodded. That was all true. But how did he explain the rest? "This might be said badly," he cautioned. "Richard asked me to help Miss Lydia improve."

"Improve what?" His sister's brow was furrowed as she attempted to understand his meaning.

"Her behaviour in public is not precisely how it should be." Though the comment was critical, Darcy kept his tone gentle. He was not attempting to disparage Miss Lydia. He could not in good conscience denigrate any of Elizabeth's sisters, most especially not the one who held his cousin's heart. However, the truth could not be overlooked either.

"Oh! I had not considered it, but I do see what you mean. She does speak more freely than I was taught to do."

"And her choices of topics are not always the best – such as asking you if you had a beau upon your first meeting."

Georgiana nodded her head thoughtfully. "I understand. It could put her in a place to be ridiculed and hurt. Richard would never wish for that."

"Indeed, he would not." It impressed Darcy how Georgiana had so succinctly stated what the jumbled mess of thoughts in his mind seemed unable to tell him clearly. "I could not have said it better. That is it precisely."

Georgiana patted his arm. "Then we have nothing to fear. I shall behave properly as I usually do, and Mrs. Annesley can assist us. I shall have her spend some time teaching me things that I already know, but that Miss Lydia and Miss Kitty might not know."

It seemed as if it was a plan which might work, but... "I do not wish to tax Mrs. Annesley too much."

"I will ask her, and if she so much as hesitates in replying, I will think of another plan that shall be just as good."

Darcy grimaced as he heard a crash in the drawing room. "I think we have found Dash."

As suspected, Dash was in the drawing room next to a vase which lay in pieces on the floor.

"It was not him," Darcy's friend, Charles Bingley, said in response to Darcy's growled *Dash.*

"Did I tell you I acquired a kitten for Miss Bennet?" Bingley added.

Darcy blinked and looked at Bingley. "You did what?"

"Before I left town, Miss Bennet was telling me about a cat she once had which had run away during a storm. She seemed to miss it a great deal, so when I arrived, I sought out Sir William and inquired if he knew where I might find a grey tabby cat. As luck would have it, he knew precisely where I might find one." Bingley lifted the drapes out of the way and scooped up a kitten. "This is Oliver. He has yet to learn not to push vases off tables."

Bingley crossed the room to where Dash sat. "Dash, this is Oliver," he said, crouching down.

When Dash sniffed the creature, Oliver meowed and attempted to climb Bingley's arm.

"He is a friend," Bingley scolded.

"You are talking to a cat as if he can understand you," Darcy said flatly.

"Who is to say he cannot," Bingley returned. "I think it would be best if they become friends."

"This is what you were doing for two days before we arrived? Acquiring a kitten?"

Bingley released Oliver who looked at Dash for only a moment before returning to his hiding spot behind the drapery.

"No, no, I was also making certain all was ready for your arrival." Bingley blew out a breath. "And that of my sister. She arrives tomorrow."

"Sir Matthew will be joining her, will he not?" Georgiana asked.

"Thankfully, yes." Bingley's eyes shifted from Darcy and Georgiana to the window. "No, Oliver. He is a friend."

"Perhaps Dash should be made comfortable in your room," Darcy suggested to his sister.

Dash had gone to attempt to make friends with Oliver, but Oliver was none too complacent about the whole idea and had decided it would be best to climb to safety.

"This might not have been my best idea," Bingley said with a laugh as he tried to extricate Oliver's sharp claws from the fabric of the drapes.

"I am certain Miss Bennet will appreciate the gesture," Darcy assured him. He sighed. "I brought Dash for Georgiana and Miss Lydia." He shrugged when Bingley looked at him. "I found it impossible to not grant their request."

Bingley laughed. "What has become of us?"

Darcy took a seat next to his friend. "We have found love, my friend, and it seems love addles one's brain."

Bingley shook his head. "No, our brains are not addled. We are just willing to do that which we might not otherwise do to see those we love happy."

"You do surprise me with your occasional astuteness," Darcy teased.

"I am impressive, am I not? If only Richard were here to tell me I was not."

Darcy sighed and nodded. How he wished the same! And he did not wish it just because then Richard could worry about Miss Lydia. Nor did he wish it just to have

Richard here to tease and taunt. He wished it because then he knew his cousin would be safe and not in harm's way.

"I suspect I will receive some news of him soon, letting me know he has arrived in Manchester. That frame-breaking bill will surely stir up more strife than it is intended to squelch."

"I cannot say I blame the frame-breakers for their anger. I have witnessed some very grim living arrangements. However, as the son of a manufacturer, I cannot condone their actions either."

Both men sat in silence for some time. Darcy tapped his fingers on the arm of his chair, while Bingley ran his hand along Oliver's back, who was sleeping on his lap.

"I am sure he will be well," Bingley said at last, putting into words what both men were contemplating.

"He has survived worse," Darcy agreed. While he disliked the idea of Richard being in harm's way at all, he knew it was part and parcel of being a colonel in His Majesty's Forces. And, to Darcy's mind, it was better for Richard to be here, in England, rather than in France, where he had been in the past. While there might be some skirmishes in the North, they were unlikely to be as deadly as a battle on the continent.

Bingley rose from his chair with Oliver tucked in the crook of his arm. "I had planned on calling at Longbourn today for a few minutes. Will you and Georgiana be joining me?"

Darcy smiled. "Without a doubt." It had been nearly a full day since he had seen Elizabeth, and there was only so long a gentleman could go without seeing the lady he loved when he was used to having her under his roof where he could see her at all hours of the day. He was not entirely sure how he was going to survive three miles of separation.

His eyes narrowed as he looked at Bingley. "Do you suppose Oliver could cause some calamity that would require both Miss Bennet and Miss Elizabeth to take up residence here?"

Bingley chuckled. "I do not think I am that clever."

Darcy sighed. "Neither am I, unfortunately, so I suppose, I will have to do as regular gentlemen do and call on her at home."

# Chapter 2

"Come in. Come in." Mrs. Bennet urged her callers to enter the sitting room at Longbourn. "It is so good to see you. I was only just telling Mrs. Long – she was here just before you arrived – how anxious I was to know if everyone was settling into Netherfield well and if you found it as pleasing upon your return as you did when you first arrived last autumn." She looked at them expectantly.

"It was just as I left it," Bingley answered. "Although there was no snow in November, so that is new."

"Is it not beautiful?" Kitty asked. "I love how the snow makes everything so bright."

"Beautiful but cold," Bingley answered. "Not that I am unfamiliar with the chill of winter having grown up in the North. I just do not prefer it."

"And you, Miss Darcy," Mrs. Bennet continued. "How do you find Netherfield?"

"It is lovely," Georgiana replied.

"Do you like the snow?"

Georgiana shrugged. "I suppose I do."

"Very good." Mrs. Bennet settled into her chair, seemingly pleased with all she had heard. Then, with a small gasp, she sat forward. "Forgive me. I forgot to inquire about you, Mr. Darcy. You were so quiet slipping in to sit by my Lizzy. I can assure you that Mrs. Long was astounded to hear of my good fortune in having two daughters so well-matched with a third in a very hopeful position. It is indeed a great blessing, I told her. However, one must not be too startled that my daughters have done so well. Just look at them. There is not a plain one amongst the lot. They are all quite beautiful. Well, then, she had a comment or two to say about Mary's disapproving looks, but I assured her that if Lizzy's odd love of books and learning could capture the affections of a man such as yourself, Mr. Darcy, that I was certain that Mary's stern looks and reprimands might be admired by someone...someday." Her brow furrowed, and she looked past Darcy. "However, it would be lovely if she were to not scold so often. There is a danger of being thought a harridan – which, of course, she is not. None of my girls are." She sighed. The furrow between her eyes deepened for a moment and then faded as she relaxed into her chair, once again pleased with all that had been said.

Darcy pondered her sigh and look of contemplation for a moment. He imagined that it was likely due to her concern about seeing Miss Mary happily married someday. He would have to give some thought to how he might assist her in seeing it done, for seeing one's daughters well-matched must be a great worry for any mother with several daughters.

"I must say that I found Netherfield much improved," he admitted. "The neighbourhood seemed more welcoming and the ladies of the area – one in particular – more beautiful than I remember."

Mrs. Bennet tittered and waved away his words with an "I should think so."

"How is Mr. Bennet?" Darcy asked.

"Papa was delighted to be returned to his book room this morning," Jane said. "However, he has returned to his bed to rest his leg just as the doctor said he should."

"Too much activity too quickly is never a good thing for one who is recovering from an injury." Mrs. Bennet's tone and look were serious. "However," she said, brightening, "he has improved so much since that first day I saw him at Darcy House. Such prodigious good care you gave him, Mr. Darcy."

"It was not I who saw to his care."

"It was your house and your physician."

Had Richard been there, Darcy knew he would have chuckled at the look of displeasure Mrs. Bennet wore at Darcy's audacity to argue with her compliment.

"It was also my dog which caused the injury." Darcy bit back a smile at seeing Mrs. Bennet's eyes narrow for a moment at his continued disagreement. "However, I was happy to be of service to both Mr. Bennet and the rest of your family. I would not be lying if I said Darcy House was exceptionally lonely yesterday after your departure. I am delighted to be here amongst you all."

That earned him a delighted smile.

"I can barely believe it." Elizabeth's tone was teasing. "I thought that you preferred solitude to company."

Darcy chuckled. "I did until I learned just how comforting company of the right sort can be." He lifted her hand to his lips, which he knew was far too forward but which he also knew would continue to delight Mrs. Bennet, and strangely, very strangely, indeed, he had come to find great pleasure in pleasing the Bennet matriarch.

"Have you had a letter?" Lydia asked.

Darcy shook his head. "Not yet. I am certain there will be one soon, however."

"You will tell me as soon as you can if you receive one?"

Darcy nodded. "And you will do the same?"

"Without question! Why I could no better keep such a thing to myself as Lizzy could refrain from reading for a full day. It is just not in my nature to keep such a pleasurable thing to myself. It must be shared with someone, and you do seem like the best person with whom to share such a thing." Her brow furrowed, and she drew the right corner of her lower lip between her teeth.

"I am certain it will contain many interesting stories

when it arrives," Darcy assured her. "Richard is a most excellent storyteller."

Her features relaxed, and she gave him a small thankful smile before turning to Kitty and Georgiana.

"As you know, she has not been quite herself," Elizabeth whispered.

"Or herself has been permanently altered by concerns beyond herself," Darcy whispered in reply. "Georgiana is altered after her first encounter with imagined love – not that either Richard or Lydia's care for the other is imagined," he clarified when Elizabeth's left eyebrow rose. "I am just saying that love, whether real or imagined, has an altering effect on a person."

"Does it?"

Darcy tipped his head and silently looked at her lovely face for a moment until she began to squirm. "I am certain it was love which caused me to enter into that scheme to see Caroline wed to Sir Matthew, and I know that it was love which caused me to expose myself to your family, which in turn has forever changed how I view the silence of my home." He squeezed the hand of hers that he still held. "They are very good changes. Even the changes in Georgiana are not all bad. She has gained wisdom, though I wish she had not gained it in such a fashion."

So much had changed inside of him since he had allowed love to rule over duty in his heart. He would not wish to return to his former self. It was as if loving Elizabeth had awakened something – had caused that something to blossom and flourish – a something that had lain dormant for some time.

"Are you unaltered by love?" he asked.

Elizabeth shook her head. "I see things so differently now. Do you truly think that is what is happening for my sister?"

"I can only suppose." Darcy rose as Lady Lucas, and her youngest daughter entered the room. He bowed and did all that was proper as he and his sister were introduced.

"So my husband was not wrong!" Lady Lucas cried. "Oh, he will be quite pleased to hear it. He will insist we have a soiree with dancing. Perhaps this time, Miss Elizabeth would be more willing to participate in the dancing." Her eyebrows flicked up as she said it. "Does Charlotte know of your betrothal?" She looked at Mrs. Bennet without waiting for Elizabeth's reply. "I am sending a letter tomorrow. I do it twice a month, you know. It is dreadful and yet not so very much to have one's daughter so far removed, although she is not so far away as some will be." She paused only long enough to take a quick breath. "Will you be remaining at Netherfield, Mr. Bingley?"

Darcy looked at the hand Elizabeth had placed on his arm before his eyes lifted to her face. "I am well," he whispered. "It just might take a little longer to get used to all the neighbours than I had hoped."

"Colonel Fitzwilliam is in Manchester."

Darcy pulled his eyes away from Elizabeth upon hearing his cousins spoken of and looked toward the group of younger ladies seated across from him just as Lydia sighed and covered her heart with her hand in a rather dramatic fashion.

"You should see him in his regimentals. He is quite handsome in a regular suit of clothing but in his regimentals?" Lydia sighed dramatically once again. "Oh, you simply must see the ribbon I purchased when in town, Maria. You do remember how you were always telling me that I should get a red ribbon to go with my sprigged muslin, do you not?"

"Indeed, a red ribbon was just what it needed," Maria agreed.

"You were not wrong." Lydia grasped Maria's hand. "Well! Let me tell you. It was quite the melee, for Mama thought one would suit, and I thought it should be another. Miss Darcy was certain I was right while Kitty thought Mama was. Do you know how we settled it?"

"No, how?" Maria leaned forward eagerly.

"We asked the colonel." Lydia wore a very pleased expression as she lifted her chin. "And he, of course, after a bit of consideration, chose mine."

"He did not!" Maria cried.

Darcy sighed. He did not find the flutterings of young ladies to be particularly enjoyable. Indeed, he found them to be somewhat tedious.

"Are you still certain you can tolerate all of this?" Elizabeth whispered.

"Honestly?"

She nodded when he looked in her direction.

"It will not be easy," Darcy admitted. "However, I do think the prize is worth the discomfort."

# Chapter 3

"Lady Lucas was wrong." Bingley dropped a missive next to Darcy's cup of tea the following morning. "This came while we were out riding."

Darcy read the invitation to a soiree at Lucas Lodge. "She did not waste any time, did she?"

Bingley chuckled. "Indeed, she did not. You will accept. Will you not?"

"Of course. I must." Darcy intended to show himself as a changed individual to the community, and, to do so, he must take part in activities where he would be amongst the people of Meryton. He had reparations to make, civilities to bestow – whether they were easily done or not.

"Caroline will likely be less than pleased to accept, but she is named on the invitation," Bingley said.

"This is the first time she will be back under your roof since she attempted to both separate you from Miss Bennet and force you into marrying another. It could be a trying time for all." Darcy breathed in the steam from his tea before taking a careful sip. He should likely let it cool longer rather than risking a burnt tongue, but the fragrance was so much more welcoming when it rose with the steam.

Across from Darcy, Bingley sighed and sank into his chair. "I will admit to being somewhat nervous to have her here, but she will be with Sir Matthew. And he seems to have had a settling effect on her, according to Hurst."

"And she arrives this afternoon?"

"Yes. But first, I hear you are off to do some shopping."

Darcy smiled over his teacup. "I tell you, Bingley, I am becoming soft."

Bingley laughed. "Not this time. I know your true reason. The militia is still in town; the winter is not yet over."

It was true. The militia's presence was bothersome to Darcy.

Georgiana and the youngest Miss Bennets wished to visit the shops in Meryton. Kitty, in particular, was eager to show her new friend what could be purchased so close to Longbourn. Georgiana had insisted that they only needed Mrs. Annesley to accompany them, but Darcy was more insistent that he join her for at least this first outing.

Wickham might be returned to his unit, and even though Darcy and Richard had pummelled him – and maybe even because of it – the gentleman might not remain quiet about what he knew concerning Georgiana, Lydia, or Elizabeth. It was better in Darcy's mind for Wickham to be met by himself and not just his sister and her friends.

"I am coming with you," Bingley added.

Darcy's eyebrows rose as he swallowed the sip of tea he had taken.

"Miss Bennet is going to attend her sisters," Bingley explained.

"So is Miss Elizabeth."

It was Elizabeth's presence that made the thought of entering shops to look at lace, gloves, hats, and the like more than bearable. Not only would Darcy be able to stroll the high street with her on his arm, but he would also get the chance to see what sorts of things caught her eye when she entered the shops. He had a wedding that was not too far in the future, and he wished to present her with something he knew she would enjoy and perhaps even cherish.

He cradled his cup of tea. His mother had a box for her broaches that had been given to her by his father. The top had been carved with bluebells, her favourite flower, and the interior was lined in purple silk because it was her favourite colour.

It was details such as these that Darcy knew he still needed to learn about Elizabeth. Of course, if observation failed, he could always inquire about such details from one of her sisters. Or, he supposed, he could just ask Elizabeth, though he did wish for his gift to be a surprise.

"I see there was more unrest." Bingley passed the newspaper to Darcy, who blew out a breath.

"I would almost rather not know," he said.

"It was in Yorkshire, not Manchester," Bingley added as Darcy began to read the account in the paper.

Sadly, the reports of damages done to property and of shots fired at protestors were becoming as commonplace as the reports of unrest on the continent.

"It is not so very far from him." Darcy sighed and wondered if Lydia ever read the paper. He hoped she did not.

A more startling thought caused him to suck in a breath just as he was taking a sip of tea. This, in turn, set off a fit of coughing and sputtering. "I am well," he assured Bingley as soon as he was able before coughing for a bit longer.

"Was there something startling in the paper?"

Darcy shook his head and took a proper sip of tea instead of attempting to inhale the liquid. "No, I was just wondering if Mrs. Bennet ever reads the paper." He pulled back from the table in surprise when Oliver landed near his plate.

"You are not allowed on the table," Bingley scolded, scooping up the kitten before it could scamper away. "I doubt she does. However, I would not be surprised if both Miss Elizabeth and Miss Mary read it."

Darcy groaned. "And Miss Mary might find it her duty to inform her mother and sisters of events. You know that kitten might find it less enjoyable to attack the tables and curtains if you did not pluck him from where he should not be and reward him by tucking him in for a pet."

Oliver was happily curled in Bingley's lap and purring.

"You scold almost as well as Miss Mary," Bingley replied with a laugh before reaching for his tea.

Either Bingley's laugh or his movement stirred the purring cat from his repose. Startled, the animal leapt up and, in so doing, caused Bingley's tea to spill. The kitten escaped the sloshing liquid. However, Bingley's breeches did not. With a muttered curse, Bingley rose. "It seems I am going to change for our outing now rather than later."

Before leaving the room, Bingley scowled at Oliver, who was hiding behind the leg of the sideboard. "You had best hope Miss Bennet likes you, or you might find yourself in the stables. Tea on my trousers. Of all the things."

Darcy could hear him continuing to mutter as he exited the room. No sooner was Bingley out of sight than Oliver slinked out from hiding and headed in Darcy's direction.

"You will have no luck with me." Darcy swallowed the last of his tea, rose, and left the room with Oliver trailing behind. "Oh, very well." Darcy stooped and gave the kitten's head a scratch, earning himself a contented purr. "Now, stay here."

Unfortunately, Oliver was as well behaved as a certain pup, and Darcy had to be quick to enter his room without company. Between animals and young ladies, Darcy was certain this sojourn at Netherfield was going to be excessively trying.

He sighed.

"And Caroline arrives this afternoon, and Wickham might be in Meryton." He shook his head at his reflection in the mirror and then rang for his man.

~*~*~

An hour later, after Darcy had changed from his riding clothes and spent a leisurely half hour reading in his room, which was blessedly free from distractions, he, Bingley, Georgiana, and Mrs. Annesley arrived at Longbourn. From here, Georgiana and Mrs. Annesley would travel with the younger Bennets while the oldest Bennets would ride with Darcy and Bingley.

"Good morning, Fitzwilliam," Elizabeth whispered as she took his hand so that he could help her into the carriage.

"Good morning, Elizabeth," he replied, lifting her hand to kiss it. "Not there," he said when she sat down on the bench next to Jane.

"Then where?"

"With me." He turned to Bingley. "You do not mind giving up your place next to me to Miss Elizabeth, do you?"

Chuckling, Bingley shook his head and entered the carriage.

"Oh, Mr. Darcy!" Lydia cried, poking her head out of the door to the Bennet's carriage. "I have a letter. I nearly forgot. I do not know how I could have. It is likely the excitement of everything." She waved an envelope at him.

"Do you wish me to read it?" he asked. "Is it not private?"

Her eyes lowered, and she blushed.

"Parts of it may be," she replied coyly. "However, if you do not read the last paragraph... He said to give you and Miss Darcy his love in that part." She still held out the letter.

"Are you certain?" Darcy questioned once more. There was no way he was going to intrude on Miss Lydia's or Richard's privacy.

"Just the beginning," Lydia said with a nod of her head.

"I promise not to read the last paragraph, and I thank you for your trust." Darcy took the missive from her. "I will have it read before we enter the first store, and then you may safely hide it away."

Lydia thanked him and pulled her head back into the carriage.

He greatly felt the honour of being allowed the privilege of reading a letter not addressed to him. And so, once he was settled into his carriage again, he immediately set about reading what Richard had written, taking care not to allow his eyes to even skim the final paragraph.

"What does he have to say?" Bingley asked.

"He has settled into his accommodations – he is staying at an inn, it seems. The room is not large, and the innkeeper's wife is not small." He chuckled at Richard's description of the jovial couple that ran the inn. It seemed his cousin may have found a friendly place to rest his head at night. As long as...

"Does he say what the innkeeper thinks of the unrest." Bingley put Darcy's concern into words.

Darcy shook his head. "There is little talk about any unrest in this letter, and what is here is couched in such a fashion that it does not appear to be of any significance. However, I suspect there will be more about that when he writes to me. Hopefully, he will include a section of the letter that I will be able to give to Miss Lydia to read. I have no great desire to see her unnecessarily unsettled."

"The paper had an account in it," Jane said. "But Lydia does not read that portion of the paper. In fact, I am not certain she knows what is in a paper other than what the society pages say. And Papa would not allow her to read anything else."

"But he allows you?"

Jane nodded. "And Lizzy and Mary. However, we have all been warned most sternly that we are not to speak of it to either Mama or our sisters."

"Papa does not wish to deal with the fit of nerves it would produce," Elizabeth added.

Darcy pulled in a deep breath and released it. "I had worried Miss Lydia might hear about things. I am glad she will not."

"Why Mr. Darcy," Elizabeth teased, "might you actually care for my youngest sister?" Her eyes were not laughing as her tone might indicate they should be.

"How can I not?" he replied with a soft smile for her. "We are to be related."

Elizabeth wrapped her arm around his and squeezed it tightly.

For her, he could weather a great many annoyances – excessively talkative neighbours, the high spirits of young ladies, and even the affection demanded by animals. However, at present, those annoyances held only a small space in his mind for he had spied a group of redcoats in front of some establishment as the carriages entered the high street in Meryton.

# Chapter 4

"Did you see Mr. Wickham in that group?" Jane whispered across the carriage to Elizabeth as the door was opened and the steps were put in place.

"I did not, but then I could not see every face. Did you?" Elizabeth did not need to hear Darcy's response for one look at the set of his jaw was all the only reply she needed. "He is here?"

Darcy nodded.

"Perhaps he will be wise and keep his distance," Bingley said hopefully as he climbed out of the carriage. "But even if he proves to be the fool we know him to be, Darcy and I will see to him."

"You will not cause a scene in the high street, will you?" Jane asked in surprise. Elizabeth could well imagine the anxiety such a thing must cause for Jane for the thought of it caused her own heart to beat a little faster.

"Not unless it is necessary," Darcy answered.

Bingley nodded. "Creating a scene is far better than allowing anything to happen to those we love."

"Indeed!" Darcy agreed with enthusiasm.

"But the talk from such a thing…" Jane cautioned as she stepped down from the carriage. She straightened her pelisse and touched her hat to see that it was properly secure as a small smile played at her lips. "I could always trip him. Who might we match him with, Lizzy?"

"I cannot think of a single young lady who deserves such a husband!" Elizabeth cried. This teasing and taunting side of Jane had always lain hidden behind the closed doors of Longbourn, so it was pleasantly shocking to have it so displayed.

"Oh, I am not entirely certain of that," Jane retorted as she placed her hand on Bingley's arm. "Mrs. Salter might have a relation who favours her."

Darcy's laugh in response to the suggestion caused Elizabeth's own laugh to die on her lips.

"I had forgotten that you have both delved into your devious sides," Elizabeth said, looking up at the formerly dour Mr. Darcy.

"If Darcy continues to be so animated," Bingley inserted before either Jane or Darcy could defend themselves to Elizabeth, "we are certain to draw a crowd to gaze on the strange spectacle of the jovial gentleman from Derbyshire."

Darcy's left brow rose, and he peered down his nose at his friend. It might have been a convincing look of hauteur had his lips not twitched in an attempt to contain a smile that would not be entirely suppressed. "You are correct, of course. I am not the man I was when I was last here." He sighed and glanced up and down the street.

"I think it was just there," he pointed to a shop opposite them and a short distance away, "where we first met Mr. Wickham in Meryton. I wanted to run him through then, which is not so different from how I feel now. However, then, I was more reserved. I had my sister's reputation to consider, and I knew few and cared for even fewer members of this village and its environs. Now, there is not only my sister to defend but also the lady I love and her sisters to consider. I fear I might not be able to conjure the appropriate amount of reserve to resist treating him now as I wished to then."

Elizabeth seemed doomed to always be provoked to smile a silly little grin every time Darcy spoke so openly of his care for her. At the moment, he seemed unaware of any shopkeepers or shoppers who might be within hearing distance.

"Why should you need reserve?" Lydia asked. She and the others had just joined them.

"Your letter, Miss Lydia." Darcy withdrew the folded missive from his pocket and handed it to her. "Again, I thank you for the privilege of reading the beginning of it."

"You did not read the last paragraph?" she asked as she slipped the letter into her reticule.

"Not a word of it."

Elizabeth watched the exchange with interest. Lydia was so different and yet the same since her trip to London. There was a softening of her boisterous edges as the small thank you to Darcy demonstrated so well.

"We should like to view some muslin." Lydia looked to her companions, Kitty and Georgiana, who both nodded. "And Miss Darcy would like to see what sorts of music might be acquired here in Meryton." She glanced at Mrs. Annesley. "If that would be acceptable to you."

"I think those are fine items for which to look," Darcy replied.

Elizabeth was quite impressed by her sister's demeanor until they were just about to go in search of their first store.

"You have still not told me why you need to gather your reserve?" She fluttered her lashes at Darcy and smiled.

"Ah... well..." Darcy began haltingly, "that has to do with the fact that a particular member of the militia is returned from town to Meryton."

Lydia gasped, and her hand flew to her mouth. "I do hope he is returned!"

"I beg your pardon?" Elizabeth's reply was quick. Why would her sister wish to see Mr. Wickham after the way he had treated them?

"Well, I should like to see the bruises the colonel and Mr. Darcy gave him. I am certain it would be very romantic to witness the defense of one's honour. And should Mr.

Darcy not be able to find his reserve, we might get to witness not just the traces of a former altercation."

"I am certain I would not like to see him or his bruises," Georgiana said.

Elizabeth did not miss the small look of apology that passed from Georgiana to her brother.

"It is not that I think myself unable to see him," Georgiana added quickly. "I just do not think it proper to find such injuries to be pleasing."

"No, not at all," Mrs. Annesley encouraged. "Nor should one wish to be reminded of one's folly."

The comment was said very softly, and the accompanying look was just as gentle.

Lydia gasped, a look of mortification spreading across her face for a moment before being tucked away. "I had not thought of it as such. You are very right, Mrs. Annesley. I should not like to be reminded of my foolishness."

"Nor do you wish to have it broadcast about," Mrs. Annesley continued in the same calm tone.

"No, no. I am sure I do not," Lydia agreed. "I am certain I do not wish to see him at all. Indeed, I wish he were still in London."

"Richard would be pleased to hear you say so," Darcy added.

That sealed the fate of wishing to see either Mr. Wickham or his bruises.

"He is not even here," Elizabeth whispered when her

younger sisters and Georgiana, accompanied by Mrs. Annesley, had moved ahead of them by a few paces, "and still the colonel is seeing to Lydia's improvement."

"It is remarkable," Jane agreed. "As is Mrs. Annesley," she added.

"Indeed, she is," Darcy agreed. "My sister was certain she and Mrs. Annesley could help me see to Miss Lydia's continued improvement as I promised Richard I would do."

This was not news to either Elizabeth or Jane. Darcy had told Elizabeth of his promise to Richard, and Elizabeth had, in turn, shared it with Jane.

Elizabeth pressed her hand more firmly on Darcy's arm at the sound of his soft but heavy sigh.

He turned questioning eyes towards her.

"I, too, wish he were here," she whispered, earning herself a smile of appreciation.

Ahead of them, Lydia was standing in front of a store peering through its many-paned window with Kitty on her one side and Georgiana on her other. Mary stood behind them with Miss Annesley, looking as if she was embarrassed to be seen in front of a shop window.

"Does Miss Mary not enjoy shopping?"

Apparently, Darcy had noticed Mary's unease as well.

"Mary prefers a list of items to be purchased and a rapid walk from merchant to merchant before meandering home while reading, satisfied to know that everything she needs will be delivered shortly," Jane replied.

"Save for the few small treats she might have purchased to eat while she walks," Elizabeth added. "Those she will carry, of course."

"A lady with purpose," Darcy muttered, "is not a bad thing."

"Unless she thinks everyone should conform to her way of thinking," Jane cautioned. "That would be Mary's weakness."

They had nearly reached the shop where their sisters stood when to Elizabeth's dismay, the group of officers they had seen, crossed the street.

"We have only just arrived back at Longbourn," Kitty was saying to Captain Denny as Elizabeth and Darcy joined her. "And we thought to show our friend the high street. Have you seen if there is any new music at the book-seller's?"

"I cannot say I have inquired." Denny shifted and glanced uneasily at Darcy. "At least, I have not since I sent my sister that piece of music last month. You remember the one, do you not?"

"Oh, indeed, I do," Kitty replied, smiling broadly. "It would be lovely if they still had a copy."

"We shall have to make certain to stop there," Elizabeth inserted before extending her greeting to the assembled officers.

Wickham glanced first at her face and then the hand which lay on Darcy's arm. "I understand that you and Miss Bennet have happy news. Allow me to extend my joy." He gave each of them a small bow of his head.

The comment surprised Elizabeth, although not because he knew of her betrothal – for, if Lady Lucas knew, everyone knew. No, she was surprised by the civility with which he greeted them and the fact that he would mention hers or Jane's betrothal at all.

"We only wanted to wish you a happy return to the neighbourhood." Captain Saunders wore a pleasant smile, though his eyes did dart uneasily toward Darcy before returning to the rest of the group. Then, he and his companions bowed and took their leave, wandering down the street toward the inn.

"Well," said Bingley, "that was unexpected."

"His bruises looked impressive," Lydia whispered with a pleased smile for Darcy. "Well done."

"We do not congratulate gentlemen on how well they can bruise another," Mrs. Annesley inserted. "Not even if those bruises are well-deserved." She winked at Lydia. "We have muslins to see."

"Muslins!" Darcy said, sending an amused smile in Bingley's direction.

"Indeed!" Bingley agreed, with a smirk of his own. "I am all anticipation" he teased.

"You poor men," Jane consoled. "What trials you endure!"

"And happily so," Bingley assured her.

"Very happily so," Darcy agreed before lifting Elizabeth's hand and placing a kiss on her knuckles bringing to mind what he had promised her while they were still in London – to endure every possible irritation for her sake.

However, as she stepped into the shop, Elizabeth was not sure if the kiss was because of the gentlemen they had met outside or the cries of delight from three young ladies admiring a selection of muslin.

# Chapter 5

To Elizabeth's surprise, Darcy seemed to be settling easily into the neighbourhood. He had greeted a few gentlemen by name when they had been in Meryton three days ago.

*"We went shooting together," he had told her.*

He had patiently borne all of her mother's happy exclamations each day when a neighbour had come to call while Darcy was also in the sitting room. Then, he had been the one to suggest dancing to Sir William when they were at Lucas Lodge for dinner last evening.

It was remarkable the change he had made, and her heart thrilled to know that he endured it all for her. She was certain there was not another man in all of England who was as wonderful as her Mr. Darcy.

Today, however, he seemed a little out of sorts. His smile was not as quick as it had been since his arrival, and he was quiet – not that silence was something which was foreign to him. It was just that it felt to her as if the silence was a heavy blanket he had to carry.

"The sun is warm today," Elizabeth said.

Darcy nodded. "It is."

Elizabeth held his arm a little more firmly, moving to walk closer to him as if somehow doing so might help him bear whatever burden he carried. His lips curled up softly as he looked down at her, and the same soft pleasure of his smile shone in his eyes.

"I have had a letter from Richard," he said after a few silent paces down the road.

Jane and Bingley, as well as Caroline and Sir Matthew, were somewhere behind them, while Georgiana and Elizabeth's other sisters were ahead of them. None were close enough to hear a word of Darcy and Elizabeth's conversation.

"I wished to tell you right away, but..." His eyes left hers as he looked toward the group in front of them.

"You did not want Lydia to know?"

He nodded. "I cannot allow her to read it. The details are," he shook his head, "disturbing, but I have promised to share with her when he writes to me."

"Was there any news which was not disturbing? Perhaps you can share that bit with her?" Elizabeth prodded hopefully.

"There were a few descriptions of his accommodations and a fellow officer or two. It was all written just as Richard would tell me if he were in my study enjoying a glass of port with me."

Elizabeth watched as a small smile played at the corners

of Darcy's mouth while, she assumed, he contemplated his cousin.

"He has been injured, but it is not severe. A few stitches above his left eye is all. There was an altercation at a tavern, and a window was broken. He assures me it will only make his appearance more fetching should it scar for it is so small and distinguished looking." He chuckled softly before sobering once again. "But I cannot tell your sister about that or the arrests or people who have died."

"Then do not tell her. Share with her the tales of the officers and tell her that the rest was about things which would surely bore her to tears. She does not wish to read about daily duties, and I am certain the awful bits were, sadly, just part of your cousin's daily duties." Elizabeth squeezed Darcy's arm tightly. How horrible it must be for him to have someone so close to him in harm's way. She had never really contemplated how it must be for some who had loved ones who were on the continent, in a far away colony where there was unrest, or sailing with the navy, let alone here at home locked in a disagreement with fellow countrymen.

"That would not be too great a prevarication, would it?" Darcy asked.

Elizabeth shook her head. "I do not believe it would be. You may tell her about his cut if you wish. I do not think that would cause her too much distress, and she must know that there are dangers."

Darcy expelled a great breath, the weight of resignation and grave duty were in the sound. "I believe you are correct. Shall we catch up to them?"

With Elizabeth's permission, they quickened their pace and were soon able to overtake the young ladies ahead of them. Of course, the fact that their sisters had stopped for Kitty to retie a bootlace did help Darcy and Elizabeth's effort.

"We must turn back soon," Elizabeth said as they reached their sisters.

"But before we do," Darcy began, "I wished to tell you that I have had a letter from my cousin."

"Richard?" Georgiana said eagerly.

Elizabeth looked quickly to Darcy. She had not thought of how his sister might receive this news. Indeed, he had not mentioned it as something which lay heavy on his heart. He had surely thought of his sister, but it was his concern for Lydia that grieved him the most.

Darcy flashed his sister a quick, tight smile and nodded. "I did not bring it to share because it was not all fit for the eyes of young ladies."

"Oh, I should think it is not!" Lydia said, surprising them all. "I would imagine that gentlemen speak to each other in letters as they do when they have their port after dinner."

"What do you mean?" Mary asked.

"Well," said Lydia as the large group started moving forward again, "we ladies are sent away, and I imagine it is so the gentlemen can use vulgar language and speak of indelicate things. Is that not what you do?"

Darcy looked from her inquisitive face to the others who also peeked at him. "I suppose, sometimes that is the case."

Elizabeth could not help but smile at his uncertain, hesitating tone and the wary expression he wore. It was as if he were uncertain what Lydia might ask him next.

"What did your cousin have to say?" Lydia asked, seemingly satisfied with Darcy's response.

"He told me about the innkeepers just as he told you. Then, he mentioned a fellow – a Captain G – who likes to sing hymns when they go out to patrol but who, after he has had a pint or two, also sings the bawdiest songs Richard has ever heard."

"I can see why that would not be something a young lady should read," muttered Mary.

"Oh, indeed," Darcy agreed. "There was one thing which happened that is not of a pleasant nature to have to report. It seems that during a disagreement between some gentlemen one night at a tavern, a window was broken, and Richard received a cut during the dispute. As a result, he required a few stitches to close the wound, but he assures me that it makes him look very distinguished," Darcy added quickly over the gasps of the four young ladies in their group.

"He is well?" Lydia asked, turning fearful eyes toward Darcy.

Elizabeth wished to gather her into her arms at the sight of her distress. She glanced up at Darcy. His throat moved up and down as he swallowed while he nodded.

"He assures me he is well."

Lydia's shoulders relaxed as she expelled a quiet, relieved breath. "That is very good news then," she said after a moment of silence. "Was there anything else?"

"Nothing I can share," Darcy answered.

"He spoke of fighting?" Lydia asked quietly.

"He did."

"I knew that there could be some," she added. "He told me before he left." She shrugged. "No one wants to lose their livelihood or their lives."

"He told you that?"

Lydia nodded. "I am not a child, Mr. Darcy." She pulled her shoulders straight. "But I thank you for not sharing any of the fightings with me aside from the colonel's injury."

They walked on for some time in silence. Elizabeth was impressed by how Lydia had accepted the news. There were no tears or fits of nerves. Her response had been more reminiscent of how Jane might react rather than how their mother might — which had always been Lydia's normal wont up until now. Lydia was improving. How had Colonel Fitzwilliam known to share such serious matters with her before he left? Elizabeth would have expected him to assure Lydia that he would be well and would return soon. She had not thought he would tell her about the grave nature of his duty. Once again, she was struck by just how very good Colonel Fitzwilliam was for her sister.

Darcy fished in his pocket and withdrew his handkerchief. Then, he touched Lydia's shoulder and gave it to her.

So, there were tears. Elizabeth had not seen them, but Darcy had. She smiled up at him as he wiped at the corners of his own eyes with his hand. Her brow furrowed. Was he thinking of his cousin?

He tipped his head toward Lydia and then touched his heart.

She nodded her understanding before laying her head against his shoulder. He was still thinking of her sister — her youngest, most troublesome sister — and his heart was touched. The thought could only endear him more firmly to her. He truly was the best of men.

# Chapter 6

Darcy settled into a comfortable chair in Netherfield's drawing room. Dash lay at his feet, and Oliver stalked them both from the far side of the room. Darcy chuckled over how the curious creature would come within feet of Dash but then scurry away as soon as Dash flinched. The fur above Dash's eyes was moving as he watched Oliver walk to and fro. Eventually, the two might become friends as Bingley predicted, but at present, it appeared as if that was not going to happen any time soon.

"That was not as dreadful as I expected," Caroline Bingley said as she took a seat on a settee. She had attended the soiree at Lucas Lodge after her arrival at Netherfield, but today was the first day she had decided to call on any of the neighbors. "The Bennets seem to improve upon acquaintance, though..." She stopped speaking when Sir Matthew coughed softly.

"There are many in this world who pose some sort of challenge to our sensibilities," Sir Matthew said.

"Oh, indeed, there are!" Caroline agreed. "Mrs. Bennet is an acquired taste."

Sir Matthew shrugged but said nothing.

"She was very welcoming of you, as she should be," Caroline added, placing a hand on her betrothed's arm. "It is not every day that she has a baronet in her home." Caroline turned to Darcy, her smile somewhat smug. "That is what she said."

"It is true," Darcy replied.

Caroline was more accepting of things than he ever remembered her being, but she had still not forgiven him either for rejecting her or for having caused her current betrothed state. Therefore, he would endure her small jabs for as long as she felt it necessary to punish him.

Darcy gave a small shake of his head when Sir Matthew raised an eyebrow in question. The man had met with both Bingley and Darcy within moments of his arrival to discuss how challenging having Caroline under the same roof as them might be. The man was exceptionally good at directing Caroline, but even more surprising was the fact that he did not seem daunted by the task. He had the patience of Job. Nothing seemed to ruffle his calm exterior.

"I am not that important," Sir Matthew said, grasping Caroline's hand which lay on his arm. "I am fortunate to have inherited a title and an estate."

Caroline's head had dipped, and her cheeks grew rosy when he had secured her hand in his.

"I am also fortunate to have fallen for such a lovely lady as yourself." His eyes smiled as much as his lips did.

To Darcy, it looked as if Sir Matthew was truly happy in his current situation.

"I think we will visit Mrs. Philips and Lady Lucas tomorrow."

Dash's head popped up almost as if he were as surprised as Darcy was at hearing Caroline say such a thing, but it was not Caroline's words that had caught Dash's attention. Nor was it Bingley's entrance to the drawing room and his subsequent scooping up of Oliver that had caused Dash to grumble. There was a carriage on the drive.

"Were you expecting visitors?" Sir Matthew asked.

"No. But it could be any one of our neighbours. There are several who have not yet called." Bingley stood expectantly in front of his chair, rather than sitting.

It was not very long before the noise of someone entering drifted up the stairs to the open door of the sitting room.

Dash was the first to move.

Darcy rushed after him, but he was not quick enough to catch him.

"Darcy, what is the meaning of this?" Lady Catherine waved at the dog who was sniffing her shoes. "I nearly fell! It is not a proper way to be greeted. Not at all. Go on with you. Leave me be," she said to Dash, and Dash being the dog that he was, cocked his head to the side, looked up at her, and moved not an inch.

"Dash," Darcy called. The beast removed his eyes from Lady Catherine to consider Darcy for a moment before ignoring him completely.

"It seems he likes you, Aunt Catherine."

"Of all the things!" she huffed. "You know how I feel about animals in the house. Dogs are for hunting, not decoration."

"Dash is anything but a decoration," Darcy said with a laugh. "And he has yet to learn to hunt. I got him for Georgiana. He makes her happy."

Lady Catherine's right brow rose as her lips pursed and she looked down at Dash. "Well, then, I suppose I must like you. Now stand by and allow me to finish my ascent of these stairs."

Dash plopped down on the step and did not move.

"I must say he obeys well when you speak correctly. I will teach you, Darcy. You are too soft. You always have been, but then, that is what I like about you." She had reached the top of the stairs by the time she had finished her comments. "Come along," she said to Dash, who immediately obeyed. "Anne is in town with her aunt. She is well. The cough never developed into anything of consequence." She looked up and down the hall. "We must talk."

"About what?" Darcy asked before making a move to lead her to the sitting room.

"I have heard tales about a betrothal. That cannot be. You were destined for Anne."

Darcy sighed. "The study is this way." He motioned down the hallway.

"I had a letter – well, no. That is not it precisely. Mrs. Collins had a letter. It contained some very unsettling news."

Apparently, his aunt was not about to wait until they had reached the study before she had her say. Of course, that was not uncommon for his aunt. When she had business to discuss, it was discussed no matter where she might be in the house. Servants did not have ears in her world. At least, they did not if they wished to retain their position in her household.

"I had thought that Mrs. Collins's mother must be mistaken. You could not possibly be betrothed to some young woman since we have been expecting you to offer for Anne for some time now." She entered the study ahead of him and paused speaking long enough to give the room a thorough looking over before sighing with resignation that it would have to do and taking a seat.

"As I was saying, I knew it could not be true, but Mrs. Collins insisted it was. Well, I knew if anyone knew the truth it would be my brother, so we – Anne and I – went to London. You were not home, which caused me no little amount of trepidation, and then, well..." She shook her head and looked most dissatisfied. "My brother informed me that the rumors I had heard were not rumors at all."

"They are not. I am betrothed." Darcy unbuttoned his jacket and reclined in his chair.

"My brother will not support me, but I had to come place my case, as well as that of your very disheartened cousin, before you. How could you play her false?"

Darcy blinked. "Play Anne false?"

Lady Catherine nodded. "She has just finished sewing a cap for when she marries. This news came as quite a blow."

Darcy doubted that very much. Anne had no desire to be Mrs. Darcy. Of that, Darcy was rather certain.

"I do apologize for your disappointment, but it is not I who has played my cousin false, madame. I believe that grievous sin falls to you."

"To me? Of all the... I dare say it does not!"

"You are the only one who has ever spoken to her about marrying me. I know for a fact that I have never mentioned it. I have done nothing to engage her affections. I have been very careful to be as circumspect as can be around my cousin."

Lady Catherine scowled. "You were kind to her."

"As I should be. We are relations." His words only deepened his aunt's scowl. "Nothing you say will move me." It was best to just end this argument before it began. "I am marrying Elizabeth Bennet."

"What is she compared to you?" Lady Catherine grumbled, stirring Darcy's ire.

"She is my life, my heart, my everything, and I will not abide one ill word to be spoken against her. If you wish to retain your relationship with me, you will measure your words carefully."

"Love," she muttered. "Young people these days think love is of utmost importance. Foolish notions. Marriage is an alliance."

"I will not disagree with you."

Lady Catherine's mouth dropped open. It was clearly not the response she expected.

"Love can be a foolish thing, but do not dismiss something merely because it appears foolish. For love is not weak. It is not easily overcome." He knew full well how difficult it had been to try to overcome his love for Elizabeth – indeed, how foolish he had been to think he could overcome his love for Elizabeth. "And marriage is most assuredly an alliance. Between two hearts."

"That is not my meaning."

"I am well aware of that fact. I will not be moved."

"You are as stubborn as an old goat just like your uncle!" she cried. "What am I to do with Anne?"

Darcy shook his head. "I do not know."

Lady Catherine sighed and patted Dash's head, which was propped on her knee.

Darcy rose. "You will stay for at least the night, will you not?"

"Well, I am not returning to London at this hour of the day!"

"Then, it would be best if I were to introduce you to our host and hostess." Darcy stood at the door with his hand on the doorknob. "You will not disparage them."

Lady Catherine lifted her chin. "It goes without saying."

"Not a foul word about my betrothal will leave your lips?"

Her eyes narrowed, and she pouted very much like a petulant child would.

"Not a foul word," Darcy repeated.

His aunt's features relaxed as she affixed a smile on her lips. "It goes without saying. I am, of course, delighted for you."

Her voice was dripping with contempt, but it would have to do.

"Since I have your word." Darcy opened the door.

"You would not do this to me, would you?"

The softly spoken comment was met with a bark.

"That is a good boy," Lady Catherine whispered.

Darcy sighed and shook his head. Apparently, if a person were in the least bit difficult, his dog would befriend them and follow them to the gates of hell and back if asked.

# Chapter 7

"I trust you slept well, Aunt Catherine?" Darcy looked up from the paper he was reading.

"Quite," she said as she took a seat to break her fast as she always did with a cup of tea, an egg, and a dry piece of toast.

Darcy had seen to it that the footmen assigned to the breakfast room were aware of his aunt's desires. She would not be toasting her own bread, nor did she expect to have to ask to be served.

"That cat," Lady Catherine's eyes followed Oliver as he slinked around the room, "has stolen my bracelet twice. He is not to be trusted."

"He also likes to pounce upon the table," Darcy cautioned. "However, I do believe you will be safe with Dash at your side. Oliver has yet to warm to Dash."

"Where is your sister?"

"She will likely be down soon. I believe she is expecting callers within the hour."

Hopefully, his aunt could be gone before the Bennets

arrived. He did not need a repeat of last evening. It had been a struggle for him to endure his aunt's cutting, veiled remarks which did a poor job of disguising her displeasure even if they did not fall on the side of being disparaging — or, more precisely, they had ceased to fall on the side of being disparaging after Darcy had asked Bingley if the empty room above the stable might be readied. That had caused Lady Catherine to hold her tongue long enough for them to all retire for the night. However, this morning, there were no demeaning accommodations to use as a deterrent to his aunt's words. She could be sent away, but likely not before she could do some damage.

"Is there no meat in this house?"

"You do not eat meat for breakfast," Darcy said, peering up once again from his paper.

"You," she called to one of the footmen, "fetch me a small bit of ham if there is any." She turned her attention back to scraping the darkest crumbs from her toast. "Georgiana seems in good spirits."

"She is."

"Is there news of Richard in the paper?"

"Nothing in particular," Darcy replied.

"She is recovering well, then?"

"Georgiana?"

"Yes, of course, of whom else might I be speaking?" Lady Catherine cut her toast into four pieces as a plate with a slice of ham was placed on the table next to her.

"Ah, that is just the thing. I was about to despair of anything proper being available in this place." She waved her knife in a circle in the air as she said *this place*.

"Netherfield is a fine estate and is run well. Mrs. Nichols is an excellent housekeeper, and Mr. Barrett excels at his post as well."

Lady Catherine pursed her lips and shook her head. "The servants can only be as good as their master, and their master," she waved her knife in the direction of the footmen, "knows little of how a master of an estate should conduct himself. No separation after the meal!"

"There was little need of separating," Darcy repeated what he had told her last night when she had voiced her displeasure over the *neglect of proper decorum*.

"There is always a need." She had finished cutting the ham into small pieces and, reaching over to take a fork from Darcy's place setting, she speared a morsel and fed it to Dash.

"He is not to be fed from the table!" Darcy cried.

"He is hungry. Just look at his eyes."

"He is a trickster," Darcy replied.

"He is a hungry trickster. Are you not?" Lady Catherine said to Dash as she fed him a second piece of ham. "That is all for the moment. I must eat my egg, and then you shall have some more."

"Good morning," Georgiana greeted as she entered the room.

"Your brother said you are expecting guests."

"I am expecting friends," Georgiana corrected.

"Friends? Here?"

Georgiana nodded as she accepted a cup of tea. "Miss Lydia, Miss Kitty, and Miss Mary promised to accompany their sisters to Netherfield today. There is a piece of music we wish to play and a dance to practice. I must be ready for my come out next season, you know."

"Indeed, you must." Lady Catherine scrutinized Georgiana as she ate the egg she had told Dash she was going to eat.

Dash pawed at her chair leg but returned to sitting attentively when Lady Catherine gave him a stern look before returning her attention to her niece.

Her brow arched, and her lips curled into a small smirk.

"Do you wish for your carriage to be readied?" Darcy asked. He did not like the calculating look on his aunt's face.

She shook her head. "I assume Miss Elizabeth Bennet is one of these young ladies' sisters?"

"Yes," Georgiana replied with a smile. "They are very pleasant."

Lady Catherine's right brow rose, imperiously this time, as her chin lifted.

"Your carriage?" Darcy tried once again.

"I will call for it when I am ready." She speared another piece of ham for Dash. "I think it would be best if I met this Miss Elizabeth since my brother has not yet exerted himself to do so."

"You will behave," Darcy cautioned.

"Perfectly," Lady Catherine said, lifting her cup to take a sip of tea. "Good morning, Sir Matthew, Miss Bingley."

She was being altogether too pleasant, and it made Darcy excessively uneasy, for Darcy knew that his aunt was rarely pleasant without a reason – or rather, a scheme to put in play. However, she gave no indication as to what the scheme might be while she and Dash finished their breakfast.

Upon leaving the breakfast room, Darcy sought out Mr. Barrett.

"Have Lady Catherine's carriage ready at a moment's notice," he instructed.

He needed to be prepared. He had warned his aunt that he would brook no disparagement of his betrothed, and while he did not fully expect her to blatantly ignore him, he also did not entirely trust her.

~*~*~

"So, you are the young woman who has finally turned Darcy's head?" Lady Catherine said after Darcy had made all the introductions when the Bennets arrived a quarter hour later.

"I suppose I am," Elizabeth replied.

"You are pretty."

"Thank you."

"There are a lot of you."

"Aunt," Darcy growled.

"It is a fact. I do not think I have seen five daughters all at once in one room," she said in defense of her comment.

"How is your father?" Bingley asked.

"He was in his study with a book when we left," Elizabeth replied.

"He seems more comfortable each day," Jane added.

"I am glad to hear it," Bingley said.

"Is your father not well?" Lady Catherine arranged herself in a chair that was close to the sofa on which Georgiana and the three youngest Bennets sat.

"Have you not heard?" Lydia asked as she scratched Dash's head. "He fell when touring Darcy House and broke his leg."

The information was met with a gasp of surprise from Lady Catherine.

"Dash tripped him," Darcy added.

"Dash did?"

The question was said with a great deal of surprise that Dash could ever do such a thing. Apparently, it did not matter that the animal had tried to do the very same thing to her yesterday on her arrival. Darcy thought to mention such to her, but it would likely not do any good.

"You really need to take him in hand, Darcy. One cannot have one's animal injuring people."

"I agree."

"As you should," Lady Catherine added.

"He has been learning to behave better," Lydia assured Lady Catherine. "He listens particularly well to Colonel Fitzwilliam and me. Actually," Lydia tipped her head, "that is not true. Dash listens well to me."

"Oh," was all Lady Catherine had to say in reply.

Lydia gasped. "I nearly forgot." She pulled a letter from her reticule. "I have had another letter." She rose and crossed to give the missive to Darcy. "Do not read the last paragraph," she whispered.

"Why is she giving you her mail?" Lady Catherine demanded.

"It is from his cousin," Lydia replied.

Darcy cringed at the admission. Lydia was far too trusting.

"Which cousin?"

"Colonel Fitzwilliam, my lady," Lydia said before resuming her seat.

"Fitzwilliam is writing to you?"

Darcy groaned.

"He has her father's permission," he interjected.

"How old are you?"

"Aunt," Darcy cautioned with a pointed look.

"I must know what sort of lady has captured my nephew's interest."

"I will be sixteen in April, my lady."

"Sixteen?" Shock suffused Lady Catherine's features.

"And your father encourages this?" She waved at the missive Darcy held. "You are out before your sisters are married?"

"Elizabeth and Jane shall marry before me." Lydia looked at Darcy, confusion etched in her features.

"Things are not done now as they once were," Darcy added with a small smile for Lydia.

"I should say not!" Lady Catherine cried. Then, with a huff — a very displeased huff — she rearranged herself in her chair as if keeping to her seat were a great trial. "Marrying where you choose, rather than thinking of your family." She shook her head. "My brother might approve of you choosing as you have, Darcy, but I am certain he will not approve of *her* for his son!" Completely overcome and not being able to resist her restlessness a moment longer, she rose from her place.

"Why would he not?" Lydia asked.

"Why would he not?" Lady Catherine's eyebrows rose high, and she looked at Lydia as if the girl was the stupidest person she had ever met. "You ask why an earl would not approve of a lady of little means whose mother is from trade? Have you no sense of propriety?"

"He loves me," Lydia said above Dash's growl.

"You are not good enough for him," Lady Catherine snapped.

Dash positioned himself in front of Lydia and barked, startling Lady Catherine.

Lydia rose, arms folded, and eyes flashing. "I think that if Colonel Fitzwilliam is intelligent enough to lead a division of men, he is capable of choosing whom he wishes to marry," she spat.

"It is not done. The son of an earl marrying someone with ties to trade?" She shook her head. "The world has turned on its head. Darcy marrying beneath his sphere? A tradesman's son becoming a gentleman? A baronet marrying a tradesman's daughter? It is not proper."

"You might wish to speak to Lady Jersey about that," Sir Matthew inserted from the corner where he sat. "Her grandfather was a banker, you know. However, I imagine he would likely agree with you since he found an earl to be less than acceptable for his daughter. And I am also certain he is not the first to think in such a fashion." Sir Matthew paused for a moment as the room sat in silence. "It seems the world has been turned on its head for some time."

"Your carriage is waiting," Darcy said softly, taking his aunt by the elbow and moving her toward the door.

"It is not right," she protested as she left the room. "This is not how things are supposed to be."

"But it is how things are," Darcy said firmly. "And if you wish to continue visiting me, you will learn to accept them as they are. I have warned you. I will abide no disparagement of my betrothed or her family. Think on that carefully as you return to town. My mother would be saddened to think you had cut yourself off from me."

"But it is not my doing," Lady Catherine protested.

"It is entirely your doing, for it is your choice," Darcy said as Mr. Barrett handed Lady Catherine's wrap and hat to her.

"But she is..."

"My sister."

Lady Catherine's eyes grew wide at Darcy's declaration.

"And I will protect her just as I would Georgiana." He waited for his aunt to say something for she looked as if she wished to, but she remained silent. "May your journey be pleasant," he added, and then with a bow, he took his leave of her.

# Chapter 8

Elizabeth kept one eye on her youngest sister and one eye on the door to Netherfield's drawing room. Lydia was sitting sullenly on the sofa. She had uncrossed her arms so that she could scratch Dash's ear, but her scowl still remained.

"That was vicious."

Elizabeth's eyes flicked in astonishment toward Caroline, the source of the whispered comment.

"There are people in this world who think they are better than others and are not sensible enough to keep their ignorance to themselves."

Caroline's head dipped at Sir Matthew's words, and a tinge of pink stained her cheeks.

"To think she thought you unfit to be my wife," Sir Matthew continued. "Utter balderdash is what it is."

Lydia brushed at the corner of her eye.

"Oh, there you are!" Bingley rose quickly from his seat and managed to capture Oliver before he could find a safe hiding place. "This is Oliver," he announced to the room.

Lydia's scowl softened to interest, and Elizabeth sighed in relief. There would likely still be some pouting and tears – how could there not be? Elizabeth was certain she would be a jumbled mess of emotions if she had been attacked in such a fashion as Lydia had been.

"He is a gift for Miss Bennet," Bingley continued.

"For me?" Jane's face lit with delight as Bingley handed Oliver to her. "Oh, he is beautiful." She made a small clicking sound to capture Oliver's attention before scratching him on the head and then stroking along his back. He stood on her lap and arched his back toward her hand.

"I acquired him before you arrived back at Longbourn," Bingley explained as he once again took a seat next to Jane. "Do you truly like him?" He scratched Oliver's head.

"He is perfect," Jane cooed.

Darcy entered the room just then, and Elizabeth shifted her attention from how her sister was playing with Oliver to him. He smiled at her but did not come to her side. Instead, he crossed to where his sister and hers were seated.

"Do you like kittens?" he asked Lydia, who nodded.

He bent to scratch Dash's ear. "We best not tell this fellow, or he will think he has lost his place."

A pleased and amused smile spread across Lydia's face.

"I will say I thought he might bite my aunt for a moment, which she would have rightly deserved."

Lydia's smile faltered.

"He is very loyal to you," Darcy added.

"He is."

"So is my cousin."

Elizabeth barely heard the whispered words which Darcy spoke as he once again scratched Dash's ear before turning his head to look at his sister.

"Were you going to practice some music, Georgiana?"

"We were," Georgiana answered. "Shall we go to the music room?" She rose.

"I think I should like that very much," Darcy agreed. "And you might even persuade me to join in the dancing if Miss Elizabeth will stand up with me."

Elizabeth nodded. She would follow him to the ends of the earth if he asked. He was crouched down now in front of Lydia, giving Dash another scratch.

"I will return your letter to you as soon as I have read all but the last paragraph," he assured her before standing and offering her his hand to aid in rising from her chair. "And," he said when she was on her feet and before he released her hand so she could join the others, "remember what my cousin said before he left Darcy House. He has made his choice and will not be dissuaded from it."

Lydia's lips curled into a small smile while her eyes glistened with tears as she nodded and whispered a quick "thank you."

While Lydia scooted from the room, Darcy's shoulders

lifted and lowered as he drew and released a deep breath. "I cannot apologize for my aunt enough," he said to those who remained in the room. "There is not one of us who she did not censure." He shook his head. "I knew she would not be happy to hear of my betrothal, but I had not considered how she might respond to Miss Lydia."

"You could not know with certainty," Sir Matthew said. "She might come to her senses now that you have tossed her from the house."

Darcy chuckled. "I did not precisely toss her from the house."

"You escorted her out the door rather quickly," Bingley said.

Darcy shook his head and chuckled softly. "Very well, I did tell her that she will not be welcome to visit me if she continues as she has been. I will brook no disparagement of any member of my family."

"Which is as it should be," Sir Matthew agreed, although his eyes were on his betrothed.

Caroline fidgeted with the seam of her skirt and, without lifting her eyes from her hands, said, "Sir Matthew is correct. You should not abide any condemnation of those you love." She blew out a breath. "I must apologize for the times I have been that small person."

Her eyes finally lifted to look at her companions when no one spoke. She shrugged. "I wanted what I could not have." She straightened her shoulders. "I believe that is all I wish to say on that for now."

Sir Matthew captured her hand, and she smiled.

"Well, I will say this bit more," Caroline continued. "Though I mean no offense to Mr. Darcy, I think what I have received is far better than what I sought, and I have no desire to become a bitter lady such as your aunt."

It was perhaps not worded in the most appropriate fashion, but Darcy still smiled and accepted her apology with grace.

"I for one, am happy to hear it," Bingley said. "You may thank me later, dear sister."

"Thank you? For what?"

"To begin with, for allowing Sir Matthew to marry you."

Caroline gasped. "Allowing? Forcing is more like the truth!"

"Do you truly feel forced to marry me?" Sir Matthew asked.

Caroline's eyes narrowed, and her lips pressed into a thin line. "No," she admitted reluctantly.

"Then," Sir Matthew continued, "I think your brother is right in expecting a thank you at some point. I know I have thanked him several times for my good fortune." The gentleman lifted her hand to his lips, causing Caroline to smile.

"Very well. You are right as you often are," Caroline

replied. "I shall have to thank you sometime, Brother. However, I do not think it will be today."

Darcy shook his head while chuckling softly to himself as he extended his hand to Elizabeth. "I believe we are expected in the music room."

"That was..."

"Surprising," Darcy finished Elizabeth's whispered sentence as he tucked her hand in the crook of his arm. "That man is a marvel."

"He is," Elizabeth said as she cast a look over her shoulder at the two couples remaining in the drawing room. Caroline was asking Jane something about a wedding breakfast. "I had worried about Jane having such a sister, but I do not think I need to worry any longer."

She rested her head against Darcy's shoulder as they ambled down the hallway. She had missed quiet moments with him like this. There had been many in the weeks she had been at Darcy House and few since her return to Longbourn.

"But then, I had also worried about my mother and sisters driving you to distraction, and I was wrong about that as well."

"They still might," Darcy admitted.

Elizabeth's cheek rubbed against the fabric of his jacket as she shook her head. "You were wonderful with Lydia just now. Even if they do set your teeth on edge from time to time as they might – for they do mine – I have no reason to worry because I know you will handle it with great aplomb."

Music filtered through the door before them.

He smiled down at her and shook his head. "I cannot guarantee that I will not ever respond inappropriately, but I have promised you that I will endure it all because I love you."

Elizabeth peeked down the hall. The door to the drawing room was closed, and no servants were about. "And how will you assure me of your promise, sir?" she asked impertinently as she looked up into the eyes of the most wonderful man in the world.

A smile spread across his face, and he answered as she hoped he would by lowering those smiling lips to hers and wrapping her in his embrace.

# Chapter 9

"Come in, my dears," Mr. Bennet called from his chair near the small hearth in his study as Elizabeth opened the door. "How many daughters are visiting me today?" He peeked over his shoulder toward the door. "My favourites," he said with a smile.

"No, Papa. I am here, too," Lydia said.

"And you are not my favourite youngest daughter? Have you given that position to Kitty? I shall have to write this down, so I do not forget if you have." He closed his book and tucked it between his leg and the arm of the chair.

"Oh, Papa," Jane chided. "You do not have favourites."

"Oh, but he does," Lydia replied. "You and Lizzy."

"Yes," her father said. "Jane is my favourite eldest daughter. Lizzy is my favourite second daughter. Mary is, of course, my favourite middle daughter. And then there is Kitty who is my favourite almost youngest daughter, and then there is you, my dear Lydia, who is and, I hope, shall always remain, my favourite youngest daughter."

"No," Lydia protested, "I am Mama's favourite, and Jane

and Lizzy are your favourites. Poor Mary and Kitty are not favourites at all; except, Kitty and I are very good friends so perhaps she is my favourite." Lydia sighed and shook her head. "Poor Mary," she murmured. "It must be dreadful to be so alone."

Mr. Bennet's left eyebrow had quirked in question during Lydia's recital of how things were. "I believe," he said, "that a daughter might be favoured by both parents and her sisters and still not have exhausted the number of people to whom she is dear."

"Do you think so?" Lydia took a seat on a footstool next to Jane.

"I am certain of it," her father replied.

"But you cannot have *everyone* as your favourite. That is not how favourites work," Lydia declared.

"Which is nearly what I said," Jane inserted. "Papa does not truly have favourites as you would think of favourites. He loves us all. It is just that there are particular things about each of us that endears us to him."

"Jane is a very wise young lady," Mr. Bennet said. "I have had my fun teasing you about favourites and trying to befuddle your mind with going in circles and will agree with Jane. She has said it perfectly."

"As she always does," Elizabeth said with a little laugh.

"Not always," Jane argued, though she grinned broadly while her eyes sparkled with amusement.

Lydia seemed either to have missed or to have chosen

to ignore Elizabeth's and Jane's playful exchange. Her face was overwritten with curiosity.

"You like something particular about me?" Lydia asked her father.

He nodded. "I do."

"What?"

Her father steepled his fingers and rested his chin on them as he studied her for a moment in silence. "More than any of your sisters, you are the very image of your mother. How could I not admire that about you, for as you know from our time in London, I love your mother very dearly. I always have, and I always will."

Elizabeth could not agree more with any of what her father said. Since spending time with Lydia at Sally's and hearing a portion of the story about their parents' courtship, Elizabeth knew just how much her parents loved each other and had come to realize just how much Lydia was like her mother. Sally had pointed it out many times, and Elizabeth had considered it in that moment and for several days afterward. However, she also knew that Lydia was not just a copy of her mother. Lydia also possessed her own special qualities. Qualities which were being drawn out and revealed because of Colonel Fitzwilliam.

"Now," her father said, "tell me about Netherfield. Does it still look as it did? Did you dance as you expected?"

Lydia nodded her head. "We did."

Mr. Bennet's brow furrowed. "That is all the report you have? Did you not see Dash? Am I to wonder about all the fixtures and furnishings?"

"Oh!" Lydia exclaimed. "Mr. Bingley gave Jane a kitten. His name is Oliver – not Mr. Bingley's. Oliver is the kitten's name."

"I did not bring him home." Jane's cheeks were rosy. "I thought it best that he stays in the home he knows for now."

"It will be her home eventually anyway," Lydia added as if no one in the room would remember that Jane was to marry Bingley. "Dash is not fond of Oliver, although I think he is merely curious about him and would really like to be his friend, but Oliver is so young. It really is not to be expected that Oliver would understand how to be a friend to Dash just yet."

"Well, that is well-thought out," muttered their father.

Elizabeth bit back a giggle at his perplexed expression.

"Mr. Darcy's aunt was there," Jane said quietly.

Lydia shook her head and looked sternly at her eldest sister. It was an action that did not go unnoticed by their father.

"She is no longer there," Elizabeth said.

"Mr. Darcy sent her away," Jane added. "She is not at all nice. In fact, she is very much like Mrs. Salter if you were to ask me." Jane's chin lifted. "She had not one nice word to say about anyone. We are all beneath her notice, and therefore, we should also be beneath Mr. Darcy's notice."

"Indeed?" Mr. Bennet's brows were lifted high in surprise.

"Lady Catherine is Lord Matlock's sister," Elizabeth said. "We are, I suppose, beneath her, though I am loathed to admit it, for she was dreadful."

"And what do you think of her?" Mr. Bennet asked Lydia.

"I quite hope the wheels fall off her carriage, and I never have to see her again."

"I must say that is a bit excessive, do you not think?" her father exclaimed.

Lydia shook her head. "Not at all. She was most rude to me."

Mr. Bennet looked to his eldest daughters for confirmation of what Lydia had said. Both Jane and Elizabeth nodded their agreement.

"I was so excited to see Georgiana – I mean Miss Darcy – when I arrived at Netherfield that I quite forgot to give my letter to Mr. Darcy until we were all seated. And then when I did, Lady Catherine," Lydia's lips curled in displeasure as she said the name, "demanded to know why I had a letter from the colonel and was not at all pleased to hear he was writing to me with permission from you. She said dreadful things, and then Mr. Darcy made her leave." Lydia pulled her lip between her teeth as a crease formed between her eyes. "Do you think it might be acceptable for me to ask Miss Darcy or Miss Bingley to teach me how to act as a lady does in London and how to manage an estate as large as Netherfield?"

The room fell silent for a minute until their father cleared his throat and began by saying, "I would rather you learn to act as Miss Darcy or Jane does. They are far better examples of how ladies with any amount of true character should behave, and I would, therefore, have you behave as they do rather than how some lady in town is supposed to comport herself. I have very little use for the likes of many of the ladies I have met from town." He blew out a breath. "As for the management of an estate, there is none better than your mother to teach you what you will need to know –"

"But she will not allow me to do things. She will do them for me," Lydia pleaded.

"As I was saying," her father continued. "There is none better than your mother to teach you what you will need to know; however, if you feel that you could learn more from Miss Bingley or Miss Darcy, I shall write the request myself."

Lydia's eyes grew wide as did her smile. "Do you mean it?" she asked eagerly.

Her father nodded. "Whether I like it or not, I will have to give you away at some point, and I would not like to think you would go to your new home feeling inadequately prepared."

Lydia leapt from her seat, crossed to her father, and threw her arms around his neck. "Thank you, Papa. Thank you."

"You will behave as a proper student should, will you not?" He asked as he held her close.

"I absolutely will," Lydia assured him. "I just do not wish to be..." she stopped speaking, released his neck, and moved to return to her seat.

However, her father caught her hand and kept her by his side. "What do you not wish to be?"

Lydia darted a look at Jane and then Elizabeth before looking down at her slippers. "Not good enough," she whispered.

"Not good enough for what?" Mr. Bennet's voice was filled with incredulity as were his eyes.

"For the colonel," Lydia whispered.

"Has he said that?" Mr. Bennet demanded. There was no missing the anger in his voice.

Lydia shook her head violently. "He would never!"

"Then who said my daughter was not good enough?"

Elizabeth was uncertain if she had ever heard her father's tone be so cold.

"Lady Catherine," Jane answered for Lydia since Lydia seemed only able to shake her head but could not form the words needed to answer.

Lydia wiped her cheek quickly.

"Oh, my dear daughter." Mr. Bennet grasped Lydia's hand between both of his. "You are now more like your mother than even I ever expected you could be." He waited until her eyes lifted to his before he continued. "There were several who claimed that your mother was not good enough for me, but do you know who is the only one who can prove those people right or wrong?"

He pointed to himself. "Me. I am the only one who can say if your mother is or is not good enough for me – which she is, of course — and the colonel is the only one who can decide if you are good enough for him — which I believe is something he has already decided. However, I understand your worry, and I will write your request to Miss Darcy and Miss Bingley tonight and have it sent tomorrow." The right corner of his lips tipped up into a half smile. "I also quite wish for the wheels to fall off Lady Catherine's carriage. My daughter not good enough for the gentleman who loves her? I think not. The idea is quite preposterous." He released Lydia's hand and allowed her to go back to her seat. "Do not tell your mother about Lady Catherine unless you must."

"Why?" Elizabeth asked.

"She may go remove the wheels from Lady Catherine's carriage herself if she were to hear of it."

"She would not!" Jane cried as they all giggled at the thought.

~*~*~

Sometime later, after the intricacies of Miss Darcy's new piece of music had been explained and both Jane and Lydia had left their father's study, Mr. Bennet looked up from his book.

"I have not done my best by her."

Elizabeth stopped reading.

"That conversation we had in the Johnson's ballroom keeps coming back to me." He blew out a breath. "Will you help Lydia find her feet? She has never lacked for confidence before now, but I can see how it is possible since her education has not been what yours was. Do I ask too much?"

"No. No. Of course not. I will gladly help Lydia, as will Jane," Elizabeth assured her father.

He sighed as if a great weight had been relieved. "Would you do one more thing for me?"

"Of course."

"Would you call someone to help me to my room? My leg is aching a bit more today than yesterday, and I fear it is because I attempted to do too much."

Elizabeth closed her book and assured her father that she would see that someone was sent to assist him as soon as possible.

It did not take long for her to find someone. Mr. Hill was just passing the study when she exited, and he sent a footman directly.

However, Mr. Bennet had only made it to the bottom of the staircase when there was a knock at the door.

"Might I speak with Mr. Bennet and Miss Elizabeth," Darcy said as he entered.

"You do not look well, sir," Mr. Bennet said.

"I am not," he answered. He held out a letter. "I have just received this and must be gone straight away."

Mr. Bennet motioned to the chair in the corridor and the footman assisted him in sitting. "I see," was all he said when he read the letter Darcy had handed him. "Of course, you must go to him."

"Who?" Elizabeth's heart was beating a rapid pace. Her father's expression was so grave, and Darcy was so distraught.

"My cousin," Darcy replied. "Richard has been injured most grievously."

# Chapter 10

"I expect my carriage to be ready when I return to Nether-field," Darcy said as Elizabeth finished reading the letter he had received from one of Richard's fellow officers and had brought to Longbourn with him. They had gone to Mr. Bennet's study as instructed by Elizabeth's father so that Elizabeth might read the news in private, and so that Darcy might take his leave of his betrothed without an audience. For both of those things, Darcy was immensely grateful to Mr. Bennet.

"Will you travel through the night?" Elizabeth looked up at him from the letter, concern shimmering in unshed tears in her eyes.

Darcy nodded. "I must get to him as soon as can be."

"You will be careful, though?" She brushed at a tear which escaped her eye, and Darcy pulled her into his embrace. "It is bad enough that Colonel Fitzwilliam is injured. I do not need you to join him," she whispered against his coat.

"I will do all that is necessary to return to you, my love," he assured her before placing a kiss on the top of her head.

She held him tightly. "Where will you take him? He cannot remain in an inn where there is so much unrest. The noise of it all would not be conducive to his recovery, I am certain."

"Bingley suggested I bring him to Netherfield since it is close enough to town for my physician to attend him if needed and for my aunt and uncle to call on him since parliament is still sitting. It makes sense."

"And the air in the country is far better for someone who is unwell," Elizabeth added.

Darcy rubbed her back and relished these few moments of comfort, storing them in his memory to carry with him as he travelled to Manchester.

He knew only a few details about Richard's injury from the letter. There had been an attack at a mill, and in the tumult, his cousin had sustained several lacerations as well as a blow to the head that had rendered him insensible. The message had been sent two days ago, so whether his cousin had regained his senses or not was unknown. However, Darcy was attempting to prepare himself for the worst scenario.

Though he did not wish for Elizabeth to witness any of the trouble in the north or the gruesomeness of any injuries associated with it, Darcy yearned to be able to have the solace he found in her presence with him on his journey.

He sighed, knowing both that he must not remain here with her much longer and that he had one more task to complete before he could leave. "Your sister needs to be told," he said softly, "but I fear that I do not know how to tell her."

"We will tell her together," Elizabeth offered.

And they had.

Lydia had been surprisingly calm during the ordeal. She had cried, of course, but Darcy had expected her to be more vocal in her grief. She had always seemed so like Mrs. Bennet, who was boisterous. He shook his head at his foolishness as he shifted in his seat in his carriage. How often would he have to remind himself that what he expected from the Bennets was often not what he received? Had not Elizabeth and Jane, as well as their parents, already surprised him enough for him to have learned that his initial assessments of them had been wrong? Was it not possible for Lydia to have a more thinking nature buried beneath her effervescent exterior just as her sister, Jane, had a scheming mind tucked neatly behind a composed smile? People were, he reasoned, made of many layers. Having been often accused of being only severe and reserved, he should have a better understanding of these things. But apparently, he did not.

He sighed and propped his head against the squabs. He

really did need to work on being more considerate of the many facets a person might possess rather than arrogantly assuming his first impression of a person was unwaveringly correct.

However, he would not ponder on that now. He would save it for later. For presently, he needed this journey to be completed quickly, and so, sleep was necessary. Travelling never seemed to take as long as it truly did when one slept for a portion of the time.

However, even sleeping as often as he could did not shorten the amount of time Darcy had to worry about his cousin or to miss Elizabeth during his trip. Two days of travel, broken only by the necessary stops to change horses had given him ample time to think about a great many things. Having finally reached Pemberley, he climbed out of his coach and stretched his back before giving an appreciative nod to his driver and making his way towards the house.

Mr. Jarvis, his butler, greeted him with Mrs. Reynolds at his side.

"All is ready," Mrs. Reynolds assured Darcy. "Your bath was drawn as soon as we heard you were at the gate, and your dinner will be in your sitting room within the half hour."

"And the room for Richard?"

"All is ready, sir. The surgeon will be waiting when you arrive with Colonel Fitzwilliam tomorrow evening."

"Thank you, Mrs. Reynolds." Darcy sighed softly as he began to climb the stairs to his room.

"He will be well." Mrs. Reynolds had apparently caught the sigh that had escaped Darcy. "We must believe that," she added when he glanced her direction.

"You are right, of course, Mrs. Reynolds. It is just not knowing what I will find tomorrow which has me troubled."

"That is understandable, sir."

Darcy continued on his way up the steps. A warm bath might help relieve some of the stiffness he felt from sitting in a carriage for two days, and a comfortable bed would not be an unwelcome luxury. Sleeping in a carriage – even one as well-sprung and richly upholstered as his was – was not conducive to feeling well-rested. Hopefully, the lack of proper rest would help him sleep well tonight.

And it did – eventually.

Darcy had lain in bed pondering life and its brevity for three-quarters of an hour before weariness claimed not only his body but his mind.

As the sun rose above the horizon the following day, Darcy woke with muscles that only ached a bit. He would take a short walk in the garden in an attempt to shake loose the remaining stiffness before climbing into his carriage today. Then he would collect his cousin and tomorrow, he would see his steward before he began the journey back to Netherfield. There was no point in being in residence even for a short time without checking on the state of his holdings.

Therefore, after his walk in the garden and before he had eaten breakfast, a message was sent to Mr. Turner informing him of Darcy's wish to see him on the morrow. Then, after a filling breakfast, Darcy was once again on his way to Manchester.

Just over half a day later, Darcy exited his carriage and entered the inn where Richard had his lodgings.

"Who is there?" Richard barked from his bed.

Darcy breathed a sigh of relief, his cousin was alive and awake, even if he did sound to be in a disagreeable mood.

"Darcy," he said as he made his way toward the bed. "I have come to take you to Pemberley and then to Netherfield." He sucked in a breath as he took in the appearance of his cousin.

"I look a fright, do I not?" Richard grumbled. "Not that anyone will give me a mirror to see the surgeon's handiwork – no matter how much I have threaten."

"The surgeon's stitches are tidy," Darcy replied. "However, there are a great number of them. This is not the wound sustained in the altercation about which you wrote me earlier, is it?"

Richard attempted to move his head but groaned and held his head still. "No. That is the cut above my left eye."

The large gash on his cheek was as fresh as it appeared.

Richard held out a hand. "If you do not mind, I could use some help in rising."

"Are you supposed to rise?" Darcy questioned. "I had thought someone was to carry you down for me. That is what I was told."

"I have two legs that still mostly work," Richard grumbled. "I can see myself to the carriage." He waved his hand at Darcy. "Now, help me rise." He winced and blew out a great breath as Darcy helped him to a sitting position. "Make sure there is ample brandy in the carriage, will you?" he ordered, a grimace still on his face.

Darcy knew that Richard's injuries were far more extensive than what could be seen above the collar of his nightshirt and robe. The fact that Richard was dressed as he was to travel was a sure sign that the rest of his body was not in a condition worthy of a uniform. Bandages were more easily covered by loose-fitting garments.

"There will be plenty of brandy. I will see to it," Darcy assured him. "Where are your other injuries?"

Richard placed a hand on his right side. "Here. My left shoulder is not in usable order. My left thigh also has a number of stitches, and of course, as you can see the once lovely features of my face have been marred." He squeezed his eyes shut. "And the room refuses to stay still." Again, he blew out a great breath.

"I have readied the carriage as best I can for your comfort, but I fear it will still not be a pleasant trip." Darcy took

Richard's hand once again to help him rise, just as two officers arrived in the room.

"We are to see our colonel to his carriage," one of the men said.

Richard attempted to take a step toward them, but he stumbled as if he had miscalculated the distance between his foot and the floor and had expected the floor to be further beyond him than it was. He sucked in a sharp breath.

"My apologies," the officer on his right said. "I did not mean to cause you pain. I only wished to keep you from falling."

Richard nodded. "Do you think you could make the floor stand still? It is dashed hard to know where to place my foot." He turned his head to the left. "Oh, there you are, Darcy. I had thought you were gone. I did not see you."

"You did not see me?" Darcy asked in surprise. He was standing almost equal with Richard's left shoulder. He should have been visible to his cousin.

"My eyes are not right," Richard admitted. "The blow to the head, you see. We are hopeful that it will clear at the same time the room stops spinning and my head stops throbbing."

Slowly – much more slowly than Darcy had ever witness Richard walk – they made their way down the stairs and to the front of the inn, and after a word of parting to the innkeepers, Richard allowed the two officers who were on either side of him to help him into Darcy's carriage.

# Chapter 11

"I beg your pardon?" Darcy turned from the window in Richard's room at Pemberley. The surgeon had left half an hour ago, and Darcy and Richard had been discussing Richard's time in Manchester.

"I am not going to Netherfield."

That was exactly what Darcy thought he had heard his cousin say, but it had startled him so much that he had to ask for it to be repeated. The surgeon had been impressed with the quality of care Richard had received and did not fear there would be any complications such as infection. The wounds were all clean and properly dressed. There was no need to remain at Pemberley. The surgeon had not thought it would be dangerous to attempt a longer trip.

"I have written to your father informing him that you will be at Netherfield," Darcy argued.

"You may write to him again. Tell him that I am well but prefer to rusticate in the country far removed from callers."

Darcy shook his head. Richard was not the sort to ever

wish to rusticate in the country. That knock he had received on his head must have jiggled something loose.

"I can write to him myself as soon as the pen and paper agree to stay in the same place at the same time," Richard added.

Darcy crossed the room to sit in a chair closer to the bed. "It is not just your father who wishes to see you."

"Mother is welcome to come visit if she wishes to make the trip during the season." He had turned his face away from Darcy while he spoke.

"And I suppose Georgiana can travel with her?" Darcy asked incredulously.

"I am certain there would be room in Mother's carriage," Richard answered. "And I think I could tolerate the three of you." His head turned toward Darcy. "But no more."

Darcy sat quietly for several minutes studying the way his cousin held his jaw firmly in position and then taking note of the way the blanket over Richard's chest rose and fell with deep, deliberate breaths.

"What of Lydia?" Darcy asked softly, breaking the silence but only for the length of time it took for him to utter the words.

Richard did not reply. He continued to breathe deeply as he stared up at the canopy above him.

"You cannot abandon her."

"She is young. She will find another."

Darcy leaned back in his chair. Something very close to anger rose within him.

"And what if she does not want another?" Darcy attempted to keep his voice from betraying his feelings. His cousin was injured and not thinking correctly. He did not deserve to feel the anger that Darcy felt at the thought of Lydia being injured in such a fashion as Richard was proposing.

"She will. Describe my appearance and tell her I am likely to lose my position in the regulars. I have little to offer her." Richard closed his eyes, but a tear escaped and ran down the side of his face toward his ear.

Allowing Richard to see himself in the mirror had been a mistake. Darcy had suspected it was at the time but had disregarded his better judgment in favour of satisfying his cousin's curiosity.

The scar on Richard's face ran the length of his cheek from nearly his ear to the almost the corner of his mouth, and it was an angry red presently with a track of neat stitches holding it closed. It looked horrid now, but it would not forever. It was going to scar, but it would fade somewhat with time.

Added to that his face was not what made him who he was. Not that Darcy could fault Richard for feeling as he did at the moment. Proper reasoning might return once some of the pain from his cousin's injuries subsided.

Darcy rose. There was little use arguing any of those

things with Richard at present. It would be better to just inform him of what was going to happen and attempt to ignore his cousin's cursing and grumbling.

"I will do nothing of the sort," Darcy said. "We are going to Netherfield tomorrow."

"I am not going," Richard yelled at the back of his cousin's retreating form.

Darcy turned from the door and went to stand beside Richard's bed. "You are going to Netherfield even if I have to contact the apothecary to acquire a potion to render you insensible."

There was no way as long as the sun still shone in the sky on a clear day that Darcy was going to allow his cousin to hide from life and lock his heart away.

"Perhaps that might be for the best anyway. It is not a short journey, and your injuries are not insignificant." He turned, once again, to leave the room.

"Why?"

The pain in Richard's tone kept Darcy from leaving, but he did not turn back to look at his cousin.

"Because Elizabeth is at Longbourn, and I will not allow you to separate me from her." If Richard was unable to care for his own heart at present, perhaps he would be able to care about Darcy's.

"Then go without me."

That would not keep Darcy from the desire of his heart, but it would do nothing for Richard's. It might be best to lay Richard's heart before him and let his cousin know that Lydia was important not only to Richard but also to Darcy.

"And," Darcy continued, "there is a young lady at Longbourn who loves you and was excessively concerned for you when I told her about my need to collect you. I gave her my word that I would return to Netherfield *with you*, and to return without you would mean I would have to break my word to her. I will not do that to her just as I would not break my word to you or Georgiana. Therefore, since I refuse to either break my word to her or to break her heart at your request, we are going to Netherfield in the morning after I have seen my steward. I suggest you try to get as much rest tonight as is possible."

And with those words, Darcy left his cousin. He leaned against the wall outside Richard's door. An injured family member was a great worry, but when the happiness of both that family member and another hung precariously in the balance, the weight of it all was nearly too much to bear. How he missed Elizabeth and her comforting presence!

He pushed off the wall and headed to his study. A concoction to help Richard sleep during their journey was indeed a good idea. Therefore, a note needed to be sent to the apothecary.

He sighed. The note to the apothecary would be easily written. The other letter which must be sent would not be so easily done. Lydia needed to be informed about the extent of Richard's injuries. Darcy knew he could write directly to her. No one would think anything of it. However, there was the matter of Richard's refusal to return to Netherfield that weighed more heavily on Darcy than any scar or loss of uniform. And because of that, he would write to Elizabeth. She would know how best to share all of this information with her sister.

"Mr. Jarvis," Darcy said when handing the missives he had written to his butler to be delivered, "my cousin is not in favour of leaving with me tomorrow. While I do not think he is well enough to manage such a feat as stealing away in the night, I prefer not to be surprised by his tenacity. Therefore, if you would inform those who need to know, that Colonel Fitzwilliam is not to be allowed to leave the house, and he is most certainly not to be given a horse or carriage for his use." It was unsettling to have to give such orders regarding his cousin. "Again, I do not expect him to attempt an escape, but I do wish to be prepared."

"It is the colonel, sir. I remember him as a boy. There is not much that could keep him from his plans."

Darcy chuckled. It was true. Richard had never been the sort to simply sit around and do as he was told.

Darcy thanked Mr. Jarvis for his understanding and then settled in a favourite chair in his study to read – or as it turned out, to look at a book with the pretense of reading while he pondered his cousin.

~*~*~

The next day, Richard glared at Darcy while Darcy attempted to ignore his cousin's displeasure at waking to find himself in the carriage. The potion the apothecary had delivered had worked well.

"Would you like another dose of medicine?" Darcy inquired.

"You know that I do not," Richard snapped. "I would like to be in a comfortable bed rather than this carriage."

"As would I," Darcy agreed, shifting slightly to make himself more comfortable. The carriage had been fitted with a board and mattress so that Richard could sit without bending his legs and if he bent his knees, it was not entirely impossible to lie down. Lying down would help with the dizziness and give his shoulder and side more rest.

"Aunt Catherine called at Netherfield the day before I received news of your injury." That bit of news should distract Richard from his displeasure with Darcy, and likely place it with someone else.

"Why would she call on Bingley?"

As Darcy expected, Richard was too curious to let a disagreeable mood keep him from discovering what he wanted to know.

"She was calling on me. It seems Mrs. Collins – Mr. Collins is Elizabeth's cousin who is Lady Catherine's parson if you remember."

Richard assured Darcy that he remembered that fact before Darcy continued.

"As it happens, Mrs. Collins had a letter from her mother, Lady Lucas, who is a particular friend of Mrs. Bennet and in that letter was news of my betrothal to someone other than our cousin Anne."

Richard rubbed his chin as he let out a long, low whistle.

"Indeed," Darcy agreed. "She was not pleased to hear the news and even less pleased that your father would not support her in her desire to see me marry Anne."

"She went to my father first?"

Darcy nodded. "Do you know that Dash took an immediate liking to her?"

"To Aunt Catherine?" Richard cried incredulously.

Again, Darcy nodded. "Well, that is he liked her right up until she spoke harshly to his Miss Lydia. Then, he asserted himself on Miss Lydia's behalf."

The sound of carriage wheels and horse's hooves were the only thing heard inside Darcy's travelling coach for a full minute before Richard asked what Darcy expected.

"Aunt Catherine spoke harshly to Miss Lydia?"

For a third time, Darcy nodded.

"About what?"

"You."

Richard's brow furrowed.

"Miss Lydia had just received a letter from you and gave it to me to read when she arrived at Netherfield." He looked Richard in the eye. "Apparently, Miss Lydia is not good enough for the son of an earl."

Anger flashed in Richard's eyes just as Darcy hoped it would.

"I assured Miss Lydia that you were not inconstant," Darcy continued. "I do hope I have not misspoken."

Again, the carriage fell silent. Darcy pretended to attend to his book while surreptitiously studying his cousin who was clearly battling a mix of emotions.

"I also told Aunt Catherine that she was not welcome in my home if she were to continue to speak poorly of one of my sisters, and then, I sent her back to your father."

Richard's eyes grew wide.

"Have you not spoken to your father about Miss Lydia?" Darcy asked in surprise.

"No. I was going to write to him about her. There was not time to speak to him before I left town." He blew out a breath. "I suppose he must know by now."

"Most likely. Aunt Catherine is not one to keep news such as that to herself."

Richard groaned.

"Would you like some medicine now?" Darcy asked with a grin.

"No, but if you have some brandy, I will not refuse it."

# Chapter 12

Lydia was sitting in the garden on the same bench she had sat on for each of the days since she had heard of Colonel Fitzwilliam's injury. From that bench, Elizabeth knew that Lydia could see the drive, and, therefore, she could see who was or was not arriving. At least, today, Lydia's good friend, Maria Lucas, had joined her while, in Longbourn's sitting room, their mothers discussed all the dreadful possibilities that might be the result of any injury sustained in battle.

"Might we go out as well?" Georgiana asked as she joined Elizabeth near the window.

"I must apologize for my mother's choice of topic for discussion," Elizabeth whispered. "Did you and Kitty have as much time to practise as you wished?"

Georgiana wore a pleased smile as she nodded. "Kitty is almost able to play that song without a single stumble."

The pride of accomplishment mingled with the joy of hearing oneself praised in Kitty's expression. "I have never played anything so well, to be honest."

Georgiana had been accompanying Bingley each day when he came to call on Jane. She and Kitty would find some excuse to not be in the sitting room. On one day, they had read lines from a play, on another day, they had pored over fashion magazines while examining the content of Kitty's wardrobe to see what alterations could be made to various dresses to make them more fashionable, and today, they had spent time working on a song Kitty wished to learn to play and sing.

Mrs. Bennet's voice had dropped to a whisper when Georgiana had entered the sitting room, but even when whispering Mrs. Bennet's voice carried.

"It is a true marvel what a bit of practice can do," Elizabeth teased. "Perhaps one day I shall try it." She wrapped one arm around Kitty's and the other around Georgiana's. "But I have no desire to practise today. The sun is warm, and I think Georgiana's suggestion to join Lydia is a very good one."

The three young ladies exited the sitting room and gathered their things to go to the garden. Just as they were starting down the path to where Lydia sat, she jumped up and, after a hasty word to her friend, ran toward the front of the house.

Elizabeth hurried to Maria. "What is it?"

"An express rider," Maria said, pointing to the front of the house.

"It is for Elizabeth," Lydia cried, waving the missive in the air.

"For me?" Elizabeth went to meet her sister. Taking the letter, she looked at the address and then, with a smile, broke the seal.

"What does it say?" Lydia asked anxiously. "Has Mr. Darcy seen his cousin?"

"He misses me."

"Yes, yes. But what of his cousin?" Lydia was wringing her hands and pacing in front of the bench on which she had been sitting as Elizabeth took a seat and continued to read.

"Oh! I can tell by your face it is not good," Lydia cried. "Will he live?"

"He is not in danger of dying," Elizabeth assured her. "However..." she paused. How was she supposed to share this information with her sister? Darcy had far more faith in her abilities to do so than she did herself. However, he had entrusted her with this news, and she would see it done. She placed the letter in her lap and, leaned forward to grasp Lydia's hand. "Sit with me."

Lydia did as she was told.

Elizabeth picked up the letter once more and scanned its content. Her protective nature told her to only reveal the bits and pieces that would not be too distressing while her rational nature told her that doing so would only lead to a greater possibility of being hurt later.

"If the colonel were to ask you to marry him, would you?" Elizabeth asked.

"Yes," Lydia cried.

"Then you believe yourself capable of facing troubles as a grown lady should?" Elizabeth asked.

"I am not a child."

The pout that accompanied the words did little to convince Elizabeth of their truth, but she chose to ignore that thought.

"Very well. You may read the entire letter." Elizabeth handed it to Lydia but did not release it. "Of course, the parts about Mr. Darcy's love for me are not to be part of any gossip."

Lydia nodded, and Elizabeth released her hold on the letter.

"There are a few new plants beginning to push through the soil," Kitty said.

"Indeed?" Georgiana asked.

Kitty nodded. "I saw them yesterday. They were not more than a few green specks in the dirt. Would you and Maria like to join me to see how much they have grown between then and now?" She smiled at Elizabeth. "I am certain after Lydia has had a read of Mr. Darcy's letter, the news that needs to be told to us will be shared."

"I would not withhold any important information," Elizabeth assured them. "Thank you," she mouthed to Kitty as the three young ladies moved down the path.

"Mr. Darcy does love you very much," Lydia whispered.

"And he loves you as you will see by his concern." Lydia was about to read the account of the colonel's unwillingness to travel to Netherfield.

Lydia's hand flew to her chest. "Stay at Pemberley?"

Elizabeth rubbed her back.

"Find another? Not wish to marry him?" She turned troubled eyes to Elizabeth. "How could he think such things?"

"How is not the right question," Elizabeth replied. "Why is the better choice."

Lydia brushed tears from her cheeks with the palm of her right hand while her left clutched the letter. Gently, Elizabeth took the letter from her and handed her a handkerchief.

"I will read this part to you."

Lydia nodded.

> I cannot blame him for his troubled thinking, but I will not allow him to hide from his heart.

Elizabeth put an arm around Lydia's shoulders and squeezed her close. "You are the colonel's heart," she whispered before continuing to read.

> Therefore, I am bringing him to Netherfield whether he wishes it or not.
>
> When you see the state he is in; I am certain you, too, will understand his wish to remain in seclusion. He has several injuries. One of his injuries has rendered his left

arm useless until it heals. He has several stitches to close wounds on his side and his upper leg. In addition to these things, he sustained an injury to his head that currently affects his eyesight. However, I do not believe any of those, save perhaps the head injury (which I will explain later), are the cause of his wish to hide.

It is his face. He has a small scar above his eye which we knew from one of his letters, as well as new large gash from his ear to his mouth on the right side of his face. It is, of course, bruised, red, and still being held closed by stitches. I will not lie to you or your sister. It looks as gruesome as you might imagine it. However, with time, it will heal.

He told me to describe this injury to your sister as an explanation of why she would not wish to marry him. In addition to that, he added that he might lose his position in the regulars. That is the part which has to do with the blow he received to his head. If his eyesight does not improve, he will not be fit to serve. He sees this as another reason why your sister might not wish to marry him.

Elizabeth peeked at Lydia who was shaking her head while silently crying.

He feels he has little to offer Miss Lydia. Little but his heart! Not that he is capable of seeing that at present. It is this knowledge that keeps me from truly being angry with him. As his body heals, so will his spirit.

I did not know how to impart such information to your

*sister, and so I am trusting you to inform her of these details as you see fit. My heart grieves both for her and Richard.*

*I am eager to see you, my love. Until I arrive at Netherfield, hold my sisters close and care for them for me.*

"And that is all there is," Elizabeth pulled Lydia close again. "Mr. Darcy said to hold his sisters – *sisters* – close," she whispered. "He cares for you very much, Lydia."

Lydia nodded.

"As does his cousin. Such injuries would cause anyone to falter and think of themselves as not good enough."

"But he is," Lydia whispered. "He is good enough." She drew a deep breath through her nose and released it slowly through her mouth. "It is as Papa said. Colonel Fitzwilliam is not the person who gets to decide if he is good enough for me." She turned toward Elizabeth with a determined look in her eye. "Only I get to decide that."

"He will be scarred and not as handsome as he was, and he might not have a uniform any longer," Elizabeth cautioned, not because she wished to dissuade her sister from thinking the colonel was good enough but to test Lydia's resolve. A handsome gentleman in a uniform – the higher the rank, the better — had always been Lydia's ideal for who would make a good husband.

"I am not stupid," Lydia muttered.

"No, you are not, but will you feel cheated by his

injuries? It would not be wrong to feel something about them."

Kitty, Georgiana, and Maria were making their way toward the house. Apparently, someone – likely Kitty – had decided they should not return to Elizabeth and Lydia at present. Elizabeth had to admit she was pleased to see such conscientiousness developing in Kitty. Kitty had not always considered much more than what Lydia's thoughts on a subject might be, or how something would make her look. However, it seemed all of Elizabeth's sisters were becoming grown women in more than just age and appearance.

She squeezed Lydia's shoulders once more. Who would have thought that Mr. Darcy, along with his cousin and sister, would be the one to work such miracles? She smiled as she thought of him standing at the edge of the assembly in the autumn, looking down his nose at everyone around him. How he had improved upon greater acquaintance!

"Are you ready to go in?" Elizabeth whispered.

Lydia rose, dried her eyes and nose once more, straightened her shoulders, and lifted her chin.

Elizabeth wound her arm around Lydia's, and they took their time returning to the house. Just as they were about to enter through the servant's entrance, Lydia stopped.

"I am scared," she whispered when Elizabeth turned toward her. "What if I am not as good as you or Jane?"

"What do you mean? Neither Jane nor I are better than you."

"Oh, you are!" Lydia cried. "You think about things that are not fashion."

"That does not make us better."

Lydia looked at the ground. "What if I discover I am not the kind of lady who can love someone who is not handsome?"

Elizabeth lifted Lydia's chin so that she could see her sister's eyes. "Do you think you are that sort of woman?"

Lydia nodded and then shrugged. "I do not know. I have never flirted with anyone who was not handsome."

"You have flirted with Mr. Ferrell, and well, he is not particularly handsome. And you are kind to Miss King despite her freckles and plumpness."

A small smile tipped up the corner of Lydia's mouth. "That is true."

"If your heart is truly engaged with Colonel Fitzwilliam, you will not find his appearance to be of great significance." She smiled reassuringly at Lydia. "Of course, we will likely not know that until we have seen the colonel, but I have faith in you, Lydia. You are not the silly little sister you were. You are becoming a fine young woman."

"Do you really think so?" Lydia's eyes were wide with shock.

"I do. Now, Mama will want to know about the colonel as will Georgiana and Mr. Bingley."

"Oh, I cannot bear to face Mama," Lydia said.

"Then, I suggest you go tell Papa what you have heard while I tell the others."

Lydia stopped half in and half out of the house, holding the door open against her hip. "But you usually tell Papa everything."

Elizabeth tugged at Lydia to get her to enter the house. "This time, I think he should hear it from you. Now, scoot. Before Mama comes looking for you."

# Chapter 13

"Are you ready for this?" Elizabeth whispered the question to Lydia two days later as they waited for Netherfield's door to open to them.

Lydia nodded and smiled, but from the way her sister clung to her arm, Elizabeth was not so certain Lydia was prepared for her first lesson in estate management. How had she never noticed any sort of unease in Lydia before that dreadful night when they found themselves at Sally's house?

"You will do well," Jane encouraged.

Jane. She was the reason, Elizabeth supposed. Not that Jane was to blame. No. Elizabeth knew it was entirely her own fault that she had not paid closer attention to her youngest sister. She had always relied on Jane to see to what needed care. In that way, Elizabeth imagined herself to be somewhat like Kitty – relying on a favoured sister to guide her. Thankfully, Jane was a sensible sister, Elizabeth thought with a smile just as the door before them opened.

The three Bennet sisters followed the butler, Mr. Harvey, into the drawing room where Miss Bingley and Mrs. Nicholls, Netherfield's housekeeper, were waiting for them.

"I thought it best to begin with a tour," Caroline said after the pleasantries of greetings were completed. "Jane will, of course, need to see the house, and well," she smiled at Elizabeth, "it would be rather rude of me to exclude one of my guests."

"I can read in the library," Elizabeth suggested.

"No, no, I am only jesting. I am nearly over my dislike of you." Again, Caroline smirked.

Elizabeth was not certain if that remark was also said in jest or not.

"I am teasing," Caroline said. "I am capable of doing so – or, I should say, I am attempting to learn to do so. Sir Matthew insists that I try to be more at ease." She blew out a breath. "However, I am not certain that teasing puts me at ease."

"If one does not like to tease, then one should not feel compelled to do so," Lydia said. "I am not clever enough to tease as Lizzy does, and so, it feels very awkward. Some of us are just not made for things such as teasing."

Caroline's eyebrows rose and her lips pursed as she considered that thought. "I must say, Miss Lydia, that I believe you are correct. I think I am far too serious a lady to ever be very good at teasing. However, I am quite good at giving opinions while others stumble over a simple 'It is lovely.'"

Elizabeth bit the inside of her mouth to keep from laughing as she and Jane followed behind Caroline and Lydia. Miss Bingley was excessively good at sharing her opinion.

"You saw many of the public rooms when you were here for our ball in November," Caroline said to Lydia. "And Jane and Miss Elizabeth have seen some of the private quarters as they were guests here for several days. However, we will make a thorough inspection of all the rooms." She stopped in the corridor just outside the drawing room and turned back toward the door.

"You will notice that this room is bright and has a good amount of air in it due to its size. These things are important if you are to have a great number of callers at one time, which can happen. I have seen drawing rooms that were nearly overflowing in London, and some of them were not bright or airy, and the need for a nosegay became particularly strong as a result." She tipped her head and studied the room before her. "Of course, you will have someone to tend to the ashes in the fireplace and others to keep the surfaces of the tables shining as well as someone to see that the fabric and rugs are tidy. There is a door at the far end, do you see it? It is nearly obscured by design."

"Oh, yes! It is very cleverly done," Lydia answered.

"That is how your servants will most often enter and exit. Well, the junior staff and below, that is. Servants such as Mrs. Nicholls and Mr. Harvey will enter just as we do.

There are lines which must not be crossed. Order cannot be retained as it should be if any maid or groom is allowed to come flouncing in however he or she wishes." She smiled at Jane. "That is my opinion, of course. A mistress of an estate must determine with the agreement of her husband as to how those lines are formed and how firmly they are held. Sir Matthew, I believe, is more forgiving of things than I am, and, therefore, I shall have to learn his ways." She turned from the room and took Lydia's arm. "One must always consider the opinion of one's husband to be the greater opinion."

"But what if he is wrong?" Lydia asked.

"He is not. Ever."

"I think it is not impossible for a husband to be wrong," Sir Matthew said from where he stood on the grand staircase. "However, I try not to be wrong too often." He bowed his good days to the ladies. "Not every rule which is parroted from matron to daughter must remain as it is. It is my opinion, that a good marriage is a friendship of the greatest kind. The joining of two people to act as one – not to become as the other but to enhance and support the other." He smiled and shrugged. "My father was a parson. I fear I have picked up some of his ability to wax eloquent on some subjects which interest me. However, I shall attempt to keep my thoughts to a minimum as I should allow you to return to your tour. I was just on my way to the library."

"To read?" Lydia asked.

"Yes," Sir Matthew replied, his lips twitching ever so slightly.

"Will you be there long?"

He nodded. "Most likely, unless something draws me away from my book."

"I only ask," Lydia said very seriously, "so that I will know to be quiet when I enter. My father does not like to be disturbed when he is reading, you see."

Sir Matthew gave a small bow of his head. "I thank you in advance for your consideration." He looked at Caroline. "You are doing an admiral job, my dear."

Caroline beamed as she watched him make his way to the library. "I have been blessed." She sighed but then looked at Jane. "Even if I did not think it a blessing at first, it is."

Jane blushed. "We selected him only because we thought he would make you happy," she said softly.

"We?"

Jane nodded. "Mr. Darcy, Aunt Gardiner, your brother, and myself. Aunt Gardiner and I were insistent that whoever was chosen would be the sort of gentleman who we ourselves would find pleasing. It was very fortuitous that Miss Darcy suggested him."

Caroline blinked. "Miss Darcy, too?"

"Yes. We all care about your happiness." Jane pulled her lip between her teeth. "As well as our own," she added.

"I was so dreadful as to have a whole battalion against me?" Caroline shook her head. "I suppose I was," she admitted. "I did try to compromise my brother to see him married where I wished. The dining room," she said to Mrs. Nicholls. "It is the second most important room when entertaining guests," she explained to Lydia as they followed behind Netherfield's housekeeper. "The drawing room is first."

"Because you have callers more often than you have dinners, is that correct?"

"Precisely. I have a feeling you will be a natural at entertaining, Miss Lydia, as long as you can learn to act with the restraint a lady must always wear."

Lydia grimaced. "Ladies are so dull," she muttered.

"No, they are not," Caroline argued. "I have been in several houses where the lady of the house was simply delightful – always seeing that her guests were comfortable and able to converse on a wide range of topics from music to art to furnishings."

"And how does one learn such topics?"

"By listening and reading. Do you paint or sew?"

"I am absolutely abysmal at painting, but my stitching is the best of all my sisters."

"It is true," Elizabeth inserted. "Lydia knows how to make even the drabbest piece of fabric bright with a few embellishments."

Caroline looked quite pleased to hear that, but her pleasure paled to the look of happiness on Lydia's face. It was not as if Lydia had never been praised for her work before. Their mother was continually going on about how accomplished Lydia was in whatever Lydia did well. However, Elizabeth thought, with a twinge of remorse, if it was not for their mother's praise, Lydia might not receive any. She knew that she, herself, had been very remiss in bestowing approval on her younger sisters. She had always been at the ready with censure but not with commendation.

"The dining room is used daily," Miss Bingley was saying. "The arrangement goes like this..." She led Lydia to the table and began to list who sat where.

"She would make a great headmistress of a finishing school," Jane whispered, guiding Elizabeth around the edge of the room.

"She does seem to know a great deal," Elizabeth admitted, a feeling of guilt pricking her again. "I did not think she knew much. I have been horribly arrogant."

"None of us are without fault," Jane replied. "I, myself, had not considered how differently Caroline must have viewed our society. We were taught to think for ourselves. Deference is a good quality, but it is not the only quality." She leaned into Elizabeth's side more. "I think we have been taught well in that regard."

"I would agree."

Mr. Harvey had entered, and Jane turned her attention to watch the gentleman set a place as it should be set.

"He is very exact, is he not?" Jane whispered.

"As he should be," Elizabeth replied with a smile. "And he shall be your butler. You are a fortunate creature."

As she was speaking, a footman appeared at the door and stood silently waiting until Mr. Harvey had completed his demonstration.

"If I may interrupt, sir," the footman said.

"Yes, Thomas, what is it?" Mr. Harvey moved toward the door.

"There is a carriage on the drive, sir."

"A carriage, you say?"

The footman nodded. "With a crest and a trunk tied on the back, sir."

"It is not Mr. Darcy?"

"No, sir, the groom who saw it did not recognize either the carriage or the coat of arms."

"Well, Mrs. Nicholls," Mr. Harvey said. "It seems we are to have guests." He bowed and left the room quickly.

"Shall I prepare a room before we know who it is?" Mrs. Nicholls asked Caroline.

"I think it is best if we wait and see what sort of accommodation is needed. A coat of arms requires a great deal of respect, you see," she added to Lydia.

"Very well, ma'am. I will wait to hear from Harvey and select according to his information."

"That would be excellent. I am certain you will choose best. You always do." Caroline gave the housekeeper a warm smile before turning back to Lydia. "And we should make our way to the drawing room to receive our caller. Please see that my brother is made aware of his guest." And with that additional directive for Mrs. Nicholls, Caroline led Jane, Elizabeth, and Lydia back to the drawing room.

They were just taking their places when the front door opened, and it was not long after that until a gentleman in fine clothing was standing behind Harvey at the entrance to the drawing room.

"Viscount Westonbury to see you, Miss Bingley," Harvey intoned.

The gentleman looked around the room, a furrow forming between his eyes. "I am looking for my brother, Colonel Fitzwill...i...am," his speech slowed as his eyes landed on Lydia. A slow smile crept across his face.

Lydia's eyes could not be wider, and Elizabeth understood why quite perfectly.

"You? You are the colonel's brother?" Lydia asked the exact question that was in Elizabeth's mind.

Lord Westonbury fumbled in his pocket. "I have a shilling," he said, holding up the coin. "Or..." he searched his pocket again, "I have a half-crown. I've been carrying both ever since our first meeting."

Lydia's mouth dropped open for a moment, but then she snapped it shut.

The gentleman looked at Caroline expectantly.

"My lord," she said with a curtsey, "may I present Miss Jane Bennet, Miss Elizabeth Bennet, and Miss Lydia Bennet."

Lord Westonbury's head snapped back toward Lydia. "You are Miss Lydia?"

Lydia lifted her chin. "I am, and it was Elizabeth who was with me when we met you, my lord."

He looked at Elizabeth. Something very like worry passed over his features. "Darcy's betrothed?"

"Yes," Lydia answered, arching a brow.

"Well, then, I suppose I should put my blunt back in my pocket. An angry, injured younger brother is one thing, but a furious Darcy is quite another."

"They are not returned yet," Miss Bingley said.

"It matters not. I shall keep my money in my pocket." Lord Westonbury's eyes roamed from Lydia's head to her feet and back. "It is a pity, though."

# Chapter 14

"Welcome back, sir," Harvey greeted as Darcy entered the door later that same day. "I trust your journey was as good as can be expected."

"It is good to be out of the carriage," Darcy admitted. It had been a long journey.

He and Richard had stopped at an inn for one night so that Richard would be able to have a good rest. His cousin had required the assistance of some medication to sleep, however, and had been nearly as reluctant to enter the carriage this morning as he had been at Pemberley the night before they had left there.

"The colonel will need some assistance."

"Of course," Harvey waved to a footman. "Viscount Westonbury has arrived, sir," he said to Darcy while he waited for the footman to reach him. "Not more than a half hour ago."

"I will inform the colonel," Darcy said, interrupting Harvey's instructions to the footman.

"The Miss Bennets are also here, sir," Harvey added.

As he walked back to his coach, Darcy wondered if perhaps he should tell his coachman to drive on for a distance so that Richard could enter the house without so many in attendance. He was just opening the door to the carriage when a furry bundle attacked him.

"Dash! You really do need to learn how to greet a person calmly," Darcy scolded as he bent to scratch the dog's ear. "I have brought the colonel back to you, but you mustn't jump on him."

Dash cocked his head as if he understood and sat patiently at Darcy's feet while the carriage door was opened. Then, he stood with his tail wagging before returning to sitting when Darcy looked at him.

"Richard, there is someone here to greet you."

Dash barked.

"Dash?"

Darcy nodded. "He is sitting just as he should."

"Well, will you look at that. And without a biscuit on his nose," Richard said as he peeked out of the carriage door.

"Your brother is also here."

"Westonbury?"

"That is what I was told."

"Why is he here?"

"I was not informed of his reason, but I would assume that it is to see you. I did write to your parents about your injury."

Richard sighed. "And they sent him?"

"That is how it appears." Darcy paused. "He is not the only one here who might wish to see you."

Richard shook his head.

"You will have to see her eventually," Darcy spoke softly.

"Please," Richard begged as he shook his head again. "I am not ready to see her."

"Ah, here is our help." Darcy ignored his cousin's plea. There was very little that could be done to avoid Richard's having to see people.

"I do not need assistance."

Darcy leveled a glare at him. "Just as you did not need help last evening and nearly fell from the carriage to the ground?"

"Yes."

"Do try to be reasonable," Darcy chided. "I am not about to allow you to fall and risk further injury or see one of your wounds torn open. You will accept the help and do so politely."

"I am not a child. You do not need to scold me."

"I do if you are going to refuse assistance," Darcy retorted.

Dash barked.

"See. Even Dash agrees." Darcy added with a smile.

"He is just eager to see me. He is not agreeing with you."

"Then, you should be quick before he gives up his patience and leaps into the carriage."

Richard huffed and moved toward the door. He paused and closed his eyes while resting his right hand on the doorframe. He was steadying himself, and Darcy held up a hand to keep the footmen from approaching until Richard once again opened his eyes.

"I can walk to the house on my own."

"Of course, you can," Darcy agreed. "But I will be at your side if the world should decide to tip and these men will not be far behind. You will, of course, accept assistance on the steps."

"Of course," Richard muttered. He placed a hand on Darcy's arm and leaned down to scratch Dash's ear.

Darcy chuckled. "If he wags that tail any harder, it shall fly off."

Richard joined Darcy in chuckling and began his slow walk to the house.

"The drive should be much closer to the door," Richard grumbled as he mounted the steps while leaning on one of the footmen.

"I will speak to Bingley about that," Darcy teased, earning a huff from his cousin.

"It is good to see you," Bingley greeted as Richard entered the house, "even if it does look like someone got the best of you. Your room is ready and waiting." He took the place of the footman at Richard's side.

"The drawing room is rather full this afternoon," Bingley continued as they climbed the stairs. "However, no one is going to exit that room until you are settled."

"That is thoughtful of you," Richard said. "I confess to not wishing to see anyone at present."

"It was not my doing," Bingley replied.

"It was not?" Richard asked in surprise.

"Was it Caroline?" Darcy asked.

"No, it was not. Nor was it Miss Bennet or Miss Elizabeth or Georgiana or even Sir Matthew," Bingley answered.

"My brother?"

Bingley chuckled. "No, he was eager to lend you assistance, but Miss Lydia would not allow it."

"Miss Lydia?"

"Yes," Bingley said as they reached the landing and began to make their way to Richard's room. "Your brother rose to leave the room, but she stopped him."

"How did she do that?" Darcy asked. Westonbury was not the sort of gentleman to be easily put off when he wanted something.

Bingley chuckled. "She told him that she would not wish to be gawked at when ill, and she was certain the same was true for anyone."

"And my brother accepted that?"

"Not at first, but after a few moments of attempting to stare her down and dissuade her from her point of view, he conceded that it might be true that one would not necessarily even want a brother or sister gawking at them when he was ill – at least, not until the ill person was properly comfortable in bed."

Richard chuckled. "Did she bat her eyelashes at him?"

"More than once," Bingley replied.

"And did she assure him that there would be some sort of reward for doing as she suggested?" Richard asked.

Bingley's brow furrowed. "I am uncertain, although she did claim that you would likely be more welcoming if he waited. And then he asked her if he could leave the room for a shilling, which I am not sure why he would do such a thing, and she replied not even for a half-crown."

Richard stopped just inside the door to his room and turned toward Bingley. "You may tell him that for a half-crown he can see me before I am properly ensconced in bed."

Again, Bingley's brow furrowed.

"He will understand it," Richard assured Bingley.

"Were Elizabeth and her sisters visiting Caroline?" Darcy asked as Richard took a seat on the bed and allowed his man to begin the work of getting him ready to rest.

Bingley nodded. "It seems your aunt's comment about Miss Lydia's not being good enough struck a cord, and Mr. Bennet has arranged for Caroline and Georgiana to assist her in learning what she feels she must learn to be acceptable to you," he looked at Richard, "and your family."

"She thinks she is not good enough for me?" Richard grimaced as he raised his left arm to allow his shirt to be removed.

"Good heavens!" Bingley cried when he saw the gash on the side of Richard's abdomen. "You are being held together with a great number of stitches, are you not?"

"There is another on his leg," Darcy said. "We are fortunate to still have him."

"I cannot disagree," Bingley said.

"Miss Lydia thinks she is not good enough for me?" Richard repeated as his nightshirt slid over his head and covered his torso.

"Yes," Bingley answered. "Miss Elizabeth has told Jane, who told me, that Miss Lydia greatly desires your approval."

Richard said nothing in reply, though to Darcy it appeared as if his cousin was pondering that thought.

"Do you still wish to see your brother? Bingley asked as Richard was settling himself in bed.

"Yes," Richard said before sighing with relief as he lay back against his pillows. "Tell him to bring his half-crown," Richard called after Bingley. "The scoundrel," he muttered. "He best not be trying to buy any more kisses from Lydia."

"Does that mean you are not giving her up?" Darcy pulled a chair near the bed.

"No. It means she does not need to be put upon by him."

"Then you are giving her up?"

"No. I am neither giving her up or expecting her to remain attached to me. I have decided to give her the choice." He closed his eyes.

"Is the room spinning?" Darcy asked.

"As is the rest of my life," Richard replied.

"Everything will right itself eventually." Or so Darcy hoped.

"If you, and not Lydia, were to choose, what would be your choice?" Darcy prodded. He needed to know the state of his cousin's heart if he were to give Richard proper assistance. He would not push his cousin to pursue a lady who did not hold his heart any more than he would allow his cousin to hide from his heart. Darcy was nearly certain that Richard had lost his heart to Miss Lydia, and from experience, he knew that trying to deny one's heart was a torturous thing.

"I would choose to reverse time and still be in London," Richard said.

"Then, you still love her?"

Richard nodded but remained silent which was just as well since his brother had arrived at his door.

Lord Westonbury approached the bed. "You look dreadful."

"It is a pleasure to see you as well, although you will need to be on the side of the bed where Darcy is if you wish for me to actually see you."

"What do you mean?" Westonbury moved to the far side of the bed.

"The blow to his head has damaged his eyesight. We do not know if it is a lasting thing or just temporary like the spinning room and unsteadiness when he walks."

"You cannot see out of your left eye?"

"No, I can see out of it as long as everything is in front of me. I just cannot see anything that is to that side of me."

"That is very odd," Westonbury propped himself on the edge of the bed, and Richard held out his hand.

"Your half-crown." Richard's tone was flat as he held his brother's gaze.

"I am not giving you my half-crown."

"You are also not going to offer it to Miss Lydia for any reason," Richard replied.

Westonbury chuckled. "You heard about Sally's did you?"

"We found Miss Lydia and Miss Elizabeth there if that is what you mean," Darcy said.

"What do you mean found?"

"Come now, Wes," Richard said, "you do not truly believe that either Miss Bennet was at Sally's for an appointment, now do you?"

Westonbury shrugged. "I suppose I had not considered why they were there. I only just found out that the pretty young thing that swindled me out of a shilling and gave me a sore nose was the lady with whom I heard you are enam-oured." He shifted on the bed. "Why were they there?"

"How did you learn about Miss Lydia?" Richard asked.

Westonbury shook his head. "No, I asked you a ques-tion first — but we could wrestle for to see who answers first. However, I do believe I would win this time."

There was only a year separating Richard and his brother, so wrestling to settle a disagreement was not an unusual thing for the two of them. They had broken more than one vase while attempting to settle a dispute in such a fashion. Richard was an inch shorter than his brother, though he was just as broad. However, shorter did not mean easily overcome, for most often, Richard had been victorious.

"You could wrestle Darcy," Richard offered.

"No, he cannot," Darcy replied. "He cheats."

Westonbury grinned. "So does Richard."

"Which is why you both usually beat me," Darcy replied. "So, let's consider me beaten in Richard's stead, which means Richard will answer your question before you tell us that Aunt Catherine told you about Miss Lydia."

"Aunt Catherine knows about Miss Lydia?"

Darcy nodded. "She was here in an attempt to talk me out of marrying Elizabeth and into marrying Anne instead."

"I knew she had gone to hunt you down," Westonbury said with a smirk, "but I heard nothing of Miss Lydia."

"Well, then, I recant. You were soundly beaten by me in our imagined wrestling match, and so you must explain how you know about Miss Lydia." Darcy had been confident that if Westonbury knew about Lydia that Lady Catherine had returned to town and told one and all at Matlock House about her.

"No, I beat you. Now, brother dear, kindly explain to me why you were looking for your lady at Sally's."

Richard drew and released a breath. "Wickham," he snarled.

"And how did you find out about Miss Lydia?" Darcy asked.

"But there is a story behind Richard's answer," Westonbury protested.

"After you give us the name of your source, we can share stories."

"You could wrestle him, and, if you win, you get your story first, but, if he wins, you tell us the name of the gossip who told you about Miss Lydia," Richard offered.

"I am still not wrestling," Darcy said. "How is it that you are both older than me and still act like you are far younger?"

Westonbury shrugged. "Because we are not you."

Darcy rolled his eyes.

"Very well," Westonbury said. "I heard about her from Mrs. Salter."

# Chapter 15

"Mrs. Salter?" Darcy repeated.

He had not thought to hear that name again, especially not from one of his relations. He had not even considered that Mrs. Salter might be a name any of his relatives would know. But then, if anyone were to know her, it would be Westonbury as he made it his business to know of as many as possible of the ladies who would be parading their charges through the season. Much could be deciphered about a daughter by knowing the mother — or so his cousin claimed.

Westonbury nodded. "Do you know her?"

"I know of her."

"You do?" Richard asked in surprise. "I cannot say I have heard the name before."

Richard, unlike his brother, only felt he needed to know those mothers who had daughters that piqued his interest. Of course, he was also more likely to sequester himself away in a library or card room to talk to the fathers and brothers than his elder brother was.

"Do you remember how I told you that Miss Bingley did not seem so bad after hearing Mr. Bennet's tale about Mrs. Bennet?" Darcy asked.

Richard shook his head slowly.

"It was the night after the ladies had come back from shopping and you were asked to choose the best red ribbon."

Westonbury laughed. "You were picking ribbons?"

"Miss Lydia needed an opinion," Darcy said.

That information did little to keep Richard's brother from chuckling further.

"She values his opinion on many things." Darcy held Richard's gaze.

"Yes, I remember that conversation." Richard's reply was quick and lacking in any emotion. However, his gaze dropped away from Darcy's.

"It was just before Miss Lydia and her sister went missing," Darcy explained to Westonbury with the hope of bringing to Richard's mind the fear they had both felt that night when they had thought their ladies were in danger.

"Yes, I know," Richard snapped. "Continue. How does that apply to this Mrs. Salter?"

"She was the lady in Mr. Bennet's story who treated Mrs. Bennet very ill."

Richard's eyes grew wide. "And you say, Wes, that she told you about Miss Lydia?"

"She did not tell me directly," Westonbury replied, rising to cross to the window. "I overheard her talking to a friend at Almack's. It seems her daughter was on the point of being happily betrothed until the fellow found someone else – with deeper pockets and a more willing charm – that is how she said it. Just like that, with a suggestive lilt to her tone. She then added that Miss –" He waved his hand in a circle in front of him as if attempting to draw a scent towards himself.

The action was familiar to Darcy. His cousin had always made that same motion when attempting to recall something.

"Oh, I cannot remember! But it matters not who she is to me. However, according to Mrs. Salter, the girl had no choice but to accept this fellow's proposal. Her willing charms had found her in a desperate state you see." He lifted a brow.

"With child?" Richard asked.

His brother nodded from where he leaned against the wall near the window. "It seems that Mrs. Salter had experienced somewhat of the same treatment when she was young. Some willing wench – I swear she used those words – stole her prize from her. And she had seen this woman in town with Miss Darcy – of all people!" He said the last part in a womanly falsetto.

"Well, that caught my attention, so I stayed where I was, twirling my quizzing glass and pretending to watch the dancing."

"She was speaking poorly of my sister?" Darcy asked. How dare the woman do such a thing!

"Not directly, but it was implied."

"She's either stupid or has no clue who Darcy is," Richard grumbled.

"My money is on stupid." Westonbury pushed off the wall. "To get to the point. After a discussion of who Darcy was and his connections – meaning our father – Mrs. Salter then said that the woman's daughters seemed to be cut from the same cloth. There was something about a compromise at a ball involving one of them, and a discussion of two others grasping far above their station. Apparently, she had heard that the youngest was vying for the affections of the Earl of Matlock's youngest son. Someone had seen them walking together or some such thing. No names were given. I had to discover the name of the youngest Bennet on my own, which was not easily or cheaply done. The servants at Almack's expect remuneration for being nosy."

"You did not just ask her?" Richard scoffed.

"She had not seen me and after speaking of Miss Lydia – whose name I did not know at that time – she then suggested to her friend that she thought her daughter might be able to do one better and snare me. Trust me, if you have ever met Miss Salter, you will understand why I was in a desperate state to be gone and not discovered by Mrs. Salter."

"Is she not handsome?" Darcy asked.

"Her features are very pleasant – her spirit is not. If I am to be tied to a wife, it shall not be a lady of her ilk." He shuddered. "And since I have no intention of being trapped by anyone, when Mrs. Salter's friend teased that Miss Salter could affect a compromise and Mrs. Salter congratulated her on a delightful plan, I found the door quickly – after enlisting a servant to discover the information I sought and having him deliver it to me in my carriage."

"That will not make it any easier for Miss Lydia to establish herself in town," Darcy muttered.

"Which is another good reason for her to give me up," Richard replied.

"Wait! If you have not formed an attachment to her, why can I not give her a half-crown for a kiss or two?" Westonbury asked. "She is a pretty thing."

Darcy folded his arm and looked at Richard, waiting to see how his cousin would explain himself.

"She is a gentleman's daughter, not some trollop," Richard argued. "You do not go around paying gentlemen's daughters for favours."

"You and Darcy might not," Westonbury teased. "Clarice was a gentleman's daughter, but she found herself in need of employment."

"Clarice? I assume you are speaking of one of the women at Sally's," Richard said.

If Richard could have gotten out of bed or even moved enough to reach his brother, who had returned to sit on the end of the bed, it looked to Darcy from the expression Richard wore and the tone he used, that Westonbury would not win such an altercation.

"I am."

"Miss Lydia is not one of Sally's women," Richard growled.

"Nor is she your lady," Westonbury argued.

"She is..." Richard snapped his mouth closed on his bellow, seeming to shrink further into his pillow as he did so.

"She is if she wishes to be," Darcy finished Richard's thought.

"What do you mean?" Westonbury asked the question of Darcy, but his eyes slid to his brother, who had his eyes closed.

"Look at me," Richard said. "Why should anyone be tied to this?"

"I still do not follow. You have never been particularly handsome."

Darcy gaped at his cousin. Did the man not think before he spoke?

"Your appeal has always been in your charm and caring nature," Westonbury said.

He did think before he spoke. Darcy's lips tipped up in pleased surprise.

"But I will likely lose my commission," Richard argued.

"And mother will be happy for it."

Richard's eyes opened. "I will need an income."

"Father will see to that."

"Not if they do not approve of my choice of bride."

Westonbury clapped his hands. "So you do like her, do you?"

"Of course, I do," Richard snapped.

"Well, she seems enamoured with you as well. There is a good deal of gumption in her. She did swindle me out of my money and gave me a sore nose in the process."

"Not to mention," said Darcy, "that she prevented Wes from seeing you before you sent for him. How many people keep him from what he wants?"

"Exactly!" Westonbury agreed. "And I am not entirely sure how she managed it. I was determined to outwit her."

"She batted her eyes," Richard said.

Westonbury's brow furrowed. "She did, but I am not unaccustomed to that."

"She is a Bennet," Darcy said. "They do seem to possess a power that few others do."

Westonbury laughed. "That is the most ridiculous thing I think I have ever heard you say, Darcy."

"It may sound ridiculous, but I assure you it is true. I helped stage the compromise of which Mrs. Salter was speaking."

The sound of a maid passing the door was the only

sound that penetrated the room for a full two minutes while Westonbury stared, open-mouthed at Darcy.

"It was necessary to be able to give me a chance of winning Elizabeth's heart," Darcy said as he pushed up from his chair. "Speaking of whom, I should like to see her before she goes home." He looked at Richard. "Do you wish to see Lydia?"

His cousin smiled sadly. "With all my heart, but I cannot."

"Then, I shall pass along your sorrow at needing to rest instead of seeing her," Westonbury said as he joined Darcy in standing.

"No, Darcy can do that."

Westonbury shook his head. "Darcy has his own lady who will claim his attention."

"You are a –"

"Yes, I am," Westonbury cut his brother's words off. "Get some rest," he added before turning to leave. "Richard," he called from the door.

"Yes."

"I am pleased you were not injured any further than you were."

"I wish I could say I am as well," Richard replied, "However, I have not yet decided if I am pleased or not."

~*~*~

"He is in a sorry state, is he not?" Westonbury said to Darcy when they were both in the hall.

"He wanted to stay at Pemberley."

"Because of Miss Lydia?"

Darcy nodded.

Westonbury blew out a breath as he stood at the top of the stairs. "I am uncertain how Mother will take the news of her son marrying someone with no standing in her circles." He cast a look back toward Richard's room. "However, he is excessively smitten."

The two cousins began their descent of the stairs.

"Go to the library," Westonbury said when they were about halfway down. "I will have Miss Elizabeth meet you there."

Darcy eyed his cousin suspiciously.

Catching Darcy's eye, Westonbury smiled. "I shall require a detailed account of the compromise you were part of in return for my service." He clapped Darcy on the shoulder as they gained the landing. "A gentleman who has been separated from the lady he fancies should not have to be reunited with her where there is an audience."

Darcy chuckled. "I see your point, but there is Lydia."

"Trust me. If she were any other man's lady, I might attempt to charm her away from him, but not my brother – or you, but she is not your lady," he added quickly.

"She is my sister – or will be," Darcy cautioned.

"And I will treat her as I do Georgiana. Now, go."

Darcy thanked him and hurried to the library. There was still a niggling fear that he should have been the one to speak to Lydia about Richard, but Westonbury had always been gentle with Georgiana. Surely, Darcy could trust him with this. Besides, he would be able to see Lydia before she left.

He made a circuit of the library while he waited for Elizabeth. Bingley did need to work on acquiring a few more books. The shelves were not barren, but they were not as full as Darcy thought they should be.

"Fitzwilliam?"

Darcy sighed in relief. She was here. He turned toward her and opened his arms, and she wasted no time in finding her way into his embrace.

"I have missed you," he said as he held her close.

"And I have missed you." She squeezed him more tightly.

"Kiss me."

She lifted her head from where it rested on his heart and tipped her face up towards him.

He cradled the back of her head with his hand and lowered his lips to hers, kissing her gently, longingly.

"When can we marry?" he asked.

"Tomorrow?" she replied.

He chuckled. "That is likely too soon, I suppose. Your mother would not be best pleased to be rushed in planning a wedding breakfast. And Richard would not be able to attend. Nor could I leave him here without me."

She cupped his cheek. "If his recovery is to be of a long

duration, I can join you here. I do not care where we are as long as we are together."

He dipped his head and kissed her once again. He was of the same mind. He wished to never be parted from her again, but that time was not yet. "When Richard is able to join us for the wedding breakfast, then we shall marry."

"And if he refuses to attend?"

Darcy sighed. "I am trusting that he will recover in mind as quickly as he does in body."

"A week will tell us more," Elizabeth assured him. "It is all very new."

"How is Lydia?"

"She is shaken and fearful. It is very unlike her."

Darcy's heart broke at the revelation.

"However," Elizabeth continued, "I will be very surprised if she does not rise to the challenge. A Bennet always does. Look at what Jane did to claim her love."

How fortunate was he to have a lady who could tease him into better spirits even in the face of such uncertainty?

"And if she does not?"

"I shall love you, and we shall face it together."

"That is a very good plan," Darcy said, pulling away from her some to smile down at her. "Now, before my cousin formulates some scandalous story about why you were absent for so long, we should return you to the drawing room."

"Should I worry about him?" Elizabeth asked as she wrapped her arm around Darcy's.

"Not overly much," Darcy assured her. "Wes and Richard are not just brothers but good friends. He is a scoundrel, but he knows his place. He will behave as he should." Darcy leaned his head towards her ear. "He also knows that neither Richard or I would allow him to treat poorly anyone for whom we cared. And I care very dearly for you, Miss Elizabeth Bennet."

"And I, you, Mr. Darcy." They had stopped outside the drawing room and, lifting onto her toes, she kissed his cheek before the door was opened and they left their private moment behind.

# Chapter 16

"Good day, my lord. How does your brother fare today?" Elizabeth asked when Darcy, Bingley, and Lord Westonbury entered the sitting room at Longbourn.

"Well enough to order me out of his room," Westonbury replied with a grin.

"He was resting when we left," Darcy added, glancing around the room.

"Our mother was needed in the kitchen," Jane said.

"Ah, I was wondering where she was."

"Was it too quiet a greeting?" Elizabeth teased.

Darcy chuckled. "In a word? Yes."

"Then, Mr. Darcy, you will be delighted to know that she is anxiously awaiting her opportunity to meet a real lord, so your desire for an effusive greeting will not go unmet," Elizabeth said. "And then, we shall go for a walk."

"Where our mother's delights will no longer be able to be heard," Mary muttered from where she sat in the corner of the room.

Elizabeth gave Mary a stern look. It was one thing to

add sardonic comments to a conversation when it was just their close family and friends who were present. It was another thing altogether when one was entertaining a person of importance whose opinion could affect the future happiness of a lady's sisters. As was normal, a stern glare did little to affect Mary, who merely stared blankly in return as if to say, "but it is true." And it was true. Elizabeth knew that her mother would not greet Lord Westonbury quietly, for the more excited their mother became, the louder her voice grew.

"Lord Westonbury, this is my sister Mary," Jane said, "and next to Lydia is Kitty. Mary, Kitty, this is Mr. Darcy's cousin, the Viscount Westonbury."

Mary placed her sewing aside and rose – reluctantly, it seemed to Elizabeth – to curtsey and greet Lord Westonbury properly.

"And tell me, Miss Mary," Westonbury said, making his way across the room to sit near her, "should I fear this introduction to your mother?"

Mary raised an eyebrow at him. "You are likely safe as long as you do not tell her that you know Sally." She leaned around him to see Lydia. "That was the lady's name at the brothel, was it not?"

"Mary!" Elizabeth scolded. "A proper lady does not speak of such things."

"And an honourable gentleman does not do such

things, and yet here we are." She gave Westonbury an appraising look but said no more.

"I am not offended," Westonbury said.

Mary opened her mouth to speak but closed it again when Elizabeth glared at her. "Then, allow me to be offended on your behalf. I assure you that my sisters do know how to comport themselves properly."

Again, Mary's brow rose as if to ask, "do we?"

Darcy took Elizabeth's hand in his, drawing her attention away from her troublesome sister. Mary was far too opinionated and outspoken at times. How anyone as wonderful as Mr. Darcy wished to tie himself to a family such as hers was at this moment beyond her! However, Elizabeth was exceptionally glad for his willingness.

"I have written to my aunt and uncle, informing them that Richard is well and has been installed in a room at Netherfield," Darcy said.

"Will they visit him?" Lydia asked.

"I would expect that, at least, my mother would visit, but I am sure my father will join her if he has no pressing matters which must come first," Westonbury said.

"And will he see them?" Lydia had been very sorry to not have been allowed to see with her own eyes that the colonel was not in grave danger.

"I imagine he will not be given the choice," Westonbury replied. "My mother is not the sort of lady to be put off."

"Is she pleasant?" Lydia was twisting her fingers in her

lap, an action that seemed not to go unnoticed by Weston-bury.

"She is, though she can also be demanding." He smiled. "However, I am certain she will be happy to meet all of Richard's new friends and relations."

It appeared as if Lydia wished to inquire further, but just at that moment, Mrs. Bennet entered the room, and Mr. Darcy rose first to greet her and then introduce her to his cousin, effectively putting an end to any previous conversation.

"A real lord – in my home!" Mrs. Bennet was overflowing with delight. "There will not be a neighbour who will not be jealous of my good fortune, I must say." She paused. "However, it would be a much more delightful thing to be called on by someone such as yourself, my lord, if the honour did not come because of the injury to our dear colonel."

"I would agree. An injury is not something someone ever wishes on those they hold dear," Westonbury said.

"My husband will be sorry to have missed your visit, my lord, but he is gone out to view a tenant's home today." She turned to Mr. Darcy. "Sir William was kind enough to take him in his cart, and I was able to send a few things for the tenant's wife in the back of it. It was really just the thing, but then Sir William is often thinking about practicalities such as that."

"Sir William is a delight!" Bingley said.

"Indeed, he is!" Mrs. Bennet agreed. "Mr. Bennet and Sir William have been particular friends for years." She smiled softly. "He never once questioned my becoming mistress of Longbourn. His wife..." She did not finish the thought. "Lady Lucas and I have become dear friends, of course. It was only natural that it should happen, you see, as our husbands spend so much time in one another's company."

"You were not friends with Lady Lucas before you married Papa?" Lydia asked.

"Oh, we knew one another, but we were no more than acquaintances."

"How very odd," Lydia said. "I had thought you were always friends."

"That is because we are such good friends now," Mrs. Bennet replied. "And it was a very little trial to become better acquainted once I was married to your father. One just presents herself as who she is even if she does not feel completely up to the challenge and eventually, one finally believes it herself." She turned to Lord Westonbury. "Would you care for tea now or after you have toured the area? Lizzy tells me that you are all to walk out. I had thought after, but I was not certain if that would be acceptable to you."

"I am amenable to after," Westonbury said.

"That is very gracious of you, my lord." She beamed at him. "I will not keep you from your walk, then, but will wait to hear about your family when you return." Her brow furrowed. "Is there a Lady Westonbury?"

"Not yet."

Her brows rose. "But there is one who will soon be?"

"No, I fear, there is not."

"Oh, that is unfortunate," Mrs. Bennet said with some feeling. "A handsome gentleman such as yourself should not be unattached."

Mary mumbled something that, to Elizabeth, sounded a lot like, "Yes, he should be."

"I apologize, Miss Mary. I did not quite catch that," Westonbury said, leaning his head closer to her.

"There was nothing to be caught," she replied, though her cheeks did grow faintly red.

"Shall we be off then?" Bingley stood quickly, much more quickly than Elizabeth had ever seen him do before. Perhaps he too feared what might come out of Mary's mouth next if they were not to leave the room quickly.

Bonnets and wraps were at the ready, so the preparation for departure was very little, and they were off quickly.

Mrs. Bennet saw them to the door herself, or more accurately, she saw Lord Westonbury to the door and made certain to tell him at least twice more how delighted she was to have met him.

"That was not so very bad," Westonbury said when they were well away from the house.

"Indeed, it was not," Mary agreed.

Westonbury stopped dead in his tracks. "Was Miss Mary just agreeable?"

"I believe she was," Lydia replied when no one else said anything.

"I try to always agree with that which is correct," Mary retorted.

"Ah, I see." Westonbury smirked at her, causing her to scowl.

"Mary, will you walk with me," Elizabeth said. It was probably best for Mary to be separated from the viscount.

"I am going to walk with Kitty," Mary answered.

"I am walking with Lydia," Kitty replied.

"My arm is not taken," Westonbury offered.

Mary looked at the arm he offered, raised a brow while giving him a look of perturbed displeasure, and then very cautiously placed her hand on it.

"Why?" Bingley whispered to Darcy as the group began walking once again. "She obviously does not like him. Why would he subject himself to what could very likely be a lecture?"

"I was thinking the same thing," Elizabeth admitted. "It is as if he wishes to provoke her."

Darcy sighed. "I cannot answer with any certainty, but I do not think he has ever met someone who is so completely unaffected by either his title or charm – at least, not a female someone."

"He will not sway her opinion," Jane said. "Once Mary's good opinion is gone, it is excessively hard to reclaim."

"It would take an act of heroic proportions," Elizabeth agreed.

Mary was firm in her resolve. That was why Mary wore dresses without a lot of adornment. She did not like flounces and ribbons, and no amount of protest or persuasion by their mother or younger sisters had ever convinced Mary that she should do more than add a row of flowers around a hem or neckline. Simply put, Mary was not overly ornate. She was as she dressed – practical, sturdy, and modest nearly to the point of being dull.

"Mary!" Lydia snapped, drawing the attention of one and all.

"I assure you that I am not offended overly much," Westonbury said.

Elizabeth's breath caught. What had Mary said while she had not been paying attention?

"A great deal of our argument was my doing." Westonbury looked at Darcy sheepishly. "I overstepped."

"You are not the only one, then!" Lydia cried. "Mary has no business speaking as she did to anyone let alone Colonel Fitzwilliam's brother. Why just think how he would feel to hear you attacking his brother!"

"I was not attacking him," Mary protested. "I was making a point – a very good and extremely accurate point!"

Lydia stamped her foot. "It was not proper. Do you wish

for him to think we are not proper? Do you truly want him to tell his parents and his brother that we are not fit to be known to them?"

"I would never –"

"You might if she continues down the path she has chosen." Lydia folded her arms and scowled at Mary.

Westonbury looked to Darcy in confusion.

Elizabeth sighed and, with a sad smile for Darcy, she dropped his arm and went to Mary.

"I think it might be best if we were to walk together."

"But what of Mr. Darcy," Mary said.

"Mr. Darcy is not causing a scene," Elizabeth replied.

"And neither am I. Lydia is doing that."

"Because you were being rude!"

"I was not being rude. I was being honest."

"The two are not always exclusive," Jane said. "Sometimes honest facts can be presented in a very unpolite fashion."

"And they were!" Lydia said.

Mary's eyes narrowed. "I would have rather stayed at home and read anyway. I only came because Lydia wanted it." She lifted her chin and began stalking silently homeward.

"We do not wish for you to leave," Westonbury called after her.

"It may not be what you wish," she retorted, "but it is what you have gotten."

"She is impossible," Lydia said with another stamp of her foot.

"Shall I go after her?" Jane asked.

Elizabeth shook her head. When Mary was in high dudgeon, there was little anyone could say to help her see reason. Later, after there had been time enough for her to calm, then she could be more easily approached.

"I could go after her," Westonbury offered. "It was my fault. I did provoke her." Again, he cast a sheepishly apologetic look at Darcy before turning to Lydia. "I must apologize for causing your unease, Miss Lydia. It was not done intentionally." He pulled a handkerchief from his pocket. "Will you forgive me so that Darcy will stop scowling at me?"

Lydia took the handkerchief from him and began dabbing at her eyes while she glanced back at Darcy, who was indeed scowling at his cousin. She nodded her head. "I should hate to see your face bruised on my account."

"You think he would hit me?"

Again, Lydia nodded. "I did not think he knew how either," she whispered. "However, I have seen Mr. Wickham and can assure you that Mr. Darcy can hit very effectively."

"Is that so?" Westonbury said as he took Lydia's hand and tucked it in the crook of his elbow before extending his other arm to Kitty. "Do tell."

Elizabeth shrugged as she met Darcy's gaze. "My sisters sometimes argue."

"As do mine," Bingley said. "Think nothing of it. It shall all get sorted out in time. It always does."

Elizabeth blew out a breath. "But the sorting out can be arduous," she said to Darcy who had reached where she stood.

Darcy took Elizabeth's hand and prevented her from walking on with Jane and Bingley. "I will speak to my troublesome cousin," he assured her before lifting her hand to his lips and kissing it. "Hopefully, he will be easily sorted."

# Chapter 17

Mary huffed as she stood beside Elizabeth, waiting to be allowed entrance to Netherfield the next day. There had been a long and lengthy discussion between Mary and her father after Lydia had told him what Mary had said on their walk.

"You are to be polite," Lydia said.

"I know," Mary grumbled.

"And apologize."

Again, Mary huffed. "I know. Stop speaking."

"Good day, Mr. Harvey," Jane said as the door opened. "We are here to see..." She looked at her sisters. "Well, everyone it seems."

"Very good, ma'am. If you will follow me."

"That lace Mama selected looked very nice on Elizabeth's wedding dress, did it not?" Jane asked Lydia. She was attempting as always to direct the conversation so that the argument from a few moments ago would be lost.

"It was lovely," Lydia agreed.

"Only two more weeks," Kitty whispered, "and we shall have to call on you here, Jane."

Jane smiled broadly. "It seems so far away and yet so close."

When he had asked, their mother had assured Darcy yesterday that she thought all the necessary preparations for a wedding would be completed by the end of the week. There was nothing to be concerned about except whether Colonel Fitzwilliam would be able to attend and if standing for a full service would be too much for Mr. Bennet's leg. Therefore, a date had finally been decided upon, and Elizabeth knew that Jane was eagerly anticipating becoming the mistress of Netherfield.

Dash was the first to greet the Bennet ladies when they entered the drawing room, but after a proper greeting, which consisted of a scratched ear, he sat down next to Lydia. Kitty and Georgiana excused themselves to go to the music room. Mary attempted to join them, but Jane, who was rarely stern, grasped her hand firmly.

"You have something you must do first," Jane whispered.

Mary blew out a breath and with flushed cheeks turned to Lord Westonbury. "My lord," she said and waited for him to acknowledge her, "I have come today with a very particular purpose. I have been made aware of the fact that though what I said to you yesterday was entirely truthful, it was not my place to say it even if no one else seems to wish to speak on the behalf of the less fortunate –"

Jane cleared her throat.

"What I am attempting to say," Mary corrected, "is that my words were out of place and so I would ask your forgiveness for my immoderate behaviour."

"My forgiveness is readily given. However, I must also apologize for provoking you to behave so." He held out his hand to her. "Am I forgiven?"

"For provoking me."

"Nothing else?" Westonbury's lips curled into a smirk, and Darcy coughed. "Yes, well, that is all for which I have asked forgiveness, is it not?" His hand remained outstretched to her.

Mary looked at his hand. Then, with a raised brow and a look that did not speak of a willingness to bestow forgiveness, she placed her hand in his.

He gave it a firm shake and then, lifted it to lips.

Mary gasped and snatched her hand away. "That is not necessary."

"I think it is."

"It is my hand, and I think it is not. Therefore, it is not."

"But it is what is polite," Westonbury protested.

"I am not to argue with you, my lord," Mary replied.

"A pity that," Westonbury muttered.

"Tea!" Bingley inserted. "I think it would be very good to have tea, do you not, Darcy?"

"An excellent idea," Darcy agreed.

"And Miss Lydia, you may help me pour," Caroline said happily.

"Wes," Darcy called to his cousin, who was still standing with Mary and offering to see her to the music room, "I believe she knows the way."

"It seems we are to be kept apart," Westonbury said with a laugh.

"It is for the best," Mary assured him.

"I am not entirely certain I agree."

"Of course, you would not. It is a logical and well-thought-out plan."

"I am not incapable of logical thinking."

Mary raised a brow and shook her head. "You have yet to prove it, my lord." Then, she curtseyed and left the room.

Westonbury flopped into a chair. "You are a dreadful bore, Darcy."

Darcy laughed. "Not everyone enjoys an argument as much as you."

"I can argue with you if you wish," Sir Matthew quipped.

Westonbury sighed. "I think I shall pass."

"I am here if you should feel the need to disagree with someone," Sir Matthew added.

Lydia followed Caroline out of the room to see that the tea service was being prepared and likely to discuss some other facet of being a proper hostess. It surprised Elizabeth how discreet Caroline was being. There was no announcement of a lesson's topic nor was there any indication that it was not the most normal thing in all the world for Caroline and Lydia to be heading off together to do something or another.

Jane took a seat next to Mr. Bingley, and the two began discussing what preparations for their upcoming wedding were being made today while she was away from home.

"Your mother does not mind that you are leaving so much to her?" Bingley asked.

"Not at all. We will do our part when we return home. Father was much more eager that we see to Mary," Jane replied.

Westonbury shifted uneasily in his chair.

"Troubles?" Darcy asked him.

"I had not intended for her to get in trouble," Westonbury whispered. "Perhaps I should apologize for that?"

"When she returns," Darcy replied.

The conversation then fell into the realm of topics commonly canvased in a drawing room – the weather, the neighbours, and the health of those family members who were ailing, namely Mr. Bennet and Colonel Fitzwilliam.

"Do you think he will see her?" Elizabeth whispered to Darcy. Lydia had eaten little yesterday or today. Between the worry over the damage Mary might have done by being so outspoken to Lord Westonbury and concern about the colonel, she had little appetite and wandered from room to room unable to focus on any task. To be honest, Elizabeth was more than a little anxious about the state of her youngest sister's mind.

"We are hopeful," Darcy replied.

"It would be excellent if he did."

"I agree," Darcy replied. "One way or the other, a decision must be arrived at eventually." He took Elizabeth's hand in his and simply held it.

"I will take him some tea," Westonbury said as the tea service was brought in. "If I cannot argue with Miss Mary, I might as well see if I can persuade my brother to be reasonable."

"Do not go to the music room," Darcy cautioned.

Westonbury leveled a severe look at him before turning away to gather the tea for himself and Richard.

"He is..." Elizabeth sought for the right word.

"Troublesome and used to getting his way," Darcy finished.

"Do I need to worry about him?" It was the same question she had asked Darcy after meeting Lord Westonbury for the first time.

"I would like to say no," Darcy answered with a sigh, "but, to be honest, I am uncertain. I do not fear for your safety or that of your sisters. However, I do fear for everyone's sanity at this point. What Miss Mary said to him yesterday seems to have struck a chord with him."

"I was shocked to hear what she had said," Elizabeth replied. "I know she does not approve of places such as Sally's."

"Which is as it should be," Darcy inserted, and Elizabeth agreed.

"And I know that she is given to moralizing, but she has always confined her speeches to those she knows well. It is truly not like her to speak as she did to a stranger – most especially, one who is due a certain amount of respect just because of who he is. I have been attempting to deduce the reason, but I have not yet discovered it."

"Have you asked her?"

Elizabeth nodded. "Her reply was not helpful." She attended to the tea she had been served. "Lydia is doing very well."

"And Caroline looks excessively pleased," Darcy added.

This, of course, led to a discussion about Darcy's aunt and Lydia's desire to do well.

When tea was nearly over, Darcy went to inquire of Richard whether or not he would be amenable to guests.

Elizabeth sighed with relief when he returned and gave her a smile and a nod before informing Lydia that the colonel would be delighted to have her visit him.

"Come, my love."

Happily, Elizabeth placed her hand in his and together, they went up with Lydia.

"Wait," Lydia said as Darcy reached for the doorknob.

She blew out a breath. "I do not know if I can do this," she whispered.

"Do you not wish to see him?" Elizabeth asked.

"Oh, very much, but what if he is too greatly altered?"

"He does not look as he did," Darcy answered. "His injuries are still fairly recent."

She shook her head. "That is not what I meant."

"Is it not?" Elizabeth asked. "I know you were worried about that." Had they not had a discussion about whether or not Lydia could love someone who was not handsome?

"I will not lie. That is still a small fear, but..." Her eyes filled with tears and she wrapped an arm around her middle. "He did not wish to see me. What if he no longer loves me?"

Elizabeth wrapped Lydia in her arms. "He will still love you."

"How can you say so?"

"If he did not love you, he would not be so concerned about not being good enough for you," Darcy replied.

"But he is!" Lydia said with some force.

"Then, you must convince him of that," Darcy replied. "His mind and heart are muddled. His life is not what it was, and it is likely that it never will be what it was."

Lydia nodded and dashed away the few tears which had escaped her eyes.

"Not knowing is far worse than knowing," Darcy added. "I know."

"You do?"

He nodded. "I thought your sister hated me and would always hate me even though I loved her dearly. That is why I took part in the scheme to see Miss Bingley and Sir Matthew betrothed. I needed to know if I had a chance. Your sister Jane and your aunt seemed to think I did. Thankfully, they were correct."

"I am also happy they were," Lydia agreed with a smile. "You are very nice when one gets to know you. Not at all as you appeared to be when you first arrived at Netherfield."

Darcy chuckled. "Thank you, Miss Lydia. I am happy to know I improve upon acquaintance. Now, shall we take on the surly Colonel Fitzwilliam and attempt to convince him that he is not unworthy?"

Lydia nodded and pulled in a deep breath as Darcy opened the door.

"Richard," Darcy said, motioning for Lydia to follow him to the far side of the bed, "I have brought you some guests."

Lydia's hand rested on her heart and tears spilled down her cheek.

"I look dreadful."

"You do," she agreed, approaching his bed. "Does it hurt horridly?" She took his hand. "I'll not move your shoulder," she added. "I understand it is also injured."

"It is not as bad as it was," Richard replied.

"The room spins, and he can see you best when you are on this side of him," Darcy added.

"I wish I could take it away," Lydia whispered. "How dreadfully boring it must be to lie here and have nothing to do but consider if you hurt more today than yesterday." She perched on the side of the bed.

"It is rather dull except when Darcy or Westonbury are here. Did you know that each swag of the flounce around the top of the bed on this side has between four and six folds?"

Lydia peered up at the material. "You are right!" She then looked at the other side of the bed. "It is the same on the side you cannot see." She sighed and smiled at him. "I have missed you, and I was so dreadfully afraid you had died."

Darcy handed her his handkerchief and then, without a word, he and Elizabeth left the room.

"And I missed you," Richard said. He wished to pull her to him and kiss away her tears, but he knew he could not. "I would understand if you did not wish for me to continue –"

"Do not say it!" Lydia interrupted. "You shall not be rid of me that easily!"

"But I am not who I was." She needed to know who she was accepting.

"Yes, you are. In your heart, you are."

Richard grimaced as he lifted her hand to his lips. "You really will accept me as I am?"

She nodded, and Richard expelled a deep breath that carried with it many of the worries and fears which had settled upon him as soon as he had woken and found his life set on its end.

# Chapter 18

Richard pushed up from the edge of his bed, where he had been waiting for the world to stop spinning. Since the room seemed to be standing still, it should now be safe to walk the short distance between the bed and the door.

Slowly, with deliberate steps, he crossed the floor but paused when he reached the door to lean his head against it for a moment to allow the room to still itself once again before opening the door.

He could not continue to stay in this room as he had for the last several days. He grew weary of seeing the same portion of ceiling and window. He wanted to attempt returning to normal, everyday life. He needed to do so, for how was he ever to be good enough for Lydia if he did not at some point get out of bed and on with his duties.

He stepped into the hallway, but then, thinking better of it as the hall seemed to waver and he imagined making a spectacle of himself by falling down the stairs, he returned to his room but not to his bed. Instead, he turned the chair near the hearth so that it would face the open door.

This way, he could, at least, catch glimpses of life while his blasted head took its sweet time healing.

With a grimace, he sat down and immediately realized that he had not moved a footstool into position for his feet. That was foolish, for he was not getting up to do it now! He would do without being able to prop up his legs until someone came into the room who would not fall over when bending to move such a piece of furniture.

"The upstairs maid sees to the cleaning of this hallway and the hearths in each of the rooms."

Richard tipped his head. Was that Caroline?

"There is another maid who sees to the hall and hearths downstairs. Of course, they will perform these duties at times when they will not be seen or will be least intrusive. One does not wish to have her private conversations carried to others."

"Would they do that?"

Was that Lydia? Richard considered getting up and going to the hall to discover what Lydia and Caroline were doing, but his body was protesting not being in bed as it was. He dared not push it further than he already had.

"Miss Bingley," he called.

"Oh, yes, it is often the servants who spread the most damaging news in town. One can never be too careful."

"How very odd."

He smiled at Lydia's tone of wonder. "Miss Bingley," he called again.

Footsteps drew nearer. And then a face appeared in his doorway. Not just one face, but two. The one he wished most to see was just behind the one to whom he had called.

"Good day, Miss Bingley, Miss Lydia."

"Why are you out of bed?" Lydia demanded. "Has the surgeon said you may be?"

"I am tired of lying there," he replied. "And I am only sitting. It is not so great a strain as one might think." His lips curled into a smile for her.

The surgeon would be here later to see if his stitches were no longer needed. He would have to remember to gain the man's approval to be up and about. He did not wish to be scolded each time he attempted to venture from his room.

"However," he continued, "before I sat down, I did not bring the footstool near enough, and it would be more comfortable to sit with my feet up."

He had not even finished saying what he had to say before Lydia was crossing the room to move the footstool.

"I was going to ask that someone be sent to see to that," he told her.

"I am quite capable of moving a small piece of furniture, and I do not think it is improper to do so." She turned to Caroline. "Is it? Should I have summoned a servant?"

Miss Bingley shook her head and smiled. "Moving the

footstool is perfectly acceptable. Being in a gentleman's bedroom is not."

Lydia gasped and scurried to the door. "Forgive me. I forgot."

To Richard's surprise, Miss Bingley smiled and said, "There is nothing to forgive. I was here to stand as chaperone. Your reputation is safe."

"What are you two doing this afternoon?" Richard asked.

"I am continuing my lessons. We have just completed the duties of the footmen and maids," Lydia replied. "There is a lot to remember, but Miss Bingley is very patient. Surprisingly so."

"Is that so?" Amusement had been so far from Richard for so many weeks that it was quite refreshing to feel it now.

"Oh, yes," she assured him seriously. "I fear I had a very incorrect view of who Miss Bingley was. She is not so cross as I had thought when I first met her. She is actually very pleasant, and I hope she will count me as a friend."

"I *was* cross when you met me," Caroline admitted. "I did not wish to be here. I preferred town."

"Do you still prefer town?" Lydia asked.

Caroline nodded. "To a degree. However, I find that the country improves when the company improves." She smiled. "I am most happy to be wherever Sir Matthew is."

"There are two chairs in here," Richard offered. "If you

were both to join me, there would be nothing improper. I would like to hear how you and Sir Matthew are getting on."

Caroline's brow furrowed. "You would?"

"I am dreadfully bored, Miss Bingley."

"Very well, then, I suppose Miss Lydia and I can conclude our lesson for today."

"But will I know enough before any other guests arrive?" Lydia questioned as she entered the room. "I should hate to be found wanting."

"You will not be," Richard assured her.

"She most certainly will not be," Caroline agreed as she sat down on the small settee that was part of the furniture grouping before the hearth.

"This will not do," Lydia said, standing before Richard and extending her hand. "We must turn your chair. I refuse to speak to the side of your head."

Richard chuckled and lowered his feet, which he had just gotten comfortable on the footstool. Then, he took her hand and allowed her to assist him in standing.

"Stand here." She had pulled him three steps away from the chair.

"I can move the chair," he argued.

"And so can I," she replied with a bat of her lashes and a smile. "You will not deny me the pleasure of assisting you, will you?"

"No."

How could he refuse when she was looking at him so hopefully and with that particular look of delight? He understood precisely why Dash did whatever Lydia asked. Refusing her would take away that look and not even a pup like Dash, who was as unyielding as they came, could tolerate seeing such disappointment.

Speaking of the creature, Dash wandered into the room just at that moment and eyed Richard's chair.

"Absolutely not!" Lydia said firmly. "The rug is very comfortable, and the colonel must have this chair."

Dash's tale wagged as he listened to Lydia, and then as soon as she was done speaking, he sat down and waited for her to help Richard to his chair.

"Come here," Richard put a hand down in invitation to Dash, who willingly came to him for a scratch.

"Now, lie down," Lydia said, pointing to the rug.

Dash's head tipped and looked at the place where Lydia was pointing before lying down exactly where he was at Richard's side.

"Oh, very well, but do not disturb the colonel." Lydia moved the footstool into place before taking a seat next to Caroline.

"That is exactly what I mean," Caroline said with a smile. "You knew precisely what was needed to make Colonel Fitzwilliam comfortable, and you were very direct in giving orders to Dash, even if he did not heed them completely.

"He'd be sacked if he were a footman," Richard teased.

"Perhaps not dismissed on the first instance," Lydia replied with a smile. "I would first speak to the butler and have him instruct the footman on what was and was not his place. A lowering of position could be tried first if the error did not correct itself. However," she sighed, "one must not have servants who are unwilling to do as they should."

"Well done, Miss Lydia," Caroline said. "You have been paying close attention."

"I wish to do well," Lydia answered.

"Why?" Richard asked.

He suspected he knew. Yesterday, they had not spoken of much except his injuries and how much they had missed each other in the few minutes of privacy Darcy had given them. And not all of those minutes had been used for talking either. Once he had convinced her that she would not injure him by kissing, there had been some time spent doing just that.

"As I said, I do not wish to be found wanting."

"By whom?"

"Well," she blinked her eyes as if surprised that he would ask such a thing, "by everyone. I should not wish for them to think you were unfortunately tied to an incapable or improper lady." She looked down at her hands. "Some might forbid you from courting me."

"I should like to see them try," he muttered.

Caroline took Lydia's hand. "If there is one thing that I have learned from Sir Matthew which I was never taught in school, it is that my success or failure is not judged by the opinions of strangers." She shrugged when Lydia looked at her in surprise. "You must first find yourself acceptable."

It was Richard's turn to blink. Caroline Bingley had always been concerned with the opinions of others for as long as he had known her. Was she no longer so enamoured with such?

"After that, it is only Sir Matthew's good opinion that I seek for I know that if I am pleased with myself and my effort, and he is equally as satisfied, then I have succeeded. Few others matter a great deal to my happiness."

"He is wise," Richard said.

"Excessively so," Caroline agreed.

Richard looked at Lydia. "Are you pleased with yourself?"

She shrugged. "I am not certain."

Caroline patted the hand she had been holding. "You will be. You only lack the confidence that comes with practice." She turned to Richard. "I was telling Miss Lydia just today when she arrived that I have decided to have her help me plan a dinner for when the countess is here. I will invite all the Bennets, and it will be an elaborate, festive affair." She smiled at Lydia who was looking a trifle uneasy. "It will be before your sisters are married and will be a celebration of their upcoming nuptials."

"That is an excellent idea," Richard said.

"We have not properly celebrated their betrothals," Caroline said.

"Nor have we celebrated yours," Lydia said.

"True! I think we should include you and Sir Matthew as honoured guests," Richard agreed heartily.

"But I am the hostess," Caroline deferred.

"Only one hostess. I believe you had another," Richard replied.

"I would prefer to not be celebrated." Caroline's cheeks flushed. "Being promised to Sir Matthew is enough. I came into this betrothal..." She paused. "My behaviour was deplorable."

"I will not press the matter," Lydia said quietly. "If you do not wish it, it shall not be."

"I wish," Caroline whispered while glancing at the door as if checking to make certain they were alone. "I wish to prove myself as a gracious hostess and acquit myself as a proper sister who is happy for her brother and his friend."

"Ah. You wish to prove yourself," Richard said.

Caroline nodded. "Do not tell anyone else. Only Sir Matthew will know beyond us."

"Of course, you may trust us," Lydia assured her. "What are friends for if not to be trusted with secrets?"

"When I first arrived at Netherfield in the autumn, I

never thought that you and I would be friends," Caroline said to Lydia.

"It is most remarkable, is it not?" Lydia agreed.

"Indubitably," Richard muttered.

Dash's head popped up as a cat crept into the room, slinking stealthily along the door.

"Have you met Oliver?" Lydia asked when she had spotted the cause for Dash's attention.

"Yes, Bingley introduced him to me."

"He and Dash are not yet friends."

Richard chuckled as he watched Oliver move around the room, carefully keeping his distance from Dash.

"The surgeon is here, sir," Richard's man stood at the door to his room. "He is waiting downstairs."

"I will see him in three minutes," Richard replied.

Caroline rose, and Lydia followed suit.

"Might I have a moment with Miss Lydia?" he asked Caroline.

"If the door is left open, I think it can be permitted," she agreed.

"Come closer," he said to Lydia as Caroline left the room. "Give me your hand."

Lydia held out her hand to him, and taking it, he bent to kiss it. "I need you to know that you will never be found wanting by me. No matter what anyone else might say. I love you."

She ducked her head and blushed sweetly. How he

wished he was able-bodied enough to stand and embrace her.

Lifting her eyes to his, she held his gaze and said, "And I need you to know that to me you shall always be enough. No matter if your coat is red, blue, black, or green." Her brow furrowed. "I am actually rather fond of blue," she said with a playful smile that made him chuckle.

"It matters not what your profession or if you can only ever see me when I stand on this side of you, for I love you. Before I saw you yesterday, I did not know if I could love a gentleman who was not handsome."

Richard's eyes grew wide. She did not find him handsome? That was a bit of a blow.

"But I did not even think about how you looked beyond the fact that my heart broke for the pain you must have suffered." She bent and kissed his lips. "And I worried for nothing. You are quite as handsome as you have always been." She ran a finger lightly down his scar, causing it to tingle as the nerves attempted to come to life. "You are just now more distinguished."

"Kiss me again."

"It is highly improper, Colonel."

However, despite her protest, she did as he asked before leaving him to wait for the surgeon.

# Chapter 19

"It is good to see you in the drawing room." Darcy looked up from the book he was reading as Richard entered the room with his brother standing watchfully at his side.

"I hear Mother is to arrive. I thought it best to look as fit as possible so that she would not send for every doctor in London."

"And a few from other locales," Westonbury quipped.

Lady Matlock had never been one to just allow her children to recuperate *as the good Lord deemed*, as her husband said it. As certain as her husband was about the fact that medication and doctors were not needed for every ailment, she was equally as certain that if doctors and medication were not needed then the good Lord would not have allowed them to exist. Therefore, if her children did not regain their health and vigour within a specified window of time – more or less mutually agreed upon between Lord and Lady Matlock – a physician would be sought.

"In fact, she might have one or two with her when she

comes," Westonbury added as he took a seat after making sure that his brother was comfortable.

"With any luck, it will only be one," Richard agreed with a half smile. "There is nothing that can be done for me that has not already been done. And so, here I am, and I would appreciate it if you would not hover so much, Wes. Mother will think I am unwell if you do."

"Have you seen yourself?" Westonbury retorted. "She will think you are unwell whether or not I am watching to make sure you do not harm yourself in your haste to ignore your current condition."

The room was spinning again, and the sunlight shone more brightly in this room than in his bedroom. Richard closed his eyes. That would help. "I am not ignoring my condition. It will not allow me the pleasure, I assure you. However, I refuse to be limited by it completely. There is a lady..." He opened his good eye and peeked around the room as best he could. No one had joined them. It was just he, his brother, and Darcy. "There is a lady I should like to one day marry. Now, that I am free of my commission, I thought it would be good to consider marrying."

Not that he knew what he was going to do rather than command a group of men. But, without the ability to see what was beside him, he was of no use to them.

"Are you certain you are rid of it?" Darcy asked.

Again, Richard opened his good eye so that he could

peek at his cousin. "I suspect so. The spinning has begun to improve, but my vision has not."

"And you fear it never will?" Darcy asked.

"Yes. As did the surgeon when I asked him."

"Ah! But that was just a country surgeon and not a physician from town," Westonbury said with a laugh.

Richard sighed. "I will consult such a person when I return to town if Mother has not stashed one in her trunk." He almost hoped that his mother had brought a doctor with her. He would like to hear what his fate would be from more than one source. It was not that he doubted the surgeon. He just did not wish to believe the man.

"Are we expecting other guests today?" Westonbury asked eagerly.

"Yes," Darcy answered. "I believe at least four of the Bennet sisters are intending to call."

"Only four?" Westonbury sounded disappointed.

"You may have to content yourself with tormenting Oliver," Darcy said dryly.

"That cat can climb all the way to the top of the drapery on that window behind you, Richard."

"Why you are proud of that fact, I do not understand. Pricks and snags from a kitten's claws do not add value to the fabric," Darcy chided.

Richard had heard how Westonbury had clapped his hands close to Oliver, and the startled creature had scurried up the drapes.

"It is almost as if Miss Mary is here," Westonbury teased Darcy.

"You should take up my commission," Richard muttered.

"We would be speaking French if he did," Darcy said.

"He needs something to do. Idleness only leads to mischief," Richard replied.

"He has an estate and eventually will have Matlock and all its duties."

"I do bore rather easily," Westonbury agreed. "There are no soirees here. There is no park in which to see and be seen. It is very dull, except when the Bennet ladies call."

His lips curled upward in pleasure but not as Richard had seen before. There was a peace to the smile where usually there was restlessness. Wes was always restless. Richard could not put his finger on it, but it was as if his brother viewed the arrival of the Bennets as something more than just a balm to boredom.

"There is to be a dinner tomorrow." Richard had heard about it from Lydia.

For the past three days since she and Caroline had visited with him for that first time in his room, she had spent at least an hour with him, reading to him or telling him about all the preparations.

"Yes, I am looking forward to it," Westonbury replied. "I hear there will be music afterward and then we will play cards. Georgie has some new song she is preparing."

"As does Miss Kitty," Darcy added.

"Both are doing very well." He sighed. "Miss Mary refuses to play."

"Does she? I thought I had heard her practising with Georgiana one day," Darcy said.

"Very well. She only refuses to play when I am in the room or even in the corridor. She makes Kitty stand guard at the door."

Richard chuckled. "She banishes you from the music room?"

"She'd likely banish me from England if she could."

Richard's head tipped at his brother's curiously perturbed tone.

"And why is that?" he asked.

Westonbury blew out a breath. "Something about Sally's. It is not on the list of Miss Mary approved places or activities."

"Which is as it should be," Darcy muttered.

"Do you know what she said to me on our walk the day I met her?"

"I am sure I could not even guess," Richard replied. He knew, however, that something said in the exchange between the two had made an impression on his brother. Darcy had said so. And as far as Richard knew, Darcy had still not discovered what had been said between the two. Elizabeth had not told him, though she knew. Apparently, it was not the sort of thing Elizabeth wished to repeat.

Nor was it the sort of thing Darcy would press to discover. Darcy was patient where Richard was curious. Richard had thought to ask Lydia about it but had not.

"That places such as Sally's only exist because of men – she did not say gentlemen, she said men – such as me who have no care for anyone but themselves." He rose from where he was sitting and scooped up Oliver before he could escape. "That was the end of our disagreement thanks to Miss Lydia." He sat down again and pulled out his watch fob to dangle in front of the kitten in his lap. "Apparently, there are men of honour such as you, Darcy, and even father – since none of you frequent such a place as Sally's – however, I am not to be counted amongst that number." He looked up from Oliver to Richard. "Is she always so severe and set in her opinions?"

"I could not say," Richard replied.

"I believe she is. Elizabeth said it would take a heroic deed to sway her opinion once it is so firmly set against someone," Darcy inserted.

The statement was met by a short burst of laughter from Westonbury. "Perhaps I do need to take up your commission after all."

"Perhaps if you started by not provoking her?" Darcy suggested.

Westonbury sighed. "Perhaps."

"We are not children any longer, Wes. You cannot throw pebbles at the girls you like," Richard said.

Understanding dawned in Darcy's eyes. "Oh, yes! I remember you used to torment any girl who caught your fancy. Do you like Miss Mary?"

"No. Yes. I do not know. I only know that it bothers me greatly that she thinks so poorly of me and that her opinion was set before she even met me. Should I not, at least, be given a chance to make a first impression?"

"Miss Bennet, Miss Elizabeth Bennet, and Miss Lydia Bennet," Mr. Harvey intoned from the doorway.

With some effort not to grimace, Richard pushed up from his seat.

"Colonel," Elizabeth said, "it is good to see you in the drawing room."

"You helped him come down; did you not?" Lydia asked Westonbury.

"I promised you I would," he replied.

"Then show me your cheek," she answered.

"You will not pinch my nose, will you?"

She laughed. "Is it necessary?"

"No." He turned his cheek towards her, and she kissed it.

"Thank you. You are a very good brother."

Richard could almost imagine her patting Wes on the head and giving him a biscuit as she did Dash. "You only helped me for a kiss?"

Westonbury shrugged and smirked. "Can you blame me? I am to keep my half-crowns to myself, after all."

"I did not say I would give him a kiss when he promised to see to you," Lydia said, folding her arms and joining Richard in glaring at his brother.

"She is correct. I was never promised a reward for making certain you did not fall to your death on the stairs."

"And he only got a kiss because there is no one here who would think it utterly improper."

"Speaking of which. Where is Miss Mary?" Westonbury asked. "She might like to know that I performed my duty as brother so admirably."

Lydia laughed. "She is in the music room with Kitty and Georgiana. I will be certain to tell her, but I fear she will still not like you. You did buy a kiss from her sister."

Westonbury's mouth dropped open. "Is that why she does not like me?"

"That and you were at Sally's," Lydia said. "What else could it be? That is all she knew of you before she met you."

"I did not know she knew of that kiss," Elizabeth said.

"Oh, she was not supposed to know, but I forgot and mentioned it on that day when Lord Westonbury arrived. I was so shocked that he was the same person we had met at Sally's that I had to tell Kitty and well, Mary happened to be there when I did," Lydia answered.

"That does make things fall into place better," Jane said.

"Miss Bennet!" Bingley said as he entered the room. "I

am delighted to see you. My sister has given me permission to enter," he added to Miss Lydia.

"What do you mean *given you permission?*" Richard asked. "This is your house. Why would you need permission to enter your own drawing room."

"You do not need to be overwhelmed the first time you are out of your room," Lydia answered. "That is why Caroline and I decided that you should be given time to get settled here without too many people or too much sound."

Westonbury laughed. "You do not need Mother. It seems Miss Lydia is filling the role of protectress very well."

Richard watched Lydia pull the right corner of her lower lip between her teeth. He also saw Darcy sit forward as if he wished to move in and care for Lydia, but then he move back purposefully and nodded to Richard. It was what he did when he thought Richard needed to address Georgiana. Lydia had become very much a sister to his cousin, and Richard would not disappoint either him or Lydia.

"I believe Mother would be delighted to know someone has seen to my care," Richard assured her.

"Do you think so?" Lydia asked eagerly.

"Yes," Westonbury said. "Do you think Miss Mary would let me hear her play today?"

"I doubt it very much," Lydia answered.

He sighed and settled back into his chair.

"Is all ready for tomorrow evening?" Richard asked.

Lydia nodded. "I have just to practice my song."

"Your song?"

She nodded again.

"I did not know you were singing."

"It is supposed to be a surprise, so I shall not tell you any more than that." Her head tipped. "Do you think your head can abide listening to several songs? You will already have endured a dinner."

"I would not miss such a treat as hearing you sing. Even if I must do it with my eyes closed to keep the room from spinning. I will imagine your lovely face if I must close my eyes," he added when her brow furrowed.

"Lady Matlock's carriage is on the drive," Harvey said from the doorway. "Miss Bingley wished you to know in advance of her arrival. Tea will be made ready soon."

Lydia's hands twisted in her lap, and Richard covered them with one of his. "All will be well. You are prepared. She might be surly at first, but she will be won over."

He had said these same words to her every day she had visited him in his room, but at present, the words felt a great deal weightier much like "you know your post, see to it" took on a far different tone when said in the face of battle rather than field practice.

"It might be a challenge, but you are equal to it," he added.

She nodded, and, upon hearing Netherfield's door open, she rose and then assisted him in also rising. Her shoulders straightened, and she lifted her chin. His Lydia was prepared for whatever lay ahead. He gave her hand a squeeze before releasing it.

"You are equal to it," he whispered once more before his mother was announced.

# Chapter 20

Lady Matlock surveyed the room, her eyes taking in every detail. It was not an unfamiliar action to Darcy. It was how his aunt entered all new rooms.

Her left brow quirked upward as she settled her gaze on him.

"Mother," Westonbury said. "May I present the room to you?"

"I believe you must, my dear. There are those here whom I have not yet met." She spoke sweetly but her eyes remained on Darcy.

"It was not feasible for you to meet them when they were in town. Lord Matlock agreed," Darcy said in answer to her look.

"Yes, well, he is not as curious as I am." She had the good grace to smile at Elizabeth. "Begin here," she said to Westonbury.

"Mother this is Fitz—"

"Oh, do skip over the people I know, Reginald." She huffed. "Why must you insist on being such a trial?"

"Because I am much like you?"

"Reginald Arthur Fitzwilliam, do your duty as you should," Lady Matlock retorted.

Westonbury chuckled. "My full name and not even five minutes have passed. That must be a record."

"Indeed," his mother replied dryly but with a smile for her eldest son. "Now, get on with it. And do it properly."

"Lady Matlock, I present to you Miss Elizabeth Bennet, soon to be Mrs. Elizabeth Darcy. Miss Elizabeth, my mother, Lady Matlock."

Elizabeth dipped a curtsey. "It is a pleasure to meet you."

"Oh, do not assume things," Lady Matlock replied with a small laugh. "Reginald was not wrong. We can be alike – difficult and trying."

"I am not unused to trying and difficult people," Elizabeth returned with a smile.

"I should think not if you have agreed to take on Darcy."

Darcy cleared his throat and scowled.

"You are so exacting, and do not tell me you are not." She turned to Westonbury. "Continue, and I do know Mr. Bingley. I should very much like to know who the beauty is beside him."

"Lady Matlock, I present to you Miss Jane Bennet, soon to be Mrs. Jane Bingley. Miss Bennet, my mother, Lady Matlock."

Jane also dipped a curtsey as was proper and voiced her pleasure in Lady Matlock's safe arrival.

"A gentleman's daughter?" she directed the question to Bingley, who nodded. "Excellent. That is just what you need to help establish yourself." She tipped her head and studied Jane for a moment. "And strikingly pretty. Make sure to have her likeness captured in a portrait," she instructed Bingley before looking once again at Westonbury.

"Lady Matlock, I present to you Miss Lydia Bennet. Miss Lydia, this is my mother, Lady Matlock."

As Darcy expected, Lydia dipped a curtsey.

"No, soon to be Mrs. Anybody?" Lady Matlock said over Lydia's greeting.

"No, my lady," Lydia answered.

"Not soon at least," Richard answered, causing Lydia's eyes to grow wide. "But I am hopeful."

Lady Matlock lifted her chin and swept her eyes from Lydia's head to her feet and back. "A trifle young, do you not think?"

"No," Richard replied. "She is perfect in every way."

"I am not," Lydia said.

"To me you are," Richard assured her.

Lady Matlock's lips twitched as if she wished to smile. "I have been attempting to bring him to the point of marriage." She blew out a breath. "However, he is stubborn." She began to peel off her gloves. "You are not what I would expect." She held up a finger to keep Richard from saying anything. "That being said, I will not discount you straight away. Someone of your age might in time learn the fortitude necessary for such a stubborn husband." She handed the first of her gloves to Westonbury and began removing the second glove. "He is a lot like his father. And, though I know you are a gentleman's daughter, the circles in which he is expected to circulate are not those to which you are accustomed." She handed the second glove to Westonbury and looked at Lydia expectantly.

Lydia's chin rose, but only just. "I believe that when my sister spoke of not being unfamiliar with trying individuals, she was thinking, at least in part, about me."

"Indeed?" Lady Matlock looked toward Elizabeth who nodded. "And only this one sister is trying?"

"No, my lady," Lydia answered for Elizabeth. "Jane is all that is good, as is Kitty, but Lizzy, Mary and myself are more challenging."

"Five sisters?" Lady Matlock blinked.

"Yes, my lady," Lydia said. "No brothers. My father's estate is entailed to his cousin, who holds the living in Hunsford, and my mother's family is from trade." She batted her lashes and smiled.

Darcy's eyes grew wide. From all the nervousness he had witnessed in Lydia over the past few days as the arrival of his aunt grew closer and closer, he had not expected such a bold reply. He wanted to look at Elizabeth to see how she was reacting to Lydia's outspoken behaviour, but he dared not take his eyes off his aunt, for he was curious to witness her response.

"And do you know how to manage a large household?" Lady Matlock countered.

"My mother is very good at what she does, my lady," Lydia responded. "And she has instructed me well. However, I have also requested and received instruction by Miss Bingley to ensure that my skills are not lacking since Miss Bingley is more familiar with town than is my mother."

Truly, Darcy had not expected her to admit that either.

"A Bennet always rises to the occasion," Elizabeth whispered.

He glanced her direction.

"Not that I am not also shocked by it," she added.

"And where are these other sisters?" Lady Matlock asked.

"They are with Georgiana in the music room," Darcy answered.

"I can take you there and introduce them to you," Westonbury offered.

"No!" Darcy said sharply.

Lady Matlock turned startled eyes to him. "And why can he not?"

"They are practising," Darcy answered.

"They can pause to meet me."

"Then, it would be best if I were to take you to them."

"Is there a reason for this?" She looked at Westonbury, who shrugged.

Darcy smiled apologetically at Lydia. "Wes and Miss Mary do not get on well together."

"Have you been tormenting the poor girl, Reginald?"

"He gets as good as he gives," Darcy supplied.

"I see. Well, then, we will wait for introductions until later." She finally took a seat.

Lydia took Richard by the elbow and assisted him in sitting, making certain he was comfortable before she took her place next to him.

"I have asked Mr. Westcott to see you," Lady Matlock said to Richard. "He was not available until the day after tomorrow, however, so he will arrive with your father. Your father cannot stay for very long, but he did wish to see you."

"I can wait until I return to London to see Mr. Westcott," Richard replied.

"Oh, but he is so very good," Lydia said. "He tended to my father when he fell," she explained to Lady Matlock. "Papa only spoke well of him, so he must be very good." She turned back to Richard. "And it is never a bad thing to seek another's opinion, is it?" Her head tipped and her lashes fluttered.

Richard scowled. "I suppose it is not."

"And you will not be returning to London until after

the wedding," Lydia added. "So, seeing Mr. Westcott now rather than later would be a good thing, would it not be?"

Richard closed his eyes.

"He might know more about how to help you," Lydia added, "or if there is anything more that you should be doing to recover."

Again, her lashes fluttered when Richard opened his eyes, and Darcy knew that is cousin was doomed to agree to have Mr. Westcott visit.

"You are correct," Richard muttered.

Lady Matlock smiled. "You might work out after all," she said. "However, I will reserve my approval for now until I have observed further."

The door to the drawing room opened, allowing Caroline, accompanied by Sir Matthew and the tea service, to enter. Introductions were made, and Lydia was called upon to help pour.

~*~*~

"That went better than I expected," Elizabeth admitted to Darcy later as they were taking a walk around the garden.

She would have to leave soon, but at his insistence, her departure had been put off for the length of a slow walk around the hedges and flower beds.

"It most certainly did," Darcy replied. "I must say I was surprised by how accepting my aunt was of everyone."

"You mean Lydia?"

"Yes, and you, to some extend, but mostly Lydia. My aunt has long spoken about how she wished to see Richard marry an heiress." It was odd really how easily his aunt had accepted Lydia. She had not even raised a brow at Mrs. Bennet being from trade. Whatever the cause of her behavior was, Darcy was happy for it. "She may have been swayed by Lydia's boldness. My aunt does not favour wilting wallflowers – that is what she calls them. A lady should be decorous but with a spine of iron."

Elizabeth laughed and hugged Darcy's arm more tightly. "Well, Lydia does have a will of iron at times, and she is working on being decorous."

Darcy kissed the top of Elizabeth's bonnet. "I am impressed by the change I have seen in her. Yesterday, she was sitting with Mrs. Annesley asking questions about a great number of things for a time, or so Georgiana told me."

"I am just as surprised by her improvement as you are, if not more so," Elizabeth said. "I should not be, I suppose, but I am."

Darcy led Elizabeth off the main path and over the lawn toward a bench across from where they had been walking. "Why should you not be surprised?"

"Lydia has always found a way to get what she wants. She wants the colonel's good opinion, and so, she will do whatever is needed to gain and keep it. I had not thought of that until recently." She sighed.

"What troubles you?"

"I have been blind to so many things."

"Such as?"

"Such as Caroline is not without sense and is very accomplished."

"She hid her sense rather well for some time. I do not think you can be faulted for not noticing it. In fact, I dare say if she did not have Sir Matthew, she would still be rather nonsensical, though possessing many accomplishments. What else?"

"Lydia is not a child."

"I think her experiences of late have played a large role in her maturity," Darcy countered.

Elizabeth shrugged. "I guess I view things through a different lens now than I did before I went to London."

"Life is changing," Darcy said softly. "And not for the worse."

"Definitely not for the worse," Elizabeth agreed, lifting her face so he could kiss her.

"I have requested permission of your father for your sisters to visit Georgiana after we marry."

"You did what?"

Darcy smiled sheepishly. "Georgiana has grown so close to them."

Elizabeth shook her head and laughed softly. "Where has the old Mr. Darcy gone?"

"The one who did not see your worth and denied his

heart? He is gone. You do not wish for him to return, do you?" He kissed her upturned lips again.

"No, but my sisters? Was not two weeks enough trial?"

He chuckled. "I think I can survive another fortnight or two."

"And has my father agreed?"

"In part. Georgiana is going to stay at Longbourn for two weeks after we leave. Then, Lydia and Kitty are to join us for a time. One for my cousin's sake and the other for my sister's." He blew out a breath. "I offered to have Mary accompany them, but your father has not decided. He might send her to your aunt's, or he might keep her at home for your mother. I believe it is the animosity between Wes and Mary which causes him to pause."

"For good reason." A creased formed between Elizabeth's eyes. "Do you not fear leaving your sister where Mr. Wickham is?"

Darcy shook his head. "Your mother – and Lydia – will not allow him to harm her." He stroked her cheek. "I never thought I would relish being part of your family. I know that sounds arrogant, and it was when I first thought it. But now. I honestly cannot imagine my life without them." He tipped his head as he stroked her cheek once more before brushing her lips with his thumb. "We do not need to stay in town for long after we marry. We could have everyone join us at Pemberley."

"Mother does not like to travel, and Jane will be here."

"We will think on it," he answered as his hand moved to cup the back of her head.

She smiled. "What has happened to your well-ordered life, Mr. Darcy?"

"It has been completely turned on its head," he replied, pulling her in for a kiss. "My heart has been broken open and filled with love for you and your family. I do not wish to have my former life back."

"And what has wrought this change?" she said as he lowered his head for a lingering kiss.

"Well," he said, "it began when you stole my heart." He kissed her again. "And over time and through challenges." Another kiss. "I learned to see beyond myself." One more kiss, this one on her nose. "However, I do believe that next to my great love for you, I would have to credit Dash for a great deal of it." He lowered his lips to hers. There was nothing in this world that he would not endure to be here with her, breathing in the lavender fragrance she wore, tasting the sweetness of her kisses, and reveling in her touch as she wound her arms around his neck.

# Chapter 21

Two weeks passed quickly. Much more quickly than Darcy had expected they would. Lady Matlock's presence, as well as that of her husband on two separate occasions, had added a liveliness to life at Netherfield that had propelled time forward at a rapid pace. The drawing room had been filled with chatter and card games. Georgiana had been called upon to play more than once. Quietness was not something which Lady Matlock sought. She was, in fact, a rather restless soul much like her eldest son. However, the busyness and noise which filled Netherfield did not bother Darcy as it once might have. Indeed, if he were to be honest, he had missed such things since leaving town and found them to be a bit of a solace.

Darcy chuckled as he thought about these things while descending the stairs at Netherfield on his way to enter his carriage, which was waiting to take him to the church. He had learned a great deal from the Bennets about what it was to be part of a loving, though somewhat chaotic, family.

"You are looking handsome, as always," Lady Matlock greeted Darcy. She motioned for him to stand in front of her so that she could straighten his jacket, though it did not need it.

"Your mother would be pleased to see you so happy." She placed a hand on his cheek. "Your father, too, but I think a son's wedding day is more a time for mothers to be nostalgic than it is for fathers."

"I should think you are correct," Darcy replied. "I know I have thought more of my mother in the last week than my father, though both have been close to mind." He was sorry that neither of them would ever know Elizabeth and her family.

"You are not alone. My husband has mentioned his sister and your father both times when he was here." She looked around Darcy and up the stairs. "Is Georgiana travelling with you?"

"No, she will travel with Richard and Westonbury." The seat next to him was reserved for Elizabeth.

"Good, then you will have a place for me."

"But –" Darcy began to protest that he was not going to share his carriage with her after the ceremony was over, but she held up a hand to stop him.

"Your uncle will see me to the wedding breakfast. I will not come between you and your bride." She gave him a wink and a smirk that was so very reminiscent of her eldest son that Darcy could not help but chuckle.

"Very well, as long as I shall be alone with Elizabeth after we have said our vows, I will allow you to accompany me to the church."

"Such a good boy." She gave his cheek a pat. "If only my boys were so well behaved." Again, she winked and smirked.

Darcy knew that while there were most certainly times when she wished her sons were as reserved as he was, his aunt would not wish them to always be so. She could be as troublesome as either Richard or Westonbury.

Her smirk faded from her lips but not her eyes as she gave him an expectant look. Obediently, he extended his arm to her and led her from the house.

"I have not yet gotten to do this with either of my boys," she said as they descended Netherfield's steps. "But," she added as they approached the carriage, "it seems I will sooner rather than later."

"How do you mean?"

Darcy was almost certain he understood his aunt's meaning. She had been very attentive to Lydia and had not had a critical thing to say. Whether she was simply keeping criticism to herself or truly approved was the true question, and frankly, it was one he had hoped to ask of her before he departed Netherfield later today.

The need to see that Lydia was well would not leave him, even if he had given over that responsibility to Richard for the past two weeks. It was only natural, he supposed since, as of today, Lydia would be his sister, and, as such, he would never truly stop worrying about her wellbeing.

"Richard spoke to his father last night," Lady Matlock said as she entered the carriage.

"Did he?" Darcy feigned surprise.

She turned and leveled a look of disbelief at him. "As if you do not know."

Darcy smiled. "I may have heard something about it."

"I am sure you heard all about it," she retorted. "As you know, your uncle has given his blessing to Richard, and so I suspect in a year or perhaps sooner, I will get to take this ride with him." She settled into her seat. "There is no rush, however. Richard must heal and find his footing in a new life, and Miss Lydia is young."

Darcy could not have asked for a better opening to present his case for Lydia if one should be needed. He would fight for both her and Richard. His cousin was making remarkable progress since he had agreed to see Lydia. His mood had lifted, and his determination had resurged. Unfortunately, his eyesight had not cleared even though he was no longer as dizzy as he had been.

"Are you pleased about the match?"

His aunt drew a breath and expelled it before pursing her lips and looking out the window. "Truthfully, she is not what I expected." She shrugged. "But then, every well-dowered accomplished debutante I have paraded before him has only ever elicited a bored pleasantness from him. Miss Lydia is not boring." She smiled as if truly delighted by that fact.

"No, she is not that," Darcy agreed.

"She is full of vitality and stubbornness." His aunt chuckled. She was obviously quite pleased with the lady whom her youngest son had selected as his future wife. "I suspect I always knew he would need someone different from what the best finishing schools produce. He is a lot like his father."

"He is, and you are not a standard issue ton-approved lady." That was how his uncle had always described his aunt when talking about what it was which had captured his interest when he had met his wife.

"No, I am not." She smiled. "Standard is boring." Again, she shrugged. "However, it is occasionally preferable to be boring. It draws fewer arrows." She had not been a part of the ton when she had met her husband.

"I believe Miss Lydia can withstand a few arrows," Darcy said. She had survived Richard's injury and seemingly had managed to win over Richard's mother, which was no small task.

Again, his aunt chuckled. "I do not doubt it, and much like his father did for me, Richard will protect her where he can." She sighed. "I was so curious to meet her after Lady Catherine told us about her, so it was a relief to have her here to greet me when I arrived two weeks ago."

"I beg your pardon?" Lady Catherine had spoken of Lydia? Why had Wes not said so?

His aunt looked at him in confusion.

"Wes said he learned about Miss Lydia from Mrs. Salter and not Aunt Catherine," Darcy explained.

Lady Matlock's eyebrows flew upward. "What does *that* woman know of Miss Lydia?"

"You know Mrs. Salter?"

Darcy pressed his lips together to keep from laughing at his aunt's unladylike description of the woman while replying in the affirmative that she did indeed know Mrs. Salter.

"Mrs. Salter was disappointed in her quest to snare Mr. Bennet when she was young. Lost him to a lady from trade."

Lady Matlock leaned forward. "Do tell."

"I cannot tell you the whole story. It is not mine to share. However, according to Wes, Mrs. Salter had heard that Richard and Miss Lydia had been seen out walking and had thought it would be an excellent thing if she could do one better than Mrs. Bennet and attach her daughter to Wes."

His aunt's eyes grew wide. "Not while I live," she snarled. "That woman is an annoyance. I will not have her be a part of this family." Her smile was a bit calculating.

Darcy was curious as to what made his aunt dislike Mrs. Salter so vehemently but having heard as many stories as he had about the woman, he was not surprised that she was not well-liked.

"Do you know she had the audacity to proclaim that no second son would be a first choice for her daughter?" his aunt said. Her look of contempt from the first mention of Mrs. Salter's name had not faded one bit.

"Where did she do this?"

"Oh, some musicale," she said with a wave of her hand. "It might have been at the Johnsons', although I am not entirely certain. Not that it matters where. It was one of those times when I was attempting to force Richard to meet several young ladies. I had not met Mrs. Salter before that evening. Well," she arched her left eyebrow and pursed her lips to emphasize the vileness of what she was about to share, "I was speaking to someone else when the mother of one of the young ladies I had introduced to Richard was talking to Mrs. Salter about her excitement at her daughter meeting the son of Lord Matlock." Lady Matlock lifted her chin. "As any sensible mother should be. Being tied to Lord Matlock is no small thing – even if it is through his second son and not his first." Her eyes narrowed. "As if one is better than the other. Oh, I know one has a title and will have a fortune, but Richard is not a prize to be snubbed."

Darcy smiled. His aunt had always loved her children fiercely.

"Well, any woman who can dismiss my son, is not worth

my time or notice!" Her lips curled into a calculating smirk. "I think I shall have to invite Miss Lydia to see the town with me when she visits. Would that not just put a bee in Mrs. Salter's bonnet."

"Indeed, it would," Darcy agreed. "But back to Aunt Catherine. You said she told you about Miss Lydia?"

Lady Matlock nodded. "She felt it her duty to tell your uncle and me about the fiery young lady she had met at Netherfield who claimed to be loved by Richard." She blew out a breath. "We were shocked at first, of course, since we had heard nothing about Miss Lydia or any attachment Richard had formed. And to be honest, we had always thought he would marry an heiress to prop up his inheritance a shade or two. It was what he had always claimed he would do, you know. However, after Lady Catherine cautioned us that no disparagement of the young woman would be allowed by you, I knew this Miss Lydia must be a quality young lady."

It was gratifying that Lady Catherine had taken his words to heart. He was not anxious to create a breach in the family, but he would have, had she not heeded his warning. "She is my sister – or will be soon. How could I do otherwise?"

His aunt shook her head. "If Miss Lydia had been a poor choice for Richard to be making, you would have attempted to sway him. You have always watched out for him. It is just part of your nature to do so. That things had progressed enough for Miss Lydia to know that Richard loved her proved that you more than tolerated her. You approved."

"I was not certain I would at first," Darcy admitted. "It was Richard who saw the potential in her from their first meeting when she asked him if he was married."

"She did not!"

"Oh, she did. She also asked if Georgiana had any beaus."

"Miss Lydia? I find that hard to believe."

"That is because she has improved, just as Richard set out to help her do before his heart became entangled — or perhaps it was as it became entangled. The Bennet ladies seem to have a power to charm a fellow rather quickly."

"They are charming, even Miss Mary when she is scowling at Reginald," his aunt said with a chuckle. "There mother is... well, she is loving despite her deficits." Her brows flicked up quickly in amusement.

"She is," Darcy agreed. Mrs. Bennet was still not an excessively intelligent woman. She was still given to rattling on in conversations and taking the longest route around a point while sometimes missing the point altogether. However, Darcy found he did not fault her for those things as he once did. "I am pleased she will be my mother-in-law." And he meant it.

"She will treat you well."

"I have no doubt of that." He moved toward the door as it was opened.

"I cannot believe you are finally getting married," his aunt said as she allowed him to help her out of the carriage.

"I am a bit in shock over that as well," Darcy replied with a chuckle.

Darcy's wedding day had been a long time in coming, and for a long, bleak time, it had appeared that such happiness as he now felt would never be his. However, as he stood here before the church ready to claim his bride, those days of sorrow seemed to fade nearly into nonexistence. It was almost as if they had been but a fitful night of sleep, disturbed by countless bad dreams.

While Darcy's journey to his wedding day had been a long one, the ceremony was, as it always is, over in what seemed like a moment, and the journey between Netherfield and the church? Well, when one was agreeably engaged in kissing and holding his wife rather than talking to his aunt, a few miles seemed more like a few feet, and the journey was rather disappointingly over far sooner than Darcy wished for it to be.

# Chapter 22

"Your mother and Caroline have outdone themselves," Darcy said as he entered the ballroom at Netherfield, which had been laid out for a lavish wedding breakfast.

There were flowers lining the center of the tables, weaving in and around platters and bowls. Glasses sparkled as they stood alongside fine china and well-polished silver. There were even ribbons tied to the chairs intended for the guests of honour.

"And Lydia. We must not forget Lydia. She has been helping Caroline," Elizabeth reminded him.

"Was this during Richard's required rest period?" Darcy still found it humorous that his cousin – a well-respected colonel in his majesty's armed forces, who was used to giving commands and having them immediately obeyed on pain of punishment, was so easily talked into spending an hour of his time alone in his room by a flutter of lashes and a pretty pout on a determined young lady.

Elizabeth laughed. "Yes, it was while the colonel was

resting. I heard about each day's progress every night at dinner."

Elizabeth glanced toward where Richard was already seated at the end of the head table, near a door through which he could make a hasty exit if needed. Lydia had insisted upon him sitting there. She was not about to allow him to become overwhelmed where one and all would notice. "They make such a good pair, do they not?"

Darcy could not agree more. His cousin was happy — utterly happy despite his injuries — and that happiness was due almost entirely to the young lady whispering something to him right at this moment.

"Then, you are no longer fearful that such a relationship will end in tragedy as you once were?"

Elizabeth sighed. "There are some things which you should likely not remember."

"Such as any time you were wrong?" he teased.

"Yes," Elizbeth replied quickly, "but that should not be hard to do since I am so very nearly always right." She looked up at him and favoured him with an impertinent grin as he stood behind her chair while she took her seat at the table near the front of the room.

Leaning down, he kissed her. How could he not when she looked so charming, especially now that she was his wife?

"Mr. Darcy, how improper!" Jane was just taking her place next to her sister.

"But an excellent idea," Bingley said, placing a kiss on Jane's cheek since she was looking at Elizabeth.

"Shall we cause a scandal?" Jane said, turning toward her new husband.

"It would not be the first," he replied before kissing her properly.

"Such changes!" Elizabeth cried. "Who would have thought that Mr. Darcy and my best-behaved sister would become such wanton individuals?"

"What about me?" Bingley said when their laughter had died some. "Are you not shocked by my behaviour?"

"No."

"No? I am wounded." He placed a hand on his heart.

Elizabeth leaned forward and looked around her sister to Bingley. "You are not as reserved as they are. However, I must say I was shocked to hear you had cut ties with your sister. Shocked and excessively pleased. Jane is worth a bit of trouble."

"I could not agree more," Bingley said.

"And her sister is worth even more trouble." Darcy wrapped an arm around Elizabeth's shoulder and squeezed her tightly to his side.

"The things you have endured," Elizabeth teased.

From lending a hand in staging a compromise to hosting her family at his house to mingling with them and their friends and neighbors here in Hertfordshire, there had been much which could have been a step too far from comfort had the prize been anything less than the lady sitting beside Darcy. However, only one of them had proven excessively difficult to endure.

"Not a one was too much except for that one night when you were missing."

But then, that one thing — Darcy's fear of losing her, even when it was simply a fear of never gaining her approval, and therefore, living in misery without her — had been the impetus to all that had happened in the past few months.

Mr. Bennet stood and tapped his glass with his knife, drawing everyone's attention and causing a hush to fall over the room.

"It is with pleasure," he began, "that I welcome two sons to my family today. Please, join me on this happy occasion in raising a glass to the happiness, health, and –"

"Prosperity," Mrs. Bennet inserted, causing a titter of laughter to spread around the room.

"Yes, prosperity," Mr. Bennet agreed. "May my daughters and their husbands prosper in love as they grow older and may their homes always be filled with as much love and laughter as mine has always been." He lifted his glass. "To the Darcys and Bingleys!"

A cheer was raised around the room, followed by the clinking of glass against glass.

"I have enjoyed this day so much," Mr. Bennet said when the room had once again stilled, "that I would not be opposed to doing it again." He nodded to Richard before returning his attention to the room at large.

"I still have two daughters yet unattached," he added, once again causing the room to laugh. "And Darcy has a sister, we must not forget Miss Darcy. It is, after all," he said with a smile for his wife, "a truth universally acknowledged that young ladies such as Kitty, Mary, and Miss Darcy, who are in possession of great beauty and generally sweet spirits, must be in want of husbands."

Mrs. Bennet gasped and clucked her tongue softly before tittering behind her wine goblet as the rest of the room also chuckled.

"I have one more duty to perform before I will allow you all to eat and be merry as is required on a day such as this. My youngest, along with the assistance of Miss Darcy, has prepared some music to start us off while we eat."

"Did you know about this? Did Georgiana tell you?" Elizabeth whispered to Darcy.

"I did know about it, but it was not Georgie who told me."

"It was not?"

Darcy shook his head.

"Miss Darcy, Lydia," Mr. Bennet motioned to the piano which had been placed in the far corner. "We look forward to hearing what you have prepared, my dear," he said to Lydia, "and we shall all pretend that it is only in honor of your sisters and not a certain colonel."

"Papa!" Lydia chided, her cheeks growing red. "It can be for everyone."

"Of course, my dear, of course," he said as he took his seat.

"Your sister did not get to sing her song the night of the dinner party for Lady Matlock," Darcy whispered.

"You mean she refused," Elizabeth corrected.

"Because Richard was absent," Darcy reminded her. "So, she asked me if I thought it would be a good idea to sing it here."

"She did?" Elizabeth's face was suffused with shock.

Darcy nodded. "Apparently, she values my opinion," he teased, earning him a roll of Elizabeth's fine eyes. "When I heard her reason for wishing to perform here today, I could not say no. It is an excellent song choice."

"Is it? You know which song she was to sing at that dinner party? She has been very guarded about it."

Darcy smiled. "I do know. Now, do you wish to know her reason?"

"Of course."

"She wanted to make a very public declaration that Richard is and always will be good enough for her."

"What is she singing?" Elizabeth's eyes were wide.

Darcy shook his head. "That I will not tell you. You must listen to discover it, and as you do, know that I would say the same to you – which is precisely what I told your sister when we discussed this. She knows that she is not just singing for herself but also for me." Miss Lydia had required a handkerchief after hearing him speak so about the sister who had been such a wonderful support to her ever since that night at Sally's.

Of course, her declaration of delight over his attachment to her sister had come at the expense of hearing how shocked she still was that he was not so horrid as she had first thought he was. It was not so painful a thing to be reminded of his poor behavior now as it might have been at one time. However, it would be far better to be able to forget such a thing than to be reminded of it. He lifted Elizabeth's hand to his lips as the first notes rang out from the piano.

"Lydia looks so calm," Elizabeth whispered.

"Love has that sort of effect on one. It is truly astounding what one would not normally do for the world but will gladly do in a heartbeat for love." He placed a kiss on the ear into which he had whispered.

Next to the piano, Lydia lifted her chin and smiled first at Elizabeth and Jane before turning her attention to Colonel Fitzwilliam as she began to sing.

*Believe me, if all those endearing young charms,*
*Which I gaze on so fondly to-day,*
*Were to change by to-morrow, and fleet in my arms,*
*Live fairy-gifts fading away,*
*Thou wouldst still be adored, as this moment thou art,*
*Let thy loveliness fade as it will,*

*And around the dear ruin each wish of my heart*
*Would entwine itself verdantly still.*

Elizabeth drew in a sharp breath, and her hand rose to cover her heart. Turning to Darcy, tears glistening in her eyes, she whispered, "It is so beautiful and perfect. So perfect."

"Indeed, it is, for I love you, Mrs. Darcy, and I always will." He was certain Elizabeth would have replied in kind if he had allowed it. However, he did not, for he could not refrain from kissing her as Lydia began the last verse.

*It is not while beauty and youth are thine own,*
*And thy cheeks unprofaned by a tear,*
*That the fervor and faith of a soul may be known,*
*To which time will but make thee more dear!*
*No, the heart that has truly loved never forgets,*
*But as truly loves on to the close,*
*As the sunflower turns on her god when he sets*
*The same look which she turned when he rose!*[1]

Today, tomorrow, next year, and until time ceased to exist, Darcy would only love Elizabeth more than he did at this moment. And when he broke their kiss far sooner than he wished and as she laid her head on his shoulder, he knew that, by marrying Elizabeth, his greatest achievement in his life had both been reached and had only begun to be grasped.

---

1. *Believe Me if All Those Endearing Young Charms, Thomas Moore*

# Before You Go

If you enjoyed this book, be sure to let others know by leaving a review.

~*~*~

Want to know when other books will be available?
You can always know what's new with my books by subscribing to my mailing list.
(There will, of course, be a thank you gift for joining because I think my readers are awesome!)
Book News from Leenie Brown
(bit.ly/LeenieBBookNews)

~*~*~

Turn the page to read an excerpt of another one of Leenie's books

# Persuading Miss Mary
## Excerpt

Would you like to know how Colonel Fitzwilliam's brother and Mary find happily ever after together? You can find out in *Persuading Miss Mary*.

### Chapter 1

"What do you mean I am not allowed entrance?" Reginald Fitzwilliam, Viscount Westonbury, glared at Mr. Nibley, Matlock House's longtime butler.

"Just that, my lord. The countess has informed me that you are not allowed entrance without specific invitation."

"But it is my home!"

Mr. Nibley did not flinch. "Not at present, my lord. Your residence is the house in Brook Street."

"The house in Brook Street?" Wes huffed and looked at the sky above him before continuing. "I fully realize that my residence is in Brook Street. However, this is also my home, and I will not leave without seeing my mother."

Mr. Nibley paused for a moment as if considering whether or not he should disturb his mistress.

Wes waved toward the house. "My mother, if you will."

"I shall see if she is home to callers."

"I am not a caller! I am her son!"

"Yes, my lord." Finally, the staid man before Wes shifted uneasily. "I only do as I am told, my lord."

Wes clenched his jaw and shook his head. "Am I allowed to wait inside while you check?"

Mr. Nibley gave a slight shake of his head. "I do apologize, my lord, but I have my orders."

"Oh, for the love of –," he stopped when Mr. Nibley coughed. "Yes, yes, I know. Mother cannot abide such language, and I promise to not resort to such as long as my mother sees me. If she will not, then I shall be forced to vent my spleen with whatever colourful language I choose and at whatever volume I wish to shout it."

The butler gave a nod of his head and hurried into Matlock House to see if his mistress was willing to see her eldest son, who was left to mutter oaths under his breath on the step and wonder what bee had flown into his mother's bonnet. She had not locked him out of the house in years!

The last time had been when a gentleman had shown up to collect a debt from Lord Matlock which had been incurred by his son, who should have been at school and not in some gambling hell. Being locked out of the house, coupled with the removal of his allowance until the sum had been repaid fully and half again, had worked well.

Westonbury never set foot in a gambling hell after that, and his bills were always paid before word of any outstanding sums reached the ears of his mother.

For most gentlemen, their fathers were to be feared, and Lord Matlock was no exception. However, Lady Matlock was a good bit more fearsome to her sons than their father for she was cunning in her punishments, which were always doled out as if they were the most natural things in the world. If one took a step off a cliff, one must experience a fall. That was his mother's philosophy. Therefore, if you stole a biscuit, you spent the day in the kitchen assisting the scullery maid.

She loved her sons fiercely. Too fiercely at times, if you asked Lord Westonbury. He shook his head and chuckled. His mother had an uncanny ability to anticipate how he might attempt to escape a punishment or to find a bit of fun. She had been sitting below his window on more than one occasion at their estate when, as a young boy, he had been required to stay indoors for some indiscretion such as tormenting the stable cats.

The door opened interrupting Wes's contemplation of his mother.

"My lady will see you in the green sitting room, and only in the green sitting room."

Just as he suspected, she expected him to decide on where they would meet, which he had been considering. His mother was not fond of the small drawing room off of the library, and that would have been precisely where he would have told Nibley that his mother could meet him. But again, she had thwarted his enjoyment by anticipating his move.

He handed his hat and walking stick to Mr. Nibley before removing his great coat.

"Am I allowed to direct myself to said room, or must I wait to be announced?"

The right corner of Mr. Nibley's mouth tipped upward but only just. "Do you wish to be announced, my lord?"

Wes chuckled. Mr. Nibley might appear to be wholly stoic, but he was not immune to the desire to have a bit of fun on occasion. "Indeed, I think I must be if I am merely a caller. Do you remember my name?"

"The name you use at every house, my lord?"

"No, the one that is precisely designed to annoy my mother."

"I think I do."

"Then, lead on my good man, and I shall not turn you out when I become master of Matlock House."

"I am sure I will not even be alive when that happens, my lord."

"I do hope that is not true. Not that I am wishing for my father's demise, of course."

"I did not think you were, my lord." Mr. Nibley began leading Wes down the hall to the green sitting room. The only sitting room on the ground floor — the room which was designated for calls and not much else.

The upper servant stepped into the room and, in a voice he might use if he were speaking to someone at the other end of a grand ballroom filled with dancers awaiting the start of the music, said "My lord, Reginald Arthur Fitzwilliam, Viscount Westonbury, the first-born and heir of the body of Lord Matlock, long may he live, to see Lady Matlock."

"Nibley," Lady Matlock scolded.

"I am only doing my duty, my lady," the butler replied with a bow before ducking out of the room.

"If he were not put up to such a thing by you, I would see him reprimanded properly."

"No, you would not," Wes said as he took a chair near where his mother was perched on her favourite sofa with a dog next to her. "Is that not Darcy's beast?"

"Beast? Dash is not a beast, are you, boy?" His mother scratched Dash's ear. "He is here to keep your brother company while he recovers."

"Then why is he here rather than with Richard?"

"Why are you here?"

Wes raised an eyebrow at his mother's coy response. "Because this is the only room in which I was allowed." He crossed his arms and leveled a disdainful look in Lady Matlock's direction. "Would you care to explain to me what I have done that has resulted in my exile from my home?"

"You are banned from the house in Brook Street?"

"Mother."

She chuckled and shrugged. "Impertinence is rather bothersome; is it not?"

"Yes, Mother. Now, if you would answer me seriously."

"I have guests."

"That is no reason for me to be stopped at the door to my home."

She shrugged again. "It is if the father of one of my guests has expressed concern regarding you."

Wes's brow furrowed. Who was visiting his mother?

"And, since the arrival of my guests, I have heard a most disturbing story from one of them."

"I still do not —"

"About you."

"I beg your pardon? You have heard a disturbing story about me?"

"Yes." She fluttered her lashes at him but said no more.

For a full minute, he only glared at her. It was a futile attempt to goad her into speaking, and he knew it. Still, it had to be attempted. "Oh, very well, what have I done?"

"I understand Miss Lydia and her sister met you in London." She lifted her chin slightly. "Quite often the ladies at such places as where you met them have been tossed out of their homes."

His waiting on the front step was beginning to make sense.

"Now, I know that there are gentlemen who frequent such places." She watched her hand stroke Dash's fur rather than looking at him. A faint pink tinged her cheeks. "However, they are not where I would wish my son to –"

"Please, Mother. I understand your meaning." He was likely as uncomfortable with this topic of conversation as she was. "However, I believe I am old enough to make my own decisions about such things."

She sighed. "Of course, you are." Her voice was just above a whisper and laced with disappointment. She lifted her eyes to him. "I only wished to make my point."

"I shall consider what you have said."

"Thank you."

"Am I reinstated as someone who can visit without an invitation?"

She shook her head. "I fear not. As long as Miss Lydia and Miss Bennet are staying here, you must be a stranger."

Wes blinked. "Miss Lydia and Miss Bennet are here?" Miss Mary Bennet was here at his parents' home? Walking the halls he had walked all his life? Sleeping in one of their guest rooms?

"Yes, I thought it good to have an ally in seeing that Richard recovers as he should, and, since Miss Kitty is visiting Georgiana, Miss Mary was sent to keep her sister company. However, there is not a lot of love lost between you and Miss Mary, so her father was concerned that being in a place where you might meet regularly might provoke her into besmirching the Bennet name. You know how it is. If someone should be calling and hear a young lady speaking plainly to a gentleman, the young lady will be the one taken to task."

"I would not provoke her."

His mother's replying look told him that she did not believe such a thing was possible, and truth be told, it likely was not. Miss Mary did not treat him as anyone else did – save for his closest family members and best friend. To her, he was merely a gentleman – not a viscount or the future Earl of Matlock. And confound it all if it was not refreshing!

"Then, am I only allowed to call during proper hours and in only this room, or will I be allowed to visit my brother?"

His mother sighed. "Your father will say you are welcome to visit your brother and join us for dinner and all those such things. However, neither he nor I will tolerate any provocation of our guests."

Wes nodded.

"I like her."

Wes's brow furrowed. "Miss Lydia?"

"Yes, her, but also her sister. Miss Mary is no wilting wallflower. I quite approve of that even if she does need a little softening."

Her head tilted to the side as she looked at him. So, this was her true purpose. She saw Miss Mary as a project of sorts.

"Just be kind to her," she added. "That is all I ask. Treat her as you would Georgiana."

That was a little bit impossible. He had never had a dream about Georgiana being in his bed. However, he was not about to say such to his mother. Instead, he dutifully assured her that he would do his best to behave as she expected.

"And if you could stop frequenting that place – Sally's, I believe it is called."

"Mother."

"I just think it would help you improve in the eyes of Miss Mary."

"I said I would consider what you had said. I will not promise any further."

She sighed. "I suppose I will have to be satisfied with that."

"Yes, you will. Now, am I allowed to see my brother?"

Lady Matlock glanced at the clock before rising. "Yes, I do believe he will be rising and making his way to the library."

"Rising? Do not tell me he is still taking a rest each afternoon." He rose to follow her from the room, but Dash stepped between Wes and his mother.

"He most certainly is. But it is not my doing." She smiled over her shoulder at him.

"Miss Lydia?"

She nodded. "As I said, I wanted to have an ally in seeing Richard recover."

Wes laughed as he followed his mother and Dash up the stairs. "Have I complimented you lately on your deviousness?"

"No, I do not believe you have," she replied with a chuckle. "There is a soiree that you must attend the day after next."

"Mother."

"You must marry someday, Reginald. The nursery has been empty for far too long."

"You forget, my lady," he said as he came to a stop on the landing next to her. "My residence is in Brook Street."

She patted his cheek. "Only until you marry. Then, you are free to bring my daughter and your children here to be with me."

# Other Leenie B Books

You can find all of Leenie's books at this link
bit.ly/LeenieBBooks
where you can explore the collections below

~*~

Sweet Possibilities and Sweet Extras

~*~

Dash of Darcy and Companions Collection

~*~

Marrying Elizabeth Series

~*~

Willow Hall Romances

~*~

The Choices Series

~*~

Darcy Family Holidays

~*~

Other Pens

~*~

Touches of Austen

~*~

Nature's Fury and Delights Novelettes Collection

~\*~

Teatime Tales Novelettes Collection

~\*~

Darcy and... An Austen-Inspired Collection

## About the Author

Leenie Brown has always been a girl with an active imagination, which, while growing up, was both an asset, providing many hours of fun as she played out stories, and a liability, when her older sister and aunt would tell her frightening tales. At one time, they had her convinced Dracula lived in the trunk at the end of the bed she slept in when visiting her grandparents!

Although it has been years since she cowered in her bed in her grandparents' basement, she still has an imagination which occasionally runs away with her, and she feeds it now as she did then — by reading!

Her heroes, when growing up, were authors, and the worlds they painted with words were (and still are) her favourite playgrounds! Now, as an adult, she spends much of her time in the Regency world, playing with the characters from her favourite Jane Austen novels and those of her own creation.

When she is not traipsing down a trail in an attempt to keep up with her imagination, Leenie resides in the beautiful province of Nova Scotia with her two sons and her very own Mr. Brown (a wonderful mix of all the best of Darcy, Bingley, and Edmund with a healthy dose of the teasing Mr. Tilney and just a dash of the scolding Mr. Knightley).

# Connect with Leenie

*E-mail:*
*LeenieBrownAuthor@gmail.com*
*Facebook:*
www.facebook.com/LeenieBrownAuthor
*Blog:*
*leeniebrown.com*
Patreon:
https://www.patreon.com/LeenieBrown
**Subscribe to Leenie's Mailing List:**
Book News from Leenie Brown
(bit.ly/LeenieBBookNews)